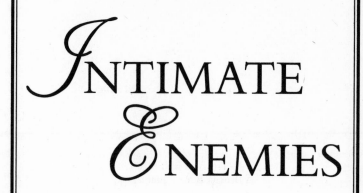

INTIMATE ENEMIES

Shana Abé

BANTAM BOOKS

New York Toronto London Sydney Auckland

$\mathcal{D}$EDICATION

For Stacey and Bob and Ted and Jenafer and Julie and Kayla and Jackie and Braeden and Nathan, and all those to come, and all those who have been. Love you.

Also my truest gratitude to Darren, Wendy McCurdy, Stephanie Kip, Mom and Dad, and especially Ruth Kagle, who kept cheering me on. They make it all work.

———⟨ഝ⟩———

The shadow of the giant shifted, and as in a dream Ari watched the dark arms lift high again—*exposing the heart, stupid move,* he thought groggily—and the wicked length of the axe was like a rushing bird across the gold, swift and silent and—unbelievably—the end.

"MacRae!" came a shout, so close and loud that even the Norseman hesitated, and the axe bird hovered over Arion, not falling just yet.

"MacRae!"

Sand exploded around him, forcing Arion to close his eyes and turn his head away, gasping, and suddenly the new call was everywhere, everything, drowning out even the death knell of the ocean. When he opened his eyes again he saw more than just the ragged boots of the Norseman—many new legs, new people. New men, fighting off the invaders. Now there were shadows all over the golden beach, sand flying, battle cries and screams echoing off the rocky dunes behind him. There were tartans and swords and the sparking clamor of metal hitting metal. The battle continued at a feverish new pitch.

And Arion, still sideways in the sand, managed to roll over and push himself up to his elbows, trying to see who else was falling around him.

The Norseman with the dead-water eyes had moved slightly away from him, lumbering after a much smaller figure, a tartan-clad creature that darted and moved like the wind, raising a broadsword that looked too heavy for him. Yet, for all his speed, it seemed the tartaned man was going to die today too, because despite his stupidity the giant had the thick brawn of a bull, Arion knew that. The smaller man would tire before the Norseman would.

There were bodies everywhere. He could see it now, how Tartan had to jump over them sideways and backward, and the Norseman just stepped around them easily. Most of the fallen were cloaked in the skins and bright silver metal of the invaders, but there were also ones in chain mail, like himself. And a few with the tartan of the newcomer, as well.

Tartan was tiring, just as Ari had feared. A misstep on something caused him to swing awkwardly to one side, and the giant gave the same laugh as he had when he had been about to kill Ari.

Ah, well, Arion thought, remote. His arms gave up the last of their strength, and he collapsed back onto the sand. *What a cold day to die.*

The Norseman shouted something incomprehensible to Tartan. Arion managed to turn his head and squinted against the blood and sweat and sand, watching the finish of the unlikely battle.

The giant lifted his arms and wielded that deadly axe above him.

The heart! Ari thought, and tried to shout it, but all that came out was a rough cough.

And Tartan whirled and moved and did the thing that Ari had thought was impossible—he ducked the blow and brought his own blade up to the exposed torso of the giant, and pushed it in. Then he let go, backing away.

The Norseman seemed frozen, no longer laughing, by God. He took a few clumsy steps backward, then fell to his knees, and then onto his back.

It was one of the last things Arion saw before the darkness came and ate him up: the fallen figure of his and torn, crawling with unpleasantness. She left it crumpled in one of the corners, by the chains.

Lauren didn't know how long she had been here—days? Weeks? She almost didn't remember how she had come here. She had been out with Da, she remembered that. He had taken her from Shot for the very first time in her life, to celebrate her eighth birthday. Da and she and a group of men had gotten on the largest ship they had and sailed to the mainland, to visit their friends there: Clan MacBain, allied with Clan Baird, allied with Clan Ramsay, allied with Clan Murdoch, allied with Clan Colquhoun. . . .

An ally was a friend, she knew that. Da had many friends.

And he had been so proud of her. Lauren had behaved properly on the voyage over. She had avoided the masts and the rigging and not caused any trouble at all, just as she knew he expected of her. The sky had been as bright as bluebells, clear and warm. The ocean wind had felt wonderful on her face, as always—clean, alive. She had loved the voyage, the water rushing past her in joyous tones and vibrant colors. She was almost sad when they docked at the mainland, but that had been overridden by the excitement of everything else.

Da, leading her off the boat to the green land before them, holding her hand. Hugs all around, people exclaiming over her, the shade of her hair—exactly like her mother's, they had said. Her smile—the image of the laird's, they said. Like Da's. Happy voices and helpful hands leading her forward into them, to the village beyond the docks.

Since they were the friends of her own clan, she had felt no reservations at all in chatting with them, letting them admire her and admiring them in return. Da walked beside her, talking in his low, gravelly voice, and it had seemed to Lauren MacRae that in that moment the world was simply a perfect place. She had her father, she had these new friends, she had her home back on Shot and the blue sky above her, and what could be finer than any of that?

Then it had happened. While they were still walking, before they could even reach the heart of the village, the bad men had come. They had swift horses and maces and swords, and Da and the rest had raced around, shouting. Hands yanked at her, pulling her this way and that, and it was all so confusing. She couldn't see anything but legs and horses, everything and everyone were so much taller than she.

Da had been howling her name, and she had shouted back, trying to run to him. But then someone new took her, one of the bad men. He had clamped a hand over her mouth and lifted her up high onto his horse with him.

Now she could see everything, all right, all the chaos and the fighting and the savage dances of the swords and maces of the different men. She even caught a glimpse of Da, battling furiously with three of the bad men, still turning his head to search for her. She had screamed from behind the hand over her mouth.

And then they had ridden away and she had been helpless to escape, though she had tried very hard. She had bitten the man who held her; she had struggled and kicked even though she was on a very tall horse, and falling to the ground would probably hurt a lot.

The man holding her had muttered something and then there was a flashing pain on the side of her head, and then . . .

Lauren had woken up here.

It was cold and damp and had frightening black shadows, and no one would answer any of her questions. It hadn't mattered if she asked politely, as Hannah had taught her, or if she yelled and called them names, cursing them with all the words she had secretly learned from eavesdropping on the stableboys. The men here would not speak to her. They would not even look at her, hunched up in her corner.

Except for one. Except for one boy.

He had come in with the laird—at least Lauren thought it was the laird, although she had not heard him called that. The odd laird was dressed as strangely as all the others, with no tartan at all, but rather a very elaborate tunic, with many colors and fancy stitchwork all over it. Yet for all the fanciness, Lauren was not fooled: This man was the cause of the death stench. It came from him, it washed out and away from him, rushing over to her in splintering waves.

As he walked into the cell, one of the guards bowed to him and called him "milord du Morgan." As soon as Lauren heard that name, she knew she was going to die here in the scary place.

The du Morgans were the clan of the devil. Everyone knew that.

The du Morgan devil had come into her prison with nothing but a sneer on his face and foul words on his lips, carrying that stench. Like all the other men, he had not looked directly at her, but rather around her, at her hair, at her clothing, at her hands. The boy walked in slowly behind him, masked with the same murky darkness that consumed the rest of the room.

Lauren stood up tall and tried not to tremble, for Da wouldn't want her to show any fear to the devil.

"Chin up," Da would have said. *"Look him straight in the eye, Lauren. You're a MacRae. You bow to no one."*

So she had stiffened her spine and glared up at the devil, though inside her stomach had been all shivery and her fingers and toes felt like ice.

And the devil had stood in front of her and talked about her—not to her, *about* her—to the lad behind him, who had stood silent, with an air of unhappiness shrouding him.

"Pathetic," ridiculed the devil, squinting his narrow demon eyes at her. "Notice well, Arion, the surly demeanor of it. Notice well the pagan color of its hair, the paleness of its skin. It is an inferior creature, all in all. Hardly worth the effort of securing it."

Lauren realized that she was the "it" in his words. She kept her head up, eyes forward, just as Da would have told her to.

"Mac-Rae," the devil smirked, making her name sound long and drawn out, a distortion of the syllables. "This is all they have to unite with their allies, this dismal female. And see how it quakes, Arion. See the weakness of its stock. Our enemy has come to a sad end indeed, to pin their hopes on this wretched child."

"I am not quaking," Lauren had said then, the first time she had dared address the devil.

But he ignored her words, just as all the others had.

"Simple," the devil mocked, dressed in his strange finery, holding a hand up to his nose, as if to block out her smell. "Weak. Common. Learn well from this, Nephew. See how easy it is to control your enemy."

The boy had not stopped staring at her, and so at last Lauren released her futile gaze on the devil-laird to glare back at the devil's nephew. He, at least, was meeting her look.

He was almost no longer a boy, Lauren could tell. He had the same lanky frame as her cousin Quinn, who was five years older than she. This boy was probably the same age, if the devil's family aged as mortals did.

His hair was coal black, and his eyes were dark and troubled.

"Our king thinks to placate us with the division of Shot," said the devil in a voice that deepened the cold in the room tenfold. "He grows weary of our island war, he says. So he panders to the Scottish king, and they drink their wine and congratulate each other on the peace they think they have scraped together. But know this, Arion: Their maps and lines and proclamations do not alter the truth. The Isle of Shot lies nearer to the coast of England, not Scotland. Our ancestors were there before the Scots. No matter who orders us to peace, the du Morgan family claims *all* of the island, and nothing will stop us from fulfilling that claim. Certainly not this feeble creature here, this little nothing."

"I am not afraid of you," Lauren had lied then, trying to inject scorn into her tone.

The devil casually crossed to her and slapped her hard across the face, sending her reeling back against the wall.

She thought she heard the boy exclaim, but her head had struck the stone and she wasn't certain. Lauren stayed there, dazed, as the shock of it wore off.

"A very little nothing," the devil said coolly. "And so easy to kill. Remember, Arion. Someday all of Shot—and all the power it represents—will be yours. This insignificant thing here is what you will need to dispatch to make it so." He turned away from her, to the boy. "Alas, however, not today. But someday. Someday soon."

The du Morgan devil had left then, and the boy had followed, throwing just one more glance at her over his shoulder before he was gone.

That had been today, Lauren was fairly certain. Time was tricky here in the scary place, and she couldn't count it out right, since it was always dark. But she thought that visit had been today.

The lamp they had left her was almost out of oil. She could tell by the way the flame grew puny and thin, a bare blue light against the heavy darkness. Soon it would be gone completely, and the blackness would take over everything. The death air would grow bolder in the darkness. Death was afraid of light.

Lauren sat down against the wall with her arms wrapped around her knees, shivering from the cold and the fear and the misery that ate away at her. She kept a fold of her tartan pressed up against her face, her cheek, breathing in the faint scent of Shot and trying to find some of the bravery she was sure must be hidden in it.

She was going to die here. What an awful thing, to die, and never see the sky again, or touch the warm sand, or swim in the ocean. Never again sleep in her corner room at Keir Castle. Never hold a starfish again, never watch dolphins weaving through the waves, never climb another tree, never see Da or Hannah or any of her family again ...

Except for Mama, up in heaven. Mama was there. Surely that had to be something.

She must have slept some, for when she lifted her head the flame from the lamp was completely gone, and the only light seeping in came from the uneven sliver of space between the door to her prison and the floor.

Lauren lowered her head again and closed her eyes, clutching the fold of tartan over her mouth, trying to hold on to her memories of her home.

$\mathcal{V}$OICES CAME TO HER IN a dream.

One of them was heavy and muttered, a man's tone. But the other was softer, womanly and sweet. The rhythm of that voice was so familiar to Lauren that she opened her eyes in the dream, the longing spreading through her in a painful ache.

"Mama?"

The lock to the cell door let out a squeak, the same sound as it always made when the key was fitted in and turned. Lauren looked over at it quickly, her heart racing. This was no dream. No, this was still the nightmare. The room was just as dark as before, and she was just as chilled. Her limbs were stiff and numb.

If this was death coming for her, she wasn't ready. But she was too cold to stand and fight.

The door opened. Light flooded into her prison, a

blinding glow, outlining the figure framed in the door-way with a radiant blur. Lauren blinked rapidly, then found the strength to stand, her back against the wall. She raised her fists.

"Oh, little girl," said the woman's voice, the one from her dream. It was still soft and gentle, and seemed to carry an undertone of music. The figure came forward, and the blur became the shape of a lady in a gown, hold-ing something in her hands.

"Who are you?" Lauren rasped, flattening back to the hard stone wall.

"Don't worry," the lady said, and the music in her words became more pronounced. "Don't worry, lit-tle girl."

When she was close enough, Lauren saw something of her face, lovely and strange, like a pixie caught down here in the dankness of the dungeon. Her eyes were large and vague; her hair fell to her waist in soft black waves.

"Don't worry," the woman crooned, lilting. She car-ried a tray. On the tray was a bowl of something that smelled like food.

Lauren's stomach betrayed her, a growl into the si-lence of the room.

The woman smiled. "See? I knew you would be happy to have me come."

She glanced around the cell, as if expecting to find a fine banquet table upon which to set her tray. Her gaze back to Lauren suggested puzzlement, then hu-mor. She knelt and placed the tray on the floor, looking up again.

"Who are you?" the lady asked, repeating Lauren's

own words back to her, but putting her faint song to them.

Lauren shook her head, wary, and tried to ignore the aroma of beef broth drifting over to her.

"Are you lost, little girl?" the woman asked now. She rose and stepped around the tray, moving toward Lauren. Her fancy gown trailed behind her, the color of summer clouds trimmed with silver. "How did you come here?"

Lauren said nothing, only watched the lady frown, faint and refined; she lifted one slender hand and wrapped her fingers around a lock of Lauren's hair.

"Oh," she said breathlessly, staring down at it. "Like . . . roses and sunset . . . melted together. I like roses. Do you, little girl?"

She seemed not to care that Lauren didn't reply, only moved her perplexed look back to Lauren's face. Her head tilted, studying her, and Lauren could only stare at her in return, appalled and captivated and starving.

"I have a mouse in my room," the lady said, slow and melodic. "A little brown mouse. I have named him Simon. Don't you think that's a good name?"

Now she appeared to want an answer, so Lauren nodded, wide-eyed. The lady watched her seriously, then shook her head, as if coming out of a daze. She took a step away from Lauren, straightening her shoulders.

"My name is Nora. I have brought you food. But you mustn't tell Uncle Ryder."

Lauren darted a quick glance down at the tray, then up to the lady's dark eyes.

"Promise," Nora said sternly. "Promise you won't tell him."

Lauren licked her lips. "I won't."

"But I don't know," Nora said, fretful now. "I don't know you. How can I believe you? You might trick me. You might tell him anyway. And then he would come. . . ." Her voice faltered and ended in a sort of moan; her eyes rolled up and then closed. "No," she whispered. "No, no, Uncle."

Her body began to sway back and forth, slow and graceful. The moan grew higher and higher in pitch, became a chant that raised the hairs on the backs of Lauren's arms.

"Blood and sea and sand and swords and song . . . *tra le la, le la . . .*"

Lauren edged sideways, moving away from her, still staring.

"No!" the lady cried, and one of her hands darted out and grabbed Lauren by the shoulder.

Back by the doorway a guard peered in. "My lady?"

Nora opened her eyes.

"Go away," she said sharply, without turning around. "I am telling this girl about my mouse Simon. You must go away. You agreed to."

"Hurry," urged the guard, and then vanished again.

"Uncle Ryder doesn't know I'm here, of course," Nora said, smiling. "He would be so angry. But I had heard of you. Arion told me of you. I thought you would like some nice food."

And Lauren, who thought she might fall down with the hunger, managed to do nothing, only stand there with the lady's hand clenched on her shoulder. Nora kept smiling her curious smile down at her.

"Come." She lightened her grip and pulled Lauren forward, toward the tray.

Lauren walked over to it almost reluctantly, though her stomach felt hollow and pained, and her mouth was watering from the delicious smell of good food. It seemed years since she had last eaten, and that had been just stale bread and a hard rind of cheese.

"Look," Nora invited, dipping down and lifting the bowl of broth. "Isn't it wonderful? I made it myself, just for you."

Steam wisped off the top of the liquid, curling magic in the stark darkness. It wafted up and filled Lauren's senses, hot and rich and meaty. It blocked out the smell of everything else: the dirt and the filth, and, most important, the death. Her hands reached out to take the bowl.

"Don't forget." Nora's voice was singsong. "Don't forget, little girl. You mustn't tell."

"No," Lauren agreed, and accepted the bowl. It heated her fingers, delicious warmth.

Nora was smiling, generous and beautiful, and Lauren felt an immense gratitude to her, whoever she was, this sad pixie person. She wanted to thank her suddenly, she wanted to shower her with words of appreciation, but her mouth would open only for the fragrant soup, and so she placed the rim of the wooden bowl to her mouth and tilted it toward her. The incredible broth slid past her lips, salty goodness over her tongue.

"Nora!"

Lauren jumped and dropped the bowl. It fell to the floor and all the wonderful broth spilled out, an arc of liquid splashing against the stones, streaming away.

"Nora!" called the same voice, young and anguished, and someone new rushed into the cell, the boy from before. He came between them and pushed Nora away from Lauren with both hands.

Nora took the force calmly, stepping back. The boy then turned and kicked the bowl that had held the broth across the room, so that it skidded and clattered up against a wall. He whirled back to the dark-haired woman.

"What were you doing?" he asked, furious and hushed. "How could you?"

"She was hungry," Nora replied, serene.

"One of the dogs," the boy began, and then stopped, shaking his head. "If Ryder discovers it— Nora! She's just a child!"

Lauren watched, spellbound, as the woman looked down at her and raised one eyebrow. Her look hinted at laughter.

"What's this?" The guard appeared again, gruff and huge, filling the doorway. "What's amiss, my lord?"

The boy spoke to him carelessly, but there was no denying the authority in his tone, even though he was so young. "It's nothing. I have a message for my sister, that's all. Leave us now."

The guard eyed the three of them, but he nodded and bowed out, leaving the empty, open doorway in his place.

"The broth you made was spilled in the buttery," the boy whispered to Nora, taking a step toward her. "The dogs came to lap it up. One has already died! The other two looked as though they would soon follow. What did you do to it?"

"It is savory," said Nora proudly.

"It is *poison*," the boy hissed back. "When Uncle Ryder finds out, he'll kill you himself! She's a hostage! She mustn't die!"

Lauren brought both hands up to her throat, gagging. She turned away from the two of them and spat on the floor, trying to rid herself of the last of the taste. Suddenly the boy was at her side, his arm tight around her shoulders.

"How much did you drink?" he asked urgently.

Lauren tried to pull away from him but he wouldn't let her, holding on tighter.

"How much?" he demanded.

"A sip!" She tore away from his grip, panting. "You won't kill me today, du Morgan!"

Amazingly, the devil's nephew smiled at her then—a true smile, swift and glad, as different from the lady's as the sun was from snow.

"No, not today," he agreed, and the gladness was in his voice as well.

"Ari?" It was Nora, now suddenly trembling, fear and panic clear in every line of her. "What—what has happened? I don't understand—"

"All is well." The boy walked to her, speaking quickly. "I think we can mend this. You need to go back to your chambers, Nora. Go now."

"Go? But . . . the little girl—she's lost, Ari, she needs our help. And I've brought her some soup, you see—"

The boy took the lady by the shoulders, nearly as tall as she. "Forget about this girl, do you understand me? *Forget her.* She's not lost. I'm taking her home now, in fact." His voice turned soothing. "All is well, Nora, all is well. Go back to your chambers."

Nora blinked, staring down into his face. The boy spoke on, the rhythm of his words steady, repetitive.

"Go as fast as you can, but walk, do you understand? Walk the entire way. If anyone stops you, tell them you must be back in your chambers to prepare for confession. Tell them the priest is waiting for you. But stay there. Don't go to confession. Wait for me. Do you understand, Nora?"

"Walk," the lady echoed, sounding relieved. "Back to my chambers."

"That's right," said the boy, and pushed her lightly to the door.

"Yes." Nora left the room, talking softly, as if to herself. "Confession, you see. I must go and confess. . . ."

The boy faced Lauren. "You. Come with me."

"Unholy demon!" Lauren circled away from him. "Touch me and I'll send you back to hell, where you belong!"

The boy stopped and considered her, unsmiling. "I won't hurt you."

Lauren let out a disbelieving laugh, slowly covering the perimeter of her cell, trying to reach the open door before he noticed.

"I won't," the boy repeated. "You have to trust me."

"Why should I?"

"MacRae!" he said, impatient. "Do you want to get out of here or not?"

"Not with you," Lauren replied, and sprinted for the door.

She almost made it. She had actually taken one full running step past the opening before he grabbed her and pulled her to him, clapping one hand over her mouth and the other across her chest. She fought, twisting and kicking, but he was older, and bigger, and stronger.

"Stop!" he grunted in her ear. "Stupid girl! I'm trying to save you!"

She kicked him again, then stomped down hard on his foot. His indrawn gasp told her that she had, at least, inflicted some pain.

"Lauren MacRae!" He bit off her name, furious. "If you want to see your father again, you had better do as I tell you!"

Lauren paused, all of the violence in her stilled at the mention of Da.

Slowly the boy loosened his grip, testing to see if she would run again, and when she didn't, he let her go completely. She whisked around to see his face, to catch the untruth lurking there.

"I know where he is," the boy said seriously. "I'll show you how to reach him. But you must obey me. Do exactly as I say."

The lie wasn't there. Or rather, she couldn't see it. In this young man's face she could detect only the appearance of sincerity. She could tell now that his eyes were not brown, as she had thought, but rather a very dark green, like the deepest part of the ocean, strangely beautiful.

He gazed back at her, just as serious as before, and then something odd happened. Lauren was looking up at him, at the youthful face that was already molding into the features of a man, and she felt a curious thing in her heart. She didn't have a name for it—heat and moment and a hard beating—and it all coalesced into something almost like . . . trust.

"Come on," the boy named Arion said softly, and reached out and took her hand. "Come with me, Mac-Rae. I can save you."

He could take her back to Da. He was the devil's kin, but he held the key to reaching Da, the only key. And they both knew it.

So she let him lead her down the cramped hall of the dungeon, past many blackened doors set low to the ground, past torches that offered surly light, past puddles and pitted stones. The smell of death penetrated everything here.

When she looked over her shoulder for the third time, the boy leaned down to her. "The guard is gone," he murmured. "Nora probably gave him coin. But he'll be back soon. We have to move faster."

They climbed very steep stairs and crept through dark, empty hallways, ducking into shadows, and once—when voices sounded abrupt and near around a corner—into an empty room, hiding behind tables and chairs.

But no one came, and soon they were going again, down smaller and smaller hallways, to another room with an open window. The boy pulled her over to it and Lauren was shocked to see that it was night out, a silver-blue night with a faint handful of stars above.

He moved to the wall and placed his hands on it, and the wall moved—opened up! Just like a door!

Lauren was still gaping at this wizardry when he grabbed her hand again and pulled her into the emptiness where the wall used to be. It was very black, blacker even than her cell had been. Lauren stopped in spite of herself, thinking of traps and guards and the devil waiting ahead for her.

"MacRae," the boy whispered, mocking. "Are you a coward, like the rest of your family?"

Lauren stepped briskly into the unknown, shoving past him until a tug on her tartan turned her in the other direction.

"This way."

They walked and walked, and even through the blackness Lauren wanted to break into a blind run, to get away from the smothering blanket of it, but the boy took up the whole space ahead of her, and she would not prove his taunt by running. She bit down on the inside of her cheek to choke back a hated whimper of fear. But her pace did not falter.

And then there was another door, and this one revealed the sky and the stars and blessed, fresh air. They left the tunnel and Lauren saw that the wizardry had taken them to a clearing in the woods, and the new door looked for all the world like a regular wall of rock, set back into a hillside. Behind them—not so very far behind—was a tremendous castle, looming with dark menace through the trees.

"Go down this path and follow that star there, do you see it?" The boy pointed to one of the sparkles in the sky, one that danced with red and green and gold. "Follow that for miles, and stay away from people until you reach the second village. You'll find your father by sunrise, if you hurry."

She gazed back at him, cloaked in the wooded, leafy starlight.

"Why did you do this?" Lauren asked.

Something in his face turned bitter, a look that held the shadow of a wearied adult.

"Just go."

"Why?" she persisted.

There was a long stretch of silence between them, and his eyes grew shuttered, the corners of his mouth grim. She didn't think he would say anything more, but then he did. His words fell flat around them.

"Don't think it was for you, MacRae. I did it for my sister. I did it for Nora. She must think you're a danger—I don't know why. You were only our uncle's hostage, to be exchanged for one of our own. But you'd be no use to us dead."

The bitter shadow on him grew deeper, and for an instant she saw an image of the man he would grow into—hard planed and masculine, unforgiving and severe. The menace of the castle behind him seemed to suit him perfectly.

"I can't watch her all the time. I'd rather risk having you free and gone than my sister punished for taking your life, even if you are a MacRae. Now go. And don't ever come back, or I may kill you myself."

Lauren turned away from him and began to run down the path, through the scattered leaves on the ground, into the obscurity of the night.

Chapter Two

*H*E WON'T DIE."

Lauren MacRae leaned back in her chair, stretching out the ache of combat that still lingered in her shoulders, and then added, "Although, he should."

The other woman in the room spoke mildly down to her embroidery.

"Be more charitable to him. It might easily have been him saving us, you know."

"No, I don't know that. I'll tell you why." Lauren pushed out of the chair, already impatient with rest, and paced around the chamber. "If it had been us out there yesterday morning, being slaughtered by a boatload of Vikings, du Morgan would have merely turned away. He would have let those Northmen do his dirty work for him, and then most likely thanked them kindly when it was over. It would save him a parcel of trouble to have us dead, and don't think he doesn't know that."

"You are too harsh."

Lauren shrugged, not replying because the only things now on the tip of her tongue were unkind. Hannah was her best friend in this world, and Lauren did not wish to be unkind to her. So instead she walked to one of the windows of her father's private solar, gazing out to what surely had to be her favorite view of Shot.

The woods, deep and dark and filled with green mystery.

The slope of the hills that turned into mountains, varied and rugged with granite and quartz.

The shoreline, deceptively calm and flat.

The ocean. Cold, endless. Sparkling indigo and green and silver.

And it was hers, all of it. Well, hers and her people's. The Isle of Shot belonged to the Clan MacRae, and had since the beginning of time. No English edict was going to change that. No English devil family could alter it. The MacRaes were here first, no matter what the English said, and so Shot would always rightfully be theirs. It was as true as the rhythm of life itself, sometimes stronger, sometimes fainter. But always there.

Too bad for her, right now the pulse was at its fainter wane. The threat from the outside had begun to wear on them all. But she was not ready to give up yet—not ever.

"How is he doing?" asked Hannah now, her voice just as gentle as always.

Lauren turned around and stared at her blankly.

"Our visitor," Hannah reminded her, looking up from her sewing. "Our guest. The Earl of Morgan."

"Oh." She turned back to the window. "I'm sure he's fine. Elias said he would recover. That's good enough for me."

"Indeed," agreed Hannah. "But perhaps you should go see for yourself."

Clever Hannah, always finding her sore points. Hannah knew that Lauren didn't want to spend any more time with the Englishman than she had to. He was most likely awake now, and demanding answers.

Lauren lifted one hand to the glassed window, tracing the outline of lead that held the panes together. Let him wait. Let him worry. Just a bit longer.

"He was defending our land, after all," said Hannah, after a pause. "He almost died for it."

"You know he thinks it's his land."

"And you know it isn't. So what does it matter? His blood was spilt for Shot. The blood of his kin, as well."

"And the blood of *my* kin!" Lauren pushed away from the window and started pacing again, giving in to the anger simmering in her with each strong step.

"Oh, Lauren." Hannah's voice was soft with sorrow. "Your father's death was a terrible loss to us all. But don't you think it might be time to let go your hatred of this family? We have a new worry to consider. We have a new enemy to vanquish from our home. It was not the du Morgans who killed your father. It was not the du Morgans who injured Quinn. It was the Vikings."

Lauren bowed her head, wanting to block out the words, wanting to block out the truth of it all.

Da, murdered by these foul invaders not yet a week ago. Her cousin Quinn, next in line to lead the clan, so seriously injured from the same battle that it was thought he might not recover.

Lauren had never been like other girls she knew. She had never willfully maintained the fantasy of a soft, sheltered life. She was a daughter of Shot, and of Hebron MacRae, the finest laird ever to head the clan. Her mother had passed away when she was young, so Lauren had grown up in the footsteps of her father, playing in the untamed woods of the island, learning to hunt and fish and even scuffle with the boys. Not for her, the confines of embroidery and looms and cooking and the safety of the walls of Keir Castle. She could shoot an arrow as straight as anyone; she was one of the swiftest in the whole clan. And, Da would say, laughing at her exploits, one of the most dauntless.

For some reason, she had thought herself inured to death, ready for it. She had thought it just a natural part of her world. What a naïve child she had been after all, even after she had grown up. All along she had thought she was so hardened, fit for anything. Yet last week Lauren realized for the first time that her life had been wildly protected—as if she had walked and walked but never strayed from the charmed luck of a fairy circle. Last week she had finally gone beyond the circle, and stepped into a harsh new world.

When the truth came, when they had carried the laird's bloodied body back to the castle, all Lauren had felt was a shaking terror, followed by a profound fury.

Da was gone. Forever.

"War is never particular about whose blood it claims, dearest," Hannah said, almost reading her thoughts. "Your Da understood that. You know he would have done anything to protect you, and to protect our home. The fact remains that this new Earl of Morgan and his men came across a threat to all of us yesterday, and they moved to halt it. You cannot fault them for that."

Lauren said nothing. She flicked a bright strand of hair out of her eyes, blinking down at the blue slate stones of the floor.

"And it could be that thanks to this English knight,"

Hannah continued, "Shot is secure another day. We didn't have a sentry for that stretch of beach."

"We've never needed one before! I can't believe those raiders made it past the rough currents offshore there!"

Hannah watched her, all calm and genuine benevolence in her chair, her hands no longer busy with the thread and cloth. Her fine silver hair was lit by the sun, her brown eyes held nothing but warmth. "But they did make it past the currents. And we have du Morgan to thank for at least slowing them down enough to repel them."

Lauren stood with her hands on her hips, scowling out the window. She didn't want to agree to this, no matter how true it was. She didn't want to give the Englishman any credit at all. He was another enemy, that was it. He was another threat to her family—a very particular one to her.

And she had lost so much of her family already.

"Lauren."

Just that. Just her name, and Hannah knew that she could not help but bend to the understated command in the syllables.

"I'll go to him," Lauren said, curt. "I will."

"You know we cannot keep him here much longer. His people have already sent demands for his return. Best to see to him now, don't you think?" She waited, then added, "It's what your father would have expected of you."

The sunlight flickered and disappeared behind a bank of clouds the shade of new steel. All the colors before her shifted to match that tint, enhancing the autumn seduction of the view.

Behind her she heard the patient silence of Hannah, her friend, her adviser.

Lauren let out a sigh. "Very well. I'll go now."

"Be kind to him," Hannah reminded her, as she was walking out of the room.

"Oh, aye," Lauren replied softly. "Depend upon it."

***

ARION DU MORGAN LAY SLEEPING in the pallet they had provided him, drifting in and out of awareness with a slow steadiness that seemed to match the sluggish pace of his heartbeat, gradually growing stronger.

Where was he? His memory was pained and dim—blunt flashes of faces and voices, potions of hot liquid, and a searing pain in his shoulder.

Blood. Sand.

He had been out on patrol with a small party of men. Aye, that was right. They were walking for stealth, because Hammond had said it would be better to walk that strange length of beach than to ride, and Ari had listened to him because Hammond knew this land far better than he did. Hammond had been born on Shot, while Ari had spent nearly the whole of his life on the mainland. This was his first visit to the island as the new earl since his uncle had died four months ago.

They had been walking on their patrol, had rounded the corner of a thick woods and heavy dunes, and then there were the Vikings, bold and astonishingly careless in their arrival, their longship in plain site from the shore.

And then, Ari remembered, all hell had broken loose.

He and his men had been spotted, and there was nothing left to do but fight or die.

Dying had surely seemed the most likely outcome. There had been only eight of them, after all, and countless, countless Vikings. . . .

After that, things got blurry. But he wasn't dead; he couldn't be. His shoulder hurt too damned much for that. Definitely alive—or was this hell?

There was something heavy and bulky tied around his shoulder and under his arm. Bandages, many of them. Dead men didn't need to be bandaged.

He remembered more. He remembered attempting to get up, trying to leave this place and search out his men. But the people here had stopped him, whoever they were—demons or angels—and gradually Ari had come to understand that his men were safe, all seven of them. They had repeated that to him enough so that he had surrendered again to the sleeping potions.

Arion tried to sit up now and immediate, unpleasant waves of blackness rolled up into his vision. When they receded, he was sprawled flat again, breathing hard, twisted awkwardly across the pallet. Slowly, carefully, he straightened himself out.

The room that held him was small but had a window which let in the fresh ocean air. Too nice a breeze for hell, he would think. There was also a great, tall ceiling, with heavy beams of wood crisscrossing the arch of it. The shadows up there seemed to shift and float in peaceful grace, silent spirits, guardian angels, perhaps, watching him . . . so this might be heaven. . . .

The door opened. Still dazed, Ari turned his head to

look and watched as one of the angels from above took shape and form and glided forward into the chamber, a vision of celestial copper-haired beauty in—surprisingly enough—a tartan.

Arion frowned. It was significant, that tartan. Perhaps even more so than the angel herself, who had walked over to him lying flat there on the hard pallet and stood silent, examining him with sober radiance.

The tartan was fixed and pinned in intricate folds over one of Angel's shoulders with a brooch of silver, then wrapped around her waist to fall in warm lines almost to the floor, covering the gown beneath. It was a deep, subtle blue, with blurred lines of emerald and teal and violet running through it. A hunting tartan, designed to disguise the form it covered in the patchwork pattern of the forest.

And that meant that this woman was no angel at all, but a hunter.

"Awake?" she asked, a single word she managed to imbue with a rich variety of inflections: scorn and disdain, danger and threat.

He sat up fully despite the streaking pain that stabbed through him and the black waves that rushed back. Ari gritted his teeth, fighting them, and felt a slow victory when they began to dissolve. He was bare chested, blankets around his waist, clearly unable to hide the fact that his breathing was strained. But Angel's eyes did not shift from his face.

Reality came back. He knew now where he was, and who she was. There could be only one possible answer. At the very same moment, Arion realized that he was nude, that his sword was nowhere to be seen, and that this enemy of his had a heavy silver dagger tucked prominently into the folds of material at her waist. It would take her no time at all to draw it—and he had no doubt that she knew how to use it.

She watched him steadily, unmoving, and Ari thought she must have sensed at least some of his comprehension, for now a slow smile curved her pretty lips, one that held no humor at all.

Angel took one step closer, keeping the smile. Her hair fell loose and free, untied from the queue she had worn on the beach—yesterday? today?—and it now covered her shoulders and back in an unbelievably rich cascade of color. It framed her so perfectly, waved and satiny in the sunlight. A breeze came and stirred it, shimmering copper, and the light showed him her eyes now, too, hauntingly familiar, the color of . . .

"Whiskey," he said.

She actually looked surprised, if only for second.

"Have you any, Lauren MacRae?" Arion asked, leaning back against the wall behind him.

She stood frozen, staring down at him.

"I have it right, don't I?" Ari asked now, moving his own glance away from her, as if unconcerned. The blankets around him fell away further, exposing not just his torso but his stomach as well, and even lower. "You *are* Lauren MacRae, are you not? Or is it Lauren Murdoch by now?"

Angel gave him a frigid smile—wholly at odds with the warm halo of her hair—and crossed to a table Ari hadn't noticed before, by the door. When she turned back she carried a flask. She pulled out the stopper for him and handed it over.

"Enjoy," she said, but the tone of her voice said, *Choke on it.*

He offered back his own smile, dry, then took a long draw from the flask.

The whiskey was good. Better than good, it was incredible, spicy and warm and smooth. But he was careful to stop after two swallows, because he knew he would need his wits to stay sharp around his adversary.

She was stunning. He couldn't think of a better word for her than that—stunning. She was exquisite and delicate and shone with all the wonderful colors he could have ever imagined on a woman—pale golden eyes and lustrous copper hair and alabaster skin tinted with pink . . . dark brown lashes and brows; her lips blood rose, full and erotic. He couldn't believe this was the child he had seen all those years ago, a thin brat grown up to be—a goddess.

But it *was* she. He knew it in bones, in his soul. Now that his head had cleared some he recognized the same bold spirit he had seen in that small girl, glowing like a living flame in the woman here in front of him. This was Lauren MacRae of the Clan MacRae, and thus one of his most hated enemies.

Ari wanted to laugh with despair and anger. Who could have guessed his enemy would have grown up to be so ruthlessly fair?

He had to pretend to take another swallow of the whiskey to cover his body's reaction to her: total greed. Quick, raging desire. He wanted her, wanted her so badly that he couldn't even look at her face for more than a few seconds at a time. It was crazed, it was deep and shadowed and endless, passion as he had never before known—or even suspected. He had to disguise the shaking of his hands.

This was insane. He must have injured his head in the battle. There had to be something wrong with him, *something* that could explain this tide of emotion that quickened through him and boiled up to his skin, this complete craving for her.

If she discovered this fault in him she would not hesitate to use it against him. And Arion realized, to his aggravation, that he would probably have to let her, that he wouldn't be able to stop her one bit. Just the thought of touching her—even her hand, her wrist, the soft, supple flesh of her arm—brought forth a torrent of dark fantasies. He closed his eyes, fighting it.

Her voice floated out into the room, velvet and smoke, utterly feminine.

"What were you doing on my land, du Morgan?"

His eyes opened again. Lauren MacRae kept her face impartial, only a glint of something cold and hostile in the lovely amber of her eyes telling him how she really felt: she loathed him. It was so obvious, and so utterly appropriate that he wanted to laugh again, but he didn't.

"Your land?" Arion murmured. "Pardon me. I was under the impression it was mine."

"You could use a lesson in geography," she replied pleasantly, and the glint grew colder. "The Isle of Shot belongs to the MacRaes."

"Odd. I seem to recall something about my family being here before yours."

"You are, no doubt, delusional. Perhaps I should confine you for your own good. Keir Castle does not have a dungeon, of course—we are not English barbarians—but I am positive I can discover a sufficiently unpleasant location for you."

Arion did look at her now, full on. "Was that a threat, MacRae?"

She gave a graceful shrug. "I don't have to threaten. You are in *my* home now, du Morgan."

Her smile was not even guarded, just clear, gorgeous spite. If the circumstances had been at all in his favor, he would have given in to the urge to lie back and admire her gall *and* her beauty.

"*Your* home," he repeated lightly. "Forgive me, Mac-Rae, my head must be muddled. When did you become the leader of your clan?"

He meant it as a casual insult, but he could see his barb went deeper than that, that he had truly wounded her. Seeing it in her caused a similar sensation in him—his heart clenched up, a stabbing ache, pain that he had pained her.

Arion was staggered by his reaction. He could not allow her to control him like this.

"My cousin is the laird," she finally said, her face showing none of her distress. "I speak for him."

He was surprised in spite of himself. "Your father?"

"Dead," she answered flatly.

Ari nodded, understanding now the source of that hurt in her. "I'm sorry."

"Aye, I'm sure you are," she said scathingly. "Very sorry indeed."

He could only shrug, knowing she wouldn't believe him. He couldn't blame her, so he changed the subject.

"I want to see my men."

"Your men are safe enough."

"Take me to them."

She had her composure back now, a careful smile on her face that couldn't quite disguise the icy anger behind it. "I think not, du Morgan. You'll just have to believe me, because you are staying here."

He sat up straighter. "Am I your prisoner, MacRae?"

"Why not? Perhaps it's your turn to play hostage."

"That would be," he said softly, letting his own threat come through in his voice, "very, very foolish of you."

"Oh, think you so?" Her smile faded but the coldness almost sparkled around her now, sharp and winter bright. "Think you so indeed?"

Arion narrowed his eyes. "Hold me here against my will and you risk a war, not only with my family on the other side of this island, but with my country. You know that both Henry and William have issued edicts against either of our families taking any more hostages. We have a truce."

"*Truce.* Is that what you call it?"

"Why," he drawled, "what do you term it, MacRae?"

"Injustice! Your 'truce' was only begun *after* I had been taken by your family as a child."

"Taken—and *freed,* MacRae. Or have you forgotten that part?"

She stilled, staring at him, unreadable. "No. I have not forgotten."

Ari met her look, caught again in the colors of her, the strange notion of this beauty grown from that little girl. They had met so briefly at Ryder's castle—yet Arion remembered this aspect of her over all else: reckless bravery and wary intelligence, thoughts upon thoughts, the true depths of her mind hidden behind that amber gaze. Then her chilling smile returned, and he saw only the woman once more.

"Yet I think you'll agree, du Morgan, that it is indeed *our* turn to take one of *you*. In the interest of fairness, after all."

"King Henry will not tolerate your hate."

"Your king," she said mildly, "is much too far away from Shot to aid you now, in case you had not noticed. All your English forces are too far. And my family has subdued yours for centuries."

"I heard it was the other way around." He was deliberately baiting her, though he knew it was not wise. It was the thwarted passion in him, perhaps, that made him say, "I heard my family has defeated yours."

"Mainlander," she scoffed, and he didn't need to see her eyes to catch the derision there. She turned away from him, walked to the window. One of her hands swept out in a fluid arc, gesturing to the view.

"All you can see before you belongs to my clan. Everything from here to the shore, from the woods to the far mountains, is ours." She looked back at him, a calm glance over her shoulder. "You are new to Shot. You grew up on the mainland with your uncle, so I suppose I could not expect you to know the truth of the island. But look around you, du Morgan. Look at my strong home. Look at the stone walls of Keir, the solid defense of it all. My family built this, my parents and their parents and all our kin. We control most of this island, even by decree of your own king. Your home here on Shot is weak and unfinished. It always will be."

Now she faced him fully again, folding her arms across her chest. Her voice was still mild, the velvet in it unchanged, but Arion was not fooled. He had seen her battle a man twice her size and defeat him. He had seen her kill. And so he knew she could do it again, if she wanted to.

"Let your own eyes determine the truth for you," said his fair enemy. "The du Morgan fortress on the other side of Shot is representative of your presence here: small and insignificant. Now, why don't you gather your nerve and answer my question—what were you doing on my land?"

Arion smiled suddenly, he couldn't help it. She was so devoutly scornful of him, yet so beguiling, with her long hair and her clean beauty and the temptation of her voice.

Good God, he was surely going mad.

He erased the smile. "I believe that beach falls exactly on the border between your part of the island and mine. So I don't really think you can rightfully claim it. If anything, MacRae, it would be *our* land."

"Yours! Are you an imbecile? You just said it's on the border! Yet now you dare to claim it as your own—"

"No," he interrupted. "I meant *ours*. Yours and mine together."

That silenced her, all right. Her eyes widened, her lips parted. She seemed stunned, and Ari watched as the natural rose of her cheeks deepened and spread, a flush of indignation that he could almost see rising through her. She took a deep breath, and opened her mouth to speak.

"I've answered your question, MacRae," Arion said

quickly, before she let loose her anger. "Now you answer mine. Why did you save my life?"

Lauren stared at him, at this bold stranger sitting up brashly on the pallet—*her* pallet, in *her* room, in *her* castle—and couldn't even find the words to tell him what she thought of him.

Idiot. That was a good one. Certainly he must be an idiot, to taunt a foe in her own domain.

Arrogant. That one suited him, too. Arrogant and sure, smiling smugly at her while he questioned her, evading her righteous hostility with own easy demeanor.

Crafty. To think to divert her interrogation of him, to hide his own sly plans for subterfuge on her land by attempting to confuse her, by daring to claim that the families actually held part of Shot together.

Deceitful. Wicked. Vile! Odious! Contemptible and . . . handsome.

Lauren couldn't deny what was such a striking truth; that would be a weakness in her, and she would not allow this man to grant her any weakness, no matter how much he troubled her.

So, yes, handsome. He sat there as calm as lake water, with his raven-black hair and his laughing green eyes—*still the color of the heart of the ocean,* she thought unwillingly—the sensual line of his lips heightened now with a faint smile. The powerful shape of him was beautifully framed against the cool stone wall behind him.

He was large and finely built—not a brute of a man, but with something more like refinement shading him. It irked her all the more, that this du Morgan could have turned out so comely; that when she meant to stare him down with abhorrence, what she saw was a strong jaw and broad shoulders, muscular arms, a flat, tapered stomach. . . .

As far as Lauren was concerned, it was all just another black mark against him.

Yesterday morning she had seen him from afar, battling the Vikings. Losing. His group had been sadly outnumbered, a very few to a great many, and Lauren and her own party were running toward the fray almost as soon as they had discovered it. In that very first pulse-pounding moment, it hadn't mattered that it was the du Morgans they were coming to aid. What had mattered was that there were aliens on Shot, the same heinous invaders who had murdered Da so cruelly. Lauren knew that her men would do anything to hurt them back, and right then she had felt the same way.

Aye, and she had seen this English knight first thing, his black hair free and tangled in the wind, the impressive size of him almost evenly matched against the giant he fought. Somehow, she had known instinctively that he was Arion du Morgan, the Earl of Morgan. It had been only a matter of time before they met again, she had always known that. She had heard, along with everyone else, that his uncle was dead, that a new enemy headed the devil family. Here at last was the boy from that nightmare in her childhood, now a full-grown man, tainting the shores of her island with his very presence.

And even that had not stopped her from aiding him.

His battle skills were sharp and true, she could tell that even from a distance. But Lauren had already seen that the Vikings did not scruple to fight unfairly, and when the arrow struck him she had not been surprised.

By then, however, her people had reached the beach, and they had joined in the fury with something close to unholy glee.

Lauren wasn't proud of having inflicted death. Almost the whole of the battle, in fact, was a blankness in her mind. Almost emptiness, like a scene hidden behind a kind of red, veiled haze. When she tried to remember those bloody moments, all she could summon was a knotted mess of emotions: fury and pain and excitement, newfound power and might. If she concentrated on it too much, she grew nauseated.

But something must have taken her arms and lifted them against the Viking. Something had moved her feet quickly enough to dodge his lethal axe, drawing him away from the fallen man. The sun and the sea and even the sand had been her allies, showing her the weakness of the giant, allowing her the will and the courage to end his life.

Yes, that had to have been the way it was. Glory and retribution.

But it bothered her that she couldn't remember.

When the red haze had cleared from her head, she had looked around again. The rest of the Northmen were fleeing, splashing through the waves to the safety of their longboat, closing ranks to heal their wounds and plan their next attack.

"Will you not answer an honest question, MacRae?" Arion du Morgan asked now, the hard lines of his face showing her only what he wanted her to see. "I know it was you who came between me and that Norseman's axe. Why?"

Lauren looked down at the floor, then up again into

the steady deep green of his gaze. "Consider it an even trade," she answered. "A life for a life."

His brows lifted, more arrogance, mingled with what might have been skepticism.

"Even though you meant only to save your sister that night in your uncle's dungeon," Lauren said, "I, at least, have honor. You managed to rescue me as well, and I have not forgotten it. Therefore, I saved you. But now we are more than even."

He laughed then, low and soft. It startled her, though she thought she managed not to show it.

"Oh really?" he asked, mirthful. "Is that what you think?"

He could infuriate her that easily, with just the contempt of his words, the easy attraction of his smile. Lauren clenched her teeth and returned his smile, a challenge. She would not give him the satisfaction of knowing he had riled her so thoroughly.

Slowly, slowly, the expression on his face changed. The hard hauteur seemed to melt away, the sharp edge of his amusement blended into something else, something more subtle, warmer. She stared over at him, watching the transformation, wondering at it in the back of her mind.

His eyes were so very green. His lashes were long and black. A vivid memory washed over her: the boy he had been, taking her hand in the cold death hall of the dungeon, telling her he would save her. The curious beating of her heart as she had stared up at him, that moment of awareness and heat.

The memory of that feeling merged with the present, swallowing her, immersing her in back then but letting her stay here now; and it all felt like a rising within her, as if she had broken free of a restraint she had not noticed before. It held her, let her feel the nervous energy of it, strange magic. Like the sparks that grew between folds of wool on a winter's night, crackling and shocking. All this from him—this man.

Lauren broke the look, her mind reeling, her mouth dry. She had to get out of here. She had to get away from him before he realized the uneasiness of her state, that he had found in her some odd deficiency, some wicked wizardry that let him confuse her.

She walked slowly to the door, making certain her hands were not clenched into the fists she wanted to make. Just before she vanished into the hallway she stopped, but did not turn around.

"I saved your life, du Morgan, and that of your comrades. It is a fact. But don't expect it to happen again. Next time, I will be the first one to cheer when they kill you."

Lauren walked out of the room, and made sure to lock the door loudly behind her.

$\mathcal{S}$HE DID NOT GO BACK to see him the next day.

Lauren told herself it was because she had too many other duties to attend to—meetings with her people, assessing the wounded from the latest battle, checking the patrols, the supplies, the fields, and the fishing nets. So many things.

She sent word to the English that their lord was nearly fit to leave. She knew they were growing more and more impatient, and despite her empty threat to the earl, the last thing she needed now was a hostage to spark a new war on top of the one with the Vikings. Her clan was already worn close to desperation, and no one understood this better than she.

With each passing day since her father's death, Lauren had prayed she would be able to retrace his steps as a leader, the great laird that he had been. He had tutored her himself, he had raised her after Mama had died, he had taught her and shaped her as surely and proudly as if she had been his son. Were it not for the accident of her sex it would be she who would lead the clan now, and not her cousin. That was not to be, obviously. Yet with Da gone, Lauren found herself pushing forward all the things that Hebron would have done.

And in the turmoil of the past week, the clan had accepted her. Most of them. She was the closest thing they had to Da, she knew that as much as anyone. It helped that her voice echoed with ideas and words she had picked up from her father, lessons learned by steady observation and her own intuition.

The new laird lay dying in Da's bed, carefully tended by the best medicines and healers the clan had to offer. Yet it might not be enough. No one had to say it. Quinn had lost a lot of blood, and he had not yet awakened from a blow to his head.

In the absence of her father and her cousin, Lauren had instinctively stepped in. It had seemed as natural as the ocean tide, and it had happened so smoothly that Lauren thought she might be the only one who had looked around one morning a few days ago in slow astonishment and realized what had happened.

It was ingrained in her as the deepest rings in the heart of an oak tree: Lead the family. Protect Shot. Save them all. Every day she would mull over each new trouble, trying to be clever, trying to think like Da.

What to do about the Vikings?

Double the patrols, instructed a voice in her mind. *Watch for them at night. They hide in the moonlight. Be ready for them.*

What about all the injured men?

Guide them. Comfort them. Inspire them if you can.

What of Quinn?

Pray for him.

And the English. The Earl of Morgan and his men?

No answer. The voice didn't seem to have a response for this new twist in her life. She couldn't even imagine what Da would say.

So Lauren concentrated on doing the things she knew she should do. She focused on her people, she smiled confidently and spoke briskly, cutting off any fear that might linger in her voice. She visited the women in the kitchens, the children in the nursery. She sat with her father's men while they brewed up plans for that night's patrols. When the day was winding down to darkness, she went to visit the chamber that held their wounded.

None had been killed in the latest fight with the Vikings. It seemed a miracle that they had all survived—even the English—because the previous two battles had been so lethal. The first had killed eight of their men, the second, ten. One of those had been Da.

Lauren walked slowly around the men lying in rows in the medicine chamber, talking to them soberly, letting them see that she was unhurt, that she was just as determined to fend off the invaders as ever. They looked up at her with hope, with grit and confidence and lasting faith. She spoke with Elias, their best healer, about each of them, finding and hoarding encouragement from his short sentences, struggling to interpret good news in the sparseness of his words.

No change in Quinn, she learned. And with that Elias fell silent, leaving Lauren to fight away her fear.

When she left it was truly nighttime, and she had to rummage in the buttery to find the remains of the supper that had been served to everyone else. She took her meal and ate it in solitary silence up at the top of one of the turrets, looking out at the savage enchantment of her island, masked in the netherlight of the evening sky. The ocean was a siren's song in the near distance, sparkling black and silver. The stars hung low above her, glittering points that melted into the horizon.

A sentry walked by and greeted her, and Lauren nodded back.

It was time.

There was a regular shift of guards both at du Morgan's door and at the door to the room that held his men. She let the guard silently unlock the one that held the earl, then shut it softly behind her.

The chamber was unlit, only the glow from the window outlining the shapes around her. She crossed to the pallet, expecting to find the form there sleeping. But he wasn't sleeping. He wasn't there at all, just the mess of his blankets.

"Spying, MacRae?"

Lauren turned quickly to the sound and found a

lighter form amid the dark, near the far wall. The bandages around his shoulder were a pale smudge against the black.

"What are you doing up?" she demanded.

"Planning my escape, of course." The night masked his face but she thought he might have flashed that smile of his, faint in the shadows.

She ignored the undertone of sarcasm in his words, instead moving away from the revealing patch of ghostly light that fell across the floor, choosing to stay in the dimness, as he did. "You will make yourself more ill. You will never heal if you do not rest."

"So?"

Another challenge. He seemed full of them, but right now Lauren was almost too tired to spar with him. It was draining enough just being around him, maintaining her feigned indifference to him, hiding the confusion he brought out in her.

"So, go ahead then," she said tartly. "Die, if that's what you want. Reopen your wounds and bleed to death. I'll no longer waste my good linen on your bandages."

He chuckled, still hidden in the cool night. "I'm sure it would please you to no longer have to worry about me, MacRae."

"Aye. I'll hold a festival to celebrate your demise. Please do hurry up with it. The dancing won't wait."

He didn't laugh this time, but walked slowly to her, until the starlight sloped across his features, becoming lost in the ebony of his hair, shining like mercury in the depths of his eyes. He wasn't smiling any longer; clearly he was an earl again, a tall knight with only a blanket wrapped around his waist and still holding all the dignity and power she had ever before seen on a man.

"Did you come to kill me in my sleep, MacRae?" he asked quietly.

She was offended, though she knew it was just another of his taunts.

"I told you before, du Morgan. I am not an English barbarian. Your life means nothing to me beyond the debt that I have repaid. But it would hardly make sense to save you in battle only to kill you the next day."

His head tilted just slightly, serious, his eyes narrowed. She felt that strangeness slipping over her again, that unexpected heat, the connection between them that felt like quick sparks, close to pain. Without meaning to Lauren took a step back, away from him, and then made herself stop.

"I have come to make you an offer," she said, after it was clear that he did not mean to break the silence. At her words she imagined she saw a new glimmer in his eyes, something bright and interested, then subdued. But he kept his silence along with that intense look down at her, almost too handsome to be true, a man made of silver and starlight and stone.

"Will you listen?" she asked over the hard pounding of her heart.

He arched one eyebrow, then nodded, not releasing her from his gaze.

Lauren took another step back, gathering her thoughts.

"I don't want your life, du Morgan, no matter what you may think. I have other concerns right now. But there is something else I want from you, and I'm willing to release you and your men in exchange for it."

She stopped, because she feared she was talking too fast, that her speed was betraying her nervousness. Finally he spoke, although he did not move otherwise.

"And what would that be?"

"Information," she said. "I want information from you, from your family on the other side of Shot. I want to know everything you know about these Northmen who killed my father. How many ships you've seen, how many men you've fought onshore, their weapons, their battle strategies. Everything."

"Where is your fiancé, Lauren? Where is Murdoch?"

The question seemed so out of place, so far from what she had been thinking about that for a moment she couldn't comprehend what he meant. Then reality came back, and with it an odd rush of disappointment.

"We sent word for his help," she said, looking away. "But his castle is inland, not very near the shore. It takes time to reach the mainland from Shot, then time again to reach his holding, I understand. And I don't have the luxury of time right now to wait for his aid."

"How long ago did you send for him?"

She let out her breath slowly, not wanting to answer.

"How long, MacRae?"

"A month," she snapped.

"Ah," he said, nodding. "I see."

"I don't believe you do," she said. "Payton Murdoch will be here, have no worries over that. He made an oath to my father to wed me, and will have every interest in arriving to protect his bride and my dowry. We are to be married in less than two months, in fact. His clan and

mine have been allies for generations, and he knows as
well as anyone that our marriage will strengthen both
families. But an army cannot be gathered in a day. Even
you must understand that. He will surely be here."

"Surely," agreed the earl, and she couldn't tell now if
it was sarcasm or irony or just boredom in his tone. He
turned away from her, showing her the broad muscles
of his back in the drama of the shadows.

"And once he arrives," du Morgan continued in the
same tone, "all your troubles will be erased, won't they?
You'll have your future husband here to take charge, to
fight your battles for you. You'll have the added force of
his clan." He turned to face her again. "But what do
you do until then, Lauren? How much time can you afford to give him, this miracle maker?"

"I don't need him to fight my battles for me," she
replied, stung. "I can fend for myself, unlike you."

"Oh, forgive me. I forgot I was talking to the grand
Lauren MacRae, great Scottish warrior."

"Great enough to save your sorry life!"

He paused, watching her, and Lauren realized he had
done it again, he had set the trap and led her to it—and
she had fallen for the bite in his words with easy gulli-
bility. He seemed to delight in tormenting her. She set
her lips together and stared at him, holding back more
insults. He would not trip her again so readily.

"You're right," he said, sounding perfectly serious once
more. "You did save me. I watched you do it, and it would
be a lie to say you were anything but great on the beach
that morning."

All the retorts she had been considering died to nothing. Was this a new trick?

"Thank you," the Earl of Morgan said. "Thank you for saving me."

She waited, preparing for the next verbal blow, the next slight, but it didn't come. He let the words hang between them, not mocking at all, not even smiling. Just looking at her. Just examining her, as if she were something new and fascinating, a riddle he couldn't quite fathom.

"You're welcome," Lauren said reluctantly.

"I don't accept your offer."

"What?"

"It won't do," he said, temperate.

"You pompous, thick-skulled, mutton-headed English *bastard*—"

"Because I have a better idea for us both."

She took a deep breath, then snapped her teeth shut, glaring.

"These Northmen are persistent," Ari said, admiring even the clench of her jaw. "And they are many. They seem quite bent on invading Shot, and these little skirmishes we keep having with them are just the beginning, I'm certain. Exchanging information isn't going to be enough to hold them back. We must do more."

Arion paused, letting that sink in, watching the emotions carry clearly across her face—disdain, anger, wariness. He waited until the wariness faded some, until curiosity crept in, keeping her tied to him despite her hostility.

"What we need," Ari said, walking slowly to her, "is one mighty group to defeat them. What we need"—he came closer, so close that she had to bend her head back to meet his look—"is a single party that can cover the whole island at once, to guard all the weaknesses with just one common eye, and one common plan."

Still she stared up at him, so lovely, so defiant. Arion smiled down at her, then made his offer in a soft, intimate voice.

"What we need, Lauren MacRae, is to combine our two families. We need to become an alliance."

Chapter Three

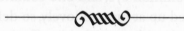

LLY WITH YOU?" LAUREN LAUGHED, a combination of astonishment and affront. "Why should I?"

"Because it's the smartest thing to do. And I don't think you're a stupid woman." Arion turned away from her, going over to his pallet. "Of course, I might be wrong."

He sat down and watched her, saw the way the silver light turned her hair to watered brilliance, lit the curve of her cheek with smooth wonder. She had not released him from her stare, scornful and dubious—but heeding. Arion saw her bite down gently on the fullness of her lower lip and felt the desire in him go spinning. He was positive she had no idea that she was even doing it.

In that sliding moment of his enthrallment, it almost didn't matter what they were discussing, it seemed unimportant. He could contemplate her all night, the succulent softness of her lips, the way her teeth pulled at the flesh there, so ripe and red, so ready to be kissed. . . .

"You are jesting," she said, breaking the spell.

"No," he replied.

A faint frown came and settled between her brows as she examined him, caught in her square of starlight.

"You must be. It is not amusing."

"It is not a jest, Lauren. It's a damned good plan."

She let out a wordless sound—frustration, irritation—and stepped out of the pale light, crossing to the door, knocking sharply. Ari thought she was leaving, just like that, and stood up quickly to stay her. Blood rushed from his head; the black waves came back, devouring his vision. He was still unwell, the proof was this. But he managed to stay standing, and when the blackness had cleared he saw that she had not left after all, merely spoken to the guard outside and accepted a brass lamp that glowed with light. She thanked the guard, then shut the door again.

Now he could see her in the colors that suited her best: the warmth of firelight that picked out the red in her hair, cast a darker rose tint to the elegance of her cheekbones. Her lips glistened, crimson stained with gold, reminding him of his fantasies, of the things he must not think about now. Ari had to look away again.

She brought the lamp to him next to the pallet, holding it up to his face, blinding him with the relative brightness of it. Arion scowled, pushing away her hand.

"What are you doing?"

She rebuffed him, freeing her hand and bringing it back, holding the light close but not too close. He allowed it now. She had to stand very near to him to keep the lamp where she wanted it, and he was too greedy to push her away a second time. The fragrance of her drifted over him, something flowered but not overly sweet . . . heated, feminine.

"Say it again, du Morgan."

"What?" he asked harshly, trying not to breathe too deeply.

"Your offer. Tell it to me again. I want to be able to see your eyes this time."

He met her gaze. "We join together to defeat the Vikings, MacRae. Your people and my people. You . . . and I."

She gave away nothing, stoic, the depths of amber in her eyes intensified by the light. Her hand was perfectly steady; the lamp did not move from him.

"Now tell me why I should aid the family of the devil," she said. "Tell me why I should consider saving you again."

"You need me, Lauren," Ari responded. "You know it's true."

She didn't reply, only kept staring up at him.

"Only united do we have any real hope of defending our home," Arion said, his voice quiet. "Together, we are stronger. Apart, we weaken ourselves. Why waste our energy battling each other when we have a mutual enemy? If we work together, we may vanquish the Northmen. We can patrol together, plan together . . . fight together, if need be."

He could see that she wanted to resist this. He could see the argument rising in her eyes, the way the faint frown came back, the way she almost bit her lip again, and then stopped. But still she did not move away, and still she did not remove the light.

"Be a true leader," he urged, almost a whisper now. "Help your people, don't hinder them. Join me."

She was overwhelming to him, hot and scented and

lovely and delicate. But also clever and strong, Ari reminded himself—and highly suspicious. He should think
of something else to woo her, something personal to
appeal to her sense of duty, of justice. Yet to his remote
dismay, Arion found that he couldn't conjure up any
further words. No words, only her, only Lauren, standing ready and sweet before him, like an offering, calm
and wild together, the promise of a heady storm in the
very essence of her.

"How can I trust you?" she asked, so softly he almost
didn't hear her.

He had his arm around her waist before he thought
to move it. It fit there so naturally, so smoothly, that
it took nothing to pull her closer to him, until her
body was brushing his despite her step back to keep
her balance.

Her eyes widened; her free hand came up between
them, pushing against his bare chest.

"If I had wanted to," Arion murmured, "I could have
killed you thrice over by now."

She hung there, unable to escape without a fight.
The flickering light behind him now showed him only
glimpses of her expression. But he didn't need to see
her face to confirm what he already knew: She felt it
too, the passion, the longing. He knew it with just the
willing sway of her body, with just the heat of her hand
against him. There was a recognition in him, a reaffirm-
ing of the primal beating in his blood, all the stronger
now for this new discovery.

Disaster. He could not give in to this. He must not.
She was a MacRae, and she was very much taken by

another man. To ignore this reality would be not only dishonorable, but exceedingly stupid. She would be wed soon to a powerful laird, one who would no doubt be displeased to find his bride even in the same room as the enemy.

Yet the hard desire crashing through him didn't care about any of that. All it wanted was what he had before him—this woman with her seductive eyes and her lips and her scent, and to hell with all the rest of it.

With great force of will, Arion eased his arm away from her. She took three rapid steps back, breathing unsteadily. It made him smile, dark and mirthless. He knew why her breathing was so short. Aye, he knew.

"I will consider your offer," she said, admirably steady, he thought.

"Why don't you?" he invited, keeping the darkness near him.

She took a few more steps away, almost as if she was afraid to turn her back to him, holding the lamp in front of her like a shield.

"But hurry, Lauren," Ari said, not releasing her from his gaze. "Hurry and decide. I won't wait forever."

She hesitated, then turned and walked briskly to the door, calling to the guard to let her out.

Ari went to the window of the room and opened the glass, letting the cold autumn air flow over him. He heard her shut the door, and then he was alone again.

"Have you lost your senses?"

Ranulf pounded his fist on the long table in the

great hall to emphasize his words, staring down at Lauren in disbelief. The other men at the table muttered their agreement.

"Join forces with the enemy? Collaborate with the devil?" Ranulf's gray-threaded beard bristled with indignation. "He'll betray us the first second he can."

"Aye," grumbled a few of the other men, elders in the clan, nodding and shooting her sharp, outraged glances.

Lauren held her peace, letting them adjust to the thought while they needed to, only folding her arms across her chest, leaning back in Da's chair at the head table. She had learned this posture from Da himself, learned that when facing strong opposition, sometimes the best thing to do was nothing at all.

Lauren had been taking Da's seat for a week, and this marked the first time she felt any resistance to it. Before now, the early-morning meetings with her father's advisers had gone as well as they could with an absent leader. She had begun to think that a few of the men here were secretly grateful that she arrived for each one, that she sat and listened and offered her own advice to the council. Until right now, when she had dared to suggest the pact that the Earl of Morgan had proposed to her late last night.

She had left his room and walked away unseeing, her thoughts snarled into confused circles, her instincts blunted and useless.

He was the wicked leader of a wicked family. He could not be trusted.

Yet . . . he was right. They would be stronger together.

Underneath all the turmoil of her thoughts was the chaos of her emotions, adding nothing to the fray but more disorientation. She felt strange and feverish, as when she had caught a terrible chill once as a child, and the world had turned to fire and ice.

Arion du Morgan had pulled her close to him and she had truly frozen, only one hand raised on instinct to protest it—and it had been a meager protest at that. He seemed not to have noticed it at all, her hand pushing at him. He had simply held her there easily, showing her the force he could exert with just one arm, solid around her back, his fingers warm on her hip.

He had captured her and then let her fall into the ocean depths of his eyes, half lidded, darkened green that mesmerized her.

And so her plan to seek the truth in him through the lamplight had gone stunningly wrong, in retrospect a telling act of lunacy on her part. She had thought to see his face and read his veracity there, just as she had done when he was a boy, in that terrible dungeon hallway.

What an astonishing mistake she had made; it had become perfectly clear to her the instant he moved. They were no longer children. Before her now was a man, and he was all solid muscle and strength—shockingly bare, warm skin, the blanket at his waist just a token of decency between them. She had lost her thoughts and then herself, lost it all to the sensation of him, leaning in so close and whispering that he could have killed her.

Fool, Lauren cursed herself. Of course he could have. *Anyone* could have, if she stood there as she had, dumb and blind and vulnerable as a babe. It was a terrible new weakness in her, something so deep and so awful that she had to bury it away completely before anyone noticed. Most especially before the Earl of Morgan noticed. If, God help her, he had not already.

She felt as if she had not slept at all last night. She did not remember sleeping. But by the time the frosted light of dawn had begun to spill over the keep, Lauren had made a decision. She would join with the devil. She was doing it for Shot. Nothing more, or less.

Nothing.

"Impossible," said Carlin, bringing Lauren back to the great hall, her father's men lined up evenly around her. Carlin's voice was no more open to change than were the others'. "I cannot believe you have been so completely deceived, Lauren."

"Think about it," Lauren said, slowly taking in the whole of the group of them. "Think of what it could mean. We would be so much the stronger. We would have eyes and ears and ready swords all across the island. There would be no place for the invaders to hide. And if we ally with the English we'll have one less enemy, at least for now—after all, they want the Vikings gone as much as we do."

That excited a new rumble in the men, a few of them turning away from her to discuss it among themselves. Ahead and all around them, the great hall was beginning to fill up. Women were bustling back and forth, getting ready to serve the breakfast, pretending not to listen. Younger men were not even bothering to pretend, instead openly taking seats near the meeting, leaning forward with their elbows on the table, alert.

"It is too dangerous," pronounced someone else, James, from the far end of the table. Lauren faced him.

"Is it not more dangerous to leave our fates to luck and chance that we will stop the next assault? I call *that* a true danger. With du Morgan on our side, we'll have stronger numbers in case of battle, and greater odds of winning."

"We should wait for the Murdoch and his clan," said James stubbornly. "He'll be coming soon. He'll be wanting to defend his bride. That's all the reinforcement we need."

"But when will he come?"

It was Ranulf again. Lauren turned to him, hiding her hope at his words. He looked to the others, speaking slowly, gravely. "We don't know when Murdoch may arrive. We don't even know if our message made it to him. Our boat might have been captured at sea. The Vikings might have killed our crew."

One of the women—Vanora, the mother of the messenger—let out a cry, then covered her mouth. Others nearby put arms around her shoulders, huddled together, breakfast forgotten.

"If the message never arrived," continued Ranulf, "then the Murdoch won't be here for nearly two more months, for the wedding."

"Payton Murdoch will come to help us," Lauren said loudly and firmly, for Vanora's sake. "I am sure our men made it to him. It just takes time."

"Aye, he'll help us, lass, and that's my point." James spoke to the rest of the room. "We don't need anything from the English. We don't need to strike any deals with the devil. Scotland's blood is plenty strong enough to defend the Isle of Shot."

The younger men were nodding; the women were silent, worried. Lauren uncurled her fingers and placed her arms on the carved wood of the chair, leaning back, thinking furiously.

Hannah walked into the chamber with a group of others, moving over to one of the tables nearby. She offered Lauren a small smile of encouragement. Lauren had already visited her in the early-morning hours to sketch out the earl's offer and to ask her opinion on what to do. Hannah had been uncharacteristically exuberant at the proposal, and that had been the final catalyst that had driven Lauren to speak.

"All right then," she said, once again capturing the attention of everyone. "How about a test? We needn't rush ahead with this. Can we not have a tentative agreement with them, say, a period of days? We work together for . . . the next fortnight. That's all. And we see what occurs. It could be that it is a trap, I grant you that, although I don't think it is."

The memory of his eyes came back to her, deep green, spellbinding. Lauren pushed it away firmly. "We strike a limited agreement, settle on a few areas we patrol together—close to the border between us. We make certain there are never more of them than there are of us in any of these areas. And we stay vigilant of them, as always. What say you?"

Voices rose and fell, everyone in the room now, not just the council, people debating and testing the idea, agreeing, disagreeing. Lauren waited, not trying to make sense of the babble but rather attempting to discern the tone of it, to see if she could sense the way her people were leaning, whether they were ready to trust her enough for this.

One voice rang out above the others, silencing the rest.

"I think it's a fine idea." The chatter died down, and everyone turned to look at Hannah. She waited for near silence, then addressed the main table. "And I think you're a pack of fools if you turn away this opportunity. It's a gift from God, it is. Hebron MacRae would have seen the wisdom of it, even if none of you do. Don't make Shot suffer for your conceit."

Lauren had to bow her head to hide her smile. Bless Hannah.

James stood up. "Now, Hannah—"

"Now what?" Hannah stood as well. "You're my brother, James, and I love you. But you have a streak of pride in you that would make a saint flinch. I'm asking you to look beyond that now. Look around at all these faces. Look at our people here. This is your chance to help us all."

The man next to Lauren turned his head away. Lauren heard his muffled laughter from behind his hand, and so, obviously, did Hannah.

"And you, Dougall! Laugh, will you? Go ahead then. And you can be the one to explain to your grandchildren why they've become the slaves of the Northmen, the ones who will steal our belovèd home."

No one laughed at all.

Hannah surveyed them, then spoke again, quieter now, her words low and intense. "Have we not lost enough good lives to these invaders? Was not the murder of a true and noble laird enough sacrifice for you? Will you now move to make his death meaningless, as well?"

The council looked away from her, to one another, to the table. Utter silence took the hall.

"Will you do it?" Lauren asked into the hush, at last rising, looking not just at the row of her father's men but at the whole of the chamber, all the people watching. "Will you have the courage to join with the du Morgans and fend off the Northmen to save our island?"

"Aye!" It was Carlin, his tone defiant.

"Aye," said a few more, and then the others joined in, one by one, all the way around the table, until it was only James who had not responded.

"What say you?" Lauren repeated severely, looking down at him, not willing to bend.

His lips pursed, his old eyes squinted, first down to the table again, then out to the crowd, to his sister, sitting calm amid a flurry of anxious kin.

"A test," he finally said, nodding. "We'll give them a test, then."

And Lauren had to sit down to hide her relief. She had done it! She had persuaded them—at least for now.

Across the room, Hannah met her look. She offered Lauren a small nod, grave. Lauren returned the nod.

She prayed to God that the Earl of Morgan had been sincere last night, because now all her hopes—and those of her clan—were riding on him. But if it *was* an evil trick, she would happily risk her own life to end his before he ruined her family.

———————— ⌘ ————————

$\mathcal{S}$OMEONE HAD BROUGHT HIM HIS clothes.

That was a relief. Lauren had ordered them taken to him this morning, but had since forgotten. When she entered his room he was pacing in the small space, dressed in his English tunic, looking restless and more than slightly dangerous. The three days he had spent at Keir had left him with a short growth of beard, which only enhanced the sharp attraction of his features. She had not dared to leave him anything honed enough to shave with.

"MacRae," he greeted her as she came forward, his voice brusque. "Where are my sword and hauberk?"

"You'll get them," she answered. "When you are off our land."

The danger in his look grew. He halted near the middle of the chamber. "I'm not leaving without my men."

"Naturally." Lauren gestured to the open door behind her.

"What's this?" he asked, not moving.

"You're leaving."

Something flickered across his face, disappointment or cynicism, she couldn't be sure. "Too much the coward to take up the fight, MacRae?"

"Your offer has been accepted," Lauren said. "We've notified your people that you are returning to them. You and your men are free to go. I'll take you to them now."

But he did not alter his stance in the center of the room. Lauren waited, knowing that this was another challenge from him, that he wanted more from her, an explanation. Perversely, she said nothing. Let him ask.

The edges of his lips lifted, almost as if he could read her thoughts.

"A ruse, MacRae?"

"We have no need to resort to ruses," she flashed. "If there is a ruse here, it's your own."

"What," he mocked gently. "Don't you trust me?"

"No."

He laughed, once again managing to throw her off her careful balance, and Lauren could have bitten her tongue in dismay. She must stay calm. She was the linchpin holding together her family's end of this wild plan, and if she let this man confuse her, he might just try to sweep her clan out of existence.

Even his smile did peculiar things to her, made her stomach drop and her thoughts distracted. Lauren fought it, focusing somewhere over his shoulder until she had the strangeness under control again.

"Very well," du Morgan said, still smiling. "I believe you, MacRae. It's not a ruse. So—show me my men."

She nodded stiffly, then walked out of the room. Arion followed, noting the solitary guard outside the door, who stared at him grimly and then fell into step behind them. He was not to be trusted far enough to roam the halls of Keir with just the daughter of the castle, Ari supposed.

Her back, he noticed, was trim and straight, finely curved underneath her tartan. She was wearing a gown beneath it again—not like in the battle, when she had worn a man's tunic under her family's plaid, a man's boots, and had fought with a man's weapon.

It was extraordinary, in retrospect, to think that a woman could so effectively handle such a difficult role, that she had fought as bravely as any man Arion had ever seen. Especially a woman with the seeming delicacy of this one.

Ari stifled a short laugh. No doubt she would not be amused to know his thoughts. Lauren MacRae would probably take the word *delicate* as an insult, no matter that to him, the rare and unlikely combination of her— refined, exquisite, bold, brave, loyal—seemed nothing less than a miracle.

Her hair swung back and forth in one long plait, smooth and neat today, much more ladylike and contained than the way he preferred it . . . like last night, loose and softly falling around her, an invitation to touch her, to sense her. To know her.

Stop, Ari thought. He moved his gaze to take in the hallway, cold stone and blue-gray darkness, closed doors and winding passageways. She had been right, the other day, in claiming that her home on Shot was so much stronger than his own. Elguire, the du Morgan stronghold here, seemed truly more of a fortress compared to this, being both smaller and unfinished—mostly due to the fact that saboteurs from Keir did their best to tear down new work each time it neared completion. The outer wall was nearly done now, but random attacks still seemed to spark up occasionally. The MacRaes, Ari knew, were nothing if not devoted to their hatred. Which made him wonder how true his lovely foe's words could be. Had her family actually accepted his bargain?

It seemed improbable. It had come to him from nowhere last night, perhaps born of his unexpected feelings for her, perhaps a reaction to the color of her eyes, or the velvet timbre of her voice—who the hell knew? After she had left, he had thought it over and couldn't believe what he had said. True, it seemed a sound enough plan on the surface. But equally true, you could not put two cocks in the same ring without expecting a fight. This was all probably just some sort of elaborate game she was playing with him, and his fingers itched to hold his absent sword.

But she stopped outside a new door, very well guarded, and then opened it for him. Arion saw that she had indeed taken him to his men, all seven of them dressed and bandaged and looking as ill tempered and uneasy as he felt.

"My lord!" Hammond was the first to recover from the surprise of seeing him, followed by the others, and for the moment Arion was caught up in the genuine gladness of seeing them all again. He was surrounded by them, each of them jostling close, looks of relief on their faces.

"Are you well?" he was asked, and he asked it back to them, until it was established that everyone was fine, that no one had been injured seriously enough to require more than some stitches and a few poultices.

"They wouldn't let us see you," said Hammond, in a low tone meant to be heard only among the group. "But we've established there's always at least four by the door, and probably more beyond. The window to this room won't open."

"Even if it did," added Trevin, "the drop to the ground is too far. It's no good to us."

Arion nodded, then looked back at the doorway.

Lauren MacRae and six tartan-clad men stood there, watching them with identical expressions of impassivity. All six of the men, Arion had already noted, were heavily armed, and even Lauren still carried her dirk at her waist.

Ari turned to his group. "Are all of you well enough to travel?"

"You think to escape?" It was Trevin, a dubious whisper. "Didn't you understand, my lord? There are too many of them, and we can't scale the wall—"

"Not that way," Arion interrupted. "We're walking out of Keir. We're going home to Elguire." He raised his voice slightly. "Isn't that correct, MacRae?"

"Aye," she said, and Ari watched as every single one of his men turned to look at her for the first time. "You'll be walking."

Something in her voice put him on alert, made his own glance to her keen and thorough. But she only smiled back at him, an angel of innocence, and Ari realized then that he must have been a great deal more desperate for a woman than he had thought, because even now, with bells of alarm pealing though him, all he wanted to do was walk over there and kiss her— hard, on the mouth. Enough to make her stop smiling at him like that. Enough to make her ask him to kiss her again.

Good God. Arion exhaled slowly through his teeth. This was getting far out of hand.

"A trick," hissed Trevin.

"Is it, MacRae?" Arion asked, calm and forceful.

"No," she said simply.

"We cannot trust them!" Hammond looked at Ari, almost stunned. "You cannot believe her!"

"Why not?" Arion asked, just as calm.

"She's a *MacRae*," Hammond said, almost spitting the name.

The men behind Lauren shifted, hands going to the hilts of their broadswords, dark looks passing among them.

"Aye, I'm a MacRae." Lauren came forward into the room, a commanding presence of strength and splendid beauty, pride clear in every step. "The same MacRae who came to your defense, English, when you were decorating my beach with your blood from theVikings. I'm that MacRae, the one who shielded you from the invaders, the one who then brought you all back here to my home and tended to you, who nursed you so that you might not die as you deserved. It's the MacRaes you should be thanking now for your lives. And it's the MacRaes who are releasing you, ungrateful though you are."

"We were fine on that beach," Trevin said to her, each word brimming with contempt. "We didn't need your help."

"You're either a liar or a fool," Lauren said flatly.

Ari placed a hand on his lieutenant's arm before Trevin could take the step forward that might destroy the fragile truce he had managed to form. "Enough," he said quietly.

"What do you mean? Didn't you hear her? She said—"

"Enough!" Ari let the temper begin to show in his voice. "I heard her. Keep your peace, lieutenant."

"My lord." Trevin subsided, though Ari could see he had to bite back more words. The other men stood silent, alternating glances from him to the Scots at the door. Arion knew that the tension in the room would break soon, one way or another, unless he managed to diffuse it.

"We're going home now," he said to them all. "Lead the way then, Lauren MacRae."

She stood there, still tense and finely spun in her anger, and for a moment Ari seriously thought it was too late, that she had changed her mind and would keep them imprisoned here, after all. But she turned away and walked out the door, some unspoken message passing between her and the guards. Two followed her; the other four stood back, waiting. The one who been guarding his own door jerked his head at Ari.

Arion stepped away from the cluster of his men and walked after her. He did not look around to see if his group fell in behind him.

If they didn't, none of this mattered anyway. If they wouldn't follow him out of this castle, then there would be no way any of them would follow a plan to join with the enemy, even if it came from the Earl of Morgan.

So he walked and listened, and was rewarded with the sound of bootsteps on the hard floor, many of them— more than four people. A very small part of him felt relief. But there was still too much at stake to start congratulating himself.

Down through the hallways they went, past doors and chambers and groups of Scots. Strangers stopped and stared at them, all of them tartan clad, all of them with wary eyes and cold demeanors, some of them greeting Lauren, most of them just silent, an army of inimical observers.

They reached what must have been their great hall, truly cavernous, even larger than the one in his own castle on the mainland, though not as richly furnished. Before he could examine much more of it they were outside, engulfed in the brightness of the day. A group of about fifteen mounted men were waiting in the bailey, staring down at them. Holding, Arion noticed, *his* men's weaponry in addition to their own.

Arion halted as Lauren walked to the only unclaimed steed. She vaulted into the saddle as easily as a man would, sitting astride and looking down at him. Her brows raised, and her smile was still divinely innocent.

"I told you that you would be walking out of here. So you are. Come."

She clucked at her steed and it turned and ambled toward the gate. The mounted men didn't move, nor did they break their looks at Arion and the men behind him.

Ari followed Lauren.

His men followed him.

And the Scotsmen surrounded them all, armed and swift and no doubt, Ari thought acidly, highly amused.

He had never been here before—never awake, at least—and now he could begin to take in the rugged surroundings of this part of Shot. It seemed wilder than his portion of the island, more wooded, less inviting. He could see why Keir was built where it was, on top of a hill amid valleys, looking down at the meadows and woods and even the shore, a clear view from here. He had to admire it all, the cleverness of the layout, the rough allure of this region.

Elguire was plainly lacking in comparison, even

though the land around it was far more cultivated. He understood a little better now why the MacRaes held on so tightly to their pride. Not that Elguire didn't have potential. Once it was finished, it would be as fine a home as any, Arion thought. And it had the appeal of being settled in a gentler area, more open fields of grass and crops, longer beaches and smoother water.

Lauren kept her horse to a slow walk, which was good, because Ari wasn't going to try to keep up with her. She was having her joke on him, and damned if he was going to make it better for her. He focused on pushing away the anger again. It would gain him nothing. He needed every advantage right now, because he truly didn't know if she meant to release him or not.

He thought she might. He thought he had read her correctly, last night and this morning, that she had some sense to her, that she was not just the summation of the unyielding arrogance of her clan. There could be no doubt she was intelligent. Ari hoped that it was enough to override whatever obvious advantage she could take of him and his men right now.

It would be very easy to kill them. It would be remarkably foolish, but easy.

She rode ahead of him with a natural poise on her mount, not looking back even once. The bright copper of her hair was like a beacon before him.

His shoulder hurt. He imagined the rest of his men were not faring much better—the battle had not been that long ago, after all. But Ari knew none of them would complain, no matter how bad the pain. He could do no less. It was going to be a long walk back to Elguire. He set his teeth and marched on.

They stayed mostly in the woods, where the ground was giving but tricky with roots and leaves. The ocean's call was constantly to the left, and sometimes he could catch glimpses of the blue of it through the trees.

No one spoke. The only sounds to be heard were the steps of the horses, the occasional songs of birds above them, and of course, the surf, crashing nearer and nearer.

Just when it seemed the throbbing pain in his arm would completely consume him, the woman ahead of him slowed, and then stopped. Ari did too, and Lauren twisted around in her saddle, waving him forward. He walked up to her, the pain that suffused him suddenly clearing, the blood in his veins alive again.

They were at the verge of a beach, he saw; the same beach where he had been felled by the Norseman days ago. Only now the other side of it was lined not with Vikings but instead with his own people—many of them—mounted and waiting.

There was a small commotion when he was spotted. Someone stepped away from the crowd, walking over to them. Gray hair, short beard, an older man with a forceful stride—Fuller, his steward, second in command.

Lauren dismounted, landing gracefully beside him. Arion turned to look at her, swathed in the gentle forest light.

"I kept my word, du Morgan." Her head tilted, indicating the mass of his people waiting on the sand.

"Aye," he said slowly. "You did."

Her look was clear gold, direct. "Will you keep yours?"

"I will."

Fuller was getting closer. Arion could see his expression from here: worry, caution, relief.

"Then tonight I will send someone to this beach," she said very softly, not moving her look from his face. "Explain your plan to your people. If it goes well, if they are amenable, then you send someone here as well, when the moon is at the apex of the sky. Agreed?"

"Agreed," Arion said.

That frown came back between her brows, a plain indication of doubt. But all she said was, "I'll be sending only one man, du Morgan. If you've been deceiving me—if this was all just a lie—then you'll be killing only one soul, at least for tonight. Tomorrow, there will be a war. Know that now."

"Don't fear, MacRae. I don't want a war any more than you do."

"I hope not," she said, sounding very sincere. She looked up and behind him, making a subtle gesture with one hand, and Ari's hauberk, sword, and scabbard were tossed down to him from the nearest Scot. He checked the blade and found it sound, then fastened the leather belt for the scabbard around his waist. A glance to his men showed them doing the same. He bent down and picked up the heavy weight of his chain mail, ignoring the jab of pain in his shoulder at the move.

Fuller was almost upon them. Lauren MacRae was watching his approach with apparent unconcern, but Ari could see the way her hand hovered near the dirk at her waist, her fingers light against the metal. The sunlight fell and lit her like an icon of fire, gorgeous reds and golds and bright warmth. She still looked for all the world like the angel he had first imagined her to be, back when he was bleeding to death from that treacherous arrow.

Arion turned around again and found Hammond and the rest ready and waiting, watching, looking to him for his next move. He motioned them to come forward.

"You'll hear from me tonight, MacRae," he said down to Lauren, and then stepped away from her, onto the sandy beach that represented the beginning of his half of this feral and untamed island that was his new home.

Chapter Four

*L*ESS THAN HALF A YEAR ago, Arion had been wonderfully unaware of the drastic changes that were about to take place in his life.

He was living in London, enjoying the fruits of his knighthood, carving out a distinct niche for himself amid the royal court as a trusted adviser to King Henry. And although the gilded edges of court life held almost no appeal for him, he still preferred it to his family's demesne, where his uncle presided as the Earl of Morgan.

Morgan Castle rested in the lush crescent of a string of fine English hills and vales, yet the earldom itself was not sizable. The mainland holdings were mostly farmland, small but fertile. It would have been enough to support any ordinary man in excellent style—but of course, Ryder du Morgan was anything but ordinary.

Arion used to imagine Uncle Ryder back at the castle, crouched in the splendor of his rooms, making his plans to destroy all his enemies, his soul growing darker and more sour with each new plot.

It was Ryder who years ago had discovered the wealth of Shot, a du Morgan holding long neglected. It was Ryder who had exploited the fruitful lands there, who realized he had grazing pastures going unused and vast farmland ready to be plowed. It was Ryder who had funneled almost all the profits of Shot back to his castle, and kept his world like that, spinning gold from the straw of the island, like some stooped troll from a dark fairy tale.

Ryder had never liked the island, only the luxury it provided him. So, over the years, the mainland holdings grew more and more extravagant, and Ryder more and more rapacious. He ruled with complete control, dispersing pain and cruelty with such abandon that Arion could not recall any man who had dared to look into his eyes for more than a few seconds at a time.

It was into this world that Ari and his sister had come, orphaned, alone.

Although Ari had spent his boyhood at Morgan Castle, it had never felt like home. He didn't like the coldness of it; a condition, he thought, not so much of the place but rather a reflection of the man who ruled it. Ryder du Morgan had no pity for anyone or anything that Arion had ever seen. Ari and Nora had lived in fear of the man from almost the very first day they had arrived there as children, after an illness sweeping the land had taken both of their parents.

Poor Nora. Tender, fragile Nora, his elder sister who had never been able to grow up.

And Ari, fully six years younger than she, had been mostly helpless to defend her from Ryder. Their uncle had never understood the slowness of her thoughts, the unique manner in which she drifted through her life. To him she was a weakness in the family, proof that their mother had been of inferior stock, that the earl's younger brother's marriage to her had been cursed from the beginning.

Ryder himself had never produced a child, even though he ran through three unfortunate wives trying. Eventually, Arion supposed, he had come to accept that his nephew would be his heir. And that was when Ari's life had taken a truly black turn.

His uncle wanted nothing less than an image of himself to rule Morgan after him—eternal oppression of the land and the people. He focused on Arion and never ceased trying to mold him into another tyrant. He would not leave him alone, forcing Ari to learn by his example. How to flog. How to cut. How to maim. How to cheat, to lie. To say and do such rash and unpredictably violent things that there could be only fear and loathing in the hearts of every single serf and noble at Morgan.

The boy he had been had cringed and averted his eyes, trying not to look, not to listen.

"Never let up," Ryder had instructed him. "You must break them, Arion. Break them until they bleed, and beg for your mercy. It is the only way they will learn to respect you."

In terror for his life, Arion spent his days hiding, closing his heart and mind to his uncle's brutal lessons. But it turned out he learned something after all: He had learned that he could never be the monster Ryder wanted for his reign.

And after the death of Nora, he had learned something new—to obscure his rage, to bide his time until he was old enough to legitimately leave Morgan as a squire.

He was remarkably lucky. The royal court had expressed an interest in du Morgan's nephew, and Ryder had been so dazzled by the opportunity to get closer to the king that he had sent Arion to London with merely delighted instructions for him to obey his elders. By the time he had come to guess Arion's secret plan, it was too late. Arion had escaped Morgan, and he was *never* going back.

London, bright and filthy and smelly, had been like a jewel to him. It represented the one thing that he had longed for: deliverance from his uncle. He had gone there and stayed there, except for battle, advancing from squire to knight to adviser. And over the years Arion had eventually accepted that this was the best that life had to offer him—false grandeur, great riches and terrible poverty together, humming plots and schemes, quick wits and a sharp sword, secret love affairs that were never very secret at all.

It had seemed the best he could do. In London he was able to think for himself, to devise his own actions and the reasons for them. He had the respect of his peers, he had the attention of the king, and he had enough women willing to amuse him until time became just a grain of sand in the memory of God.

It was enough, he used to think as he lay awake in the deep of the night in his bed, or his current lover's. Aye, enough. It would do, this strange and fleeting life. It would have to.

But still, he was left hollow somehow. Even amid

fawning crowds, Arion had always understood that he was ultimately alone—perhaps just as much as his uncle was. He remained surrounded by people, yet none of them ever truly mattered to him. None of them ever came close.

From that isolation in him there came a void that seemed to grow with each passing year, with each flattering smile and every glittering bit of praise he received. The void was a mixed blessing, devoid of true emotion, nothing like fear or dread or happiness surviving in it.

Near the end, about five months ago—after over a decade of his London life—Arion had begun to suspect that the void would swell to eat him whole. And he found, to his distant wonder, that he didn't even care.

Then Ryder died. Ari didn't really believe it at first; he thought it a new scheme of his uncle's to get him back to Morgan. Ryder had never stopped trying to reclaim him after he fathomed that his prodigy did not plan to come back. But no, it was true, the old demon was dead.

Arion realized, with a sort of sick jolt, that he was now the Earl of Morgan. It was fully expected that he would return to his home to take up his duties. Even the king had called him into a private meeting to wish him a good journey back to Morgan.

There was nothing else Arion could do. If Henry told him to go, he had to go. Never mind that he never wanted to see that castle again. Never mind that the thought of encountering Ryder just in the marble image on his tomb was enough to turn his stomach.

So, Ari went. Once back at Morgan, the first thing

he did was kneel in the chapel and pray for the soul his sister. Then he prayed for the damnation of Ryder. He did not bother to pray for himself—he didn't think God was listening, anyway.

Slowly it began to sink in: He was the new earl. All the people of Morgan stared and whispered and watched him as if he might sprout horns the moment they turned away. Each hallway held an unwelcome memory, each chamber a face he wanted to forget. People jumped at the mildest of his commands. Women seemed almost to tremble when he came too close, surreptitiously hiding their children behind their skirts. Arion pretended not to notice.

He held meetings, trying to think of things to say and do to assure them that he was not his uncle. But it wasn't until he tried consulting the steward, Fuller, that he reached any level of success.

It took a full month to get the man to relax enough to sit when Ari did. It took another month to get him to laugh at a quip. Slowly, the steward began to thaw to him. While Arion struggled daily with his new role and tried to oust the memories that haunted him, gradually the people of Morgan began to change around him as well, growing less stiff, a little more friendly. It was taking time. But perhaps it could be done. Perhaps he could show them that he could rule without the brutality that had stained his uncle's life.

He worked, he talked, he studied and adapted to suit the land. It seemed almost . . . good.

But that was just an illusion. He knew that, aye; it was just a shell over his true self. Because Arion still lay alone every night—a different bed, true, and no woman beside him any longer, but the same void still slowly devouring him. It would not let him go. It was his own personal demon, large enough now to be a fatal one. Ryder was surely laughing at him from hell.

Ah, but then . . . but then *she* had come to him. Born of blood and sand and blinding light: Lauren MacRae, all grown up from the spirited child he had admired and pitied when he was a boy. She had challenged him and taunted him and teased him until Arion thought he might go mad with it, and that had been only three days of her.

Not until this afternoon, after he had left her and traveled back to Elguire, did Ari realize that at Keir there had been no void. At Keir it had been banished, faded away to nothing when confronted with her overwhelming luminescence. Instead of the void, he had felt things so sharply that he almost didn't know himself.

Who was this man who burned for a copper-haired woman, one who might kill him without a second thought? Who was this man who craved possession of her, who fantasized about her touch, about her scent, about burying his face in the luster of her hair and claiming her as his own, over and over again? Who was he now, this stranger inside him, who felt pain and hunger and admiration for her with bleeding hurt?

Who was he, Arion du Morgan, without the numbness of the void that had saturated all the years before her?

It was a great conundrum, a knot as intricate as any he had ever fashioned from his life.

He had sailed to this island with a small army of men, ready to defend it, ready to do battle to ward off the threat his vassals here had reported to the mainland. Arion was not his uncle, no. He would defend the island, or die trying—not to protect the wealth of it, but to save the people. *His* people. He had actually even looked forward to it, a good fight, something the void had not yet managed to swallow. And he had gotten his fight, and nearly lost his life from it. Until she came.

Arion had looked into the amber of her eyes and knew then that he had found a new lost hope—the daughter of his enemy, future wife of another man. The void shrank and paled before her. It was laughable; it was a travesty. The only woman in the world who could touch him was forever beyond his touch.

Today Arion roamed the halls of Elguire and managed to keep up the facade of calm leadership, even as Lauren's image haunted him. He knew the things to say to soothe the people here. He knew what to do to make them think he was worthy of their trust. No doubt it was because Ryder had hardly ever bothered to come to Shot, but these islanders of his had almost none of the reservation he had encountered back at the mainland. They had welcomed him wholeheartedly—and the aid he represented to them.

It had taken only a few days for Arion to realize that his aid was not going to be enough. Shot was doomed.

The Vikings had decided to pluck out this island from the chain of many that wandered up the coast, perhaps because the Isle of Shot was one of the largest, or the most fertile, or the farthest from the mainland shore. Any one of those reasons might have been enough to incite attack; all three might make it irresistible. Ari knew that over the centuries there had been sporadic conflicts with Northmen on Shot, but only now had they decided to attack in earnest. It was clear they meant to take possession. And one of the most appealing elements of this place—its sprawling vastness—was also its greatest vulnerability. There was no way the du Morgans could guard all of it all the time. Not while worrying about the Scots as well.

The MacRaes, he had been told, were involved in their own clashes with the Vikings on the other side of the island. Perhaps luck would take a hand and they would all kill each other, someone suggested, not really joking. There was no love lost between the two groups.

Elguire was fine and strong, in parts. The western half was whole, thick with stone and strong lumber. The southern and northern parts were almost completed. The eastern edge of the outer wall, however, was a disaster, rubble and broken wood, remnants of the ongoing war with the other family who lived on Shot. It was not only the longest section of the wall but the part closest to the cover of the forest, and to Keir.

The keep itself was almost complete, thank God, but the outer wall was slowing them down. They had a patrol on it at all times, but it wasn't enough. When Arion arrived he had tripled it, and then ordered work on the wall to continue night and day. It was a deficiency they could not afford.

He walked there now in the waning light of the late afternoon, stepping around the stones in the bailey, noticing how most of them had been picked up and readied again for permanent placement. Men greeted him, leaving off their duties for a moment to come over and see for themselves that the earl was well, that he had survived his tenure with the enemy for almost three entire days. He smiled and reassured them, being careful not to comment on the MacRaes other than to say he had been well taken care of, because he didn't want to shade these men against his plan, and he wasn't yet sure how best to present it to them.

So he made his rounds, talking with Fuller, who had noticed the bulk of the bandage on his shoulder but said nothing. He would wait, Ari knew, for Arion to mention it first, and then offer whatever aid he thought he should. Ari liked his steward, this quiet and thoughtful man, and was grateful that his uncle had not managed to completely poison everyone he had touched back at Morgan.

"Looks good," Ari said, his glance taking in the men who labored with the stone, slowly and steadily building up their defenses.

"Aye," replied Fuller. "It's been coming along, since the MacRaes have found themselves distracted with new woes."

Arion didn't look away from the men. "This woe of theirs is ours as well, my friend."

"Aye, my lord," said Fuller, with a careful lack of emotion.

"I'm glad you agree." Ari began to walk again, moving away from the contained commotion around them. He kept his pace slow, so that the older man would not have to work to keep up. "Tell me. What would you say is the mood of the people here—whom do they hate more, the MacRaes or the Northmen?"

Fuller didn't respond immediately. He walked beside Arion, looking down at the rough grass of the ground they covered. "I cannot say, my lord."

"You cannot say? Why? Because you don't know, or because you don't want to tell me?"

The steward seemed almost to smile, but his reply was sober enough. "I cannot say because there is no way to know." He lifted his gaze, faded blue eyes that took in the surroundings. "The MacRaes have been our enemy for so long, I don't think anyone here considers it much anymore. They are the enemy because they have always been so. Oh, you might point to petty fights along the borders, or insults hurled at passing groups—even the occasional undermining of this wall here—but our two kings have done what they could to stop true bloodshed between us. Yet the hatred remains."

Arion nodded, not saying anything, so Fuller continued.

"But with the Northmen it's easy to understand the threat. They want our home, our land, and our wealth—and not just that, but our lives and those of our loved ones. They have no respect for our island or our way of life, which is not something you could say of the Mac-Raes. In fact, I would think that there is one factor that both families share, and that is that both love this land and how we live on it."

Fuller stopped, sounding almost puzzled by his own words.

"I have an idea," Arion said.

"It won't work, my lord."

They both paused outside the heavy wooden door that was the entrance to the keep.

"Why not?" Arion asked, not at all surprised that Fuller had anticipated his thoughts.

"I was born on Shot, my lord. I don't think you knew that. I grew up here on the island; married and buried my wife and our child here. It was only in the past few years that I went to the mainland to serve as steward to your uncle. What I'm trying to tell you is, I know as well as anyone the mood of these people, and although you might say there is no new bloodshed between us and the MacRaes, no one has forgotten the past. No one will. And they will never join a cause that might benefit the MacRaes."

"But what of benefit to us?" Arion asked quietly. "If we band together we are stronger in the face of the invaders. We will save ourselves, not just the MacRaes."

Fuller glanced away again, shaking his head, and Ari felt his heart sink. If he could not convince this man, who had become his closest ally among his people, he hadn't a chance with the rest of them.

"Think on it," Arion urged. "You know I'm right. Without their help, Shot is a lost cause."

Fuller let out a long sigh, and as if in reply a breeze came and swept around their feet, bending the grass. At last he looked up, and Arion could see the reluctant agreement in his eyes.

"I'm not saying you're not right, my lord. I'm just saying it's going to take something terrible to convince them."

"All right, then." Arion walked to the door of the

keep, stepping into the sheltered darkness inside. "I'll think of something terrible."

———————————⟨∾⟩———————————

HE WAITED UNTIL THE EVENING meal, when the sun had softened to a faint lavender light, and everyone had eaten enough to take away the sharp edge of irritation that could come with hunger. He waited until enough mead and ale had been passed around that wits were still alert but not quarrelsome.

Arion himself ate almost nothing, nor did he touch the ale. He sat there and turned his thoughts over and over, gazing out the high window at the other end of the great hall, watching the clouds skim by in shades of pink and purple and dusky blue.

He idly considered what a heavy notion it was to own something. About how this wild, rich island was his—part of it, at least. The land, the animals and people. The responsibility could be crushing, if he let it. As he watched the sky beyond the arched window he wondered if it might even be said that the clouds belonged to him, with their dusky magic, and then gave a private, rueful smile at the thought.

Arion was overlord, for better or worse. He had faced danger before, and death, and sacrifice. He knew the pain of loss, the obligation of success. He had risen high enough in court to understand how the power of a man might turn in a heartbeat, how clever words could change minds. How even a single look could alter fate itself.

He had known too many men to rise to the favor of the king with cunning and guile and betrayal. Men of noble title, and ignoble dispositions. He had never wished to become like them, had indeed spent a good portion of his life striving to prosper in exactly the opposite manner. Even now he wasn't certain that he had been successful. Was it possible to be a man of might and integrity together? Was it possible to clutch leadership in the palm of your hand without losing honor?

Not to Ryder, Earl of Morgan, nor to most of those cunning courtiers.

But he was Arion, not Ryder. He was not any of those men he had seen and tried not to emulate.

He was the new Earl of Morgan, and this was as good a time as any to become that man. It was well nigh time, in fact, to put the lessons of his past life to good use.

The noise of conversation around him was a combination of cheer and buoyant aggression, certainly nothing subdued. By now everyone knew what had happened on the beach with the Vikings. There was vast relief at the safety of the men, underscored with tension, fear, and resentment. The MacRaes had come and interfered, Ari heard said. The MacRaes had spoiled the fight for our boys. The MacRaes had kept them prisoner at Keir. The MacRaes, the MacRaes . . .

Fuller, sitting nearby, looked at Arion with worried eyes but said nothing, just continued to eat his meal.

Arion ran his fingers over the coolness of the pewter goblet in front of him, filled with untouched ale. He stayed silent until there was a drop in the noise around him, one of those unplanned moments when it seemed no one had anything more to say. When it came, Arion looked up and said loudly:

"Benedict Morgan. I understand I am to congratulate you on your recent marriage."

A young man sitting at a table not too far away appeared startled, then pleased. The attractive girl next to him blushed and smiled down at her hands in her lap. She looked to be no more than fifteen.

"Thank you, my lord," the groom replied, and the people in the hall began to laugh and call out more felicitations.

Arion stood up, raising his goblet.

"To the happy couple. May they always prosper on our island."

Before anyone could repeat the toast, Arion quickly lowered his goblet. The beginnings of sound died all around him. Everyone stared.

"Alas, I cannot drink to it," Arion said. "I'm sorry."

Gasps came from around the room. The young man named Benedict began to turn red—astonishment, humiliation.

"My lord?" he choked out.

"I would sincerely like to toast your future happiness," Arion explained gravely. "But it would be a lie. And I don't lie."

Benedict stood up at his table, and the hush in the room was so complete that Ari heard the ragged anger in the man's breathing.

"My lord does not wish to offer his blessing to my lady wife?" Benedict asked, each word measured, almost disbelieving.

"Your wife is lovely," Ari said. "Under other circumstances, I would say you are truly fortunate. But I'm afraid her very beauty is what is going to endear her to the Northmen, when they come. You'll lose her soon enough, I think."

The room exploded with comment, people expressing their shock and ire at Arion's words.

Fuller, off to his right, leaned back in his chair, watching the chaos with him.

Several men were standing, arguing to him, speaking so loudly over one another that Ari couldn't make out what they were saying. Arion's soldiers from Morgan looked uneasy, muttering among themselves, shifting along the benches on which they sat.

Arion set down his goblet on the table and raised his hands. The noise thinned out, everyone staring at him as if he had lost his mind, and then finally there was quiet enough for him to speak again.

"You came to me for help." He spoke calmly, firmly, the way he had learned in London worked best with adversaries. "You sent word to your overlord that you were being attacked, that people were dying. It was the right thing to do, and as your overlord, I have come to defend you. You should know that I will die defending you. But that is all I can do. The Northmen will keep coming. We will not be able to defeat them as we are."

Again the explosion of sound, of comments and opinions that drowned out one another, but with a little less hostility this time.

Good, Ari thought. They were beginning to lean in the right direction.

"My lord!" It was a new man, big and burly, a thatch

of blond hair. "What do you mean, my lord? Are you saying the Vikings will win? That they'll take over Shot?"

"Aye, that's what I'm saying." He held up his hands again to stay the comments. "I'm being as honest with you as I can be. You are my people, and as the Earl of Morgan I am pledged to protect you as best I can. I have fought beside the king. I have earned my knighthood on the battlefield with him, and I have seen enough of war to know when one is lost before it even begins. Our battle here on Shot with the Northmen is fated to fail. We do not have enough time. We do not have enough men."

"Not enough men?" he heard repeated, a few voices, incredulous.

"That's right. The Isle of Shot is too large for us to patrol at all times, even our half of it. You know it as well as I. It's how the Vikings keep sneaking past our guard. It's why they keep coming back."

A woman stood. "But, my lord! To say we are going to lose—"

"We *will* lose," Arion interrupted, hard and cold. "It's just a matter of time."

"The king!" said the burly man, reckless. "The king will send help for us, will he not? We are his vassals, and he has taken the same pledge to defend us in times of need!"

"The king has no men to spare," Arion said. "Believe me on this. He has wars of his own that plague him, that drain his coffers. We're fortunate he hasn't called away any of our own men to replace the deaths left from his battles. The king will not be able to aid us."

He didn't have to do anything now to gain quiet.

Every single person in front of him was silent. He thought he recognized the numb despair on their faces, the desperate looks they exchanged with one another. Such emotions had dwelled in his own soul for so long now.

But perhaps he had redemption for them all.

"No, we will not win against the Vikings," Arion said, slowly surveying the room. "Not like this. Not alone. But there *is* a chance of getting the help we need. . . ." He let his voice trail off, as if uncertain whether he should continue.

"But—you just said, the king has no men to spare," said one of the men.

"That's correct. Alone in this battle now as we are, we will fall. Our women will be forced to serve these invaders. Our children will be slaughtered or put to labor. But," he shrugged, "at least it will be an honorable battle for us, before that happens."

There was a collective moan in the room now, denial and fright and blustering outrage. The man named Benedict shouted out his next question over the noise.

"Then what was the help you spoke of, my lord?"

"The only help we have available," Arion replied. "The help of the only other people in the world who care as much about Shot as we do. The help of the MacRaes."

For the space of a heartbeat it seemed the room had gone dead. Ari had never experienced a moment of such complete suspension, when everything around him just stopped—no breathing, no words, no movement. Just unequivocal astonishment. Then:

"The *MacRaes!*" It was the name on everyone's

tongue, repeated with varying degrees of derision and fury and disbelief. Arion let it wash over and around him, not trying to stem the torrent of emotion, only standing firm amid it, a rock in the ocean of their rancor.

"Never!"

"Outrageous!"

"We would rather die!"

"Would you?" Arion shouted out now, his voice deep and powerful. "Would you truly rather die? Because that's what will happen!"

People began to subside, muttering. Arion gazed around the room, letting them see his face, serious, unyielding.

"Are you truly so willing to throw your lives away? The Vikings have already had a fine taste of our blood. How many men have you yet buried due to this outside threat?"

Everyone here knew the answer—far better than he did, in fact: dozens. Arion had lost only faceless vassals, islanders he had never met. But these people had wept over their lovers, husbands, sons, brothers. He wanted them to remember that. He wanted them never to forget.

He pointed to Benedict in the crowd, speaking more quietly now. "Would *you* rather die, Benedict Morgan? Would you condemn your bride to die with you?"

The young man said nothing, only throwing one agonized glance at his wife.

Arion continued, relentless. "But as I said before, I doubt she will die at your side. She'll become a favorite of the Vikings instead, fair as she is. And if she does not submit to them, you may be sure they'll kill her, and they will not be kind about it. While you, brave man, will be naught but blood and bones, no help to her at all."

Benedict placed an arm around his wife, who turned her head against his shoulder and began to cry softly.

"How many of you would choose such a fate for your wives, your daughters, your sisters and your mothers? How many? Tell me now, so that I will know the faces of the men who would sacrifice their families for their vanity."

Silence filled the room again, strained, broken only by the muffled weeping of Benedict's wife.

Arion met the gazes of those who were staring at him and said clearly, "I have come here to lead you! I have come here to fight for you, and your home! But do I lead an island of fools? Shall I lead you all to your deaths, or to your futures? The choice must be yours."

Murmuring broke out, dubious tones, people shifting in place. He heard them whispering the name of their old enemy, but it was softer now, less emphatic.

"How could we?"

"How could we trust them?"

"Fight *with* them, *beside* them? The *MacRaes*?"

"The *MacRaes*," Ari called out, "are our one true hope to save Shot. The *MacRaes* have just as much reason as we do to defend our island. If they lose their side of Shot to the Northmen, we are finished. There will be no hope for any of us. We will be destroyed, one by one, until the last of us are dead or enslaved. But if we join forces with them—willingly, eagerly— we might stave off this terrible fate."

Fuller chose now to stand beside Arion, remaining close behind him, his arms crossed over his chest.

"The Earl of Morgan is right," he said. "We must do this thing. We must join the MacRaes, for the sake of Shot, and for all of our souls."

And slowly, gradually, Arion saw the realization take over them all, the undeniable logic of it beginning to drive out the prejudice. It came as a softening of the anger, blurred lines of fear and confusion now mingling with tentative hope. Men dropped their heads and frowned or stared blankly around them. Women looked to one another and gave small nods, clasping hands.

"We must do it," repeated Fuller, plain and strong.

Arion saw all his people begin to nod, a reluctant agreement.

"Very well." Ari raised his goblet once more, looking down at the tearful face of the new bride. "I lift my drink to you, young mistress, in sincere and hearty hopes of your well being in the future. God bless your union."

"God bless!" echoed the people in the hall, uncertain, muted.

But everyone drank.

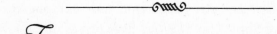

$\mathscr{T}$HE NIGHTTIME DARKNESS ON SHOT had a unique kind of crispness to it, Arion thought. Brisk and welcome, not yet bitter from winter. The shadows that draped and fell over him and his mount were clear and sharp in the moonlight, even though the moon was just a curving sliver above him. Stars seemed brighter. The richness of the midnight sky seemed deeper, bluer than it had back on the mainland. It was another example of the unexpected beauty of this place, of this island he found he was beginning to care for more and more.

His horse was black, to blend better with the shadows. Ari kept the gait slow and smooth, in no hurry. The moon was not yet at its apex. He had time to sit and think and let the horse take him to where he needed to be.

Arion knew that he was risking a great deal, not even so much with his own life but with the well-being of an entire people. It was a weighty matter, and he did not want to leap into it without first contemplating all that might go wrong. But he had considered it and considered it, and uniting with the MacRaes truly seemed the only hope of salvation against the savagery of the Northmen.

They might fail anyway. It could be that even joined as a common force, they would not be strong enough to defeat a relentless line of invaders. But he believed it was the best chance they had.

And he could not deny that the thought of working with Lauren MacRae, instead of against her, was exciting, a challenge he actually looked forward to.

Careful, Ari thought, shaking his head. *Don't be distracted by her face.* He should not forget where her loyalties lay. Her blood ran deep and true to her family.

But what a pleasant pastime it made, riding alone to meet her liaison, considering what it might be like to kiss her full lips, to taste her sweetness, to run his hands through her hair, letting the rare color of it wind through his fingers with rich sensuality. . . .

The beach appeared deserted, as did the flat of the ocean beyond it. No Viking ships tonight, at least not here. Ari glanced up and found the moon, still not as high as it should be, so he led his steed to the deception of a spot of dappled moonlight beneath a cluster of pines, then settled back in his saddle to wait.

The ocean swelled and shrank again from the shore, with enough noise to mask most of the other sounds around him. Arion listened anyway, intent on honing his skills.

An owl, about thirty paces behind him, he guessed, calling out soulfully for a mate.

Wind, brushing the tops of the trees around him with occasional rustling, delicate and subdued.

His horse, lifting his head, turning his ears to the wooded grove across the long line of beach ahead of them, let out a soft snort of air.

Ari looked, seeing nothing at first. But then he caught it—the way the shadows shifted near a space between two trees, patches of ghostly light slipping over something solid and large. Another horse, a hooded rider on it. They halted just where the woods met the sand, as Ari had.

He gathered the reins and took his steed out into the open moonlight, nothing but sand dunes and tufts of sea lavender to hide him now. After a moment, the other rider did the same.

They approached each other slowly, cautiously. Ari couldn't yet see the man Lauren had sent to him. The hood was large, and the cape connected to it covered him completely. But as the distance between them grew shorter, he didn't have to see the face of the other rider to know who it was.

She had come herself. She had shunned handing off the task—and the risk, Ari supposed—to anyone else. He was not surprised, though the anticipation in him now was heightened almost to exhilaration.

She rode a horse that matched the moonlight instead of the night. It suited her well, he thought, a stroke of boldness that complemented her spirit, disdainful of hiding.

Lauren brought her mount up to his and then stopped, pushing back the hood.

"du Morgan," she greeted him, nodding coolly.

"MacRae," he replied, nodding back, hiding his amusement at her reserve. "You gamble much for someone who doesn't trust me."

He could see her choose not to respond to this, almost as if her thoughts were open to him, no secrets. The wind twined between them, stirring her hair from its coif, stealing loose strands to dance around her face, beckoning him to touch her. Lauren's hand came up; she pushed back the errant strands impatiently.

"Well?" she asked. "What news have you?"

"They agreed," Arion said. "We will join with you."

Obviously this was not the answer she had expected. Astonishment flashed across her features, a bare second, and then she masked it by turning her head away from him, as if to scan the ocean. If he hadn't been examining her so closely he wouldn't have caught it at all.

"Excellent," she said, turning back to him, perfectly composed. The playful strands came free again, now brushing her lips. Arion watched them, helpless to look away, while Lauren continued to speak, appearing not to notice his distraction.

"I should tell you that my clan would agree only to a test period, however. A fortnight, nothing more."

"Why didn't you mention this before?"

She actually smiled. "I didn't think your people would accept your plan. So it didn't seem to matter."

His steed shifted sideways, restless, and Ari brought him back near hers with a calming hand, though there was a rising irritation in him. "Such faith you have! And what happens after a fortnight, MacRae? Two weeks of cooperation and shared goals, suddenly followed by a renewed animosity between us?"

She looked down at the mane of her horse, then out at the water again. "I don't know," she said softly, and the wind took her words away from him and made them thin.

He stared at her and she ended up staring back, both of them arrested in the moment, blind to the wind and the sea and the stars. Arion felt the desire welling up once more, a natural reaction to her nearness, but this time he gained no pleasure from it. Her beauty grated on him, that she could be so close and never his, that she could command that any truce between them would be only temporary at best.

It hurt him somehow, though he knew it was absurd, and unwarranted. His ache for her turned sharp, cutting; nothing like pleasure but more of frustration, and pain.

"It appears we have a bargain, then," Arion said, trying to keep the myriad of emotions from showing in his voice.

"Aye," she finally replied. "It appears we do."

He edged his mount even closer to hers, until they were almost side by side, then held out his hand, palm up. Lauren merely looked at it, then back up to his face.

"In England," he lied, "we seal a bargain like this."

She hesitated, then mirrored his move, allowing him to take her hand and bring it close to his face. He bowed his head and pressed his lips against her skin—not on the back of her hand, the way he should have done. Ari raised her palm and kissed her there, in the center of it, so that her fingers curled up and touched his cheek, and he could feel the heat of her wrist so near to him, the scent of flowers and woman tantalizing him.

When he lifted just his eyes to see her she was perfectly still, staring at him, aghast. So Arion moved his lips down farther, over to her wrist, and the beating pulse that fluttered there made him smile against her, a wicked satisfaction. Let her consider *this* when their fortnight ended.

Lauren snatched back her hand.

"A very strange custom," she said, and the velvet of her voice seemed roughened, shaken.

"On the contrary," Arion replied. "You'd be surprised at how many good unions begin in such a way."

She pushed her mount back to put space between them, pulling up her hood at the same time, until the shadows hid her face, and all he was left with was a woman on a horse, her breathing a little too shallow for normal.

"Tomorrow morning, du Morgan, we will have a patrol at the eastern meadow with the rock oak. Do you know the one I mean?"

"Aye. I've seen it."

"Bring your men—or send them, I don't care—to that rock oak at dawn, and we will begin this ... union."

"Very well," he said.

She turned her steed and galloped away, quickly absorbed in the depths of the forest leading back to Keir.

Arion, alone now in the sand, smiled grimly to himself. He knew what Lauren MacRae didn't, or wouldn't admit: The union between them had already begun. He could only pray to God it didn't kill him before the Vikings did.

Chapter Five

————— ⟨✿⟩ —————

*T*HE ROCK OAK WAS THE only one of its kind
on the island, an oddity that Lauren had always thought
had been dubbed with a reversed name, since it was not
an oak at all, but really a stone that was shaped as one.

It was distinctive on Shot not just for that quality but
because it was the only thing of any height in the eastern meadow, a lone mark against the sky and the ocean,
a heavy twist of mottled rock in reddish brown and gray
and clear quartz.

Lauren had always considered it beautiful. She supposed it was a strange quirk in her, that she found po-
etry in things where others found only practicality. A
river became a ribbon of liquid gold, instead of an ob-
stacle to cross. A storm was the pageantry of nature, instead of a cursed nuisance. Lightning was fascinating,
not frightening. Thunder was thrilling, not the wrath of
God. The distinctive taste of sea salt, the rainbowed interior of mussel shells, even the cries of the sea birds
that circled their ships were all things of wonder to her.

And the rock oak was one of the best wonders of
them all. It thrust out from the waving meadow grass,
dark against the green and yellow ground, completely
out of place. It stood taller than she—taller than anyone

in the clan, for that matter. Stone bark, rough in some places, smoother in others, just like the bark of an actual oak tree. But instead of branches coming out of the top, it was cut off, as if a capricious giant had come and snapped it in half. As a girl she used to climb up the trunk of it to sit on the top, and there, on the uneven table of its crown, she had discovered the circles of alternating color that started small and spread out, like rings on the surface of a pond.

A whim of nature, at least to Lauren. To everyone else, it was just a good place to meet, a distinctive marker for that part of the island.

They gathered next to it now and watched the sun come up over the water, mostly silent, a group of young warriors and older ones. Their horses were still fresh, slightly restless, shifting in the grass.

Lauren, who had dismounted to wait, leaned back against the rock oak and tried not to yawn. When had she last had a good night's sleep? She had no idea.

"Mayhap they won't come," said Rhodric, one of the men who, yesterday, had expressed more doubt than most at this scheme. He was the youngest son of James, and apparently he was even less ready to accept an agreement with the enemy than his father was.

"They'll come," Lauren said. "They have every reason to."

No one replied. They just kept scanning the horizon, a few holding up hands to block out the bright light of the new sun.

A slow commotion at the southern edge of the meadow drew everyone's attention. It was the sound of horses, many of them. A dark, hazy line became heads, torsos, and then horses, at least forty men, all converging on the group by the rock oak.

There were only thirty of the MacRaes.

"They've outnumbered us," someone muttered.

"It's all right," Lauren said, hoping it was true.

One rider broke away from the rest and took the lead. Lauren didn't bother to remount to meet him. She strode across the yellow and green grass, walking up fearlessly to the large black stallion.

"You're late," she said.

The Earl of Morgan gave her a disgruntled look. "This meadow is closer to Keir than Elguire."

"Is that all it was, du Morgan? Or were you having second thoughts?"

He swung out of the saddle, coming down close beside her, but Lauren refused to take a step back.

"Second and third and fourth, MacRae," he said to her, offering that dry smile of his. "Yet here we are."

"So I see."

One of them would have to move. She had to bend her neck too much to meet his look, but he seemed not to notice, only stood there with that smile, so close she could follow the pattern of threading at the collar of his tunic. Each stitch was precise, exact, she noticed—and then she wondered who had sewn them for him.

A sweetheart? A betrothed? Some English beauty, no doubt, with flaxen hair and sky-blue eyes . . .

This was unseemly. Lauren took the step away, using her arm to sweep back to her men as a cover for it. "We are ready to ride with you. I have some information from this morning's early patrol, however."

"What is it?"

"A longship was spotted off the northeastern coast. At least one, perhaps more. My men said it was too far off to be certain. They've been watching it, but the Vikings made no move to come inland."

"Are they still there?"

"Aye, as far as I know."

"Then let's go," he said.

It didn't take long to reach the lookout point where the longship had first been spotted. A narrow hill atop a steep cliff, more of just a rock face, really, marked with stunted bushes and no path to speak of. Trees and bushes grew thick along the edges of the cliff on either side of the outcropping, which hung thin and pointed over the fury of the ocean below.

They found the guards' horses first, tied at the bottom of the incline. The hill was too steep for riding. Two of her men remained up there still; she saw them both staring out at the water. They always kept scouts in pairs now, ever since the disastrous attack that had killed Da. One to mark the progress of the boat, the other to ride back to Keir to warn of the impending assault.

When they heard the group approaching, one of them walked down the hill, searching the crowd until he saw Lauren.

"It's still out there," he said to her, and Lauren dismounted and tied the reins of her steed to the same scrub as the scout had. When the man began the climb back up the hill, Lauren followed, then looked back at the earl, still mounted.

"Well? Aren't you coming?"

He looked around him, then dismounted, handing

the reins and his shield to one of his soldiers. Lauren began to climb again.

The view from the top of the craggy incline was spectacular, if windy. From here she could see out to forever, to the endless line of the water meeting the sky, blue on blue, with perfect, even whitecaps farther out. Marring the symmetry of the scene was the faraway form of the longship, brown and red and white, the curving prow of it unmistakable even from this distance. All of the oars had been lifted from the water. Rounded metal shields lined the edge of the hull, flashes of brilliance against the sunlight.

The two most approachable beaches on Shot were always well guarded: Keir overlooked one, Elguire the other. Otherwise the shoreline was rocky at best, deadly at worst. Yet these Vikings weren't near a beach at all. It made no sense.

"What are they doing?" Lauren asked, almost to herself.

"They're waiting," said a voice at her shoulder, firm and authoritative.

"For what?" asked one of the scouts.

"I don't know," the earl said. "That's the bad part."

Her braid was already coming loose; Lauren put both hands on her hair to keep it from whipping around them, still staring at the menace of the boat, almost motionless amid the waves. "There's no place to land here," she said. "It's all cliffs on this part of the island. They won't be coming this way, unless they're crazed."

"No," Arion agreed. "And there's just one boat. We've already shown them we can defeat one boatload of men. Mayhap they're waiting for more of them to arrive."

"Why here?" Lauren asked.

"It's almost the exact middle between Keir and El-guire," Arion said. "Perhaps they chose it for that."

"But there is no haven—" Lauren began, then exchanged a long look with the scouts.

"What?" Arion asked, curt.

"No haven off this shore except for the caves," she finished.

"Caves? What caves?"

"The cliffs here are riddled with them. But they're mostly very small, and they fill with water at high tide— they're too dangerous even to visit, much less dock in. It's why we haven't patrolled here as much as the beaches."

She inched farther up the incline, past both of the scouts and the earl, until she lay against the slope of the hill at the very edge of it, leaning her head down over the top. The drop would be quick and staggering from this rock, nothing below her but air and then the churning water, crashing up against the cliffs. She craned her head to the left, seeing only white froth and waves, nothing unordinary. Then she looked to the right, and found Arion beside her in an identical position, leaning over the edge of the rock, following her look.

"Refreshing," he commented, as the wind came up hard and slammed against them, smelling strongly of the sea.

She ignored his sarcasm, creeping up even farther over the brink, so that her elbows were braced against what was almost the underside of the stone, and her head hung far down, her braid falling past her to point to the sea. If she looked straight down it was a dizzying distance to the swirling blue.

"Careful," said the earl, now sharp. She felt his hand on her back, and then her arm, holding her in place.

"I'm fine," Lauren said, but she didn't dare try to shake him off. She kept searching the water below.

Nothing. No Vikings down there, as far as she could see; no boats of any kind. But the sunlight coming off the water made a jumble of the waves, blinding her in spells, so that she had to squint to close out most of it. She gave up on the ocean and started looking down at the face of the cliffs instead, at the layers of shadows against the pink stone, chips of white sparkles shimmering at her.

The shadows were deep and impenetrable, easy camouflage for the natural cave openings pocketing the bluffs here.

"I think that's enough," the earl said, and began to pull on her arm. "Come up, Lauren, and we'll talk—"

"Look!" She did shake him off now, taking back her arm and pointing. And then she lost her balance and tipped forward, toward the seething blue water.

Firm hands pulled her back, stabilizing her. She heard him swear at her under his breath. "Come up!" Arion demanded, pulling at her.

"No, look! Don't you see it, du Morgan? Open your eyes!"

She pointed with her other hand, right to the betraying shadow, turning and finding his face until he scowled and tilted his head to follow her finger, partially blocking her view.

His black hair billowed up around them, brushing her cheek, tickling. He had not let go of her arm.

Lauren spoke into his ear. "That shadow there, beyond

the rock that looks like a seal. It's moving. Do you see it?" She tried to go lower than his head, then higher, to find her view again. "It's the tip of a boat, du Morgan! A rowboat, I would say, from that longship of theirs. They found their way to one of the caves, but the tide is rising, pulling at the boat. That's why we can see the end of it."

The wind was a steady howl around them now, the echoing crash of the ocean seemed all too near. He hung there with her, motionless now, and Lauren managed to find a space to look around him at the very tip of the rowboat, a bobbing speck of color against the darkness.

"Yes," Arion said at last. "I see it. You're right—it's a boat."

He looked back at her and she at him, their faces so close together, enthusiasm and thrill between them. His hair blew around them again and then mingled with strands of her own, ebony on copper red, creating the illusion of shelter around them.

All at once the elation of discovery in Lauren turned to something else, something that had nothing to do with the boat below, a spiraling sort of intensity. She met the earl's look—altered now as well, not so open as before—then watched as his eyes dropped lower, down to her lips.

Lauren pulled away, and her hair freed from his, and the wind and the sun came back between them. She scooted down the incline of the hill until there was all solid rock beneath her, shaking her head to rid herself of the strange potency of his look. When she turned around he was standing at her side, and the men in front of them were showering them with questions.

"It's a rowboat," she said, to no one in particular. "They've found one of the openings in the cliff face."

"Are you certain?" asked Rhodric.

"It's there," answered the earl.

Rhodric didn't look at him, keeping his gaze pinned to Lauren.

"Are *you* certain, lass?" he asked again, almost a drawl.

The earl did not shift beside her, but Lauren felt the insult go through him, a subtle tensing of his muscles. She clearly saw the affronted looks passing back and forth among the English soldiers ahead of them.

"We *both* saw it," she said to Rhodric, trying to put a warning in her tone. "It's almost directly below us. The stern is just barely showing past the cliff. If the seas weren't so rough there, we wouldn't have seen it moving at all. They must have rowed in very early this morning, before our patrol got here."

"We need to get down there," said the earl to her.

"And how to you propose to do that, du Morgan?" sneered Rhodric. There was no denying the challenge in his voice now.

Lauren took a quick step between Arion and her kinsman. Since she was higher on the hill than Rhodric, her head was almost level with his. She fixed him with a severe look. His hazel eyes held scorn, unwavering anger.

"Do you seek to thwart your father, Rhodric?" Lauren asked mildly.

"Don't be a fool," he whispered to her, darting a look at the earl behind her.

"Then do you seek to thwart the council?"

"Lauren, you have no idea what these men—"

"Do you?" she interrupted, speaking over him. "Do you seek to thwart the wishes of your own laird, my cousin? Is that it?"

"You know that Quinn would never approve of such a—"

"I know that he would!" Lauren flared. "I know him better than you do, I would say! And I also know that our council has approved of this plan, and they speak for him! So if you think to ruin our peace, Rhodric, I wish you would do it elsewhere. I have other things to worry about now. There are Vikings right below us!"

She pushed past him, walking away down the hill a little too fast, her heart in her throat. Rhodric was one of the best swordsmen on Shot, and no one knew it better than he did. If he truly wanted to start a fight here, he would do permanent damage to their relationship with the du Morgans. She could only hope that she had made him understand, and that he was not so hotheaded as to forget that there were more of the English than there were of them.

She went to her horse and listened, hearing nothing but the wind, so she turned and looked back up the hill. Rhodric and the earl were taking each other's measure, two large men, neither of them yielding to the other. The edges of her vision showed her all the men with hands on sword hilts, English and Scots alike, their attention riveted on the scene above them.

Please, she thought frantically, an aimless prayer. *Don't do it. . . .*

And then Rhodric took a backward step down the hill. Just one step, enough for the Earl of Morgan to walk by him, which is what he did, passing the other man with supreme unconcern, appearing totally indifferent to the threat in the air.

Rhodric turned and stared at the earl's back, a wrathful promise of future conflict.

"We need to get down there," Arion said again to Lauren. She had been so worried about Rhodric that she hadn't even noticed the earl coming straight to her. "How do we do that, MacRae? This is your side of the island."

"Yes." She raised a hand to her eyes, trying to put her thoughts back together.

"We'll have to go down the tunnels through the opening up here," offered one of her clansmen, brisk and practical.

Arion looked at the man, then back down at her. He raised one elegant brow, an unspoken question.

"The caves are vast and confusing," Lauren said, raising her voice, explaining to everyone. "We haven't fully mapped them out, because they are of no real use to us. They are difficult to access, and they narrow and widen unpredictably. Most of them flood with the tide."

"Could the Vikings find their way up here from where they are?" asked an English soldier.

"Aye," Lauren admitted. "It's possible. The cliffs themselves are too tall and too steep to scale; we do know that. But there are a few cavern tunnels that rise to the surface of the island. We've gone down through them a number of times, just to see what was there. So the

Vikings could discover the same route we did, I suppose, if the cave they are in has a full connection to one of the main shafts."

"Where is the exit?" Arion asked.

Lauren lifted her hands in the air. "Almost anywhere. We've discovered many shallow openings in the stone around here. But we've found only one that is wide enough for a man to fit through."

She looked around at the men, all concentrating on her, each one at last considering the same goal.

"I'll show you," Lauren said to them all. "It's not far."

---

*T*HE OPENING WAS MUCH SMALLER than what Ari had expected, and if Lauren MacRae had not paused beside the deep crevice of rock that made a ravine in the earth, he was sure he would have ridden by it without noticing it.

The ravine was worn stone, obviously a flood channel from the rains, and the grass and brush around it grew tall and thick. Ari followed her as she scrambled down the stepped ledge of the trench. A group of soldiers fanned out behind them; Arion had already sent some of them to search the surrounding woods. The two sentries had stayed behind at the ledge of rock overlooking the ocean, keeping vigilant watch on the longship.

Lauren covered the uneven ground of the ravine with ease, he couldn't help but notice. Her steps were swift and almost silent over the gravel that littered the gully. She stopped beside what appeared to be merely a fold in the stone. When Arion got close enough, he could see a strange oval darkness against the rock, almost sinister, thicker than the other shadows around them.

"This is it," she said, one hand on the curve of the entrance. "Only a few people will be able to go, and you won't have room for that." She gave his shield a dismissive glance. "The way is deceptive, and most of the tunnel is too narrow to walk side by side. We should leave some men here to guard the entrance."

"Agreed," said Arion, and turned to the man nearest him, issuing instructions. Lauren did the same, speaking quietly to one of the Scots. Ari watched the man walk over to his horse and take something bulky from a sack near the saddle. He returned and handed it to Lauren. It was rope, battered and faded.

She noticed Ari's frown. "Some of the drops are steep," she said, "and this will help to keep us all together. We're going to have to hurry to beat the high tide." She took one end of the rope and handed the rest to him, then began to duck into the cave.

"Wait a minute." Arion had her by the arm before she could vanish into that ominous opening. "What are you doing? Have someone else lead."

Lauren shot him an impatient look. "I'm the smallest of us all. And I know these caves better than most. I spent a whole summer once mapping them with my father. No one here is better qualified than I am to lead."

He didn't like it. It felt wrong, but to say that to her would be nothing short of idiocy. She would only laugh at him and go anyway. It made Arion irritated, then annoyed with himself for being irritated. It was not his duty to be her nursemaid. If she had no sense, it would not be his fault if she stumbled across the enemy and got killed before she could draw breath. She knew the risks, obviously. She had flaunted her power and her knowledge of this land from the moment he had met her.

Fine. She could lead. If she ended up as a sacrifice to the Vikings, it would be no one's fault but her own.

But what he said was, "We don't have a light. We can't go down without one."

She looked amused. "Just follow me, du Morgan."

Lauren stepped into the oval and was immediately engulfed in the vacuum of it. The rope in his hand grew taut. He loosened his grip on it, and it began to slither through his fingers into the cave after her.

The rest of the men were waiting for him. Ari handed the coils of rope to the soldier nearest him. "Take up the rear of the line and hold on to that," he said, "and don't let go."

"Aye, my lord," said the man.

Arion stalked into the darkness.

He let his hand drift over the roughness of the rope at his side, using it as a guide to find her—lightly, because it was obviously old, and many of the fibrous strands were separating from the whole of it. His palm skipped over them; he ignored the bite they left against his skin.

It was utterly black inside the cave, a close kind of suffocating nothingness, no way to tell where the walls might be but for the fact that his shoulders kept grazing them. Lauren had been right: It would be impossible to walk down this tunnel any way but single-file.

He heard her ahead of him, her steps still agile and

sure. He fancied he could even hear her breathing, slow, steady.

When he sensed he was close enough to her he grasped the rope again, then reached out and placed a hand on her shoulder.

"What are you doing?" Her voice floated back at him, eerily disembodied, yet clearly with a trace of vexation.

"Indulge me," he said. "Pretend I can't see a damned thing."

"Can't you, du Morgan?" He heard amusement again.

"No. Apparently unlike you, I do not have the eyes of a cat."

She gave a soft laugh. He would have missed it had he not been so close to her now.

Behind him came the louder sounds of the other men, none so surefooted as the woman ahead of him. There was distinct cursing and muffled thumps, arms and feet hitting stone. At least he was not the only one blinded.

"Almost there," said Lauren, whatever that meant.

They walked farther, and Arion sensed they were descending, but for now the grade was gentle enough. Since he couldn't see anything anyway, he closed his eyes, focusing on feeling the space around him, trying to find his bearings by concentrating on his other senses.

Small space, getting smaller. Strange odor, cool and musty, with the tang of salt underlying it. A steady commotion behind him, and ahead . . .

Heat. Adventure. Sweet curves, firm flesh. A delicately boned shoulder, warm beneath his hand. The whisper of her tartan against the oversized tunic she wore. Confident, airy footsteps, her legs encased in leather boots that laced up the sides, all the way up to her knees, perhaps, and then higher than that would be just softness, just the creamy line of her thighs—

"Halt." Lauren slowed enough to let her command filter past her, and Arion came out of his daydream with a jolt. He repeated the word, heard it go down the line until everyone stopped. She moved, dropping down so that he was no longer touching her, and he heard sounds coming from where she must be kneeling.

The musty smell was much stronger here, unpleasant but not unendurable. A spark of light took him by surprise, showing him the confining tunnel around them in one quick white flash, and then it came again, only this time it caught on something, and the *whoosh* of a fire began.

Lauren stood up and turned around, holding up a thick torch that flamed at the end.

"We keep the light this far in so no one will be tempted to go exploring when just passing by. We've lost several children over the years to these caves."

Ari nodded, looking around.

"From this point on it gets more dangerous," she continued. "We're going to have to make a sharp descent. The tide waters fill most the tunnels below this level, so be careful. The ground will be slick. Don't fall."

"Is that concern I detect, MacRae?" Arion asked.

"Just practicality." She gave him her cold smile. "If you injure yourself, we'd have to back half the men out of the tunnel to free you. I'd rather not waste the time."

They stood in a cramped cavern where the shaft they had been following split into three directions, all of them looking uncomfortably small to Arion. He ignored her barb, concentrating on the openings before them. None appeared too promising.

The first was a rough circle of stone, but set up high in the arch of the wall. They would have to climb to reach it. The middle one was lower but had a sickle shape; it looked almost impossible to walk in. The third was too squat for anything but crawling.

Lauren held the torch up high, then bent and picked up the rope again.

"This way." She chose the sickled tunnel, and had to twist sideways to slip though. Ari watched the flame of the torch reflect back at him on the pale stone around them, a dragon's tail of black smoke beckoning him forward. The rope began to slide past his fingers again.

Arion sighed, then approached the stone. He exhaled a little deeper, managing to squeeze into the opening. Cold stone pressed into him on both sides; he had to turn his head to the side and grope the walls with his hands to keep moving. It was almost unbearable. Grumbling voices behind him told him that the other men were experiencing the same problems.

After what seemed aeons, the stone slowly began to release him, though it seemed they were going almost straight down. As the walls grew farther apart, he could breathe a little easier. Eventually, he was able to face forward again, though he had to hunch over to accommodate the lowering ceiling. The smell of the sea grew stronger, and the damp, slimy green leaves attached to the walls they walked past could only be seaweed.

They passed many other openings in the cave walls, but Lauren didn't veer off to any of them, only kept on in this interminable curving shaft, lower, lower into the earth. Even she was going more slowly now, picking her way carefully around the slippery, uneven cave floor.

The ceiling dropped farther. Then it shrank again, and he was almost having to bend double to walk, using his hands on the walls for balance. Since Lauren had slowed he kept right behind her, certain that at some point on this insane journey she would skid and fall into the bowels of the island, though he didn't see how he would be able to help her. Most likely they would go plunging down into some pit together.

She was compensating for the lowering space by tilting sideways, though she didn't have to bend as far as he did to escape the cave ceiling. The muscles in his legs were beginning to ache. He could only imagine how she was holding up.

"Lauren," he began.

She whipped around and put her free hand over his mouth, silencing him with a fierce scowl. The men behind them bunched up at his sudden halting, and Arion turned and waved an arm at them, indicating that they should stop.

"Stay here," Lauren mouthed, silent, and handed him the torch.

He didn't understand what she was about to do until she began to wrap the rope around her forearm, all the way down to her wrist. He handed the torch back to whoever was next in line behind him, then grabbed her arm and shook his head at her.

She tried to free herself and he held on harder. He wasn't going to let her go forward alone. It was plain that she thought them close enough now to the cave where the Vikings hid that the light would be a detriment to them, and any noise at all might give them away. Ari came up close and put his lips next to her ear.

"I'm taking the lead now."

She let out a huff of air, perhaps exasperation, then moved so that she could whisper back, her breath warm on him. "You don't know the way. You don't know the opening. And you wouldn't fit anyway."

He kept his grip on her firm.

"Be reasonable, du Morgan!" Her words were hushed, but the tension in her was marked. "Let go of me!"

"I'm coming with you."

He heard her draw in air through her teeth, and he pulled back so that he could look into her eyes, letting her see that he meant what he said.

There was a smudge of dirt on her chin, and the loosened hair around her face had become waving curls that seemed to match the color of the fire. Her eyes deepened to golden brown in this light, very serious. She was so beautiful, even now.

"Stay far behind me, then," she said, the lightest of sounds. "Don't interfere."

Arion let go of her arm. She moved off into the darkness ahead.

He turned and indicated to the man there that he was to wait, and listen, and give the rope enough slack. The soldier nodded.

The cave got, if possible, even smaller ahead, but strangely enough, they were moving up again, rising above the level where they had left the others. Eventually Ari was forced to give up walking and begin to crawl blindly, adding bruises and scrapes that stung in the salt water puddled on the stone, silently reciting every profanity he had ever learned. The tunnel went on and on, slowly leveling out.

All his previous fantasies of her had shriveled away; right now all that Lauren MacRae represented to him was pain and a sore back and bleeding palms and a certain faith that she was going to get them killed, probably very soon. He couldn't see her any longer, but Arion considered how nice it would be to catch up with her, so that he could wrap his hands around her swanlike neck and squeeze.

The darkness around him began to lighten—not from torchlight, but something more like daylight, cool blue suffusing the tunnel. He rounded a curve and found the object of his ire lying on her stomach on the tunnel floor, staring down at what appeared to be a hole in the ground. Her face was dramatically lit with the unearthly new light, and she was slowly moving her head, searching whatever was below her.

He was able to creep up beside her by overlapping her, and she shifted over as far as she could, not bothering to look at him.

Fresh air wafted up around him, the promise of the outside world so close.

Directly below them, not too far down, was what appeared to be a significant grotto opening out to the ocean. A small, rocky ledge to the left was all that was not submerged by the pulsing water. And on the water was the rowboat, so close he could make out the sinewy lines of the animal carvings along the prow.

Arion leaned out farther over the opening, so that

he could see the whole of the space below them, all the way back to the jagged entrance of the grotto.

He lifted his head and looked at Lauren, and she stared back at him, dismayed.

The boat was empty, and so was the cavern.

The Vikings were loose on Shot.

Chapter Six

$\mathscr{L}$AUREN TUGGED ON THE ROPE until she felt it give, then gathered up the slack and began to creep over the edge of the hole.

Predictably, the Earl of Morgan pulled her back.

She forestalled his argument. "It's the only logical thing to do, du Morgan," she said, still a whisper, because she wasn't sure if the invaders were nearby or not. "One of us has to go down there. You're too heavy for the rope."

"I think not, MacRae." His face hung over hers. He moved until his body pressed her back down to the stone, so that she couldn't escape without a struggle. "Time for a retreat."

"Don't be stupid! We have to be certain they're gone!"

"Suppose they aren't," he said, the calmness in his voice beginning to fray. "Suppose they're hiding, Lauren—that it's an ambush. Suppose they're just waiting for a fight, and all they get is you."

He was right. She knew it, but she was right, too. She couldn't leave here without knowing absolutely that what she saw below her was the truth. In fact, it would be better if it *were* an ambush, that the Vikings were trapped down there. Because the alternative gave her chills of terror.

"We have to be sure," she said to him, because she didn't know what else to add.

His lips were pressed to a grim line, the green of his eyes somehow vivid, enhanced by the ocean light.

"I can't let you do it," he said at last.

"I have to," she said, softer now, close to pleading. "You know I do."

He didn't move, and he didn't release her from his gaze, though she thought she saw some change in him at her words, a streak of what might have been pain behind his steady look.

"Let me go, Arion," Lauren said, and his name slipped out almost gently.

Now there was no mistaking the change in him, a swift intent, his head lowering to hers. He kissed her, his lips claiming hers roughly, his hands coming up to frame her face.

Lauren felt all her being rise up and dissolve, shock and pleasure and complete desire. He tasted of salt and desperation; his fingers trembled against her cheeks. His lips were firm yet soft, caressing hers, and the desire in her made her free hand come up around him, pulling him closer, tangling in his hair.

He made a wordless sound, shifting again, covering more of her body, and his weight and form felt welcome, urgent. He was all hard muscles and unyielding lines, pressing into her, and she reveled in it, she wanted more.

His tongue was stroking her lips now, urging her to open her mouth, and so she did, and Arion let out another sound, masculine and low.

It hummed through her and found an answer, the

stinging delight of him, how she couldn't get enough of him, taste enough of him. He was pain, he was the sparking joy, and she fell spinning into the desire, letting it fill her until there was nothing but Arion.

He dragged his lips from hers and began to kiss her cheeks, her throat, his breath hot and rushed against her skin, pushing against her now in a slow rhythm that made her weak. Lauren closed her eyes and tilted back her head, allowing him more, eager for whatever he had to give her.

She felt him take a deep breath against her neck, sudden coolness, and then he stopped, still pressed there, unmoving.

The world came back to her in excruciating detail— the hard stone against her back, the dampness of it soaking through her tartan and tunic. The turbulent lapping of the water below them, sloshing against the cavern walls. The warmth of this man's body, covering hers.

Arion lifted his head. She stared up at him, at the appealing planes of his face, the fall of ebony hair the only softness to him.

He said slowly, "My God."

Lauren placed her hand against his shoulder and pushed lightly. He moved off her with almost insulting speed, backing up into the tunnel, leaving her completely. The shadows took away his expression, but she could imagine what he was feeling. It couldn't be anything less appalling than what was racing through her.

She had embraced her enemy—she had *loved* it, she had wanted more of it. She would have done anything for him in that moment; he had held her captive with ern rocks, stunned, unable to move her arms or her legs. Everything was murky and dim, heavy and cold. She couldn't think of what she was supposed to do—move, fight, breathe—

Don't breathe!

The current was sucking her toward brighter waters, the open ocean. If she was swept out there, she might be hurled against the cliffs or, worse, pulled out to sea.

Lauren kicked and began to struggle, pushing off the rocks with all her strength, fighting the pull of the current. The grotto was much deeper than she had thought, and the surface was not close. With one last, hard shove, Lauren gave herself up to the flow of the water, just trying to move up. After what seemed an eternity, her head cleared the water. She felt cool air on her face and took a deep, coughing gasp of it.

Something dark and blurred went by her and instinctively she grabbed at it, fingers slipping and then catching on slick stone. Water rushed back into her face, blinding her, and she turned her head and pulled herself closer to her anchor. She heard her name being shouted, a man's voice.

Lauren looked up and around. She had managed to grasp one of the last jutting bits of rock that stood between her and the mouth of the grotto; it lay near the end of the ledge she had seen before. From above she had thought the cave to be shallow, but now she saw that her guess had been wrong—in fact, it was quite deep. The farthest stone the Vikings could tie their craft to had been near only the middle of the cavern.

Close to the center of the ceiling was the opening she had come through, the splintered end of the rope

still visible. Booted feet were descending through the
hole, followed by large, muscular legs, a heavy tunic.

"No!" Lauren tried to shout, but the water clogging
her throat made it nothing but a rasp. She coughed, clinging to her stone. "Don't come down here! There's no
time! We won't be able to—"

The earl dropped through the opening, disappearing
with a neat splash into the dark blue waters. She looked
around frantically at the rippled surface of the cave water, searching in vain for any sign of him.

Damn him! If he had hit his head on one of those
underwater rocks, she was *not* going after him! It would
be exactly what he deserved, for doing something so
witless, for risking his life to come after her....

He didn't surface. Lauren began to drag herself along
the ledge of stone, still looking, and when she was almost to the center of the cavern again she took a deep
breath and dived down into the dimness once more.

Perhaps it was that her eyes were better adjusted, or
that she had been just too confused before, but now she
discerned the outline of the grotto floor, the strange
and twisted shapes of the stone that reached up and
then dipped down, the swaying clusters of seaweed that
grew in the niches. She even saw the tenacious bands of
starfish clinging to the edges of the cavern walls, rough
masses of barnacles or mussels hidden in the grooves.
But she did not see Arion.

The current was her foe again, pulling at her feet,
taking the folds of her tunic and tartan and using them
against her, making them heavy, resistant to her swimming. Where was he? If he had been dragged out to sea
she might never find him....

She had to rise to take in air, this time keeping one hand against the hull of the Vikings' boat to keep her steady as she panted. Her hands and feet were already numb; she barely felt the hardness of the wood beneath her palms. Lauren went back down.

Still nothing. Only the shadow of the rowboat above her, the seaweed dancing below and alongside her, showing her the rising push of the tide. Could he have become caught beneath a sea rock? Trapped, running out of air, unable to free himself—

Something yanked at her hair, pulling her backward, and then an arm came around her neck with brutal force, leaving her flailing in the water, towing her up with abrupt speed.

They surfaced together, Arion's arm still tight around her neck, and Lauren had both hands on it, trying to pull him off her. She felt him swimming with strong, powerful strokes, bringing them both up against something solid. It had to be the ledge again.

The arm around her neck loosened, then let go. Lauren turned just as Arion grabbed her tartan, and then the collar of her tunic, hauling her up close to him. He kept one hand on the ledge, the other holding her to him, water sloshing around their necks. In the next second he was climbing up it, dragging her along, and Lauren was scrambling to find holds in the smooth stone where there were none.

After a struggle they were on its narrow top, sitting slumped against the wall of the cavern, panting, with the ocean lapping over their feet.

She was exhausted. There was no feeling left in her fingers or feet; her hair hung down in clumping strands around her, dark red against the sodden mess of her tartan. A look over at the earl showed her a similar view. He was dripping, the black of his hair plastered against him, sea water gleaming off his skin. There was a clear, coming storm in his eyes.

"What is wrong with you?" he demanded, and all the wrath from before was still there. "Are you deranged? What a stupid thing to do—"

"Me?" Lauren sat up straighter. "You English lunatic! Everything was fine until you had to fall in after me!"

"Oh, yes, I could see that. You were perfectly fine, trusting a rope that obviously wouldn't hold even a child! You were fine in that water, drowning!"

"I was *not* drowning! I was looking for *you!*"

"Certainly you were," he mocked. "That's why you were floating there like a sack beneath the water—to *save* me."

Lauren stumbled to her feet, water running down her, all the coldness in her banished in her fury. "I shouldn't have wasted my time on you! You're nothing but a heartless, insolent—"

In a flash he was standing as well, drawing his sword with a look that choked off the rest of her words. He moved so quickly that she barely saw the blur of his arm, pushing her up against the stone and then behind him, sending her reeling to the ledge. It happened too fast for her even to break her fall, and her shoulder took the blunt of the force, a streak of fiery pain running through it all the way down her spine.

Behind her was a scream, truly savage, and then the sound of sword against sword, sharp strikes, again and again. She rolled over and curled up, trying to avoid

Arion's feet as he lunged and shifted over the wet
rock, battling a Viking who had come from nowhere.

Lauren dragged herself out of Arion's way and stood
again, drawing her own dagger. She wasn't wearing a
broadsword today, not even the light one Da had had
made for her, because she honestly had not thought the
invaders would attack again so soon.

She would not allow Arion to pay for her mistake.
Her dirk was sharp and deadly, and she was skilled in its
use. Lauren stood as far back as she could on the ledge,
giving Arion room, ready to leap into the fight when
she was needed.

The Viking was yelling, every clash of the swords
prompting a new scream from him, a thick and in-
articulate sound, his eyes wide and bloodshot. Arion
fought silently, ceaselessly, countering each blow with
one of his own, slowly edging the other man back,
away from Lauren. She followed them, keeping her
eyes pinned on the Northman, waiting for any opportunity to help Arion.

The water was rising. There could be no doubt about
it. Minutes ago it had been below the table of the ledge;
right now they were splashing through it as it seeped
up over the rock. In minutes the entire block of stone
would be submerged—and then the cavern itself.

The Viking kicked out suddenly, taking Arion by surprise, sweeping his foot behind Arion's ankle and knocking him down to one knee, raising his sword and then
plunging it down to Arion's chest. Lauren leaped forward, dirk raised, a scream on her lips, but before she
could reach the invader Arion twisted to the side, allowing the Northman's sword to slice through the water and

hit the rock, a terrible clanging sound, almost embedding itself in the ledge from the force of it.

In an instant Arion had moved with lethal speed, shoving his own sword up at the other man, plunging into the water to make the blow.

The Viking stared at the length of steel that pierced his chest, hot blood bubbling up to cascade in ribbons all around the wound. He raised his eyes to Lauren's and she stared back at him, frozen, both of them connected for one unlikely moment in their mutual horror. Then the Viking took a lurching step to the side and fell, headfirst, into the waves. His body slowly sank into the water, a cloud of scarlet blossoming up from where he vanished.

Lauren lowered her dagger, feeling sick.

"My lord!" The words were strange and disembodied, echoing around her.

She turned blindly, trying to block out the sight of the blood, then looked up to the jagged ceiling. Faces crowded the opening above her, men she knew and men she didn't, all of them anxiously scanning the cavern.

"Lauren!" shouted one of the Scots.

"I'm fine!" she answered, and only then had the presence of mind to look around for Arion.

Once again the water was unbroken, only now it was up to her shins, and the tug of the current was tangible again.

"Where is the earl?" someone called, and she shook her head, taking a few steps forward, searching for any darkness beneath the surface that might be a man.

Lauren heard demands to lower the rope, and she

her footing; only Arion's quick clutch at her elbow kept her from sliding beneath the water. When they looked up again, the opening was deserted.

"I hope you weren't thinking of going into whatever tunnel access the Northmen did to escape," Arion said, seeming almost cheerful. "I don't relish having to fight all of them at once."

"No." Lauren splashed past him, bracing herself against the cavern wall for balance. She spoke quickly, because her teeth were starting to chatter from the cold. "I don't think there's any other w-way out of here but for that hole in the ceiling and the entrance to the s-sea. I th-think that man was waiting here, guarding the boat until his crewmen r-returned. Look, he could have hidden b-behind this rock here and we wouldn't have seen him f-from our vantage above."

Arion came behind her, wrapping his arms around her. The violence of the water seemed simply to part around him.

"You're freezing, and you haven't stopped bleeding. We've got to get you out of here."

"I know." She couldn't control the shivers now, fighting the urge to hug her arms to her, still trying to keep them moving. The water sloshed up to her waist; the cavern entrance was a half-moon ahead of her, shrinking rapidly. Lauren pointed to the boat. "We . . . have t-to leave . . . in that."

Ari didn't bother to argue with her, to tell her all the reasons why it was going to be impossible for them to fit the mass of the rowboat through what was left of the opening of the cave. Her lips were blue, her teeth were clenched together so tightly he could see the muscles in her jaw. At least the rowboat would be dry. If nothing else, he might be able to maneuver it over to the opening in the ceiling and hoist her through before the water crushed them.

She was in no condition to run, however. One look into her eyes told him that. The amber of them had become vacant, glazed, and the blood from the gash on her forehead still dribbled down her cheek in vivid color, dripping off her chin to mingle with the salt water.

The rowboat was bucking in the water now, the line that held it tied to one of the jagged rocks taut with tension. The only way to get over there was to swim, and Arion knew that Lauren wasn't going to be able to do that, either. He put her in front of him, wrapping an arm around her neck again, then pushed off into the waves, dragging her along.

It wasn't far to the boat, but the difficulty was the roughness of sea, now frothing up at the end of the cavern in wild bursts, spray everywhere. His first try at holding the rim of the rowboat failed; it jumped out of his reach just as he leaned in for it, and then it came back down against him with a painful shove, knocking him sideways. Both he and Lauren went whirling in the water.

He caught it on the second try, finding the wooden edge and grabbing on tightly.

"Lauren! I need your help!"

She stirred against him.

"I need you to lift your hands and try to hold on to the boat. Can you do that?"

She said nothing, but her movement grew stronger.

She was attempting to reach the boat. He helped her, pushing her up close, both of them rocking wildly. Ari saw her hands rise and flatten on the side of it, white skin on dark wood, too far down to reach the edge.

He let go of her and quickly moved back, then forward again, a rising surge with the water, taking her under her arms and lifting her as high as he could, straining. The wave receded and he fell away with it, but Lauren stayed. She was clinging to the rim of the boat. One more swell and he was back with her, arms around her legs, boosting her up higher. She kicked out and he had to let go, dropping back into the water, submerging beneath a particularly large wave and then coming up again. Ari looked up in time to see her disappear over the edge of the hull. She had made her way in.

He was getting tired. That was a bad sign, that the cold was sapping his vigor, making the work of getting himself into the Viking boat a clumsy and painful process. He managed to get both hands on the edge, and hung there, waiting for the next big wave to lift him up. It happened almost too soon; Arion hurled himself out of the water, wrapping one arm and a leg over the wood, precarious.

Two hands were pulling at him, tugging him in, and Arion found the strength to drop the rest of the way into the rowboat, trying not to fall on Lauren and not succeeding all that much.

He lay there for a moment, unable to move, and stared up at the rough edges of the ceiling, which now seemed to descend upon him, closer and closer in awful, nauseating dips and peaks. Something new blocked his vision—Lauren, pale and bleeding and long red hair, worry in her eyes.

Arion sat up, assessing the situation.

One rowboat, one pair of oars, out of the water. The rope, now stretched to the breaking point, the only thing keeping them reasonably still. The opening to the cave— far, far too tight now for them to fit through.

One woman, hunched and shivering in a soaked tartan, arms wrapped around herself, staring back at him in a poignant combination of dread and hope.

Arion clambered up to the front of the boat, drawing his sword and severing the rope with one quick slice. Immediately he was knocked backward with the release, as the boat rode a new swell forward into the cavern, then came crashing up against the end of the rocks.

He staggered back to Lauren, shoving her down to the bottom of the craft as he took the seat near the oars, then maneuvered them into the water.

"Stay there," he ordered, fighting to keep them from another crash.

She didn't listen, of course. Arion shouldn't have been surprised that instead of lying sensibly on the floor of the boat—the safest thing to do right now—she rose to her knees and peered behind him, at the thin opening that was left to them in the heaving sea. Arion didn't have time to push her down again. It was all he could do to move the craft at all. It wasn't designed for such harsh conditions, and the oars were awkward in the stiff coldness of his hands.

"Get down!" Lauren shouted suddenly, and when he

didn't move she hit him with her fists, pushing him to one side, making him lose his grip on an oar.

A rock from the ceiling the size of a man went grating past him, barely missing his torso but catching one of his thighs, tearing his tunic and hose, scraping the wood of the seat with a low groan. But the boat kept moving.

"There's more," Lauren said, her voice a rasp over the turmoil of the waves. "Don't get up."

Arion looked behind him and saw that she was right. If he tried to take his seat to row again it would be fatal. They were high enough now so that the long, pointed rocks hanging from the top of the grotto were a clear threat. Another came by, a new scraping sound against the planking, and Ari had to move again to avoid it, lower down in the boat.

The current was taking them where they needed to go, out of the cave. If only they didn't get smashed by the rocks first.

"Come on, come on," he heard Lauren whisper. He turned his head and saw her crouched down, holding on to the oar he had lost. She was facing the opening, transfixed on it, her lips moving almost silently.

Another rock, this one huge, large enough to block out all the light, and Ari lifted his hands above him and tried to make the boat go past it faster, pushing at it. When it cleared, he was staring up at the sky.

He wanted to shout out his victory, he wanted to jump up and celebrate to the sky and the clouds, the open sea around them now. But before he could do any of this, the boat came to a grinding, shuddering halt, and a wave of ice water broke over his head.

"What happened?" he shouted, clearing the hair from his eyes. He looked around and Lauren was missing— but no, he spotted one foot sticking out from underneath the mouth of the cave. The rest of her was blocked by the thick stone that pressed down against the hull. Her foot drew in, and then all of her was gone.

The rowboat had stopped only partially outside the cave, trapped. It was obviously caught on the other side, but the water had not let up its ferociousness. Wave after wave was now breaking over the hull, splashing into the boat. Another minute of this and they would sink.

Arion flattened himself and crawled back to the front. He found Lauren leaning over the side of the craft, clinging to the neck of the wooden beast whose head curved into the prow of the boat, hacking away at the wood with her dirk. She was making less progress than the rock itself, which was slowly splintering the wood with each jolt of water.

This was what had halted their freedom, this Viking carving, a snarling beast with a thick wooden neck. It resisted all attempts to separate it from the rest of the boat, as if it were a cursed extension of the invaders themselves, determined to drown the inhabitants of this island.

They were at the very limit of any hope to escape; soon the water would crush the boat in its rush to flood the cavern. But if the head of the beast was torn off by the current, it might take the entire prow with it, and the craft would sink instantly.

Arion copied Lauren's position on the other side of the boat, squeezing up through what was left of the opening, hanging off the side and using just his legs to hold him.

"Go back!" he yelled at her, and unsheathed his sword. She looked at him silently, then shifted down again, out of his sight.

Arion lifted his sword and came down on the neck, again and again, hacking at it, until chips of white wood were flying around him, and the head tilted down, bowing to the force of his blows and the unyielding pressure of rock. Spray from the ocean stung his eyes, a painful blur, and still he didn't stop, only kept stabbing at the beast. He halted just before it looked like it would snap, the wood giving off an eerie groan, almost as a real monster might under such an assault.

Arion let go of the boat and dropped into the sea just as the neck gave way, and the head cracked off and fell into the water with a heavy splash. The rowboat, safe from flooding, slid past the opening in grinding spells, out into the open sea.

Water buffeted him but he managed to sheathe his sword again. Arion took a deep breath and dived under the water to follow the boat, thinking of nothing but Lauren right now, alone in the craft, looking for him. She would be looking for him. He had to surface. He had to go to her. He couldn't give in to the heaviness invading him now, the cold, the dark, the endless deep....

Lauren, Lauren . . . gold and copper and red roses . . .

It wasn't that he found the surface but more that it found him, a rapid brightness, a buoyancy that took him and tossed him up, right up to the clean air, where he could breathe. And there was the rowboat, and there was

Lauren, leaning off the side again, half standing with a hand shielding her eyes, searching.

Ari made it to the boat and she helped him back in, though it wasn't easy for either of them. And although he was close to the end of his limits, he did a quick scan of the area around them, to see what new danger might present itself next.

The cliffs, ebbing in the distance. The mouth of the cave, nothing but a narrow slit in the rocks, then it was gone. The rowboat was caught in a current that was taking them away from that danger but still somewhat parallel to the shore.

The Viking longboat, moving away from Shot, a shrinking dot on the horizon. Apparently they had abandoned their lost crew.

He was too tired to do anything more. Arion lay on the bottom now in the water there, beyond movement, letting the autumn sun come down on him and slowly steal away the chill. Lauren was folded up beside him, unmoving, the sound of her breathing soft in his ear. One of her hands lay peacefully across his chest.

Clouds floated by in milky puffs. The sky was otherwise empty, cool and infinite.

Arion turned his head to the side, and what he saw there made him sit up quickly.

Lauren had collapsed in an awkward position, her eyes closed, her lips not quite as blue as before but still far too pale. In fact, all of her was too pale. Ari leaned over her and unfastened the silver brooch that held the soaked tartan to her, then unwrapped it from the intricacy of the folds around her. The wool cloth fell away with a wet heaviness, all the colors darkened to muted tones, testimony to her struggle in the water.

Arion lifted her up and gathered her to him, holding her close, trying to gauge how badly she was chilled—if he should panic yet at her lassitude or not.

She didn't open her eyes but did let out a low murmur, protest or reassurance, he couldn't tell. Her head rested against his chest, bowed, and all he could see now was the curve of her shoulder, drying strands of her hair beginning to float up with the breeze. He ran his hand down her arm, feeling the dampness of the tunic she still wore, wondering if he should try to remove it.

He probably should. She would warm up faster without it. That had to be more important than her modesty.

But when he reached for the hem down by her shins—obviously the tunic was too large on her—she stirred again, and tried to brush his hand away.

"Lauren, you have to get warm," Ari said. "I'm trying to help you."

"No," was all she replied, but she did not try to move from his arms.

He let out his breath in frustration. "Your tunic is too wet."

She laughed weakly. "So is yours."

She had a point. Arion gave up on the tunic and instead relaxed back against the seat behind him, keeping her close. He felt surprisingly good, considering all that he had just been through. Yes, in fact, he felt better than that. He felt . . . wonderful.

The sun was bright and promising above them, the wind not too strong, smelling of salt and freshness and Lauren.

He looked down at her again and found her looking up at him, a faint pinkness at last returning to her cheeks, her lips. Her eyelashes had dried into star points around her eyes, whimsical and dramatic all at once, framing the gold with dark brown, so captivating.

Her hair blew up and caressed his chin, his cheek, a silky skimming over his skin. It was not an invitation but his body responded as if it were: a quick hardening, the craving for her that could overwhelm him just that quickly, like a sunburst, total heat.

He watched her eyes widen, almost as if she felt it as well. Yes, there was a definite shift in her. She seemed to soften against him, her head tilting back, her hair sliding down his arms. It was just like before, when he had lost his reason in that tunnel shaft and kissed her, and she had kissed him back, passionate, responding. Oh, it had been so perfect, so incredibly arousing. . . .

Arion lowered his head, his lips dropping down to hers, their breath mingled.

Lauren pulled back with a jerk, until his arms tightened instinctively, stopping her from leaving completely. She stayed there, still close enough to him that his body ached for her, but she was shaking her head, and her hands were braced against his wrists.

Obviously, it had been perfect for only one of them.

Ari let her go. She moved away from him, as far as she could in the confines of the boat, not meeting his eyes but instead looking down and away. There could be no mistaking what was now a blush across her cheeks.

"Lauren," he tried, but she only shook her head again, a hand coming up to cover her lips, as if she could press back what she wanted to say to him. Her eyes lifted and then moved beyond him, behind him.

"Look!" she cried, pointing.

He did, following her hand to see the shoreline of the island, a minuscule beach crowded with people, most of them waving and shouting.

Ari saw the blue and green tartan of the MacRaes on a great many of those people, and plainer tunics and hauberks on the rest.

His gaze moved back to Lauren and this time she didn't look away. Her face appeared carefully blank, smooth nothing. But her eyes revealed the truth. He saw the shame there, and the desire.

Arion found his place on the seat behind him and wordlessly began to row them to shore.

Chapter Seven

*T*HE WOMEN AT THE LOOMS were talking about her.

Lauren couldn't ignore it, though she was too far away to actually hear their conversation. She was walking from the keep to the stables, looking for Hannah, when she passed the weavers sitting snug in their own building, a stone and thatch place that held the precious quantities of wools and dyes and people who created the woolen trade the MacRaes were known for.

Lauren knew how to use a loom. She knew every step of the process, in fact; being the daughter of the laird had not spared her from having to learn the technique that all the women of the clan knew and passed down from generation to generation. She could even produce a fairly passable blanket, as long as the pattern wasn't too demanding. Otherwise, it had been long ago agreed that her skills might be better placed elsewhere.

She had not minded at all. In fact, it had been a great relief to her when, at the age of twelve, both Hannah and Da had excused her from the weaving. No one had been happier than Lauren to bid good-bye to that painstaking work. Instead she had focused on all the things it was thought she should know as the future wife of a laird—supervising the castle, the meals, the cleaning, the supplies, the trading and accounts. So many things, all in preparation for her role as the wife of Payton Murdoch. And since Lauren had wanted her clan to be proud of her, she had truly worked hard at mastering these skills. But even as a child, her hidden heart had always longed for a life that could never be hers.

She wanted to be a boy.

Not really *be* a boy. Rather, she wanted their freedom. She envied them their loud games, their thrilling hunts, their open ways and thoughts and authority. As Hebron's daughter she knew she had been granted a great deal of privilege, learning things that usually only males did. She went on those hunts. She joined in those games. She spoke her mind, perhaps too freely. But she couldn't imagine living any other way. She couldn't imagine shutting herself away from life, to be sheltered and hidden and relied upon to do all the necessary things the women did that never seemed to be appreciated.

As a result of this—her spirit at odds with the firm line of tradition—Lauren always felt that she had set herself up for a dual life, with one foot on either side of who she was supposed to be. Yes, she would be the bride of Murdoch, and she would honestly try to fulfill her duties as his wife. But she was also wild Lauren MacRae, whose soul burned for adventure and independence.

Eventually, one of these people would have to suffocate so that the other might survive. She knew, deep down, that the wife of Murdoch was going to win. Because to do otherwise would be to dishonor the memory of her father, and Lauren would never willingly do that.

After her capture and release from Morgan Castle as

a girl, Da had swiftly arranged her betrothal to the son of one of his oldest allies. The Murdochs held a good portion of the lands that ran along the jagged mainland shore parallel to Shot. Over the years a handful of marriages had taken place between the two families, yet none would be as significant as the daughter of a laird wedding another laird.

Lauren understood this. Da and Hannah—everyone—had impressed upon her the importance of the union. How good it would be for the clan. How strong it would make Shot, securing them a solid Scottish army in the face of the English. And Lauren had trusted in her father and all the rest, sliding along the path chosen for her without open protest, although sometimes she had secretly wondered at her own future, what it would be like to leave Shot, to become a part of a new clan. A strange and frightening thought, but she had been careful not to mention it aloud.

"You will abide," Da would tell her, with a sad smile. "You are resourceful and courageous, my Lauren. I know you will learn to love your new home. And your husband."

Lauren had always nodded and agreed, never giving voice to that private fear of her own weakness—that she would not be brave enough or strong enough to survive away from her island. She knew to act happy, to ease the small wrinkles of worry on Da's face that he could not quite hide from her.

So it took her by surprise this morning to hear the weaving women say her name in tones of scandal, to catch the gossip that rose over the steady clicking and thumping of the looms, hands and mouths busy.

Her feet slowed by themselves just outside the door, where she could not be seen. Lauren stopped, confused, and then bent over and pretended to adjust her boot, as if she had found a pebble in it.

". . . the Murdoch will be coming soon, and what will he think, do you suppose?"

"That Lauren's as wild as the wind. So she is."

"Ach. She's got her mother's passion for life, that's all it is."

"But Payton Murdoch won't know about that. Something's got to be done about her, I say."

This prompted several chuckles.

"And what would that be, Michal? Do you propose to tie her down, to stop her from roaming the island, perhaps?"

"It isn't seemly," insisted Michal. "It is not her duty to patrol. She should be here at Keir, minding the castle. She should be preparing for her wedding, I say!"

Lauren knew every voice that spoke. She had grown up with these girls, she had been tutored by their mothers. How sharply painful it was to hear their criticism, even if she did deserve it. She should not eavesdrop; no good would come of it. But she did not move.

"Michal's right," said someone else, Clara, mother of three. "Lauren should stay here. We've got enough to do for this wedding, and it doesn't help that she's always off running with the men. You heard what happened to her last week, how she fell into that cavern and knocked herself silly. That Englishman had to save her, and how does that make us look, I ask you?"

"As though we cannot offer a proper bride to the laird of the Murdochs," finished Michal darkly.

"You fuss over nothing," said a steady voice, and Lauren was slightly cheered to hear the tones of Vanora, one of her mother's old friends. "Let the girl alone. She's always had a free spirit."

"That's well enough for a child," retorted Michal. "But she's a grown woman now, a bride. If she doesn't change, she'll only shame us!"

Vanora clicked her tongue, reproving. "She won't shame us."

"How do you know?" challenged someone.

"Because," said Vanora, and then paused. "Because she is Lauren. That's all."

Lauren straightened up, turned around, and walked back the way she had come, so that she wouldn't have to pass the open door to the weaving room.

It had been six days since the fiasco in the cavern, and she had just started patrolling again only three days ago. Three days of rest, that's what she had told herself she needed. Three days to recover from the near drowning, from the pain in her shoulder. From the sight of that Viking with Arion's sword sticking out of him.

Three days of rest, and she had been about driven mad with it. True, the first day had actually been a necessary reprieve; she had spent almost all of it asleep. But the next two had been just added time. Her shoulder was not that sore. She was no longer tired. Yet she waited to return.

Just to prove that she could. Just to prove that she did not need to see Arion du Morgan right away—in fact, that she didn't need to see him at all.

The hunt for any remaining Vikings had been unsuccessful, and it was widely believed that they had managed to drown themselves in the caves beneath Shot. None had ever come up from the passageways, and there was always a guard there now, just to be certain. A sort of drab quiet seemed to have settled over the people, as the worry from this latest threat slowly paled beneath the steady cadence of daily living in their strong castle.

So Lauren had lingered at Keir. There were chores enough to keep her busy. There were the council meetings she still attended, stubborn about her place in Da's chair, though she was now drawing some looks. There were the wounded to visit, to encourage to recover. There was her cousin Quinn in Da's bed, still asleep—though the healers told her he would swallow broth, a good sign—still unknowing of all the strange and terrible changes that had taken place since that fateful battle in which he had been felled.

And there were the meals and the supplies and the cleaning and the trading and the accounts. Each task performed with perfunctory attention, each moment she spent at them seeming a dull, dragging eternity. But she made herself do it.

Most significant, perhaps, there was the matter of her wedding to attend to.

She knew it was looming close, an unaccountably dark thread on her horizon. She should be happy about it. She should be proud and thrilled to marry the laird of the Murdochs, to join his family and strengthen her own. She should be.

But Arion du Morgan stayed with her still, for all her devotion to duty. He lingered as an unwelcome phantom in her memory, not releasing her, ever. Not even in her dreams.

She saw his eyes in the green woods. She saw his hair on the raven's wing. She heard his subtle laugh in the call of the ocean. His smile was the sunlight, a stray beam to light up the darkness of gloom around her.

At night, when she tossed and turned on her pallet—the same one he had slept in, since she had placed him in her room—at night it was the worst. She could close her eyes, she could pull the covers over her head, but still she felt his kiss, her terrible secret, and the longing in her for more of him.

It was not merely immodest, it was a calamity. She couldn't want more of him! However smoothly they worked together now as allies, the Earl of Morgan would return to being her enemy soon enough. She would walk away from him and into the embrace of another man—a laird she had never met, a fellow countryman who was vital to the success of her clan.

She could not indulge in the wicked pleasures of stolen kisses. She could not risk her future on such frivolity.

Yet she couldn't let go of him. She couldn't release that feeling he had given her, the sparks, the heat, the wild attraction. Arion had kissed her and she had changed forever. But he was not for her, that English knight with his enthralling eyes and soft lips.

Now Lauren knew what true duty was. Now she understood sacrifice.

She waited three days to see him again, steeled up in her tartan, wrapped in her responsibility. And when she went back on patrol, he wasn't even there.

The earl was off to the far side of the island, she was told when she managed a casual inquiry to one of her clansmen. He had left his steward in his place, a man named Fuller, who offered calm suggestions to the patrol, and issued his own orders in a deceptively mild voice. Lauren consulted with the earl's man and rode beside him and never once mentioned Arion. It was Fuller who finally did, only once, saying nonchalantly that the earl sent his regards and hopes for her complete recovery.

She had replied with equal indifference, sending the same back to him.

No new sightings of longships. No reports of stray Vikings wandering around on Shot. She wondered if perhaps they all really had drowned in the caves, as it was said, or gotten so lost there was no hope for them. Either way, it set everyone in the patrols on edge, this absence of the enemy, and tempers were starting to show.

Rhodric was especially problematic. He wore a permanent scowl now, and the looks he threw to the English party were nothing but sullen. Lauren recognized the trouble brewing, and this was why she went to find Hannah after the third day's patrol. Hannah was his aunt and knew the moods of him. More important, Hannah always had something encouraging to say no matter how dire the circumstances, and right now— after overhearing the weavers dissect her behavior to find her wanting—Lauren discovered she could use some encouragement.

Hannah was in the storeroom, braiding herbs into looping circles with two girls to help her. She looked up at Lauren with quiet welcome from across a long table littered with loose stems and leaves. The girls on either side of her offered shy greetings.

Lauren remembered this from her childhood, as well. Tending to the multitude of herbs in the storeroom was considered a punishment for some slight infraction. She had spent many an hour in here over the years, braiding everything from garlic and onions to rosemary and lavender. Lauren briefly wondered what mischief these two girls had found, then felt a pang of envy, quickly pushed aside.

"May I speak with you alone?" she asked Hannah, and the older woman nodded.

"That's enough for now," said Hannah to the girls, and they dropped their braids onto the table with careless curtsies, almost skipping from the room, delighted grins between them.

"I sense they'll be back soon," Lauren said, watching them run off.

"Aye," Hannah said. "They do remind me of you at that age."

Lauren smiled in spite of herself, approaching the table in front of her. She picked up one of the long, leafy stems from the sorted piles, held it to her nose.

"Sage," she guessed.

"Correct."

Hannah continued her work, her fingers slow and steady, twining stem to stem to stem, until she had a thick loop of silvery green. Lauren followed suit, her hands remembering exactly how to handle the soft leaves, the pliant stems. It was soothing, familiar work, and so for a while she just let the rhythm of it take her thoughts, finding almost a peace in the lull. Hannah knew her well enough to let her speak when she was ready.

The storeroom became quiet, the smell of the sage mingled with all the other scents, the fading sunlight giving the air a faint glow near the ceiling, where endless rows of fantastic herbs and spices hung from wall to wall.

"Hannah, do you think I've been . . . too bold?"

"In what way, lass?"

Lauren shrugged down to her hands. "In any way, I suppose. For instance, with the patrols. Do you think I should be staying at Keir, waiting for the Murdoch?"

"Do you?"

"I don't know. I mean, no. I don't think so." One of the fat leaves snapped off in her fingers. Lauren tossed it aside in frustration.

"Are you unhappy on patrol?" Hannah asked.

"No. I think it's going fairly well, actually. Almost everyone gets along now. There is no doubt our strength has doubled since we joined with the du Morgans. Shot is the better for it."

"It was a fine idea," said Hannah serenely.

"Aye," Lauren muttered, remembering the man who had thought up the idea. Another leaf broke off the stem she was plaiting. "It's just that there are some people who seem to think otherwise. They think I should confine myself to Keir. That the joining with the English was folly."

"There will always be dissent in such a large and

complex clan as ours, Lauren. Expect it, learn from it. That's what your father did. But do not let it worry you unduly. Follow your heart, and the fine principles you have in there. Don't allow yourself the chance to live in regret that you did not."

Lauren looked up, alerted by something in Hannah's tone, but her friend's face was as tranquil as ever, revealing nothing beyond gentle concern.

"What if my heart tells me something my principles do not like?" she asked slowly.

Hannah stopped her braiding. "Then you have a problem," she said, somber. "One that must be fully examined. But I know you, my sweet Lauren. You'll do what's right."

Of course. Of course she would. Lauren nodded and kept her gaze fixed on her hands again, on the intertwining pattern of the sage. Her heart felt heavy, slowed with a strange sadness, even though she knew Hannah spoke the truth.

"Rhodric is going to stir a mutiny against the joining," Lauren said, still to the sage.

"I will speak to James again," Hannah replied, her voice perfectly normal. "He understands what is at stake here, even if his son does not. James will have a word with him."

"Thank you."

"You needn't thank me, lass. It's what I *should* do. All of us have a place in the clan. All of us have obligations. I do not mind that this would be one of mine."

Lauren heard the lesson in the words and could only nod again, blinking down at the tender leaves, which for some reason were now blurred and indistinct. After a moment, she wiped the back of her hand across her eyes, as if to rid herself of perspiration, then went to work on the sage once more.

--------------⟨ᴏᴍᴍᴏ⟩--------------

A WEEK, LAUREN FOUND, COULD be a remarkably short amount of time.

She had made a genuine attempt to listen to Hannah's counsel. She had cut back on patrolling, riding out only on those that didn't stray too far from Keir. The fact that the earl had not returned from the other side of Shot had nothing to do with her sudden decline of interest in long patrols, Lauren told herself.

Their fortnight of truce was ebbing ever faster, each new day one day less that her clan would accept any sort of peace with the du Morgans. Lauren knew it, and she knew how precious the remaining time was. Yet it seemed the Earl of Morgan cared little enough for their agreement—he did not even trouble himself to join the men he had assigned to work with the Scots. So why should she be nervous that their time was almost over? She wasn't! Let the fortnight die away. If he didn't care, neither did she.

The men were finding nothing, after all. No reports of any strange happenings, and many said that the Vikings would not be back at all.

Maybe they were right. Maybe everyone was right but Lauren, who felt a strange pressure constantly at her back and couldn't let go of the idea that the absence of the Northmen was a battle strategy, designed to lure Shot to complacency. Clearly, however, she was the only one who thought so. Many of the clan were not attempting to hide the fact that they would be relieved when their bargain with the du Morgans ended, and they could resume their open distrust of this enemy.

Lauren remained at Keir, trying to think of her future, trying to remember who she had been before Arion du Morgan had torn back into her life.

And time ticked past, and the days slipped away, and it seemed she truly might never see him again. So be it.

She knew what Da would have expected her to do.

He had arranged a marriage for her, set the date, negotiated the dowry, and kissed her cheeks to congratulate her on it. He had explained to her countless times why it was so important for her to wed the laird of the Murdochs. Even though Da was gone now, Lauren intended to honor his wishes.

The women of Keir were delighted that she began to consider the wedding again. They welcomed her back with approving nods and sharp smiles, and Lauren let them envelop her in the frenzy of their plans for her impending union with Payton Murdoch. Their enthusiasm was enough to carry her, she thought, and didn't try to understand why she was so indifferent to it all.

"Turn the other way, lass," instructed the seamstress, and Lauren moved without thought, arms raised, staring blankly at the wall before her.

"Oh, it fits like a dream!" exclaimed someone, and Lauren heard several women agree.

Sunlight etched through the glass of her window and

lit her chamber with golden brilliance. She stood in the center of the floor, arms still high, as the seamstress hummed and clucked and tucked a few more pins into the loose gown that draped her.

"Lovely," said Vanora, watching with the others.

"Aye," said the seamstress. "You're lucky, lass, that Murdoch's mother was such a close size to you. Had she been smaller, it would be an awkward fit."

"But it suits you well," interjected Hannah, walking around her, and Lauren left off her contemplation of the wall to meet her friend's eyes. Hannah smiled at her, then walked over and fingered the cloth of one of the sleeves, soft wool the color of sand.

"You'll make a fair bride," Hannah said.

"And with the jewels the Murdoch sent, what a sight you'll be," sighed Clara.

Lauren let out little laugh, then smothered it. Only Hannah noticed; she gave her a glance that said she understood what Lauren was feeling.

Two months ago Payton Murdoch had sent a trunk across the sea for her. It had been delivered right before the invaders first came, with great fanfare and protocol from the captain of Murdoch's personal guard. That man had huffed at Lauren and eyed her up and down while she had stood in front of him and everyone and endured it. The captain had announced that the laird of the Murdochs sent his greetings and well wishes to his future bride, and honored her with this chest of goods to prepare for their wedding.

In the chest had been four things.

His mother's wedding gown, carefully folded into many layers.

The Murdoch tartan that would go over it, taking the place of her own after the ceremony.

A brooch of polished silver, carved into the shape of a rowan twig, the badge of his clan.

A ring, heavy and thick, also silver, set with three large rubies that gleamed like frozen blood in the light.

Lauren had worn the ring only when she had to, and at least had had the excuse that she could not work properly when having to care for such a precious item. Everyone had seemed to accept that, and she had put it away with a sigh of relief.

She could not say the same about the brooch, however, and so over dinner with the captain, Da had ceremoniously removed the elegant golden brooch of her own clan to pin this new one on her. The color of it remained a distraction to her for weeks afterward. Even now she could find herself startled by the glint of silver at her chest, instead of the gold that had been there all her life before.

The wedding dress and tartan, obviously, had not been a concern until recently.

The marriage was drawing near. Assuming, of course, that Murdoch intended to show up and claim her still, Lauren thought sourly. He could send an army of men from the mainland to guard a bit of jewelry and cloth, but her clan's pleas for aid against butchery remained unanswered even a month and a half later.

Spirits remained high that he would still come, however, and privately Lauren agreed with them, though not for the same reason as they. She figured that Payton Murdoch would want his ring and brooch back, if nothing else.

So she stood there in her chamber with a strange mixture of dejection and laughter coursing through her, and kept a faint smile firmly in place as the women of her clan admired her and the gown and the vision of their splendid wedding to come.

Lauren tried not to think of the wedding. Da would not be there for it, so no matter how splendid it might be, there would always be something dark about it for her.

She tried to imagine what he would say to her now, if he could see her in her bridal gown. Would he smile at her? Would he hug her close, and tell her how proud he was of her?

She had to hope so. She had to believe that he would. If only he were here . . .

"You're a bit taller and thinner than Murdoch's mother," pronounced the seamstress, stepping back to admire her work. "But it will do, I think."

"Your Da would be so pleased," said Vanora softly.

Lauren turned her smile down to the ground, holding on to it with gritty determination.

Eventually the women collected their needles and pins and sewing baskets and left her alone, whisking away even the dress, to be labored over with careful devotion until it was perfect.

Murdoch's ring was a heavy weight on her hand, and she pulled it off her finger as soon as they were gone, taking it over to the cushioned box that held her own few pieces of jewelry. She placed it carefully beside her old brooch, the golden one that held the intricate, twisting lines of her own clan's badge, then shut the lid. The silver twig of rowan was waiting for her on her pallet, and she changed into her regular clothes and then pinned it back in place, trying to find an angle for it that pleased her. At last she gave up, exasperated. Nothing about it looked right on her, and perhaps it never would.

Supper would not be served for a few more hours, but because she was restless and slightly apprehensive of her own thoughts, Lauren left her room and began to wander down the hallways of Keir, thinking vaguely of going to the buttery and helping with the food.

But she walked by a door that had not been closed carefully enough, and what she heard there made her pause, then suck in her breath.

". . . won't tolerate the du Morgans much longer, by God. When this is over, I say if they step foot on our half of the isle, we show *them* what we would have done to those Northmen!"

Lauren pushed the door open slowly to reveal Rhodric, his back to her, James and Ranulf standing in front. The older men were listening, arms crossed, as Rhodric continued.

"We've got only three days left of this *agreement*." He made the word a sneer. "But it's three days too many. I'm not the only man who wants to see the backs of those English."

"No doubt," said James, his tone heavy. "But it is still an agreement, son. You will heed it until the fortnight is done."

"I'm telling you, we don't need them!" Rhodric slammed his fist into the flat of his palm. "This alliance never should have existed in the first place!"

"Oh, truly?" said Lauren, not moving from the doorway.

All three men turned to see her for the first time, and their expressions ranged from embarrassment in the elders to bluster in the younger man.

"This talk does not concern you, woman," said Rhodric, with clear derision.

James immediately stepped over to him, grabbing his tunic and pulling him close, face to face. "Never address her like that again, do you understand me?"

His son glowered for a moment, but then nodded, glaring at the fire in the hearth. "Aye," he muttered. James released him, pushing him away with a slight shove.

"It was merely idle conversation, Lauren," Ranulf said into the silence. "Pay it no mind."

Lauren stepped into the room. "Rhodric is right about something. The alliance will be ending soon, by our own terms. It's time to think about what might happen afterwards."

Rhodric still would not look at her, but she had the attention of the two other men.

"I think we should renew the agreement," she said calmly.

"God's blood!" Rhodric exploded. "Are you mad?"

James grimaced, and Ranulf was already shaking his head.

"Listen to me," Lauren said. "Everything about this joining has worked so far, barring"—she looked at Rhodric—"minor discontent. You cannot deny that we have been safer and more informed since the du Morgans began to work with us. We are a stronger force now. We are the better for it!"

"Well, lass," began Ranulf.

"There are no Vikings, Lauren, none at all!" Rhodric

threw his hands into the air. "You would tie us to our enemy just to fend off the clouds! There is no more threat!"

"Of course there is!" She crossed to him, more than ready to argue. "Just because we succeeded in shaking them off up until now doesn't mean they won't be back!"

"You're suspicious of the wrong people! It's the English you should be worried about, not the Vikings!"

"And how is that?" she demanded.

"The moment this alliance ends, they'll be at us, and don't think they won't," replied Rhodric, looking away from her to his father and Ranulf. "They've been trying to quiet our misgivings the whole time. When the moment is right, they'll attack us! It's what they've been after all along!"

For a moment Lauren just stared at him, speechless. Then she said, "I think *you're* the mad one, Rhodric MacRae. Only a madman would consider such a witless plan!"

"*I'm* not the one who ran to the leader of our enemy, Lauren," Rhodric spat. "I'm not the one who listened to his false words and let him court me away from my own clan! I'm not the one who pretends to be loyal to the family while letting the Earl of Morgan woo me with lies! I'm not the one who finds any reason to see him, to stay near him! I've watched you with him, I've seen you—"

"Enough!" bellowed James. "I've heard enough of this!"

Rhodric fell silent and Lauren stood there, mute,

faint, feeling the blood drain from her face, feeling the betraying, leaden knot of guilt expand in her stomach.

Oh God, he knew.

Rhodric *knew* about her feelings for Arion. Somehow, he knew!

She managed to look at his face and found him staring back at her, flushed, breathing hard, anger and something more in his eyes, wounded pride.

"It's not true," she breathed, cold with fright.

"Of course it's not, lass." Ranulf placed a heavy arm around her shoulder. "The lad was mistaken. Weren't you, Rhodric?"

Rhodric didn't reply. He kept staring at Lauren, finding that guilt in her, seeing it, she was certain, each damning word of his echoing through her, adding to it.

"*Weren't* you, son?" James spoke the words with pointed emphasis.

At last Rhodric nodded his head, just once, and the other men seized on it with sighs of relief.

"Hotheaded, just like his father when he was a lad," said Ranulf with a forced smile.

"It's a fact," agreed James, another false smile. "Don't let it worry you, Lauren."

Ranulf was urging her to the door. She walked with him in wooden steps, trying to find her breath again. "And never mind about the end of the agreement, lass. We know how you feel about it. I cannot help but agree with you that it seems to have worked out well enough. When the fortnight ends, the council will consider your idea to renew it."

"Aye, we'll consider it," added James from behind her,

but Lauren already heard the verdict in his voice. Rhodric had gotten to him first.

---

*T*HE VILLAGE WAS REMOTE, ONE of the farthest from Keir on all of Shot, nestled up against the base of a mountain, great fields spreading all around, sheep in clusters in the meadows. The name of the village was Dunmar, and the MacRaes who lived there had the all-important job of tending to the largest herds of sheep on the island.

It took almost a full day to get there from Keir, a hard ride with twisting trails and steep edges near the hills—one more precious day, leaving only two to the alliance.

Lauren cherished every moment of it, every second of freedom and beauty on her mount, on her way to investigate reports of missing sheep from the herds.

It was more than what they would occasionally lose to a wild boar, or a bog, or even a cliff, the messenger had said. It was a slow, steady loss, one sheep a day—no carcasses—and Lauren knew what that meant.

"Vikings," she had said to the men at the council meeting that morning.

"Or du Morgans," Rhodric had thrown in from the other side of the room, scowling.

Lauren had not bothered to look at him again. She couldn't risk letting him see the guilt in her once more—or the icy fear he gave her—so she had pretended to ignore him. And fortunately, no one

English, he would have to fight her every step of the way.

For the first time, Lauren found herself devoutly glad that the Earl of Morgan was so far away.

It was a group of about thirty who made their way up the final path to Dunmar, past golden meadows and autumn trees, all eyes turned up to take in the sight of the misted mountain ahead of them.

Dunmar had a long, rudimentary wooden fence encircling the majority of the structures in the village; tall, pointed spikes that were buried deep in the earth. Several large, penned areas inside of it were for the sheep, to guard at night. The fence was relatively new, put in only a few years ago to spite the du Morgans, and Lauren wondered if the earl's steward knew of this.

She rather hoped not. She was coming to like this Fuller, his quiet demeanor, his polite ways that guided a sharp mind. When he offered ideas she invariably found them sound, and told him so. Though he spoke for the earl, Lauren found that she felt none of the nervous discord with Fuller that Arion brought out in her. A strange thing, to find something like easy goodwill in a du Morgan.

It would be a step backward for them both to insult him now with the obvious gesture of the spiked fence. But if Fuller knew of it, he said nothing, only allowed Lauren to lead the party to the gate, which opened for them as soon as they were seen.

People came forward and greeted them, eyeing the strangers warily, though of course they had been told of the agreement. Lauren dismounted and found her-

else took him very seriously, and the comment ha
passed.

It would not be the du Morgans stealing these shee
In the past, yes, they had certainly plagued the vi
lage, knowing Dunmar's defenses were not as strong
Keir's. And the MacRaes always managed to retaliate
some way or another. Plenty of sheep had crossed ar
recrossed the border between them over the years.

This time, however, Lauren was certain it was the i
vaders, most likely the ones that had been left by t
longboat, now scattered about on Shot. Apparently th
had not drowned, after all. Not all of them. It wa:
problem that demanded immediate action, and Laur
found herself ready for it.

Anything to escape Keir now, and the massive b
den of all the things that pressured her to stay: l
wedding, the women, even that thick ruby ring in l
chamber.

So Lauren had ridden out right away with a pa:
of her men and a few of the English, since Fuller l
insisted that they come as well. Any threat to Shot w
threat to both families, he reminded her, and Lau
had been forced to agree. But both had left behind
majority of their factions to keep up the regular patr
which they could ill afford to underman.

Rhodric was one of the party going to Dunmar. I
ren could not refuse him, not without a scene. l
had shrugged when he insisted upon going, as if l
didn't care one way or another. If he meant to sp)
her, there was nothing she could do about it. But l
planned to disrupt what was left of the bargain witl

self wrapped in a solid embrace—her cousin Kenna, daughter of her mother's sister, who had wed one of the shepherds of Dunmar and lived in this outpost.

"I'm so happy to see you!"

Lauren laughed and leaned back, examining the other woman's bulging stomach.

"You haven't changed a bit, I see! What's this, number five?"

"Six," said Kenna proudly. "A girl this time, I'm sure of it."

"Well, five boys are likely enough." Lauren linked arms with her cousin and then looked around, searching until she found the face she sought.

"Any of the herd gone missing today, Cormic?"

"Naught," replied the old man, acknowledged leader of the village. "At least, not yet."

It was Cormic who had sent the rider to Keir to warn of the strange loss of sheep. He came forward to her now in slow, dignified steps, the setting sun turning the white of his hair to rosy gold, an illusion of youth. When he was close enough he became the familiar elder she had known all her life, a seamed face with deep brown eyes, the edge of a smile always just tucked away, it seemed. Only right now he was not smiling.

Lauren released Kenna and greeted him properly, offering a small curtsy, even though she wore a tunic, and it most likely looked ridiculous. Cormic just nodded, then took in all the others behind her.

"A fair number," he commented, and Lauren couldn't tell if this was approval or not.

"If it is the Vikings stealing the sheep, there can't be

that many of them. We've had only one boat sighted recently, and we think there could be only a few men that might have made it to the shore."

"I hope so, lass," said Cormic, and turned away from her, walking back up to the village.

Kenna noticed Lauren's frown. "He's worried," she whispered, coming close. "He won't say it, but he's afraid we'll lose people next. And he doesn't like the English at all, you know."

"How astonishing," Lauren said wryly. She glanced over her shoulder and found Fuller standing close by. "Bring your men and mounts up to the village. We'll be spending the night here, since it's so close to dark now. I'm going to leave a group of men outside the gate, keeping watch. You may do the same, if you like."

Fuller nodded.

"Come." Kenna tugged on Lauren's arm. "Time to sup. Come see my family. And I want to hear all about the wedding. I can't wait for it!"

Lauren was taking the first few steps up the grassy slope to the center of the village when she heard the commotion behind her, raised voices, the thunder of hooves. She pulled away from her cousin and went running back down to the gate, joining the crowd gathered there, the hairs on the back of her neck raising.

"What is it?" she asked, because she couldn't see over the heads of her kinsmen. No one answered her, but the feeling in the air around her was ominous. She ducked and elbowed her way to the front of them, nudging her way forward until she could see for herself the reason for the stiffness in the men around her, the antagonism in their stances.

A mass of horsemen were racing across one of the meadows, up to the wooden wall, still too far away to be readily identified—but it didn't matter. Lauren knew who was leading that pack, and so did everyone else around her.

The Earl of Morgan rode his midnight destrier with almost unnatural grace, his hair loose and flying in the wind, the last of the sunlight blanketing him and his group in such a blood red that they might have been riders from the underworld, come for a final, murderous battle with the mortals of Shot.

As he came closer she could see a strange wad of cloth secured to the back of his saddle, bouncing with the gait of the stallion. But no—it wasn't cloth at all.

It was a lamb. A dead lamb, limp and broken, tied behind the earl.

Lauren was not the only one alarmed by the sight. All around her the men were drawing their broadswords, edging toward the advancing horsemen, narrowing their eyes.

"The devil family," she heard someone say, and the phrase was taken up immediately.

"Lucifer's own!"

"Damned English!"

"Thieves!"

"Demons!"

"No," she said loudly, breaking away from the group, turning to face them. No one even glanced at her; all eyes were fixed on the riders.

"They are not the devil's own," Lauren called out, and it was only then that she noticed Fuller and his men on the fringes of the crowd, the look of danger clenched around each of them. They had their swords out too, but they were facing her clansmen, already grouped into fighting formation.

"They are our allies now!" Lauren said urgently. "You will not harm them! You will not threaten them! They are here to aid us!"

"They have the sheep!" exclaimed someone. "They have the stolen sheep!"

"It was them all along!"

"Aye!"

"No!" she cried again. "It *wasn't* them! I know there's a good reason for this! Everyone, keep your head!"

By now she could hear the horses slowing, coming up behind her, heavy breath and snorting, skittish hooves. But she did not turn around, because she could not afford to lose this test. Everything depended upon it.

"What's this, Lauren MacRae?" inquired a smooth voice at her back, understated menace in every inflection.

Lauren still did not turn, offering a hard gaze to Cormic, who stood silent. "We've been discussing the loss of the sheep, du Morgan. I see you've found something from the Vikings."

Let him understand her, she prayed. Let him follow her lead, and turn the focus of danger away from him, to the Northmen instead.

She heard the creaking of leather, perhaps his saddle. Something soft and heavy landed close behind her, stirring the dirt. With just a slight turn of her head she saw one sad, thin leg of the lamb, awkward against the earth.

"It was about half an hour distant from here," said du Morgan. "I think you'll find the cuts were clean, made with a very sharp knife."

"An *English* knife," muttered one of the Scots.

"Now, how would a Northman do that?" inquired the earl, with silky danger. "I assure you, we English keep our blades close to us at all times. *We* have sense enough to guard against thieves."

Lauren turned around to see him, spoke before anyone else could. "So you found their camp?"

He was still edged in red, high above her on his steed, watching her.

"No," replied the earl, after a moment. "Not that. Only the loss of this lamb, abandoned near the edge of a woods."

"Where?" she asked.

"If we might dismount," Arion suggested, aloof, "and enter your fine village, perhaps we could discuss it, as promised allies would."

He met her look with cool inquiry, the threat of his men behind him. Lauren turned around again, facing her kin, the angry faces, the tight looks of distrust.

"We welcome you to Dunmar, du Morgan," she said clearly. She found Cormic again amid the faces and focused on him, waiting for him to add his approval. But still the old man said nothing, only looked from her to the mounted man behind her, his expression shadowed.

"Oh, is this a welcome?" asked the earl now, in the same tone. "How unusual. In my country, such a greeting does not include the threat of swords."

Damn the man. He was obviously no help to her.

Lauren spoke again, this time straight to the elder in front of her. "You are most welcome here, Earl of Morgan, in the name of my father, Hebron MacRae, and of my cousin Quinn MacRae. Is it not so, Cormic?"

Cormic's lips grew thin and sour, as if he had tasted something unpleasant. For a long moment he did not speak, and Lauren felt moisture bead up on her forehead despite the coolness of the night. She gave up demanding and instead implored him with her eyes. He could not be so shortsighted as to start a war now. He *must* not. . . .

"Aye," Cormic finally conceded, almost a snarl. "You're welcome here, Earl of Morgan, you and your men."

He turned around and walked away before anything more could be said, leaving the Scots around her to slowly loosen their tension, exchanging looks. They began to put away their swords. Lauren saw Fuller's group do the same. Only then did she turn again to Arion.

He did not dismount but stared down at her, now a man of twilight shadows, the red light faded to dusk.

It would not surprise her to find the prince of darkness so handsome, she thought suddenly, remote. Surely he must be so, to be the lord of temptation, yet Lauren imagined that even the devil would find it hard to compete with this earl, with his long black hair and his hard green eyes, such strong features, masculine radiance embodied in every line.

"And how are you, MacRae?" he asked now, a softer voice, just for her.

"Well enough," she managed to reply.

He came off his mount with fluid ease, and one by

one his men did the same. Fuller was beside them now, bowing. Lauren looked at him, startled, having almost forgotten the conflict that had been barely averted.

Arion could do that to her, just so easily. He could make her forget the whole of the world, every other single thing in her life, with just one entrancing glance from his ocean eyes.

Splendid. Just what she needed, she thought acridly.

Lauren drew back slightly, assessing the scene around her to ensure there would be no immediate trouble, allowing the earl and his steward to converse in private.

A few of the Scots had come over and hefted the lamb, carrying it back into the heart of the village, talking in low voices. The rest of her people were moving off in slow gatherings, plenty of looks being thrown behind them at the new arrivals, plenty of words passing back and forth about it all. Lauren was grateful she could not hear them.

Only Rhodric stood still amid the movement, watching her, and she stared back at him coldly until he turned away, joining his colleagues.

Kenna was suddenly there, pale and brave with her husband behind her, offering Lauren her arm again. Lauren took it, then addressed Arion.

"There will be a supper at the common house at the top of this hill." She looked to her cousin for confirmation, and got a quick nod. "The stable is over there, to the right. Come up for the meal when you are ready. We can discuss your discovery after we eat."

Arion gave a half-bow of acknowledgment, almost

too grand for the moment, which Lauren ignored. She
began the walk back up the path with Kenna.

"I was going to cook for you tonight in my own
home," Kenna murmured.

"I think it might be better if I joined everyone in the
common," Lauren murmured back.

Kenna gave a slight smile to the ground. "Well, I think
the view will be nicer there, anyway."

𝒯HE MEAL WAS NOT AS uneasy as it might have
been. Many of the Scots had already taken their evening supper, but more than a few lingered, just to keep
an eye on the newcomers, drinking and talking in pockets of conversation. In any other situation it might have
been difficult to tell that there was anything amiss, other
than the fact that the room was divided neatly down
the middle, Scots on one side, English on the other.
Rhodric, Lauren took pains to notice, was pointedly
absent.

She helped to serve the food herself, guessing correctly that none of the women would be keen on approaching the strangers without some encouragement.
So she took the first bowl of mutton stew and walked it
over to the earl, who sat at a packed table, watching her.
Lauren placed it in front of him, then turned away to
find Kenna at her side, two more bowls in hand. After
that, others began to join them, offering the meal mostly
in silence, getting silence in return.

It was the children who kept the situation in hand,

Lauren thought privately, and not without some amusement. Kenna's boys, old enough to be mischievous, young enough to be openly curious about the strangers among them. They led the other children in the room with their happy outbursts, excitement and interest bubbling up around them.

Lauren ended up sitting with a group of them, getting lost in their questions, laughing with them, answering as best she could without becoming too involved in her explanations: What was it like to live at Keir? Was the castle really as high as the clouds? Could she talk to the angels? Could she count the seals on the beaches there as they did here? And who were these English? Why did they look so strange? Why did they glare so?

"They're just hungry," Lauren said. "Like you and me. Now, who took my bread, I'd like to know?"

And the meal passed slowly with moments like these, until the time when Lauren looked up and around and was satisfied that the strain cloaking everyone was finally beginning to dissolve, even though the partition of the groups was still quite precise. Someone tugged on her sleeve and she began to glance down at her young inquisitor, another question to be addressed, but as she did so her gaze skimmed across the earl's, sitting stoic across the room. In one timeless moment their eyes connected.

He was not eating. He did not drink, or talk, or look away from her. He seemed caught up in a brooding reverie—nothing very pleasant from the expression on his face—unblinking, staring at her. The smoky, golden light in the room did not reveal him very well to her, but Lauren did not need more illumination. Just the connection they made in that heartbeat of a moment was enough to suspend her, to make her lose the time and place around her. All the other people faded away to a blur of noise and light, nothing significant. He alone stayed sharp in her vision, not releasing her from his look, still and strong and unwavering.

She felt her breath grow longer, slower. She felt her stomach tighten, her skin seemed to tingle.

She felt the hot desire pass from him to her as if there were no space between them, as if they were standing alone, close together, pressed flesh to flesh. The longing for his physical touch was unrelieved, became a sharp ache throughout her whole body. The blood began to pound through her, making Lauren go warm and then cold, then warm again—too warm.

He smiled. Subtle, slight, so barely there that she might not have seen it at all. But she felt its power, what it did to her, so knowing and sure. It was not just his recognition of what she was feeling, Lauren knew that. His smile suggested something more, something much more perilous to her: mutual acknowledgment of their link. That she could do the same to him, make him feel these things. That he burned for her, as well.

A boy pulled hard on her arm and the moment broke apart into pieces, falling and then gone. Lauren looked down, flushed and dazed, trying to remember where she was and what she had been doing.

Childish voices were scolding her for being so absent-minded, more questions peppered the air around her. Lauren swallowed and smiled and made some comment, she didn't even know what, but it seemed to content them for the moment. The children turned away long enough for her to dare to look up again, searching.

But Arion was no longer watching her. He was gazing down at his food, brooding once more.

Chapter Eight

———— ⚊⚊⚊ ————

$\mathcal{L}$AUREN WAS TO SPEND THE night in a pallet on the floor of Kenna's cottage, surrounded by sleeping children who breathed with heavy innocence into the night; soft, baby snores coming from at least two of them.

After the meal, she had met with the earl and a mix of their men, a large group of them discussing the finding of the lamb. She had stayed on one side of the circle and Arion on the other. There were no more long looks between them. Indeed, there were no looks at all. She kept her focus grimly on the men around him. It was an exchange of clipped words, sparse information:

The lamb had been found to the west of Dunmar, far from any flock. There had been a faint path leading back into the woods there—most likely the earl and his men had startled the Northmen, causing them to flee without their kill. The final agreement among them all was that it would be best to send at least one group out to scout the area and pursue that wooded path.

She had divided up her men for the series of patrols that would take place later that night, sentries and riders out to watch for any signs of Northmen closer to the village. It was decided that she would join the third patrol herself, the one that wouldn't leave until after dawn. Secretly, Lauren was glad about the timing. A good night's rest sounded welcome.

Kenna and her husband had offered her their own pallet, sequestered off with a blanket in a nook of the room, but Lauren had refused, not wanting to put her cousin out of her own bed. It was enough that they shared their home, Lauren had said, pointing out that everyone else had to sleep in the common, so surely she was already princess enough here in their fine cottage.

They had laughed, as she had meant them to, and retired with quiet good-nights, bidding their sons to *try* not to kick their guest while they slept. The boys promised to do their best.

Lauren had thought herself spent from the tiring day but found herself awake long after her small companions had drifted off. The darkness was not quite complete. A faint aura of moonlight crept past the shuttered window above her, and although it was dim at best, Lauren found it yet another reason why sleep eluded her. The room was too bright. The pallet too hard. Her body too sore.

One of the boys kicked her.

She sat up carefully, pushing back the blanket, getting up without disturbing the rhythm of the children's slumber. Since she was still fully dressed, Lauren had no worries about groping in the strange surroundings for proper clothing. All she needed was her cloak to fight the night air, and she found that on a peg by the door. She slung it over her shoulders, then slipped quietly out of the cottage.

Out here the moonlight was much more pronounced,

making it relatively easy for her to see the details of the landscape—the other buildings, dark and quiet; the pens filled with drowsy sheep, heads lowered, bundles of white pressed together on the ground; the line of the new wooden fence, broken only by the tower for the sentry near the gate, and another at the opposite end of the village. Lauren began to walk over to the one by the gate.

"Fine night," said a deep voice behind her.

She turned with a hand over her heart, wide-eyed. Arion had come up without a sound. Lauren saw his eyes drift down to note her nervous gesture, but instead of remarking on it, he merely lifted his own hand, offering her a mug of something.

"Fine whiskey," he added, when she did nothing. "Your people have a gift for it."

"Why aren't you sleeping?" she heard herself ask.

"Why aren't you?" he countered, still offering the drink.

Since she didn't want to answer that, she took the mug, lifting it to her lips, inhaling the scent of the strong liquor, its bite curling over her tongue. She wasn't used to it and so had only a sip before handing it back to him.

Arion took it from her solemnly, not looking away. It was the whiskey that made her head feel suddenly strange, Lauren told herself. Nothing more.

But the moonlight fell with silver flattery across his features, almost teasing her with his good looks. His eyes were black and deep out here under the night sky. He lifted a hand again, the one without the mug, and moved it toward her face.

Lauren took a rapid step away, out of his reach, and saw his lips twist up into something that was not a smile.

"How is your head?" he asked, masked and pleasant.

"I beg your pardon?"

"You hit it rather hard, as I recall. You were bleeding quite a bit."

"Oh." She felt stupid and flushed again. She should not have had the whiskey. "It's fine."

"May I look?"

Lauren tucked her hands behind her back, clenching her fingers together where he could not see. "Why?"

The twist in his lips tightened, then relaxed away to nothing. "Still don't trust me, MacRae?"

"All right then," she said crossly. "Go ahead, if you insist on it."

He closed the space between them, coming very near, and she fought the urge to shut her eyes, to hide from him, as if that could help her now. His hand came up once more and grazed her skin lightly—*sparks, pain, burning heat*—pushing back the hair from her forehead, every inch of him now attentive and calmly serious.

She stared at the hollow at the base of his throat, trying not to move at all, trying not even to breathe. She found his pulse and couldn't look away, following the strong steadiness of his heartbeat until she felt it reverberating through her, her soul echoing it, a tandem vibration that sank in down to her bones.

"You're right," Arion said, very quiet, his voice sounding strained. "It looks much . . . better."

She couldn't help it; she gazed up at him as he was

looking down, her head tilted, his hand still touching her. He was so near that she did close her eyes now, surrendering to it, feeling the passion and not even caring.

They were at Dunmar. They were standing out in the open. Anyone could see them. *The sentries, Cormic, Rhodric . . .* she thought vaguely, and then even that drifted away.

None of it mattered. Only he did. Only Arion.

His fingers were threading through her hair. His breath was warm and close, tinged with the spice of her family's whiskey. It brushed her lips, tantalizing—and then was gone.

Lauren opened her eyes. He had moved away from her, harshness on his face now, then he turned to the side and stared out fiercely into the shadows.

She felt herself grow cold with the night, aware all at once of her vulnerability in this moment, the wind carrying the coming winter, the unforgiving light and dark of the moonlight.

Sweet Mary, what had she been thinking? She had nearly let him do the thing that could destroy them both. If anyone had passed by, if *anyone* had seen . . .

The night appeared empty, however, when she glanced around, fighting the hard pounding of her heart and a rising sickness in her throat. When she looked back at him he had not changed, still so handsome, and so completely forbidden.

Shame came and added to the cold and fear, shame at her own weakness for this man, shame at her unbidden yearning for him.

She was Lauren MacRae. She had a destiny to fulfill,

a future to secure for her whole clan. And it was absolutely not with the Earl of Morgan.

So then with the shame came despair, that she had ended up in this unenviable position, her whole being wanting something that would harm so many others dear to her. It was a grievous burden, settling over her with weighted sorrow, making her tired and chilled and angry. It wasn't fair. But she had always known that fairness was not a frequent part of life.

She heard him let out his breath in a kind of prolonged sigh, hard and frustrated. At last he looked back at her, and she held up her head to meet that look, though a good part of her wanted nothing more than to duck and turn away.

"What does it mean, your pin?" he asked.

His words made no sense to her at first, and she found herself puzzling over them as if he had spoken in some secret language, unfamiliar sounds strung together at random.

"Your pin," Arion said again, gesturing impatiently at the silver twig near her shoulder, only just revealed by the fall of her cape. "Your brooch. It's different from all the others in your clan. What does it mean?"

"Oh." She glanced down at it, the odd, long shape of it on her, and felt the heaviness of it suddenly pressing down on her chest. "It's . . . it's the badge of the Murdochs. It was a gift, from their laird."

He gave her a strange smile, tense and sharp. "So you wear his mark."

"It is my honor to do so."

"Clever," he said, and the anger she had noticed

before seemed to be growing, turning to scorn. "He ensures that you remember your obligation to him every day, doesn't he?"

"It is apt," Lauren said, reacting to his tone. "I wouldn't expect you to understand."

"Why? Because I am a du Morgan? You called me an English barbarian, yet I would never force a woman to wear my emblem."

"I am not forced to wear it!" Lauren exclaimed, goaded. "I choose to!"

"It doesn't suit you," he said coldly. He walked over to her and flicked one lean finger at it, his nail clicking against the metal. "Your own family badge is better."

Without warning the pin sprang loose from its hold on her tartan, releasing the tight folds of material it had contained. Lauren gave a small cry and tried to hold it in place, clutching at the cloth. A sharp jab pricked her hand; the needle-sharp point of the pin had stabbed her in her haste.

She pulled her hand away and let the tartan fall to her waist, finding the prick of the pin on the edge of her palm, a tiny bead of blood coming up. She put it to her mouth and sucked on it, glaring up at the earl.

The brooch of rowan clung to the fallen tartan for a moment, then fell between them into the dirt.

Arion had not moved at all since touching the brooch, and now remained very close, staring down at her, his expression frozen between that scorn of before and something very familiar to her—heat and want, bright desire.

Lauren moved her hand away from her mouth.

She watched him come out of his reverie with just

a downward glance, away from her. He bent to the ground and picked up the fallen twig of silver, handing it to her carefully.

"It's not strong enough for you, Lauren MacRae," he said, and she understood his double meaning.

I know, came the thought, unbidden, but instead she replied: "It would be, if left alone."

"A pity you'll never find something better." Arion glanced around them now, as if bored.

All her previous sadness evaporated in the face of this, his unyielding arrogance. What had she been thinking, to find herself pining for this man? He was nothing but a coldhearted Englishman, one who found pleasure in harassing her however he could. She must be touched, to think that she could ever long for someone so purely designed to disdain her.

He seemed to have nothing more to say, only took slow drinks from his mug of whiskey while she attempted to fix her tartan and the brooch, an air of tight control around his eyes and mouth. He could have been made of ice and snow, Lauren thought. Just his words could touch off an endless winter in her heart.

"What were you doing so near Dunmar?" she asked into the silence, seeking refuge in her own anger now, the one thing that held off some of the cold. "You took a foolish risk, riding up like that, unannounced."

Arion shrugged, still not looking at her. "My group has been out here for days, Lauren, while you stayed hiding in your castle. Fuller sent word you were headed this way, and why."

"I wasn't hiding!"

He slanted her a sardonic look.

"Oh, of course. While you were *recovering* at Keir."

Her tartan was right again, the silver brooch in place as securely as she could make it. Lauren tucked her hands under her cape now, hugging warmth to her. "Why were you over here on this side of the island, anyway?"

"I suspected there were Vikings out here, at least ten, perhaps more. We've been trying to track them."

"What?"

Now her fury was pure and loud, and her voice attracted the attention of the sentry above them, who turned around and called out to them. Lauren waved him off wordlessly, staring at the earl. He appeared perfectly genial now, a mercurial shift in his mood, obviously pleased that he could stir her so easily.

"You knew a week ago there were Vikings here," she said, disbelieving, "and you said nothing about it to us?"

"Well, at the time it was only a guess," he said. "There was no point in involving you without some measure of proof."

"Proof! We've had sheep disappearing for days!"

"And there you have it," finished the earl. "So I came."

She stared at him, fuming. One of the sheep called out from the pen. Another answered it, a mournful bleating.

"First round of the night patrol is due back soon," said Arion casually. "I was going to meet them. Will you come along?"

Lauren gave a short nod of assent and strode off to the gate. After a moment she heard his footsteps behind her, and then beside her, but she did not look over to confirm his presence. She felt him there as sure as anything, an undeniable sensation, still sparks, still heat. Yet now it heightened the anger in her all the more.

He was far worse than she had first thought, beyond even their personal enmity. Perhaps Rhodric had seen the truth about him after all.

Days—he had been out here for *days,* knowing of the possible danger to her clan, saying nothing! It was intolerable. The Earl of Morgan had taken their agreement and managed to interpret it conveniently to his needs. He had moved behind her back. He had acted on his own without giving her or her people the benefit of his suspicions. He would make this alliance work only as long as it suited him to do so. She had been an idiot to think that she could trust him.

And the desire for him, still blooming inside her, was nothing but an extension of her idiocy. She must not succumb to it again.

The sentry opened the gate for them just as the patrol was riding up. It was a combination of Mac-Raes and du Morgans, an even number of each, and with one quick scan of their faces Lauren could tell that they had not found the invaders. She didn't know whether to be relieved or not.

They came forward into the compound, horses steaming with sweat, a mass of noise and bleak expressions and tired postures.

"We found the trail by the dead lamb, going off into the mountains," said one of the English soldiers to the earl. "It led us to the place where they must have camped. But the ashes from their fire were cold. They've moved on. We didn't pick up a new trail."

"They're hiding in the hills," said one the Scots. "We'll need daylight to track them properly."

There was a new group of men coming down from

the stables; the second patrol, fresh for the end of the night. Lauren saw Fuller among them, Rhodric, more familiar faces than not. The first patrol was now passing by them, some dismounting, more of them going directly to the stables.

Arion turned to his steward. "Wait for me here. I'm joining you."

Lauren spoke up. "As am I."

He looked at her sharply but she lifted her chin, daring him to argue. Dunmar was her village. This was her part of the island still. Let him try to stop her.

But he didn't. Arion simply shrugged again, then moved away up the hill, headed for the stables. Lauren began a stately walk after him.

SHE RODE A HORSE THAT wasn't happy about the slow pace on the trails, and it was a silent struggle to keep her gelding from trotting off the narrow path they followed. He was a handsome fellow, chestnut with a dark mane and tail, but it was wearing to keep him constantly in hand, and Lauren was beginning to think that she might have made a mistake in joining this party.

The exhaustion that had avoided her before was upon her now in full force, making her eyelids droop, her muscles ache. The moon had set a while ago. It would be morning in a few short hours, and the new darkness around her became all the more devious without the pale light. Thank goodness she had not taken the lead.

She had let the earl do that, along with a man from the first patrol who was guiding them.

They were riding much farther out than she had expected. Already they were an hour away from Dunmar, on their way to find the abandoned camp of the Northmen. She could not recall ever having been here before. It shouldn't have been surprising, since she had spent most of her time at Keir, only visiting the outlying villages with Da about twice a year. But still, she had not expected this kind of complete alienation from her surroundings. It was unnerving, and made her fatigue all the more pronounced.

They were following a mountain pass, going deeper into the heart of the sole range on Shot, three jagged peaks sharing a common base, a place where neither MacRae nor du Morgan had a settlement. The land here was considered too rough, the soil too thin for crops, the grass too scarce for grazing. There were plenty of trees, however, which added to the strange shadows around them. Their roots became protrusions in the winding path that made the horses stumble; their leaves and pine needles rustled into unexpected noises in the wind, which made her gelding tremble with nerves. More than once she had had to rein in sharply to keep him steady.

And still they rode on, mostly single-file, treading deeper and deeper into the wild territory. Although there was no snow on the trail, it felt like true winter up here already. When she looked up and around, however, she could find the snow, waiting to spread down from the tops of these mountains, waiting for charcoal clouds to come to them, soft, covering it all, snow white on the ridges, snow white on the trees . . . the path . . . silent, endless blanket of snow, bringing peace, bringing hush. . . .

Arion would suit the snow, she knew that. He would suit any season; he would complement the trees and the stars and the wind and daylight. He could laugh away the cold, he could charm the sun from behind the clouds. He could make her forget all the hardships of the world. . . .

He could smile and cause the birds to sing. He could take her hand and hold it and bring her to him, giving her his warmth, so solid, so comforting. She could rest in his arms forever and a day, her head against his shoulder, his fingers stroking her so gently, so wonderfully. He could rock her close to him and whisper all the secrets of her heart to her, because only he would know them, only he would see that deeply into her spirit. Only he would care enough to—

Lauren came awake with a little gasp, catching herself from tipping out of her saddle just in time. She looked around to see if anyone had noticed, pretending to adjust part of her tartan.

She couldn't tell. The man directly behind her returned her look with inquiry, but she just nodded and turned back around.

By God, she was weary. When would they get there? She couldn't see the front of the line any longer; the trail was too twisting, and the jutting rocks and trees around every corner blocked her view. In the distance a pair of owls exchanged an eerie ballad, but there were no other sounds, just the horses, just the clinking of armor. Her fingers felt stiff with the cold. Her neck felt like it had turned to wood, rigid and unyielding.

She could be back at Kenna's home now, asleep on a pallet, tucked away under a soft blanket. She could be at Keir, safe in her own little room, sleeping soundly on her own pillow. But no, she had to come out here, she had to let the Earl of Morgan goad her into riding with this group, to ensure that he was not trying to deceive her, that he was not attempting to hide information from her. That he was not going to fool her without a good fight on her part.

Was that really why she came? whispered a voice inside her. *Was he truly hiding anything at all from her? Or was it just what he said, that he was taking precautions, that he was waiting for proof? Why was she so suspicious of him? Did it have anything to do with how she really felt about him, how she couldn't stop thinking of him, how she wanted him to touch her even though she hated herself for it?*

Lord, what was she doing?

For the first time since her father's death, Lauren felt beaten. She did not belong here. She did not have the stamina for this. She did not have the right to try to lead her clan like this.

All the gossip back at Keir had been right about her . . . she should have stayed home. She should be waiting for Murdoch right now, she should be thinking of him and their wedding, and not of this English earl, not of these terrible, clashing emotions that swept through her and left her empty and pained, bruised. She should have let a man take over her father's role. She should have realized she could never really succeed in a world devised to favor men in every way. She was a farce, a fraud. She was so tired.

Lauren brought a hand to her eyes and closed them, wavering in the saddle, close to tears and trying desperately to hide it. Too many wild thoughts, too many conflicts born of them.

Da would be ashamed of her now, for allowing such weakness to overcome her.

Lauren lifted her head again, letting the realization filter through her.

Da would have expected better of her. Da had never coddled her, and he had never expected her to follow rules that made no sense. Da had been proud of her uniqueness. Da had encouraged it.

When she had come racing into that mainland village as a young girl, that night that Arion du Morgan had given her her freedom, Da had cried out and run to her, hugged her close and kissed her. When, after the initial shock and tumult had died away and she had a chance to tell everyone what had happened—how she had been taken, the devil-laird who had come, the boy who had stolen her out of the dungeon, her all-night run through the woods that had brought her to him—Da had turned to everyone around them and exclaimed, "See what a treasure she is, my daughter! See how clever and brave!"

He had taught her in every single way how to be honorable, how to think for herself, how to lead. Lauren knew that—how could she have forgotten? He would have expected her to do exactly what she did after his death. He would have wanted her to manage the clan as she could, until Quinn was better, until the threat to them all was removed. It was what he had been training her for all her life, she realized with a start. Da had given her this gift, and she wasn't going to waste it.

She straightened in the saddle, feeling more alert, a little more heartened.

The horses were beginning to slow, bunching into a group near a plateau in the path, a thickening of the line of dirt that became almost a small valley.

"We'll have to walk from here," said one of the English, and Lauren dismounted with the rest of them, walking her steed to a nearby tree and wrapping the reins around a branch. Then she gathered her cloak closer to her and joined the group standing around Arion.

"You can see the rest of the trail from here," said one of her men, pointing up to a faint, ragged line that depressed the grass going up a steep hill. The way was tight and narrow through trees and bushes, and Lauren understood why they had to walk instead of ride. Like so much of Shot, this part was not yet tamed for people. It would be a hard climb up the slope. It looked rocky and uneven, but on top of that, it hugged the side of the mountain so tightly that in some places they might have to inch sideways to stay on the path. The way ahead loomed dark and sharply hazardous.

She heard Arion giving orders on who was to stay with the horses and keep watch for trouble, so she quickly looked around and picked out a few of her own men, indicating to them that they were to remain here as well.

The earl was observing her actions, inscrutable. When she finished he walked over to her, casual, as if to consult with her before heading up the trail. He spoke softly down to the ground.

"I won't ask if you're ready for this, MacRae." His voice was so quiet she had to take a step closer to hear him, attempting the same composure, as he continued. "You barely made it this far at all—I saw you fight to stay awake. Do us both a favor and wait here until we return."

She lifted her head and gave a slight smile. "No."

He seemed to expect this response, his face blank, but there was something new in his voice, something short and irate. "You'll only pose a risk to everyone if you come. We don't know what's ahead. It could be dangerous. You're not alert enough for this, and you know it."

"I'm going up there, du Morgan. I feel fine." She kept her smile in place.

He took a long breath, releasing it slowly, as if to stem the anger. Then he gave a curt nod, turning away from her, heading up the path into the canyons of the mountain. The other men fell in behind him. Lauren waited until near the end of the string of them. When she looked around there was only Fuller left. He smiled at her, offering to let her go first, so Lauren did.

It was a difficult walk, nothing gentle, but in spite of Arion's suspicions, Lauren had been telling the truth: She was no longer tired. She felt fine, she felt refreshed. She felt ready for whatever was at the end of the path.

Ahead was nothing but dim shadows and the breathing of about twenty men, the occasional sound of rocks skittering off the trail to go bouncing down the side of the canyon in sharp clatters. Every now and again she caught a muttered curse.

Behind her Fuller was quiet as usual, and Lauren found herself thinking that she was glad he had taken up the rear, that his calm presence was a sort of reassurance to her. He was skilled and capable. If anything approached them from behind, he would know.

The sound of a river echoed steadily stronger. Down at the bottom of the gorge she could make out a crooked line of water, pearly lavender. It made her look up past the mountains, realizing that dawn was almost here. At some point during the hike the sky had paled from its heavy black to something softer on the eastern edge, a welcome respite from what surely had become the longest night in her life.

The trail grew a little easier, following a smoother part of the land, flatter and more stable to walk on. Soon it ended in a rounded meadow, shelter amid the trees, a spent campfire plainly visible.

The men approached it with swords drawn and Lauren followed suit, pulling out her broadsword, walking cautiously forward. Something about the setting didn't feel right. She couldn't say what—it was a strong sense of apprehension, nothing she could articulate, so she kept silent, examining the landscape as closely as she could.

The light was turning color, less purple, more pink, a stronger glow that still held plenty of shadows in the woods around them, plenty of chances for the enemy to watch and not be seen. Lauren edged farther into the meadow, going over to where Arion stood next to the campfire. It was filled with bones, charred and discarded—the missing sheep, she knew. He kneeled and touched the ashes.

"Stone cold." He looked up at the guide. "You found no sign of where they might have gone?"

"It was too dark before," said the man. "But now . . ."

"Yes—now." Arion stood up, searching the ground. As he looked, others followed his lead, stepping carefully around the site, swords still raised.

But there was nothing. At least, nothing that Lauren could see. Admittedly, she was not the best tracker, but she knew enough to understand that finding the men who had made that fire was not going to be an easy thing. They had covered themselves well—no obvious paths, no bent twigs, no marks in the dirt, no freshly scuffled stones. Yet no one stopped looking, and the horizon was gradually growing brighter to the east.

The feeling of apprehension did not ease, but truly there seemed no cause for it. Men were scattered to every corner of this field, and no one could claim to find anything unusual. A few ventured slightly into the woods, but again, no discoveries. Arion refused to give up, however, and his men followed his command silently. Some of the Scots looked to Lauren, waiting for her reaction, so she nodded to indicate that she agreed with the earl, although privately she thought the path was far too cold to follow.

A heavy oppression hung around them all, growing thicker with every passing minute. The sun rose higher, warming the sky if not the air.

A single bird began a song of quick, shrill notes.

"I'm done with this farce," announced Rhodric,

sounding disgusted, on the other side of the meadow from Lauren. He straightened up from where he had been crouching, a scowl on his face. "There are no Northmen here. Mayhap there never were."

"What do you mean?" asked one of the earl's men.

"I *mean*," said Rhodric, in a clear and carrying voice, "that there never were any Vikings here, English. That your fine and fancy lordship over there most likely stole our sheep, and made this fire himself to draw us out here, to leave our village unprotected. We're on du Morgan land now. Don't think I didn't notice."

"Rhodric," warned Lauren, beginning to cross the grass to him.

"Don't you defend him to me!" Rhodric rounded on her. "You've been supporting him from the beginning, and it sickens me, Lauren MacRae! Your father would be mortified right now at the disgrace of your loyalties!"

She stopped, stunned amid the sunlight and the venom of his attack.

"That's enough," said Arion, walking slowly and deliberately closer to Rhodric. "If you wish to challenge me, boy, then you talk to me. Otherwise, leave Lauren out of this."

"He calls her by her given name," shouted Rhodric to the others, raising his sword. "As if she were his whore, and not the daughter of Hebron, who would cleave him in two for it!"

An ugly muttering began to rise from the men.

"Rhodric!" Lauren pushed her way past the others until she was in front of him. "What are you doing?" she demanded, furious. "How dare you say such things?"

"How dare *I*?" echoed Rhodric, laughing. "How dare *I*? How dare *you*, Lauren MacRae? How dare *you* fall to the side of the English? How dare *you* forsake all you know that's right and proper, and forget your father and your home for this du Morgan, who would kill us in an instant if he thought he could?"

"You're crazed!" Anger and bitterness carried her a few steps closer to him. "Hold your tongue, before you make even more of an ass out of yourself!"

The muttering of before was becoming more distinct, names and words becoming clearer, terms of insult and distrust and unrest.

"You're naught but a woman, weak and gullible," said Rhodric down to her, with scathing contempt. "You'd sell your body to this devil for the price of the souls of your own clan!"

And then he pushed her away from him.

It wasn't that hard a push, but it was enough to catch her off guard, to send her falling back into the grass, trying to hold on to her sword and her dignity at the same time, which was impossible. It happened almost slowly, a strange fall, with plenty of time to feel the full impact, to hear the distortion of the sudden silence around her. She landed with a bruising jolt; the force of it jarred her sword loose from her hand and emptied all the air from her lungs. She rolled backward, knocking her head against the ground, seeing bursts of orange light on the edges of her vision in a brief, fiery dance.

Lauren blinked and took a deep gasp of air. When she opened her eyes again, time had done a trick and speeded up, frightening and swift, and Arion had tossed his sword to the ground and charged at Rhodric. The two of them went flying in a tangle of oaths and smashing fists. Others swarmed between her and them—more fights, more hitting and cursing and all the tension of the past few weeks exploding into fury. The entire meadow became a tumult of violence.

She lifted herself up and gazed around her, perplexed and still winded, barely managing to get out of the way of two men tumbling past her, beating each other bloody. There was a dull roar coming from everywhere and nowhere, a war sound, but instead of sword striking sword it was flesh striking flesh, as it seemed that one and all had abandoned their blades and their wits in favor of pummeling each other.

Lauren stood, swaying, looking around at the writhing mass of them, appalled.

A scream came from one side of the meadow—a sound that made her swing around instantly, groping for her fallen sword. She knew that sound, and with the floating sense of moving through a dream, knew what was about to happen.

From the woods poured a storm of Vikings, a truly terrible sight, and Lauren screamed in response, a wordless warning to all the men around her, who continued to battle one another, blind to the onslaught coming toward them.

She found her sword in the grass and began to run toward the invaders, still screaming, matching their own sound, and by now some of her clan and the English had broken off, scrambling up to follow her. But they were slow, all of them too slow, and the invaders swept over and around them, still giving their awful call, striking ruthlessly at everyone in their path.

She met one of them and blocked a blow that would have fallen on the back of a downed man, turning the Northman's attention to her, his eyes widening and then narrowing as he took her in. He offered her a fearsome smile, showing a row of yellowed teeth. His sword came back up and he swung it around to her. Lauren blocked it again, the force of it quaking through her, but she barely felt it at all. She felt light and fleet together; she felt empty and focused at once. All that mattered was that this man be stopped. She must be the one to stop him.

He was taller and less agile than she, but he was also stronger, and his sword was heavier. Each blow he gave her sent a buzzing numbness up her hands, made her invent new twists and turns to incorporate the power of it into her movements, trying to work with the force as she had been taught, not against it. He moved clumsily—she managed a glancing blow along his ribs, causing him to grunt and step back in surprise. He squinted at her again, judging her anew. Lauren felt her lips curl back in a savage smile, and then he was upon her once more.

Around them were new outbreaks of battle, her clan and the du Morgans united again to fend off this threat. But that was a distant recognition in her. Lauren had no time to be grateful that her group was no longer fighting among themselves. The Viking was steadily pushing her back into the woods, the way he had come, and now it was all she could to do fend him off. She nearly managed another blow on him but he moved in time, and lunged at her. She jumped over a small boulder protruding from the brambles around them and heard the Northman's sword go singing as it hit the stone. There was an opening in his defenses; she darted in but the Viking moved away from her, anticipating it, laughing.

Lauren had to step over a root to evade the next thrust, but she lost her balance and staggered against the trunk of a tree. Now the Northman managed to get close enough to rip her tartan, sending a long flap of it falling down to her waist.

The Viking paused, staring at her, and she realized that he had cut her tunic beneath as well, tearing it apart to reveal a triangle of her skin just above her left breast, pale white and streaked now with red—a thin smear of blood.

They looked at each other, and she could mark the instant the change in him took place. It was nothing obvious, but Lauren knew with full certainty that the invader had just altered his intent with her—she read it in his eyes and then in his smile, cold and leering.

Lauren pushed herself off the tree trunk and swung wildly at him, missing but not caring because it made him back away from her, and it took the leer from his face. She swung again, coming closer, and the Viking said something to her and raised his sword.

In the distance she heard her name being called, but the voice was faded and held no promise of aid. The man in front of her now wasn't trying to strike at her any longer, only deflected her blows easily, almost calmly walking her farther back into the woods.

Her sword had become a burden of weight, her breath was short and pained, but she didn't stop, and she didn't hesitate, because she knew that the moment she fumbled, he would be upon her . . . and then he would win.

The woods were thick, and maneuvering around all the brush and trees was growing more difficult. She kept having to give quick, frantic glances around her to see where she was stepping and still he did not stop, only kept walking to her, that smile back in place, his own strength obviously untapped.

The men calling her name had not stopped, and Lauren thought that perhaps they were even coming closer, but she knew—and so did the Viking—that they would not find them in time.

She tried one last, desperate thrust, aiming for the exposed stomach of the man when he dropped one of his arms, and she realized too late that it was a hoax, meant to lure her to do exactly what she did. She fell in too close and the Northman simply grabbed her wrists, dropping his sword to painfully squeeze her fragile bones there, forcing her hands to open. Her broadsword fell to the soft dirt. The Viking yanked her up close to him, releasing one of her hands to capture her hair at the base of her neck.

Lauren took her free hand and swung at him, connecting with his jaw beneath his beard, rocking them both backward. But it was not enough force, and he recovered, shaking his head, laughing again. His grip on her had not loosened at all.

He said something new, and his breath was rotting fish, and his beard was dirty and scratchy, and the tightness of his hold on her hair was making her eyes tear.

The invader twisted the arm he still held behind her back, and now he was so close that she could not help but be pressed up against him. She tried to kick him but he lifted her up until her feet were off the forest floor and she had no purchase at all, her head forced far backward with his grip. The canopy of trees was green and gold and scarlet above her, a slur of colors through her tears. Lauren cried out and gave a mighty twist in his arms, almost succeeding in gaining her freedom, but the man tightened his grip until she couldn't breathe. The world grew dim and muted.

Something happened. She heard faint sounds in the back of her mind, grotesque noises that made no sense to her, rumbling, deep. They changed with the intake of her breath, fading away to nothing. Lauren realized she was turned around now, staring ahead at the dusky lines of the trees around her, and there was something large and warm behind her, and something cold and sharp at her throat.

She was half standing, half falling against the Viking, and he had an arm around her chest, hard. His other hand held the edge of his sword against her neck. His breathing was harsh in her ear.

Ahead of her were men coming past the shadowed lines of the tree trunks, all of them staring at her. She knew these men . . . her clansmen, swords out, the unmistakable red of blood decorating the blades. And the other men, she knew them as well. They were du Morgans, but their expressions were identical to her family's—wrath and caution mixed together. Standing before them all was one figure, large and dark, slowly edging closer. He was the one saying her name.

"Can you understand me, Lauren?" Arion spoke in a low monotone. "Lauren? Are you hurt?"

"No," she whispered, and the hold on her grew tighter. The Viking shouted words that made no sense, but it was clear from his voice that he was close to ruin, and he knew it. He dragged her back, away from Arion and the rest, and Arion lifted his hands to show them empty, not moving.

"We've got to rush him," said someone, and Lauren saw that it was Rhodric, sweaty and covered in dirt, his sword held ready.

No, Lauren tried to say, but the sound would not come out.

"No," said the Earl of Morgan, not looking around at anyone else, only at the man behind her. "We can't take that chance. He could kill her before we got there."

"He's going to kill her anyway if we don't move," hissed Rhodric.

"Stay back," ordered Arion, such a biting command that even Rhodric subsided.

"He's taking her to the cliff," cautioned a new voice—Fuller.

"I know," said the earl. He took one careful step toward Lauren and the Viking, hands still up. The breathing in her ear grew louder, but the man did not move away.

"All we want is the girl," Arion said, reasonable. "Release her, and you will live."

"He doesn't understand you!" Rhodric spoke through clenched teeth.

"Perhaps he does," Arion replied, very calm. "He can

understand my meaning, at any rate." He took another step toward them.

The Viking shouted out a garbled string of sounds, bellowing in her ear, and pulled Lauren back again, four huge steps, prompting Arion to halt once more, his face dispassionate, his eyes piercing.

"Sweet Jesu," said someone. "He'll do it. He'll kill them both. Look at him."

She couldn't understand what that meant until she angled her gaze downward and saw, strangely, the sky beneath her. But it wasn't truly the sky, just the reflection of it, clear blue threading through the canyon right below her. They were at the edge of a very steep drop. Far, far down was the river she had glimpsed earlier this morning, catching heaven and showing it off through the rocks.

If the Viking took another step back, they would both go falling to their deaths, long before they even reached the river.

She quickly looked back up at Arion and found him fixed on her.

"I'm all right," Lauren said, which surprised even her, because she was most certainly *not* all right, but she had needed to take away the look on Arion's face. She couldn't bear to see the veiled panic there, the tight fear for her.

So she did the only thing she could, which was to remove her hand from around her waist, where she had palmed her dirk, and shove it back behind her, stabbing the Viking with a quick and brutal blow, pushing the metal in as far as it would go.

The man jumped, and she felt the sting of the blade at her throat along with his sudden roar of fury, but he had moved away from her enough that she could turn and jerk out of his grip, an ungainly sideways step. The Viking grabbed at her again, now wavering against the sky, but he missed, cartwheeling backward, falling away, still yelling.

Lauren caught herself and stood motionless, holding her arms out for balance, perched on the very end of the ledge of dirt that had kept her from falling as well.

She didn't dare even to breathe, but it had worked! She looked to Arion and found him staring at her, as still as she was, and everyone else. But there was no joy on his face, like what was beating through her. There was panic again. In one abrupt move, he lunged for her— too late.

Lauren felt the ground beneath her feet crumble away, astonished, and then there was nothing there at all, and she went plunging down to the end of the world.

Chapter Nine

—— ༄ ——

𝓢HE WAS HAVING A DREAM of sunny places, open fields and warm skies, and the clouds were pearls and the trees had leaves of sparkling emeralds. Swans floated by in lapis-blue ponds, with onyx eyes and smiling beaks of gold. The sun was a rounded cabochon of topaz, glowing with light.

Lauren felt safe and comfortable here, despite the fantastic surroundings. She slept in a meadow of soft grass and heather. She drank nectar from flowers with long, elegant stems.

Arion was here. He offered her the nectar, said her name in whisper tones, touched her face and smiled at her as she looked up at him.

What a vivid dream, the nicest one she had ever had. Lauren settled back into the welcoming grass—smelling of cleanness, sweet and fresh—and closed her eyes again, deciding to nap beneath the bright sun.

Time passed. She didn't know how long. Long enough so that the sky faded away and became a canopy of cloth above her, and the grass became a blanket wrapped around her, with furs by her head.

Only the sun and the swans and the clouds and the trees stayed the same: topaz and onyx, pearls and emeralds, all carefully sewn into a tapestry that hung nearby, a brilliant pastoral scene that fooled the eye with its detailed richness.

It gradually came to Lauren that she was lying in a bed that was not her own, in a room that was not her own. When she turned her head to see why this might be, a terrible stab of lightning exploded though her, blinding her, nearly killing her, and she moaned with the pain of it.

"Don't move," said a voice to her left, where she could not see. "You need to stay still, Lauren."

She knew who that was. Lauren tried again to turn her head, back to the left, but this time the lightning blocked out everything else, and she actually felt herself slide into oblivion as it happened.

No dreams now, only that discontinuation of time and life; everything empty, everything gone.

When she looked up again, the canopy above her had not changed. It hung from wooden beams that had been polished and carved into long, twisting lines, as if the tree had grown into one of the braids she had made of the sage. The cloth against it was slate and silver, cool winter colors that soothed the pounding ache in her head.

Lauren moved very slowly, expecting the lightning but getting only more of the ache. She searched the darkened corners of the room, and found a shadow that shifted and then separated from the rest.

Arion came toward her, reached out a hand and lifted her own, bringing it to his lips. She felt the new growth of his beard rasp her there, brief and prickling.

"You look terrible," she said, but her voice was so

slight even she barely heard it. Nevertheless, he smiled down at her, still holding her hand.

"So do you," he replied cordially.

Lauren carefully managed to turn her head again, away from him, looking around at the rest of the room.

"You're at Elguire," Arion said, before she could ask. "We brought you here after the fall."

"Fall?"

He paused for a moment, until she looked back at him, waiting. "Don't you remember, Lauren? You fell down a cliff. It was hell getting you back up, I assure you." He spoke lightly but his eyes were deep and serious. "That was yesterday."

"But . . . ." Something he had said came back to her, alarming: "I'm at *Elguire*?"

"One of the advantages to being on du Morgan land," he said. "My home was closer than yours."

"Elguire?" Lauren repeated again. She could not stop the word from circling around her, a threat and certain cause for worry. Elguire—home of the enemy, seat of the devil family—her clan would be appalled; they would come, they would battle for her—

She began to sit up but his hands were immediately at her shoulders, gently pushing her back.

"Let me go!"

"Lauren!" Arion leaned over her, frowning. "Do not try to get up. You're almost more bandages than woman at this point, and I won't allow you to harm yourself."

There was no sense in fighting him. He was much stronger than she was, and besides, the pain came rushing back, flooding her head until she had to close her eyes again, breathing quickly.

After a while she felt his hands lift from her, but she remained where she was, struggling to keep her senses straight.

"I must go home to Keir," she said to him, when she could.

"That would be unwise."

She opened her eyes and found him standing very close, the cloth of slate and silver hanging like clouds above him.

"Am I your prisoner, du Morgan?"

He gave her the smile that was not a smile, and there was no humor in his eyes. "No."

Just that. No explanation, no reassurances beyond it.

"I can't be here," she tried. "You must understand. I have to go home."

"No," he said again.

She could hear the wind now, an intermittent brush against the glass of the windows in the room, but nothing else—no birds outside, no voices in the hall-way. Nothing. It was as if the rest of the world had vanished, and there were only the two of them left from it all. It felt odd and eerie and strangely like something she had always half expected in her deepest dreams—that they would end up so alone together, perhaps forever.

Lauren shook her head at the thought. The pain came back, and with it, the reality.

"My family will be worried," she said. "How did I come here?"

Now Arion sat on the edge of the bed, carefully, so that the feather mattress tilted a very little, and she didn't have to shift to make room for him.

"You don't remember, do you?" he asked, but it was more a statement than a question. She felt the alarm in her climb, something dark and unpleasant lurking just beyond her reach, at the edges of her memory.

"Remember what?"

"Let me ask you this: What *do* you remember, Lauren?"

"Well . . ." She looked down at the blanket covering her, the color of charcoal, the wool of it fleecy. "We were at . . . Dunmar. To find the Vikings . . ."

—his face, the dinner, the heat between them, the cold night, the near kiss by the sentry tower—

"And we rode out with the second patrol." Lauren noticed her hands against the deep color of the blanket, so pale, almost too thin. Faint scratches crisscrossed the backs of them. There was a bandage wrapped up her left forearm. "We found that meadow, and the campfire. And then Rhodric . . ."

She stopped, not because she couldn't recall what had happened but because it humiliated her, that her kinsman would say the things he had, would disgrace her so openly in front of everyone else, especially the Earl of Morgan.

"I know," said Arion, his voice telling her nothing of his thoughts. "Go on."

"Then there was fighting," she finished. "Your family and mine. Everyone went mad, I think."

"And after that?"

The dark lurking thing came closer, creeping out from corners and closed doors in her mind. She didn't want to open those doors. She didn't want to know what was waiting there for her.

"I don't know," Lauren said, trying to sound convincing.

"Are you certain?"

"Yes," she stated. "I don't know."

He didn't respond to this, only studied her lying there, so close she could reach out and touch his hand, if she wanted to. But she didn't. Instead she turned her head away, trying to rid him from her vision, wishing she were anywhere else but here right now.

The dark thing hovered, not banished, pressed up taut against her, waiting.

"I want to go home," she said tightly. "My clan will hold you responsible for keeping me here."

"Your clan is aware of where you are, Lauren," he said. "They helped to bring you here. They agreed that it was best for you to recover at Elguire, at least right now. We have a good healer, and a broader access to medicine than Dunmar. None of your bones were broken—a miracle— but still you were hurt, and are unfit for travel. Even your foolhardy Rhodric agreed to it. So, you will stay here."

She felt trapped and betrayed, an uncontrollable reaction to his words and the thing that was pressing ever harder against her, pushing, pushing, relentless.

"There were Vikings hiding in the woods there." Arion stared down at the floor. There was something new in his voice, ire or pain, she couldn't tell. "They had to be from that rowboat in the caves. We think they were scouting the island, planning to rejoin the Northmen on the longship once they had discovered how many of us there are on Shot, the locations of our villages, our fortresses. We surprised them that morning, and they attacked. There were still more of us. We de-

feated them. But a good many of our men were felled
before we had the wits to fight back."

She looked up. "How many were felled?"

He sighed, and even that sounded angry. "Twelve.
Five of yours. Seven of mine."

*—she struck at the Viking and he blocked her easily, smil-
ing, walking toward her with that leer on his face—*

"They came from the forest," she said slowly, as images
formed and scattered across her memory. "They waited
until we were distracted, and then they charged." She
shook her head, feeling ill. "There were . . . so many."

"Aye," said Arion, grave and soft.

Lauren felt so peculiar. She felt as if she had split
apart into two different people, and one of them was
feeling a sickening rush of emotions, guilt and wrath
and remorse—but the other was merely standing back,
surveying what was happening with a cool detachment.
She moved to sit up and this time Arion helped her, his
hands firm and impersonal, until she was propped up
against the massive wooden headboard, and the charcoal blanket fell to her lap.

The details of little things struck her with great
importance:

She wore a loose gown the color of heather, with
tiny flowers embroidered on the cuffs.

The bed was very high off the stone floor. There was
a rug of many colors covering the area nearby.

All the windows were securely closed, and the wind
outside had not ceased.

The Earl of Morgan was gazing at her face, and his
eyes became the color of the sea in a tempest, nothing
calm at all.

"You were right," the removed Lauren said, matter-of-fact. "I should not have gone to the meadow. I was a danger to everyone. I allowed myself to be taken by that Viking."

Arion looked taken aback for a moment, then said, "Lauren, you were the one who saw them before anyone. You called out to warn us all."

"If it had not been for me, he would have had no hostage."

"If it hadn't been for you, he would have killed many more than he did."

The dark thing pressed harder against her, storm and fright. It was howling her name.

"But—I killed him." Lauren wasn't certain if she meant this as a question. She looked down at her hands again. They were shaking. How strange.

"Yes," the earl said, and nothing else.

"I—" The shaking was spreading, she couldn't stop it, though it embarrassed her, as if she were being unpardonably rude.

"We were at the cliff, and I had my dirk . . . I suppose it's gone now." She laughed, treble and tearful at once, and then choked it off, horrified at herself. What was happening to her?

Arion was there, close—too close—and she pulled back from him, trembling.

"What is it?" he asked, making no move to come near again. "Lauren, what's wrong?"

"That man," she said, in a voice that matched her shaking. "He was going to kill me."

"Yes," Arion replied, urgent. "He would have. You did the right thing."

Lauren shook her head and brought her hands up to her face, covering her eyes, bowing her head, trying not to laugh and cry at the same time, which made no sense at all. She felt something warm and hard around her back—his arm, drawing her to him now, holding her to his side, a hand stroking her shoulder, her hair. She leaned her head against him, no longer fighting it, and felt the dark thing boil up and spill over her, thick and black and oily, smothering.

She tried to breathe against it and felt the air within her turn into a sob, and then more of them, a prolonged misery of tears. She clung to Arion and he was still and solid beside her, but she barely noticed it, because the dark thing was so immense.

Blood and sea and sand and death and death, her father's face. . . .

Arion was saying things to her, low murmurs and sounds that were not words, comforting, patient. He kept her close and held her there tightly, which was good, because otherwise she might go flying away, she might shatter into so many pieces that she would never find herself again.

She heard her voice, whisper thin, her words tangled with grief and fear: "I see him. I see his *face,* as he died . . . and it's *Da's face!*"

"No," Arion said, sweet and gentle. "No, Lauren."

"And the other one, the first one on the beach—I killed him too, because they killed Da, because he was murdered by them and I wanted to murder them back— but it was *his face,* and I *killed* him—"

He rocked her slowly. "You saved my life, my love, and then you saved your own. It was all you could do."

"Da," she cried against him, a soft muffled lament, "oh, Da . . ."

Ari put both arms around her and held her even closer to him, until her head was against his shoulder and he could rest his lips on her hair. She was chilled and flushed, quaking so violently with the force of her sorrow that he truly feared for her, that she would harm herself further, that she would go so deeply into that place of pain she had made for herself that he would not be able to help her at all.

But he couldn't think of anything else to do. It was plain that she was still shocked from all that had happened, and it might hurt her further to try to bring her out of it. So he just held her and kept rocking, saying things he hoped made sense, things that he hoped would reach her past all the tears. She kept one fist closed around the front of his tunic, as child might, seeking comfort.

Eventually she relaxed into a heaviness against him, trusting and dear, and he slowed his movement and then stopped, not releasing her, unable to let go.

He could tell by her breathing that she had fallen asleep, which was hardly surprising. She was not well; she had awakened to confront both him and her hidden fears, but her body was not yet healed from all that had happened to her. Poor, brave Lauren MacRae.

Her hair was a fall of copper skimming over his arms. Her skin was dewy now, pale, the chill of before warmed away. He laced his fingers through hers, carefully freeing her hold on his tunic, then laid her back onto the pillows so slowly that she didn't even shift from his hold. As Arion pulled up the blankets to cover her again, she sighed and moved her hand across her chest, but that was all.

He lifted his own hand to brush away a few burnished strands that clung to her face, then made himself stop. He backed away from her, leaving the room.

⸻

*T*HE WOMAN FROM KEIR DID not come as soon as Arion had hoped, and when she finally did arrive at the gate of Elguire, the sun was already high in the sky of Lauren's second day there.

Ari was vaguely surprised by her age. He had been expecting someone more of Lauren's years, he supposed. But this woman was much older, dignified and proud atop her roan mare. She did not travel alone, but instead had an escort of eight men flanking her.

Arion met her in the bailey, walking up to the group of them, nodding to the faces he knew among her guard.

She dismounted with the help of her men, a stately woman with shining silver hair and doe eyes. He could only imagine what the beauty of her youth had done to the men around her. There even seemed to be something of Lauren about her face—perhaps the straightness of her nose, or the same elegant cheekbones. He was probably imagining that. Hell, he was seeing Lauren everywhere now, so deeply had she touched him.

"So, here is the Earl of Morgan," said the woman, surveying him. She raised one hand to him and Arion bowed over it, amused, in spite of himself, at both of them.

"Madam," he replied, since he did not know her

name. All Ari had been told was that there would be a chaperon arriving from Keir for Lauren, to stay with her until she was well enough to leave on her own.

Elguire had been housing a parcel of the Scots who had been on that fateful patrol two nights ago—stubborn about remaining near the promised bride of Murdoch— and Ari honestly didn't think anyone would be happier to see them depart than he was. Suspicions and barely controlled tempers had been running high on both sides since the unconscious Lauren had been carried into Elguire. And although the MacRaes had come and hovered over her every few hours, they still managed to stir up trouble the rest of the time, though Ari doubted it was entirely their fault.

He had had to argue to bring Lauren here. He had had to threaten, in fact. She was bleeding from an assortment of wounds, deathly white, and Ari had been more than willing to fight them all to get her to Elguire, so that she might be saved.

As he had watched her fall he had honestly thought, in that sick, horrible instant, that she would be killed. That when he raced to the rough new edge of the cliff he would see nothing of her at all; she would be gone to the depths of the canyon. He did not remember running to the cliff. He did not remember scrambling down the soft dirt, barely managing to keep his balance. He remembered calling her name, that was all, and it became a chant, a litany, a prayer as his very soul seemed torn from his body at her loss.

But she was there. Below him—far below them all, her body draped limply against one of the few thin pine trees growing out of the side of the mountain. Her tartan had saved her. It remained stretched and taut over the branches and her body, preventing her from plummeting the rest of the way down.

They had managed to raise her. That was another moment that was not quite clear to him now—shouts and hasty plans, a rope, a struggle to be the first to reach her. It seemed to take an eternity to get down to her, and all the while he kept his fervent stare on the colors of her tartan, sweating, straining, finding a new prayer for its strength, and that of the tree. He himself had carried her back up the cliff.

After they had her safe again, the dispute began about where to take her to treat her injuries.

She lay there, bleeding into the dirt, and Arion had stood over her and told them all that he was taking her to Elguire, and damn them if they tried to stop him. He had his sword out, streaked red with blood, his words coming rough and fast. This was his land, and he was the Earl of Morgan, with the might of his king behind him. If the Scots wanted a war they would get one, but he was taking her anyway, and they would have to fight him right now to prevent it.

And the men around him had taken one another's measure once more—Ari had kept his gaze straight on Rhodric as he spoke—until finally the Scots begrudgingly agreed that Elguire was closer.

So they had come here.

Ari had known better than to insist on carrying her himself in his saddle. He handed her up to one of the Scots, and they all rode like hell to reach his home.

The Viking had managed to miss the vein in her neck, but Ari's hands were still sticky with her blood, drying in the wind to a deep reddish brown that chilled the deepest depths of him every time he looked down. The entire ride he was sweating, frantic, not even realizing that he was still praying ardently to God for her life until they had placed Lauren in his bed and the healer had come.

He was praying. He, Arion du Morgan, who had thought that God was merely a word that meant endless tithings and obedience to the church. Yes, he had prayed for her. The realization of it left him humble and shaken.

Perhaps God was listening, after all. Perhaps the prayer worked, or perhaps it was just that the decision to take her to Elguire had been the right one. Either way, Lauren lived, and she recovered, and she awoke.

"Where is Lauren?" asked the Scotswoman in front of him now, and Ari came back to this moment, focusing on her again.

"She is within. May I escort you . . . ?"

"Hannah Elizabeth MacRae." She placed one hand delicately on his proffered arm, turning to her outriders.

"You are done here," she instructed them. "Rest as long as you must, but then return to Keir, along with our other men." Hannah looked back at Arion. "The men from our patrol are ready to leave, I hope?"

"Quite," answered Ari, repressing a smile.

She nodded, then faced the keep again. "Very well."

He wanted to look back at the mounted men but didn't. They seemed to have bowed to the will of this woman with perfect ease, and to look back would imply a kind of distrust he didn't want to offer. Besides, Fuller was nearby. Ari had seen him on the fringes of

the crowd, watching the proceedings with close attention. Fuller would handle any problems.

Ari began to guide her to his chambers, and Hannah
MacRae strolled beside him with the perfect hauteur
of a queen. He had to admire it, how she went past staring people and loud rooms with equal indifference.
The deep blues and greens of her tartan shouted out
her difference here, yet she seemed to fear nothing, only
kept moving through the hallways with pure serenity
about her.

He had seen Lauren practice this look. Now he knew
its origin.

"The latest report on Lauren claimed that she was
not gravely injured, only enough so that she must rest a
few days," said Hannah, still walking.

Arion hesitated, then said, "That's true."

She threw him an astute look. "But there is more, isn't
there, your lordship?"

He debated about what to say to her, not certain if
he should reveal what Lauren had said through her tears.
After all, he really had no idea who she might be to
Lauren—a near-stranger, perhaps—or even a spy for her
fiancé. Yet he knew he should say something. He didn't
know how Lauren was feeling this afternoon, after the
trauma of the morning. He had left her sleeping but
she might be awake by now, and still grieved.

Hannah pulled away from him and stopped in the
hallway.

"If there is something truly wrong with Lauren, I insist you tell me at once," said the woman, stern. "Do not
spare me, Earl of Morgan. No one cares for that girl more
than I. Tell me what it is."

He could see the worry behind the command of her, and that was enough to persuade him to speak.

"Lauren had trouble remembering what happened to her," he said cautiously. "When she did begin to remember, it . . . upset her."

"Ah," said Hannah, watching him keenly.

"She was badly battered from that fall down the cliff," Arion added, trying to explain. "I'm certain her head was struck more than once."

"How exactly was she upset?"

Ari looked around the hallway, people passing back and forth on both ends, many throwing them curious stares. He took Hannah into the nearest room, thankfully deserted, and shut the door behind them. Gloom instantly filled the chamber. The windows were shuttered, and there was no fire in the hearth. The air felt heavy and cold. Arion leaned against the door, then continued.

"The Northman who held her was going to kill her. She pulled her dirk and struck him with it. She was so brave. . . ." How vividly he remembered *that* moment, colors so intense they hurt his eyes—the blue of the sky, the red of her blood. How his hands and feet had been weighted, slow. How his entire existence had seemed to hinge on that wild man's sword at her throat, how he couldn't breathe or think but only react, his life depending upon getting her away from him. And how Lauren had smiled at him—*smiled* at him—and tried to reassure him, even as there were thin streamers of scarlet running down her neck from the blade.

"She killed the invader," stated Hannah to the empty

air of the room, nodding. "I know it already. That is
what upsets her?"

Arion let out his breath, trying to push away the terror of that moment. He felt tired suddenly, his whole
body weary, and he brought up a hand to rub his temple, trying to battle this away as well.

"She told me that she sees her father's face on the
man she killed. Not just on that one, but on the other
Northman too. On the beach that morning, when she
first came—" *to save me,* he almost said, but didn't—
"When she came with the others of her patrol, and she
killed the Northman there," he finished. "She said they
both had his face."

"Ah," said Hannah again, and again she nodded. "I
understand."

Neither of them spoke for a good while, allowing
the silence to expand in the cool air, almost as a shield
to further inquiry.

Ari saw that there was furniture in the room, thick
and dim, a table with chairs, a cabinet of some sort with
jars and pots stacked on the shelves. The floor was bare
of rugs or rushes, left instead to just plain, cold stone.

"Has Lauren mentioned anything to you about the
death of her father, du Morgan?" asked Hannah.

"No."

He watched her walk to one of the chairs, where
she sat down with a faint sigh, arranging her skirts
around her.

"Forgive me. I must sit for this tale."

He stayed where he was, against the door, actually glad
that there was more space between them. Something in

her voice told him he was not going to like what she was about to tell him, and he didn't want her to see his reluctance.

Yet she said nothing, apparently content once more with their silence, and Ari found his thoughts drifting to the woman upstairs in his chamber, how she had last looked when he left: a sleeping princess from a fable, marble and flame and roses in his bed.

"Hebron led the patrols after the first longship was spotted off our shores," Hannah said eventually, mellow and sad. "He was the laird of our clan, and none would refuse him. He had done so much for us all. He was shrewd and wise and charming and brave—he was everything a laird could be for his people, and all of us knew this. Unlike some leaders of men," she looked at Arion, albeit briefly, "Hebron was beloved. But no one was closer to him than Lauren.

"So one dark day the Vikings came to shore, and they caught him unawares, and there was a fight. A terrible, terrible fight. We supposed that the Vikings had identified Hebron as the leader, for they singled him out and came after him so fiercely that he had to die. He died bravely, of course. But he did die."

Her voice wavered now, and she paused, smoothing her skirts again. Arion heard her sigh once more, and her words grew softer. "They did not just kill him. They tortured him. They maimed him—and then he was beheaded. No one could do anything to stop them that day. We lost that battle, as we lost our laird. It was a storm that finally drove the invaders off, and the sight of our reinforcements arriving.

"Lauren was at Keir, waiting like the rest of us for our men to return. And when they did, it was she who ran out to meet them before any of us. You can imagine what she saw that night, du Morgan. You can imagine how it must have been for her, to see her father cut down as he was, carried back home in pieces."

Ari closed his eyes, bowing his head.

"She never cried," said Hannah, almost reflective. "She never stopped to shed her grief. She buried her father with the rest of our dead, and she stepped into his place and tried to carry his hopes and determination forward, to help the clan. But I never saw her cry."

Hannah fell silent, letting the chill in the air take over the room again, and it sank into Arion's bones and left him breathless, frost settling over his heart. That Lauren, his beautiful, remarkable Lauren, had suffered such a loss, had seen such things . . .

"She has cried now," he said at last, down to his booted feet.

He heard the woman get up out of her chair, the faint rustling of her clothing as she walked over to him. He felt her place one frail hand on his arm, a timid warmth against the cold.

"Then I am glad, Arion du Morgan," she said. "It was time."

———————— ⚬∞⚬ ————————

HE WATCHED THEM REUNITE WITH the feeling that he should be elsewhere, that he should not be here in his own chamber staring at the embraces they shared, or listening to the words of relief and fondness they exchanged.

But Arion did not leave. In fact, he pretended to make himself useful by going to the fire in the hearth—which had indeed burned itself low—and slowly building it up again, taking such exact care with his placement of the logs that anyone truly watching him would have laughed. It was a transparent stratagem, no doubt, but the two women in the room seemed to give it no notice.

If Lauren was still distressed, she gave no sign of it. She smiled and even laughed a little, brushing off her injuries to inquire about Hannah, and Keir, and all her clan there.

When he turned around they were sitting together with the ease of old friends, holding hands, Hannah perched on the edge of his bed.

"I have good news for you," the older woman was saying. "Quinn is awake, and aware."

"He is?" Lauren's voice was still slightly rasped, but the happiness in it was clear to Arion.

"Aye. It appears he'll recover. Elias said he can be up within a few days, if all goes well."

"That's wonderful!"

"We've told him of all that's happened since he's been asleep. About your Da, and the battles—the beach and the caves and Dunmar."

"Oh." The syllable was small, deflated.

"James informed him of the joining with the English." Hannah glanced over at Arion, then back at Lauren. "Quinn said he wants to speak with you."

"Oh," said Lauren again, and this time Ari heard gloom.

Someone knocked on the door, and both women immediately looked to him, standing idle by the now blazing fire. Ari walked over and opened it.

"Your pardon, my lord." It was Fuller.

"Yes?" Arion didn't move from the doorway.

"I thought you might like to know that the fourth patrol will be riding in soon. In case you wanted to meet them."

Ari stared at him, baffled. Fuller knew that Arion always met the patrols when he could, and both of them knew perfectly well that the next one was not due in for over an hour.

He lowered his voice. "Is something amiss?"

"No, my lord. Not that I know of." But the steward seemed almost nervous, his eyes shifting from Arion's to the room behind him.

"Fuller Morgan."

Arion turned at the words, spoken with quiet emphasis. Hannah had risen from the bed and was walking toward the doorway, a warm smile in place.

Ari backed away and Fuller came into the room, meeting Hannah halfway.

"Hannah MacRae," said the steward. He took her proffered hand in both of his and just held it, not smiling back.

Arion looked at Lauren and found the same puzzled expression on her face as he was certain he was wearing. She was sitting up, intent, watching the curious scene unfold before them.

"It's been many years," said Hannah.

"Aye," replied Fuller, not releasing her hand.

"Hannah?" Lauren recovered from the astonishment before Ari did.

"My dear." Hannah turned around and walked Fuller over to the bed. "Have you met the earl's steward?"

"Yes," replied Lauren. "But I didn't realize that you had."

"Why, we're naught but old acquaintances, isn't that so?" Hannah looked at Fuller, who nodded, slow and deliberate. They stayed that way, staring at each other, two people so obviously lost in each other that now Ari did feel like an intruder—not a welcome feeling, especially considering the circumstances.

"What a delightful happenstance." He crossed to them, trying to judge the situation. Lauren appeared thoughtful; Hannah, still composed. And his steward had the look of a man who had found a lifeline, and had no intention of letting go.

Arion, God help him, knew that feeling too well. He wasn't going to be the man who crushed it in the only person who had shown him an ounce of friendship since he had inherited his title.

"Perhaps you might show Hannah MacRae our ..." Ari paused, trying to think of anything that might seem appropriate, but Fuller only nodded once more, and drew the woman's arm through his own with solemn courtesy.

"Aye, my lord," he said, walking away with her, to the doorway and beyond. But there Hannah stopped, not pulling away. She glanced back at Lauren, an unspoken question.

Ari saw Lauren nod and offer a half-smile, leaning back against her pillows. Hannah turned again to Fuller, and the two of them faded off into the torchlit shadows, no words between them.

When he looked at Lauren again she was still staring at the empty doorway, her smile vanished. After a moment she glanced down at the covers of the bed, and then slowly up to him. The gold of her eyes was clear and lucid, no trace of the tears she had shed earlier. Yet there was a pensive air about her now that made him want to comfort her still, even though he knew she would not welcome it.

"How are you?" he asked, trying to find some way to set them both at ease.

Instead of answering she turned her face away from him, a delicate blush spreading across her cheeks. She bowed her head and the fullness of her hair fell forward, disguising her features.

"I feel better," she said, low.

"Good." He stood there awkwardly for another moment, then went ahead and sat down on the feather mattress where he had before, when he had held her and rocked her to sleep. She did not raise her head, but neither did she protest his move. Her copper hair curled and rested across his blanket, bright warmth amid the darkened colors of his bed.

"Lauren," he began, "I want you to know I'm sorry about your father. I didn't realize—"

She cut him off, speaking over him. "You told me this morning that men died in that battle in the meadow. Who were they?"

Arion paused, watching the gleam of her hair, since

she still wouldn't look up at him. "I don't know the names of your kin who died," he said carefully. "Your friend Hannah will, however. Shall I go get her?"

"No." Now she looked up again, and Ari saw that the blush was still there. "Leave her be. Let her have her moment with Fuller."

Arion nodded, agreeing, thinking of the two of them, the mystery they presented.

"What of your men?" Lauren asked now, softer than before. "Who were they, the ones who died?"

Ari turned his gaze to one of the walls, to the window that showed him an empty sky framed in stone. "Good men," he said shortly. "I don't know their names, either. Men from Shot. Men who died defending their home."

Now it was Lauren who nodded, silent. Her eyes met his, steady and calm despite the conversation.

"I should know their names," Arion said, almost to himself. "I should know them."

"You are still new here," she said, surprising him with her defense. "And there are many of your people on this island. It takes time to remember faces and names."

"I should have known them," he said again anyway, and then quelled the tired sigh that wanted to come.

One of her hands reached out, rested lightly on the back of his own. She said nothing more, only left her touch on him, and Arion felt it burning through him as if she held a flame to his skin.

He got up abruptly, stalking away from her, walking away—anywhere but near her, when just her touch could cloud his mind, making him dazed and careless and his thoughts inappropriate. He ended up near a table of dark oak, heavily carved, with drawers and wrought-iron handles and a polished top. He remembered this table, strangely enough. He remembered it from this very room, when he had been summoned here as a boy, his uncle's companion on one of the visits to the island.

Ryder had sat there and written notes to himself, detailing his thoughts out loud on the best—the most cutting and cruel—manner in which to take over all of Shot. Arion had been made to stand before him. It was a test; one of the many Ryder had subjected him to every day of his miserable life with him.

"They have a castle," Uncle Ryder had said, his tone didactic, lecturing. "What do we do?"

"Breach it," suggested the young boy Arion had been, hesitant, afraid not to answer.

"Correct. But there are many of them and fewer of us here. What do we do?"

"Outwit them?" tried Arion.

"How?" demanded Ryder, not looking up from his notes, his face empty.

"Poison," ventured Arion, trying desperately to guess the correct answer from his uncle's lessons. "Fire. Ambush. Siege. War."

"Very good." Ryder held the feather quill motionless, staring down at the paper, and Ari knew that meant that the next question would be the true one, the one that he had to get right or else risk his uncle's punishment. He felt his stomach do a sick lurch, and curled his fingers up into his palms until the nails bit the flesh there, so that he could keep his composure.

"And there is something else to this situation, Nephew. They have a weakness."

"Exploit it," Arion said instantly.

"It is a child," said Ryder gently. "A little girl, a princess to them. She will marry someday, unite them with another clan, making them all the more powerful. What do we do?"

"Kill her," Arion had replied, without even blinking.

Ryder looked up finally, and his face was still empty, but that was good. No wrath right now, no striking hand, no whippings or slaps or confinement for Ari today—or for Nora.

"Yes," his uncle had said, and then patted Arion on the shoulder. "That's correct, Arion. Excellent."

The wood of the tabletop now looked to Arion precisely as it had in that harrowing moment, just as finely polished; it even had what appeared to be the same inkwell resting on one corner of it, silver and brass in the shape of a gargoyle's head.

Ari wondered if that conversation with his uncle had taken place before Lauren had been kidnapped or after. It had to have been before. Yes, before, because he had never heard of Lauren MacRae until that day.

What would Ryder du Morgan think of that little girl, the child he had wanted to murder, resting now in his bed in this very room? Ari found a dark amusement at the thought.

"Your fortnight is over soon, MacRae," said Arion to Lauren, speaking down to the table. "Tomorrow, in fact." He waited, then added, "You'll not be able to leave here before then."

He heard her shift in the bed but she said nothing. He did not turn around to see her face.

"What do you think your clan will do when the alliance expires?" he asked, and heard an ominously familiar rhythm in his question—slow, paced to coach an answer. "Would they fight to gain you back?"

"Would they need to?" Lauren asked, wary.

Arion shrugged, still finding that black amusement, but it had turned sour somehow, growing bitter in his blood. He wondered for a bare instant if this was something that Ryder would have felt, this wild anger at nothing and everything, this buried hurt that made him want to hurt in return.

He was his uncle's nephew, after all. Perhaps some of that ruthlessness would be of use to him.

He wanted something that was not his. Honor and reason dictated that he conquer the want, that he vanquish it for the good of everyone.

But he was the Earl of Morgan, a man with a noble title and considerable authority to go with it. He had extensive lands, he had armies, he had a king who would—with the proper persuasion—grant him almost anything he requested. Indeed, for all intents and purposes, out here on the remoteness of Shot he spoke for the king, and that made him just as strong.

For the first time, Arion had a cold taste of how power truly felt, and a clear vision of what it could mean, if wielded the way he wanted to. How it might satisfy this thing in him that called out for a woman beyond his control—at least until her clan killed him to get her back. It was a vast, whirling darkness, and he felt himself drawn to it with almost overwhelming force.

This would be his last chance to capture her before she vanished into her people, became lost amid them before she left the isle—and his life—forever. He had not truly considered it until this moment, staring down at the inkwell. Soon she would be gone, and all that luminescence about her would be gone as well, and he would be left empty and alone and with that bitter thickness in his blood, until it froze him dead, or he wished he were.

Arion faced her again, leaning against Ryder's table. "Naturally, I would prefer peace."

"We all would." Her figure was slim and shadowed amid his pillows. He could see the caution in her more clearly than he could hear it. Her voice was even, but there was a kind of tenseness about her, her hands clenched together on her lap. "There is no cause for fighting among us."

"I could not, however," Arion continued, "allow you to leave Elguire until it was judged you were well enough to be moved, no matter what your clan said. I am the overlord here, and you are in my country. I am responsible for all the souls in my demesne. Right now, that includes you."

"I cannot imagine it would take more than just a day or two until I am sound again."

"I can imagine it," Ari replied. "I can imagine it quite easily. You were seriously injured. I'm surprised you lived, in fact. It could take . . . weeks until you are healed. Or longer."

"I'm sure something can be arranged," Lauren said, the tension in her becoming more pronounced. "I'm sure we can reach an agreement."

"Aye," he said. "An agreement."

And she stared over at him from the luxury of his bed and Arion saw her now, at last, see into his thoughts, understand what he was contemplating, what he might do. He saw the warm blush that had graced her before go draining away to nothing, leaving her pale and wide-eyed, lovely and worried.

He gave her a smile that he knew would not reassure her, but he couldn't help it. It was the bitterness, the hurt and want in him that made him do it, and these were the things in him that made him walk away from her now, over to the door of the room.

"Rest well, Lauren," he said. "We'll discuss our agreement again tomorrow."

Then he left.

Chapter Ten

———————— ❧ ————————

*L*AUREN AWOKE TO A ROOM that was unfamiliar to her, filled with gilt and tapestries and an enormous bed that swallowed her up as if she were a sparrow in a swirl of clouds, lost amid the softness.

But in the next heartbeat she remembered it all, every moment of it, yesterday with the Earl of Morgan, her tears, his comfort . . . and then Hannah, and Arion again, and his strangeness, the edge of wildness that had come over him as he had talked about the end of the alliance.

She sat up, scanning the room, wincing when she moved too quickly, and the pain rushed back. A figure in one far corner moved and stood; Lauren's breath caught and then released. It was Hannah.

"Good morning, dearest," said her friend, coming toward her. "How do you feel?"

Lauren had to yawn and shake her head, then she looked around the rest of the room anyway, just to be certain Arion was not somewhere she could not easily see, a silent observer.

"He is not here," said Hannah.

"No," Lauren replied. "Of course not."

"It would not be appropriate," Hannah said now.

Lauren lifted one shoulder in a shrug, to show how little the subject interested her.

"Do you think you are well enough to step out of the bed?" Hannah moved closer. "I do not wish to hurry you unduly, but we should think about when you might be well enough to return to Keir. Everyone awaits us there."

"Hannah." Lauren put her hand on her friend's arm. "Today is the last day of the alliance, isn't it?"

"Is it?" asked Hannah, appearing unconcerned. "Why, I suppose you're right."

Lauren raised a hand to her head, rubbing, fighting the sensation of dizzy apprehension that was filling her. "Tell me this: What was the talk, when you left Keir? What was the council saying? Will they renew our agreement with the du Morgans?"

Hannah said nothing, but Lauren didn't need the words. She could see the answer in her eyes.

"Oh no," she whispered, and moved her hands to cover her own eyes. The apprehension turned to dread, sharp and lancing, and she couldn't even speak for a moment, so great was its hold on her.

"The Earl of Morgan sent a day gown for you," said Hannah, after a long pause. "Won't you see it? You cannot go home in what you have on, and we do not have your tartan."

"They're fools," said Lauren, biting. "I cannot believe they would let our agreement die."

"I do not think," said Hannah softly, "that *that* is what they truly wish to have die."

"What, then?" asked Lauren.

Again her friend said nothing, only looked down at

her, and there was sadness and knowledge behind her expression, compassion. Lauren felt her heart shrivel into something dry and cold.

Rhodric had won. He had told the council of his discovery—of how she felt about Arion—and even though they had professed not to believe him, Lauren knew now that he had stirred them into doubt. And because of the doubt, everything would be ended.

"It took a great deal of convincing to persuade them to send only me to companion you," said Hannah, reading her, as she always did. "And they agreed only because they trust me, and they know me, and they honestly do not wish you to be ill used by anyone. They cherish you, Lauren. They want what is best for you."

Arion had to know. He had to have realized by now what was about to happen. It would explain his mood yesterday, the chilled finality of his words. The alliance was ending. They would not be able to see each other again. Unless . . .

Unless she had read the strange air about him correctly. Unless she had accurately perceived in him what she feared even to consider, the desperate depths to the green of his eyes . . .

He had left her alone with her fears, her imaginings of what he was capable of, and even Hannah had stayed away until that evening, when Lauren had been asleep again because the exhaustion and the pain would not cease. She had roused briefly enough to see the figure of her friend, and then . . . this morning.

"Come," said Hannah, so gentle. "Look at the gown. Let me help you dress."

The day gown was an English fashion, created from a

very heavy material that Lauren could not name. It was composed of a thick outer garment with long, slashed sleeves, and slits in both the front and back of the skirts. A plainer gown apparently went beneath it. After some struggling and a bit of guessing, they had the foreign thing on her, and it actually fit.

Hannah seemed speechless, looking her up and down as Lauren leaned against the bedpost, trying not to appear as faint as she felt. When her head cleared she glanced down at herself. The color of the outer gown was a deep amber, soft and gleaming with stitches of darker gold. The gown beneath it, revealed in coy glimpses behind the slits, was a rich, royal blue, also gleaming, also thick and fine.

It was clearly a gown for someone more important than she was, Lauren realized, an English princess, perhaps. It felt strange on her, confining and weighted, such a contrast from the relative looseness of her usual gown and tartan.

"Well," pronounced Hannah, and then she said nothing more, because it was impossible not to be impressed with the grandeur of it. Their eyes met and both women broke into smiles, then laughter. Lauren held up one of the sleeves, displaying the long sweep of it.

"Who could work in such a thing?" she asked, and Hannah laughed again and shook her head. The moment faded away, leaving them in silence once more. Lauren shifted, and the gown rustled in stately folds, formal and stiff.

Hannah crossed to one of the tables in the room and came back with a looking glass in her hands. She held it up so that Lauren could see herself in it, a dusky reflection.

It was not she. It could not be, that woman there, with her long, tangled red hair and her pale cheeks. It was not she in such English finery, looking like a noble stranger from that other land, a rogue queen who had run away from her court.

Lauren stared at the image, fascinated, seeing a glimpse of someone she had never known before— a woman with her own face, yet who wore the clothing of the enemy, who looked like she belonged with them.

"I met Fuller Morgan over thirty-five years ago," said Hannah quietly, not moving the glass, not taking her gaze from the vision of Lauren in the gown. "It was a thing of chance, of pure blind fortune, that had us both become lost in a sudden storm one afternoon. I took shelter beneath a tree, terrified of the lightning, the thunder. I was but fourteen. And then there he was, running out of the storm, an Englishman coming toward me, soaked with rain. I was too afraid to even move. But he was kind to me, gentle and sweet. He smiled at me and took my hand, and that was the end of my fear. Storms have held no threat for me since that day."

Lauren stood still, listening, the woman in the glass just as intent.

"We arranged to meet about a dozen times over the next year," Hannah continued. "And each time was more precious than the last, and more magical. I did not think of the future. I could not. I thought only of him, and of what might be."

Slowly the glass lowered, and the English queen tilted

and then was gone. Only a flash of gold at her feet remained in the disk of it.

"What happened?" Lauren asked, still not moving.

Hannah bent her head and smiled to the ground, then back up at Lauren. "Only what you might think. I was already betrothed, of course, and I ended up marrying the man my father chose for me. There was nothing else I could do, not without disgracing my family. Fuller understood. Indeed, within a year he was wed as well, to someone from his own people. And the years passed, and he stayed over on his side of Shot, and I on mine. Even after my husband died, years ago, I never ventured out again to that place where we used to meet when I was a girl."

"Did you ever . . ." Lauren hesitated, then finished her thought. "Did you ever regret your choice?"

"No," Hannah replied. "I never did."

Lauren turned and walked back to the bed, touching the covers, trying not to give in to the hot stinging behind her eyes. She heard Hannah come up behind her and then beside her. The older woman reached out, placed a finger under Lauren's chin to raise her head.

"Until yesterday," she said. "When I saw him again at last, and realized what it was that I had missed all my life."

The stinging grew, became moisture that Lauren had to blink away.

"You are the daughter of Hebron," said Hannah softly. "And the bride of Murdoch. But I fear for you, my darling. I'm afraid for your future, of what you might be forced to become. You are as precious to me as my own child could have been. I do not want to see you destroyed."

Lauren moved into her embrace, and they held each other, and the tears still came.

"What should I do?" she whispered, wiping at her eyes.

"I don't know," said Hannah, mournful. "I don't know what to tell you. I don't want you to do something that will mar you for the rest of your life. I understand your heart, child. And I understand the power of your feelings." She leaned back, taking in Lauren's face. "But I do not think you will be able to live with yourself if you injure your clan. I don't think you can do that. You are perhaps the most loyal person I've ever known—along with your father. You could not live with such a betrayal in your soul."

Lauren felt herself go still and empty, the words surrounding her, sinking in. She felt the confines of the gown as if she were suddenly in chains, everything heavy on her, everything important. It had taken Hannah to tell her what she had known all along—that she could never turn her back on her own people to save just herself. That she could never leave Murdoch and run to the side of a man who was untouchable to her.

Da had set her path for her. She must continue to follow it.

The stinging was gone, her mind felt clear and pure, perhaps for the very first time since she had seen Arion du Morgan as a man. She stepped back from Hannah's arms, nodding, calm. She looked around the room and realized again its unfamiliarity to her, and why that must remain so.

Hannah looked strained, worried, so Lauren gave her a small smile and kissed her on her cheek, reassuring.

"I think you should go find your Fuller," she said. "A lifetime is a long time to have to wait, and the day is well begun already."

But Hannah did not move, so Lauren gave a wider smile, and another embrace, this one quicker, impatient. "Go on. I'm fine. You are my sanity, you know. But now I need to be alone. Go find him. I'm sure he's waiting for you, wherever he is."

After a long minute Hannah moved away, clasping Lauren's hand in a final squeeze, so dear and kind. At the door she turned around, and Lauren only waved her on.

"Be certain to rest," Hannah instructed. "We'll be leaving soon."

"I know," replied Lauren. And finally Hannah left.

THE SUNLIGHT WAS CAPRICIOUS, COMING and going through silver clouds, and Lauren watched it all from a cushioned seat on a bower at the window, her back to Arion's chamber, her head tilted against the stone.

Her hands rested loose and empty on her lap, very white against the sapphire and amber of the gown she wore, and the view before her seemed as mysterious and foreign as the clothing on her body.

It might not have been Shot out there, so different was it from her half of the island. Before her now was nothing of the ruggedness she knew; instead she had miles of long meadows, rolling hills, lone trees that stood scattered like sentinels around it all. She saw the beach from here, too, again so mild and clement, smooth and tame, with water that rolled up to perfection at its edge.

The clouds were fat and curled, tumbling and racing over the ocean in hypnotic form, highlighting long rays of sunlight that broke between them.

Since she had been expecting him, the click of the door opening was not surprising to her. But Lauren could not help the depth of the next breath she took, a brace for fortitude, for what she was about to do.

"What peace surrounds you here," she commented, not bothering to look at Arion.

She heard him walk forward into the room, across the thick rug, until he stopped behind her, not too close.

"Could you ever live in such a peace, Lauren?"

The breath in her became stabbing, painful, but she managed to say lightly, "What a question to ask me! I am certain Payton Murdoch's lands are as peaceful as these."

She waited, counting out the seconds before she turned her head to him, took in his face.

That was a mistake. There were no secrets there now, nothing hidden from her as he usually did. What she saw there was a need as raw and as powerful as what she felt, deep green eyes that pierced her, that stripped away her pretense to leave her bare and vulnerable. Lauren shifted her gaze down to her lap.

"An interesting gown you've offered me," she said. "But strange and uncomfortable, I fear. I would like my tartan back, if you please."

"I cannot give it to you."

She affected annoyance. "You would keep my own clothing from me now? To what purpose?"

Arion shrugged. "Your tartan was ruined in battle, and your fall. I don't even have it any longer. I sent it back to Keir with your men."

Lauren pinched one of the folds of amber cloth; it almost stayed in place, so heavy and unyielding. "Is this your sister's?"

"No."

"I would feel odd, wearing the gown of a woman who wanted me dead."

"Nora's clothing is back at Morgan, I should think."

Lauren dared to look up at him again, striving for nonchalance.

"She never comes here?"

"No," Arion said again. He examined her face, his look dark and hidden once more, as she was used to seeing. "Nora is in the family crypt at Morgan."

She couldn't disguise what this news did to her, and it was too late to try. She felt his pain go through her, a terrible sorrow for his loss, even though it was for someone who had tried to kill her.

"I'm sorry," Lauren said, genuine. "I didn't know."

His eyes became shuttered; he looked away from her, out to his view. "It was years ago."

She felt her bravery slowly begin to unravel, her resolution faltering. This was much more difficult than she had imagined.

It had seemed the only right thing she could do, the only solution that might spare them both from the unacceptable connection between them. She would let him know, beyond all doubts, that she did not want him. That she could never be anything to him other than someone whom fate had thrown at him for no purpose at all. She had to convince Arion that she cared nothing for him, that her heart and hopes belonged to the man she would soon wed.

What a simpleton, to think it might not be so horrible to fool him. It was worse. It was agony.

"I don't really think she meant to kill you, if it matters," Arion said indifferently. "Nora was prone to fits and visions. She spoke to voices in her head. I believe that you became something else to her than you really were. She was the most gentle girl I have ever known. She never would have tried to harm you had she been right in her mind. She couldn't bear to kill even a mouse."

"Yes," said Lauren, remembering. "She told me that. She had a mouse in her room—"

"—named Simon." He gave a short laugh, mirthless. "They were all named that. She would not let them set traps in her chamber."

He looked down at the floor, so like the young boy who had come into the dungeon cell with his uncle, troubled and lost.

"In the end," he said, "the only living thing she ever managed to harm was herself. She ended her own life, not so very long after you left Morgan. She hanged herself from her bed with one of her gowns." He indicated Lauren's in a short gesture, his voice rough. "It looked nothing like the one you wear now."

She had to turn her back to him. She had to hide

her face, to disguise the pity and sadness and distress that his words gave her.

This was absolutely not what she had wanted to happen between them. He was trusting her with this devastating news, he sounded almost as if he were confessing to her, asking for mercy, or forgiveness, she couldn't say which. His memories of his sister seemed to explain at least some of the constant ache that appeared to shadow him. She didn't want to share that with him now—or ever. She could not afford that. It would be the thing that broke her.

Lauren pushed off the bower and walked away from him, trying to keep her steps steady and firm.

"So, whose gown is it, then? Not your sister's. Perhaps a friend's?"

She looked over her shoulder at him. Arion stared at her, hard lines and tautness.

"Perhaps," Lauren suggested, still blithe, "your lover's?"

"No," he said, tight lipped. "I don't know whose it is. I told a maid to find you something. That's all."

"I cannot ride home in it," she said. "I'll need something else."

"Is that what you're considering? Riding home?"

"Naturally. Our alliance has ended, Earl of Morgan. I'm sorry to say it, but it's true. I must return to Keir, to my clan. To my wedding. My husband will be arriving soon."

"Your husband," he scoffed, taking just one step to her. "Not yet, Lauren. You're not wed to him yet."

"I am, you know. In the minds of all who matter, I already am."

"Not by any law *I* recognize," Arion stated. "You seem to forget something, my sweet. You're not in your own country any longer, you're in mine, and I rule here. I'm not convinced you should be allowed to leave."

"I am fine now. I thank you for your aid, du Morgan. I am certain Payton Murdoch would thank you as well. But see me walk, see me stand. I am able to leave. Therefore, I must. Your English ways do not suit me at all—not your home nor your clothing—not anything, really. To stay here with you any longer would be . . . offensive to me."

He stood silent, an outline of a man, and she could almost feel the anger from him, waves of it rushing at her, cold and menacing. Lauren felt her throat grow tight. She became keenly aware that she had crossed a line at some point, that her words had gone far beyond her intended effect to make him scorn her, to disdain her. She had found a barb and stabbed him with it, and now it was too late to reverse it.

"Offensive?" he repeated, deadly soft. "Do you think so?"

She actually could not say anything. She could not even try. Fear and panic wrapped around her chest, constricting her.

"Is it offensive to shelter a woman in need? Is it offensive to comfort her, to hold her as she weeps?"

He took another step toward her, and Lauren could not move her feet to flee. The fright had taken her legs and rendered them immobile.

"Are those things offensive to you?" Arion asked in a smooth voice, danger in every word. "Because I had thought it would be something far beyond those simple acts. In fact, Lauren, I had something else in mind entirely."

Again he took a step, and then another, and now he was right in front of her, and she had to tilt her head back to see his face, because she had to see him, even though what was there left the fear running feral through her.

"If I am offensive," Arion said down to her, "for these innocent things, then I have no reason not to go further. I am already damned, am I not?"

She shook her head—again, too late. He seized her by her shoulders and pulled her to him, enclosing her in an embrace that felt like steel, and his lips were hard against her skin. Lauren tried to twist away but he wouldn't let her, crushing her until she couldn't move any longer, and then he kissed her on the lips with bruising force, nothing loving or calm, only hurt, only pain.

Yet within her was the spark that still wanted him, still hungered for him, and Lauren felt it bloom and grow in her, responding even to this angry moment, softening her for him, taking her imprisoned arms and wrapping them around his waist, where she could reach him.

He had not stopped the kiss. It was as if he couldn't feel her beyond the ire in him, beyond the way he held her, rough and untamed, hot and masculine.

"Am I offensive now, Lauren?" he asked against her cheek, and one of his hands slid down to cup her buttocks, pulling her against him, allowing her to feel the hardness of him. He did not let her answer, he claimed her lips again, sucking at them, his tongue invading her in a way that sent mindless chills all through her body.

The room slipped and tilted; she found herself on her back on the floor, the rug beneath her. Lauren gasped out loud but Arion had covered her again that quickly, his body demanding over hers, ardent. He was resting between her thighs, boldly moving there with his body, making the gasp turn into a whimper at the back of her throat. A new fire was burning through her, confusion and passion becoming mingled in a heated song that came from him, from his touch, the way he held her, controlling her, mastering her.

It was too strong to resist. This was Arion, the man she had been dreaming of for what seemed forever, and so the wound in him had to become her own, or else she would perish in this fire alone.

So Lauren held on to him and kissed him back, not caring about anything else, and this at last was the thing that made him stop, held in place as she pressed up against him, every bit of him rigid.

His breath was rapid and shallow, rasped in her ear. She felt a wetness on her face and thought it might be her tears, reflection of the passion that had taken her.

Arion leaned back, looked into her eyes.

"You can't leave," he said, intense. "I won't allow it."

"Am I your prisoner, after all?" she asked softly.

"Is that what you want?" His words were harsh and broken. "Is it?"

Yes! shouted her mind, but she kept her lips pressed together.

Yet her hand moved without her will, coming up to slide through the ebony of his hair, feeling the softness of it, so appealing. It was her hand that pulled him back down to her, as simple as that, just her hand, a very slight pull, and then the desperation around him broke away, and he found her lips again.

This kiss was different, tender and achingly sweet, a pledge of something she was afraid to name. It matched the song still beating through her, it made the sparks of his touch turn wanton, leaving her defenseless, open to him. Arion slowly dragged his mouth across hers, tasting her again with his tongue, and Lauren felt a cry rise and catch in her.

It was he who moaned instead, who took his hands and held her face as he ravaged her lips, each touch like fire, like lightning, bright and fierce.

"Is it what you want?" Arion asked again. He moved to kiss her throat, then farther down, to the crescent of flesh that showed at her chest, soft and hard at once, his fingers tugging at the bodice, pulling it lower, lower, licking her skin, and Lauren thought she might go mad with the pleasure of him.

He found her breast through the gown, his hand palming it, squeezing gently, then he placed his mouth over her nipple and scored his teeth across the cloth.

She cried out, hushed and excited, and his hand came up to cover her mouth, cutting off the sound. Then he did the same thing again, but to her other breast. Lauren closed her eyes and tried not to scream.

His hand left her mouth, replaced again by his lips, a sensual caress against her, and she felt the stiff amber gown bunched up and pushed aside, the roughness of his palm on her bare leg, gliding up, finding her thigh.

He lifted himself from her and came back down in one swift move, only now the gown was around her waist, and there was nothing between her and him but his clothing, which felt appallingly thin. He held her tightly, fighting her new tension, and her eyes were wide and stunned, her lips parted on a protest that would not come.

Arion began to move, the same rhythm as before, and it surrounded her and wrapped around her even tighter; it was liquid fire and light, it was essential and unsatisfied, but oh, it felt so good.

"Is this it?" he asked, panting against her, moving his hand between them to touch her in her most intimate place. "Is this it, Lauren? Tell me."

She gave a breathless cry, and again he smothered it, closing it off with his kiss, not releasing her, building the sparks, the fire, building. . . .

"Tell me," he grated against her. "Say it."

"Yes," Lauren said, trying to feel more of him, helpless to prevent the words from escaping her. "Yes, oh, please . . ."

"Yes," Arion agreed, triumphant, and she felt him press even harder against her, his fingers covered in her wetness, teasing her, and she knew then that she would have sold her soul to let this feeling go on forever, never to stop, but if it didn't, she would surely die from it.

"Yes," he ground out. "Yes, you're mine."

The end came with shattering strength, a dissolving of light and sound and all that she was, the pulse of the ocean coursing through her, drowning her until she lost everything, all her senses, to him, to Arion.

She was crying. She couldn't stop, silent tears that were all she could express of what had just happened to her, the loss of her security, of her world.

Arion remained over her, tense and, she knew, battling his own will right now. And she lay there beneath him as open as a flower, yet still he did not move.

When she could, she raised her eyes to his and found his faced closed off, remote. He lifted himself off her with controlled suppleness, standing to straighten his tunic and hose, hiding his arousal.

Lauren sat up as fast as she could to push the amber skirts down again, though they were now hopelessly wrinkled. From there she stood, unsteady, then took a few blind steps over to the bed, away from him. He had not looked at her again.

"Would you go to him now?" Arion asked, his voice uneven. "Could you, Lauren MacRae?"

She brought her hands up to her lips and felt the aftermath of his kisses—tenderness, swelling. She took a deep breath and inhaled his scent, intoxicating.

There were no words to soothe him. There was no truth she could say to him without wounding him again, or her. There was no painless answer to the devastating problem her life had become.

Lauren could only say hopelessly: "My clan. My people."

It meant so much to her, yet she knew it would be almost nothing to him. So she turned around to see him, to let him see her, so that he could understand what he was asking her to sacrifice.

"My *family*," she said, and felt those odious tears rise again.

He stared at her, his mouth turned to something bitter and awful, his eyes stark green. She saw that he wasn't ready to give up yet, that although he could guess what it meant, he was stubborn, and he was proud. He would make her declare it beyond all doubts.

"They *need* me," Lauren said. She had to sit on the edge of the bed for support, because her legs refused to hold her up any longer. Arion didn't release her from his gaze, ruthlessly honest, brutal.

Lauren lifted her hands in the air, a supplication to him to free her from that severity. The tears were in her throat. "Please understand. I made a promise."

Sunlight came loose suddenly in the room, a pale golden wash that flared up around him, obscuring him, the tempest of his emotions, the anger and suffering for her.

A knock sounded on the door. Neither of them moved, neither of them spoke.

It came again, then the door eased open to reveal Hannah, stepping forward into the room, her eyes bright and sharp. She looked to Lauren and then to the earl. Her manner remained smooth and tranquil, and she stopped near the bed.

"There is a storm approaching, Earl of Morgan. I would like for Lauren and me to depart before it hits."

Arion did nothing for what seemed an eternity to Lauren. The sunlight around him had not changed; he remained a man of shadow and darkness.

"Yes," he said finally. "It would be wise to leave before the storm blows in full force. I will have your mounts ready for you in a few minutes, and an escort for you back to Keir. Do not tarry. Or you will be forced to remain here."

Hannah nodded. Lauren could only close her eyes, trying to shut out some of the light and dark that was him.

Chapter Eleven

*S*HE HAD RIDDEN HOME IN the gown of gold, after all.

In the end there had been no time to change, and Lauren had thought it prudent not to ignore Arion's veiled warning. They left as soon as they could—she and Hannah and some of the earl's men, and he had not even come out of Elguire to bid them farewell. She had not seen him again. And now, Lauren supposed, she never would.

Her heart was cold steel, her soul the shade of gray that matched the clouds that hung low above them, threatening winter. But she had kept her back straight, and she had not cried again.

It had caused quite a stir, the group of them approaching Keir, an English guard for one woman in a tartan and another in bright sapphire and gold. Arion's men had halted before they had actually reached the gate of Keir, as had been previously agreed; now that the alliance was over, they would not find a likely welcome from the Scots. She and Hannah had ridden alone up the final path to the castle.

People had flocked over to see her, to touch her, to eye the gown and the bruise on her head, to help her off her steed and usher her back into the walls of her home.

Lauren moved through them in a blur, trying to smile and talk to them as they were to her, trying to appear as normal as she could. There were happy faces and sterner ones, women and men who each and all had an opinion about her, about what had happened outside of Dunmar, and where she had been for the past few days.

She tried to remember that they cared for her. That they did love her, and they did need her, as she had claimed to Arion. But for the first time ever in her life, Lauren found herself doubtful, examining them carefully, seeing things she had not noticed before.

How eyes met over her head, and silent messages were exchanged.

How words became fast and furious when she moved away.

How they watched her. How closely they observed her.

Lauren realized, walking with them into the keep, that she was no longer completely in their confidence. That since the Vikings had come, and Da had died, and Arion had first kissed her hand, she had grown into the thing she had always privately feared she would—a creature of two worlds and of none, a woman with no true home, because her spirit was so impossibly torn.

It seemed laughable in sane daylight. It seemed ludicrous, to think that her people would not trust her.

But stepping into the cradle of the castle, the shadows crept over her eyes and her heart, and Lauren could more easily believe all the whispers that trailed her, a cloak of public caution that followed her.

If only they knew . . . if only they had any idea of what had actually happened between her and Arion . . . She prayed to God they never would.

She asked of Quinn and was told he was resting, he was better—but nothing else.

More than a few of her clan were viewing the golden gown with plain hostility, and it was James who finally growled down at her, "What is this thing you wear, lass? You look like no proper MacRae."

"It was just for the ride," Hannah assured them all, her hand on Lauren's elbow. "We go to her chamber now, to change."

Her room was her haven, sweet silence and no lasting stares, only Hannah, busy finding and setting out one of Lauren's regular gowns, and the square of blue and teal and emerald that was her tartan.

"You had best change," suggested Hannah mildly, when Lauren made no effort to do so.

"I know," Lauren replied. But still she didn't move.

"I will assist you." Hannah came forward and began to untie the laces of the English gown, and Lauren allowed it, numb, letting this dress from Arion peel away from her body, and then the sapphire one, until she stood shivering in her bandages on the stone and Hannah wrapped her up again in the softness of what she had always worn, and always would—sturdy Scottish clothing, everything fit and fine and seemly. The brooch of rowan was again at her shoulder.

The rogue queen's gown lay crumpled on her pallet, and Hannah bent over now and began to fold it up.

"No," Lauren said, stopping her. "I'll do it. You must be tired. Go rest."

"Are you certain?"

"Aye." Lauren nodded. "I'll see you for supper, no doubt."

"As you wish." Hannah offered her a short embrace, ending it with her hand cupping Lauren's cheek, smiling at her. "It's good to be home, isn't it?"

"Aye," said Lauren again, and then Hannah was gone.

She gazed down at the English garment before her, still resplendent despite its undignified state, glowing so richly. Lauren went and turned the lock on the door to her chamber, then reached for the dirk she always wore at her waist. Her hands grasped at nothing; she had lost the dirk down the gorge with the Viking she had killed. Very well.

In her jewelry box was another dirk, very much like her old one. A little thinner, a little longer, more tarnished with age. Her mother's. Lauren picked it up now, examining the blade. It appeared honed enough.

She sat down on her pallet, lifting the heavy hem of the amber cloth to her lap. Lauren turned it inside out, examining the stitchwork there.

When she had found the right spot she took the dirk and made a small hole in the material, where the cut of the cloth was widest from the hem, and from that hole she made an incision, the sharp blade of the dagger slicing almost with ease.

Lauren held up her prize: a narrow strip of fine amber, slight enough not to be missed from inside the gown, significant enough to her that she could curl it up into itself to make it small and tight. She took it back to the jewelry box and pushed aside Murdoch's ring to place the cloth behind her clan's badge, rolled away and hidden beneath the metal.

Not good enough. Winks of amber peeked past the brooch, and so she used the dirk again, this time to cut a nearly invisible slash near the seam of the lining of the box, and then tucked the English cloth down into that, smoothing it until there was no hint of anything improper.

She closed the lid, then fixed the dirk to the leather belt at her waist, where it belonged.

The jewelry box would accompany her when she left for the mainland, off to her future with the Murdoch. She would keep it with her always, and put away the things there that she should—her wedding ring, the rowan brooch, whatever trinkets or baubles he might see fit to give her.

And only she would know the secret hidden there. Only she would know about the stolen strip of gold from an English queen's gown, and that she had been that queen for just a day—for an English knight who had awakened her heart and then burned it to ash . . . the day she would carry with her for the rest of her life.

---

*D*INNER PASSED AND SHE ENDURED it, and surely it was not her imagination that everyone seemed a little heartier around her now, dressed as one of them again.

Lauren took her usual seat at the head table and felt a sad surprise to see her father's empty chair. She had not been gone so long, but already the memory of his death had faded.

It was an enchantment, perhaps, cast over her by the Earl of Morgan, to ease her pain. It could be no less.

When he had held her and let her release her tears to him, all the fears and wrath from Da's death had seemed slowly to dispel, leaving only the sorrow behind, only the grieving for him.

It was a keepsake from her enemy, unexpected, unprecedented. When Arion had wrapped his arms around her and taken in her anguish, she had felt such a heavy relief from it all. She would never have guessed it possible, what he had done. Yet it had been real, and the proof was that she was able to sit beside the empty seat of the laird and feel almost none of the barrenness of before, none of the blank numbness.

But she was sore and fatigued and it must have shown, for people were kind to her, courteous now, and after just a few bites of grilled fish and bread Lauren had to retire, back up to her room, where the darkness was a close companion, and the clouds beyond her window glowed pale and ghostly in the night.

She slept.

Morning came and the air left no doubt as to the winter approaching. But when she looked out her window there were only the same clouds as before, low and bubbling against Shot, dark grays and pearls surrounding the landscape.

The council would be meeting this morning. She must not miss it. Perhaps she could persuade them against Rhodric. Perhaps she could convince them anew that the du Morgans were potent allies, vital friends on Shot. It could be her final gift to Arion, the tempered goodwill of her people before she left the island forever.

Lauren dressed in a hurry and rushed down the stairs. She could tell by the light in the sky that she would be late but not too much so. She rounded the corner of the entrance to the great hall and stopped, slightly breathless, staring at the scene before her.

The room was filled with people, many more than was normal for the meeting. The elders of the council were discussing something among themselves, a few heads nodding, a few shaking. Their voices were rumbles across the room to her, deep and serious as they always were, but that was not what had halted her.

Her father's chair was no longer empty. Her cousin Quinn sat there.

He spied her across the distance and waved her forward, and Lauren obeyed his command, though her mind seemed mired in astonishment. Yes, it was Quinn, much paler than before, and so much thinner, but it was he, her father's heir.

Quinn was in Da's chair. She could no longer sit there for the meetings. She could no longer take his place. She could no longer speak her thoughts, give voice to reason, echo the spirit that had been Hebron.

Quinn was the laird, awake again.

And Lauren understood—instantly and inexorably—that she was nothing more than a woman once more, bride of Murdoch, key to a very different sort of alliance than she had hoped.

It was confirmed in every face before her, in varying degrees of satisfaction, or pity, or musing quiet. She felt it pound through her, the insurmountable fact of her future and her role in the clan. Almost everyone had noticed her by now, turning to look, to judge her.

"Lauren," greeted Quinn, and he alone had a smile for her. He stood awkwardly and came around the table in stiff steps, and she moved across the hall to embrace him, blinking at his chest.

"How do you fare?" she managed to ask, pulling back.

He smiled again and she saw Da in a second, the same way his eyes narrowed in humor, the same easy spirit. "They tell me I'll live, though if I see even one more leech, I'm not so certain."

His face sobered, and he bent his head to her, private words. "Your Da," he began, and then shook his head.

"I know," Lauren said, holding his hands. "It's over now. He'd be so proud to see you here."

Both of them fell quiet; Lauren heard the expectant silence of the elders behind them, watching, a few shifting around in their chairs, taking drinks from goblets.

"Well," said Quinn now, with every bit of Da's charm. "We're having a meeting, lass. You're a bit too early to break your fast, but mayhap you can convince the cook to offer you something—"

"I'm here for the meeting," Lauren said firmly.

And instead of the resistance she had been expecting, Quinn only shrugged and turned away, not looking at her, which was her first clue that he had known all along why she had come, and that he was not yet ready to ban her completely.

The elders were not so compliant. They threw her bristled looks while Quinn sat again, their hands knuckled together in opposition.

Lauren took a seat on a bench as near to them as she could, next to a few of the warriors she knew. She waited while the meeting dragged on, discussions of things that seemed ridiculously unimportant to her right now— fishing conditions, whose boat needed repair the most, the amount of wool stored away at Keir for weaving, the date of the wedding coming up. . . .

She glanced up from where she had been resting her chin on her fist, drowsing in spite of herself, and found still that none of the men were looking at her, although they discussed the arrival of the Murdoch in tones of such certainty, and the fact of her marriage in words that made it seem as if it had already happened.

Disconcerting, and vexing. But when the council had worked out the details of the celebration that bothered them—had they enough swine fattened, had enough ale been prepared?—all the men began to push their chairs back and rise, a sign that the meeting was over.

Lauren quickly stood.

Quinn acknowledged her with a nod, forcing the other men to sit again, pinched lips and shifting eyes.

"What of the alliance with the du Morgans?" she asked them all. "You didn't discuss that."

"We did," replied Quinn. "While you were at El- guire." He hesitated, then said, "I'm sorry, Lauren."

"But—"

"It's over, lass," said Quinn now, firmer. "It worked for a time, but now it is ended."

"But the meadow!" she said anyway, disbelieving. "And the Vikings there! We fought as one! We de- feated them only because we were united!"

"We would not have had to fight that battle were it not for your alliance," claimed James. "Those Vikings were on du Morgan land. It would have been their fight alone."

"They were stealing *our* sheep, from *our* village," Lau- ren retorted.

"And *our* lads died for it on *English* land," said Ranulf now, curt. "We've lost enough men for the du Morgans."

"You must not do this thing!" Lauren stepped around the table in front of her, addressed them all. "You must not be so shortsighted as to let this end, when the threat is not yet over!"

" 'Must not?' "

It was the voice she least wanted to hear, Rhodric, standing up from a table on the other side of the room. " 'Must not?' " he repeated, light and mocking. "You cannot tell the council what they must and must not do, Lauren. Leave this work to the men!"

His words began a slow wave of comment around the hall, approval and masculine nods. Rhodric glanced around, then looked back at her, superior. "It is not your place to question the decisions made here."

"I am a member of this clan! It *is* my place to question them, when I think they are folly. And this would be naught but folly! We *need* the du Morgans, we need their cooperation. Without them, we will only lose more men!"

"It was a trial, Lauren." James glared down at the audience, his eyes skipping over her. "We knew it from the start. Do not argue to change the laird's mind."

"The laird—" Lauren began hotly, then stopped herself, realizing what it was she was about to say.

The laird would want this. The laird would want his daughter to show the clan peace, and strength through unity.

But not *this* laird, apparently.

The hall was utterly silent, locked in agreement against her, and Lauren felt the futility of her argument. Every face before her was closed and tight, shut against what-ever she might say. No one would listen to her.

She stood alone, feeling like an outsider again in front of these people, men and women she had known her entire life. They turned away from her now, stone cold and rigid, every one of them, even Quinn.

Lauren shook her head, perplexed and hurt, and then walked out of the hall, leaving everyone, everything. They let her go without a word.

She found herself wandering without direction through the depths of the keep, lost in her sense of surprised misery, isolated from the one thing she had always assumed would hold her dear and close: the clan, the MacRaes, her very own kin.

The day was dark and cold and inside Keir it was no less so, with torches and lamps that gave off only short stabs of light. She knew every inch of it, every slate-blue stone, every room, every turret. She knew all the views from all the windows, and which areas were best in summer, or winter, and which had the strongest drafts, and which the nicest tapestries. She had spent the whole of her life here, laughing and lov-ing and growing.

Today was the end of that. Today she became a stranger to it all, because, God help her, she didn't even know herself any longer.

Run away, whispered a wicked voice inside her. *Run to him. Leave it all. Be with him, only him, and find your happiness. . . .*

Lauren stopped, putting her hands over her eyes, lean-ing against a wall of the hallway, pressing back the urge to surrender to that selfish want.

"Lauren?" It was Vanora, coming up to her with concern. "What is it? Are you ill?"

"No." Lauren straightened up.

Vanora studied her for a moment, then said, "I'm glad I've found you here. We were just about to go looking for you. Your gown is ready."

"My gown?" Lauren thought of the amber and sapphire dress, lying flat over one of her chests in her chamber, ready to be returned to Elguire.

"Your wedding gown, lass. Come try it on. We're all eager to see it on you."

And she indicated an open door that Lauren had just walked past, light spilling from it, faint feminine voices.

Lauren allowed herself to be pulled in.

They surrounded her and congratulated her, they stripped her of her clothing and put Murdoch's on her, and Lauren examined her wedding dress impartially, distant from all the praise that the other women were expressing.

It fit well now, altered for her figure. It looked acceptable. It was plain but not too much so, it was decided. And with the tartan of the Murdochs over it, surely it would be a lovely thing to see.

They pulled out the tartan and folded it over her—brown and russet and thin blue lines—and then someone brought out a mirror and held it up to Lauren's face, showing her the reflection there.

A Scotswoman stared back at her, pale and unsmiling. She wore a tartan that looked too stiff on her, and a gown that bleached the color from her cheeks. She was duty and common sense, honor and obligation. The woman in the glass was as far from a rogue queen as could be. The woman there would never hold soft dreams for an English knight, not for any reason.

". . . would be better. What do you think, Lauren?"

"Hmm?" She wrenched her eyes away from the pallid figure in the glass.

"Swine or swan?"

Lauren stared at them all blankly. One of the women clucked her tongue in impatience.

"Roasted suckling or feathered swan, Lauren? For the first course of the wedding feast."

She tried very hard not to sigh. "It doesn't matter."

"Of course it does!" It was Michal, indignant. "We cannot insult the Murdoch with an inferior meal! Now, I know that you wanted the swine, Clara, but think how lovely it would be to present the swan, cooked and stitched back up in her own feathers. You know we've managed that before, and it worked so well. I think it was for Enid's wedding—"

"No, no, you're thinking of Arlene's wedding. . . ."

Lauren stared out the window, at the roiling mass of clouds, the skeleton outlines of the trees near the keep. It would snow soon. The first snow of the season, soft white dust covering the island. She had always looked forward to it as a girl. Right now, however, it just seemed unbearable.

"Swan, then. We all agree. And swine to follow, of course. Naturally, Clara will make her special mulled wine, and Judith her gull pies—"

"I have to go," said Lauren suddenly, her fingers working at the tartan, to get it off her.

"What are you doing, lass? Stop! Stop, I say! You'll

ruin it, tearing at it so!" The seamstress slapped her hands away, glaring.

"Where do you go, Lauren?" asked Vanora.

"The patrol," she improvised. "I'm riding out this morning with them. I'll be late."

It happened again, that knowing connection of eyes all around her, beyond her. Lauren felt her fingers grow cold, but she pretended to ignore it all, moving away from them, fussing with the gown. Someone came up before her, blocking her way. She looked up to meet Michal's irritated gaze.

"You'll need to be at Keir when your fiancé arrives," stated Michal, a clear challenge. "You cannot keep running off like a heathen to fight with the men whenever you want. The Murdoch will be here any day, and how are we to explain to him that you're gone on some foolish ride, instead of greeting him properly as you should?"

"Explain to him that his bride is off defending her home," Lauren said tartly. "If he wants some simpering maid, I'm afraid he's going to be sorely disappointed."

"Well, that's what I expect," snapped Michal. "That he will be disappointed in you! Any man would be, to find his bride so uncivilized!"

Lauren lost the last shred of control on her temper.

"Then let him marry someone else!"

There was a shocked silence all around her. No one moved, every face was turned to her in stunned disbelief. And then:

"Lauren! You don't mean it!"

She didn't want to answer that. She had to.

"No. Of course I don't mean it." She took a deep breath and released it slowly. "But I do have to leave now. I am riding out on patrol today."

Again came that stilted silence, laden with meaning that was not meant for her to understand.

"Did you discuss this with anyone, lass?" asked Vanora, concerned.

"Yes," Lauren lied.

"We thought you would be spending more time here, at Keir," countered Clara, looking to Michal. "We thought you'd be more interested in your wedding."

"Well, I am interested. But I'm needed on patrol."

"That's not what James said." Michal folded her arms across her chest, victory in the tilt of her head. "He said that you weren't going to go on patrol any longer."

"That it was to be only the men from now on," added Clara. "You're to stay at Keir until the Murdoch comes, preparing for your wedding. That's what he said, and the laird and the council agreed. They will not allow you on patrol."

The lie stayed caught in Lauren's mouth, freezing her tongue in place. She was finally trapped, and she knew it.

"Oh dear, she's going to faint," said someone, very distant.

Lauren swallowed and fought it, moving away from them all. "I'm all right! I'm only a bit tired, nothing more."

"Of course you are," comforted Vanora, and guided her over to a chair. "We'll get you right out of this gown, and then you'll go back to your chamber for a good, long nap. All this excitement can be so wearing, I know. And you, poor lass, not yet healed from all that's happened, I'm sure. . . ."

Lauren let them minister to her again, focusing on the gray outside, trying to stay calm amid it.

———————— ⟨ᴔᴘᴪᴔ⟩ ————————

Sʜᴇ ᴡᴏʀᴇ ᴀɴ ᴏʟᴅ ᴄʟᴏᴀᴋ, gray like everything else about her now, thick and with a tattered hem. It had been one of her favorites of them all, perhaps because Da had given it to her, or because it was so sturdy and warm. For some reason she had put it away for more than a few seasons. But now it was perfect again, and the hood of it not only kept her own heat close to her but aided in her anonymity.

Not that she was hiding. She had no need to hide. Indeed, it would have been impossible anyway. She had to be seen to claim her horse from the stables, and one of the lads there helped her to saddle her mare with nothing but solemn stares. She thanked him briskly, then trotted out to the gate of Keir.

The gatekeeper nodded to her, and ordered the gate lowered so that she could pass. That had been her greatest fear, that she might be forcibly kept here, that they might actually mean to make her a sort of pampered prisoner.

But all the man said was, "Where you off to, lass?"

"Black Beach," she replied, which was the truth. She was not actually running away. She just needed to feel the air on her face and taste the ocean wind again. She needed to be as alone as she could, to sift through her thoughts. But she would be back.

"Don't stay too long," instructed the man. "Snow's coming, and the day is short."

"Aye," replied Lauren, and spurred her mount on.

Black Beach was aptly named; although the sand remained the same color as all the rest on Shot, a mellow gold, it had a variety of large and jagged boulders rising from that sand, black as pitch, odd shapes and chunks that made riding it a hazard at best, impossible at worst.

So she dismounted, letting the mare walk beside her, and lifted her head so that her hood was pushed back by the wind and she could see the beauty all around her.

Keir was not very distant, a magnificent shadow over the woods behind her.

This beach was long and wildly crooked, the boulders that heaved everywhere making it that much more challenging to find a clear path in the sand. The mare was having difficulty, so Lauren led her over to a bush and tied the reins to a branch, making certain that her steed would have shelter from the constant wind.

The mare bent her head and began to nose around at some dried strands of grass that had grown nearby. Lauren walked back out to the beach.

There *was* a storm coming, she could see it now eating up a corner of the sky, vicious black clouds from the gray. It was moving remarkably swiftly toward Shot, sweeping closer over a heavy ocean mist that lingered offshore. Indeed, as Lauren paused at the edge of the water, she could almost mark the distance being closed, counting out the seconds as the storm grew, and grew.

It would be a cold one. She felt that already, she heard it in the howl of the wind and the angry crash of the surf before her. It seemed to suit her mood, however, so she did not turn back toward Keir. She walked on.

As a girl she had played games amid these black boulders with the other children of the clan, hiding games, climbing games, races. The largest of the rocks had names: Auld Blackie, Big Lad, Fiona's Gown, Giant's Head. . . .

A spray of water caught her by surprise. The tide was rising rapidly, spurred on by the wind. It came again, catching her up to her ankles this time, and Lauren jumped away from it, clutching her cloak and gown up to her knees. She was not fast enough, and the water tugged at her with icy fingers, then fell away.

Time to go back.

She didn't want to. She was freezing and now wet on top of it, her eyes tearing and her nose and lips almost numb. But she didn't want to go back just yet.

Lauren had a sense of being in a moment of decision, of standing on top of a hill and looking back from where she had come, and forward to where she was to go. Here on this zigzagged beach she realized why it was she had braved the bitter weather. She was saying good-bye to it all, to Arion and her clan and the place that had always been her home.

Snow began to fall, light and delicate despite the wind, stark white against the black boulders surrounding her.

She was walking through a tunnel made by two tremendous rocks that tilted against each other, marking a natural turn in the beach, from facing south to facing west. These two rocks—dubbed Turning Point by some long-ago MacRae—formed an arch that was about as tall as a man and twice as long. For a few seconds, as

Lauren entered it and became encompassed by the stone, the wind stopped, the snow ceased. It was utterly silent.

She paused and closed her eyes, feeling relief that at last she was able to hide, to become invisible to everything else in the world, even the elements.

Then she took a step out of the tunnel, and looked out onto calamity.

Men were on the beach before her, moving through the drifting snow. Many, many men, an army of men, pulling boats up to shore, splashing through the waves, wielding axes and broadswords and quivers of arrows. The wind turned and brought her their voices, gibberish, low and secretive. Row upon row of longships sliced through the mist and the waves, the black sky behind them speckled with white, and before Lauren could even think to turn and run for help, she was spotted.

One of the Vikings pointed to her and gave a shout. She didn't wait for the others to look. She whirled around and slid in the sand, kicking it up behind her, pushing off the tunnel walls in her haste.

She was running so fast that the boulders were a true danger, but she could not slow down. She had to make it back to Keir. She had to warn them.

The snow blinded her, cold wetness in her eyes. Her foot struck a rock and she fell hard onto the sand, breathing in the grit, but Lauren launched herself back up and took off again. She could hear her pursuer behind her now—heavy, running steps. When she dared to risk a look at him he was much closer than she had thought, his teeth bared in a grimace, massive and bearded and gaining so fast.

Her mare was standing alert where she had been

left, looking at Lauren with alarmed brown eyes as she scrambled up the mild slope to the brush. Her speed spooked the mare, which yanked at the reins and whinnied in distress as Lauren tried frantically to untie them.

They were knotted too tightly now; the mare had not calmed. The man was closer, so close, almost upon her. . . .

Lauren took out her dirk and cut the leather straps with trembling hands, freeing the mare. Then she was knocked down to the sand, and the dirk went flying. Her horse galloped away.

She rolled instinctively, bringing her hands up to defend herself, but the Northman was much larger, capturing her easily, nearly crushing her with his weight. She managed to jab at his throat to make him cough, but that was all—then he had both of her wrists locked in one of his hands. He struck her across the jaw with the other one.

She saw bright blue light that dissolved to darkness, amazingly painless. And then the weight on her vanished, leaving only the wind to tug at her cape, howling in her ears.

What had happened? She must have fainted, or it had never been real at all, no Viking, no invasion—

Someone called her name, curt and cut off, and Lauren lifted herself out of the sand to see Arion struggling with the man who had hit her, blood on both of their faces, sand flying around them as they rolled and fought.

Arion yelled her name again and she got to her knees, disoriented. She saw his head turn to see her rise; it seemed to give him a renewed fury. His attention fell back to the Northman, a force of untamed power that could not be stopped. The other man was weakening, his face shining red with blood, his eyes puffed and split. Arion was growing stronger, if that was possible, and with one final blow the Viking fell away, dead or merely unconscious, Lauren didn't know.

Arion clambered to his feet and ran to her, pulling her up with a quick yank, and Lauren went into his arms and lifted her head as though it was the one thing she had been waiting her whole life to do.

His kiss was bloodied and hard, quick and filled with salt and sand. He leaned back and kissed her forehead next, holding her to him tightly, and she was holding him just as close.

"Did he hurt you?" Arion asked, still breathing hard.

Lauren shook her head, a crazed mixture of joy and fright racing through her.

"You've got to get out of here." He pushed her away, the look on his face severe. "Run back to Keir."

"No," she said, though she knew he was right. "I won't leave you!"

"Get out of here!" Arion gave her a little shove toward the woods, back the way her mare had run. "There aren't enough of us here to win this battle, Lauren! We're going to need your help! You've got to get to Keir!"

She wanted to argue; she wanted to take his hand and pull him away from the violence with her, but she knew that both of these wants in her were wrong.

"Go," he said, much gentler. Snowflakes began to grace his hair, his shoulders, in feathery layers. "Please, Lauren—go. I need you to be safe."

Then his eyes moved past her, to the Turning Point, and Lauren saw the change in him. It made her turn around and take in what it was that made the green of his eyes so dark and resigned.

"Damn," she heard him say.

The Vikings were pounding through the black stone tunnel, running straight toward them.

Chapter Twelve

———————⟨∞∞⟩———————

ARI COULDN'T BELIEVE THEIR BAD fortune.

His patrol had been near the border of the island on his orders, some foolish whim of his to bring him as close to Lauren MacRae as he could without igniting a new war between the families.

But instead of discovering Lauren on patrol, they had seen the Viking longships, a great line of them appearing all at once, cutting through the thick ocean mists to land on Shot.

He had done what he could. He had sent his swiftest man back to Elguire, to gather his army, and the rest of his patrol had marked the passage of the Northmen in almost prosaic silence, following the ships as they made their way closer to shore, even when it meant they had to cross onto MacRae land to keep the Vikings in sight.

There was never any doubt that there were not enough men on his patrol to take on the many who had to be manning those ships. It would be only time, really, that would tell him the odds of the battle. He could not allow the invaders to gain too much ground on Shot, and at some point he would be forced to confront them. But how soon before Elguire sent help? And would the patrol from Keir see the ships as well?

Yet none of his men wavered, and none suggested retreat until their numbers were stronger. In each face Ari had seen the same stoic determination as that which filled him. When the Vikings landed, they would engage them in battle, until either every one of them was dead or help had arrived.

No one wanted it to be a slaughter, however. To waste lives on an unplanned attack would be foolish. So they had watched and followed, guessing where the invaders might land, deciding that the obscure beach with the black boulders studding it would be the most likely place—merely because it was so *unlikely* for a sane man to try to land a boat there.

It was hidden and sheltered from the view of both Elguire and even Keir, yes, but it was also a gauntlet of peril for any wooden craft, razor-sharp rocks residing just beneath the water.

And sure enough, it was there that the rowboats from the longships headed. It was there that they dragged their crafts to shore, infesting a place where they would not so easily be seen from the woods or another shore.

Arion and his men tried to count the Northmen as they drew close to the beach, since once on Shot the numbers became confused as men scurried in and out of the rocks.

Ari gave up counting at two hundred. And, God curse it, there were more ships coming.

He watched with grim humor as it finally began to snow.

Arion had gathered his group together, seriously rethinking their suicidal attack, when Fuller wordlessly took his arm and pointed back to the beach.

Ari turned, sharp eyed, and what he saw there made his heart lurch up into his throat.

A woman stood framed between two huge stones, her hair loose and blowing against the black of them in a beckoning copper wave, the snow a slanting curtain of white before her. But for her hair she was perfectly motionless, staring at the invaders, surprise and wonder on her face.

Dear God, it was Lauren. And she was about to die.

One of the Vikings gave a shout and pointed to her. Ari saw her at last gather her wits and turn to bolt. But he knew she didn't have a chance.

He was running to her without thought. He was breaking past the last of the bush and scrub, racing to get to her before the man chasing her did. Some part of him at least remembered stealth, which was probably what saved him. He didn't leave the bushes until the last minute, not giving the Norsemen a chance to see him until he was beyond them, and far from where he had left his own group. It was the warrior part of him, no doubt, that took over when his rational thoughts went blank, went running around in looping circles that had just one phrase repeated, over and over: *save her, save her, save her. . . .*

Ari had fought before, and well enough to live through this. He was not going to succumb to death now. Not before he reached Lauren.

And it was the warrior in him that had quelled the threat to her, that had pulled the filthy Viking off her, rage and fury scoring through him.

He thought he had won. He thought he had done it, he had managed to save her.

But now he saw that all he had done was delay their deaths, because the line of men screaming for them across the beach would absolutely kill them both. The woods were too far to reach in time, and there was no one nearby to aid them.

Arion picked up his shield from where it had fallen in the fight with the Viking, then pushed Lauren behind him, readying his sword. He heard her breathing, quick and shallow, and then she was down on her knees in the sand, sifting through it for something. He didn't dare look away from the men to see what she was doing. Then she was back beside him, a glint of sharp silver in her hand—a dirk, her only defense.

At least he had kissed her once more. At least that.

"I love you," he said to her, and from the corner of his eye he saw her look up at him, startled.

"What?" she asked, but there was no time for him to answer. The first of the men was there, and he was already swinging his sword.

It was war, a familiar monster to Arion, and he knew the steps by heart, the advance and the retreat, the cunning and the brutality. He was fighting three at once, and then four, and then five, and still he was managing to keep Lauren behind his shield, away from them. Part of him noticed that she was holding her dirk aloft, ready to strike, but it was a distant recognition. The battle was his world now.

A blow to his arm, barely felt. Screams and words that made no sense, and then another blow, this one to his shoulder, and another, to his ribs. Lauren was busy now as well—in spite of his best efforts, a Northman had gotten around him to her, and she was fighting like a wildcat, making the invader hesitate, so quick with her dirk that Arion couldn't even follow her movements.

But they would get to her, and to him. It was just a matter of time.

From the woods came a new call, one he knew well: the sound of his own men from the patrol, breaking past the line of trees, running toward him and the rest of the invaders, forcing their attention to shift to face this new threat.

Two of his five attackers fell off, one with a deep gash down his front that Ari had managed to inflict, and then one more was gone, drawn away into the conflict with his men. That left two for Arion—the one who still fought him, and one who fought Lauren.

Ari heard her cry out and then she stumbled against him; she had been hurt, and he felt it split through him as if it were his own flesh. He gave an agonized shout and quickly killed the man before him, then leaped aside and took down her assailant, a rushing lethal blow that was over before he realized it had begun. The man fell to the sand with a heavy, muffled sound.

Ari reached for Lauren, trying to hold her, to bring her to him.

"Where is it?" he shouted over the noise, his sword dipped in bright scarlet. "Where did he wound you?"

Her arm was bleeding, almost the identical location where he had been cut, but on her how it weakened him. How it made him hurt for her.

"What was it you said, before?" she shouted back to him now, cradling her arm.

A man came tumbling into Arion and they both went falling to the ground, clashing blades, his shield flying away, useless. Arion finished it as quickly as he could but it still wasn't quick enough. When he looked up again, Lauren was battling another Northman. She had picked up the axe of one of the felled around her and was swinging it with skilled concentration, her hair flowing with the storm wind. The man in front of her was dodging her, looking to grab the axe. Lauren managed to strike him once, near the arm. He edged away but came back, still trying to disarm her, to find a chance to stab her.

Arion rose to his feet and was immediately hit by another man, and then another. He lost sight of Lauren in the flurry of snow and sand.

There was no feeling in his left arm. He didn't bother to look down to see what had happened. He could still grip his sword, and that was all that mattered. The men before him were tenacious and fierce, but Ari knew he had the natural edge.

All they wanted was the land.

But Arion had much more at stake. He had Lauren, and that was everything.

It gave him the strength to kill them both, messy and cruel or quick and merciful, it made no difference to him. Let them all die. He was going to save Lauren.

His hands knew how to move; his sword cut and tore and jabbed and sliced. He managed to catch glimpses of her beyond the fury, still standing, still wielding her axe, though she was not able to hold it as high as she should.

He killed the last Northman almost easily, then jumped over the body, searching through the wind. He found her by her hair, a banner of fire in this icy world, and charged over just in time to see her swing again.

The Viking staggered and went to his knees. Arion pushed him the rest of the way down, then dragged Lauren to his side, searching wildly for shelter for her.

She stared up at him, blood smeared across her face—her mouth and forehead and cheekbones—from where he had kissed her.

"What was it you said?" she demanded again.

His men were losing, and losing badly. Even worse, he saw no way to get Lauren away from this atrocity. They were outnumbered and surrounded, with more invaders joining in, death in their shouts, insanity in their eyes. There seemed an inexhaustible supply of them, and it filled Ari with deep despair. He would not be able to rescue her after all.

"What was it—" She began again, but the rest of her words were drowned out by a new sound, a new call. It was a rising surge of voices, the battle cry of a throng of men, and from the woods now rushed a promise of new blood: dozens and dozens of tartan-clad warriors, brandishing their own insanity with broadswords and mace and morning stars.

Arion pushed Lauren back until they were both against one of the massive boulders, wind and war baying around them, and then he turned to her, holding her shoulders.

"Stay here," he ordered. "Do not move from this rock."

"No," she said, grabbing at the sleeve of his chain mail, slipping. "What are you doing? Wait for them to advance, to break through—"

"Do not move!" he called again, edging out into the storm.

And again it was nearly effortless to fend off those

who were trying to reach her, to set himself up as her guard until finally he discerned a face he recognized through the snow and the shouts. Without losing sight of Lauren, he yelled out to the man.

"MacRae! Over here!"

The impetuous youth named Rhodric threw him a wild glance, fighting off two men. Ari joined in, and the men were wounded and then gone. Ari stopped the Scot from sprinting off to a new fight.

"Lauren is over there!" he shouted, using his sword to point at her, vivid against the rock. He supposed her arm was too badly hurt to support the axe any longer. She was stemming the blood with the hand that still clutched her dirk, ready to fight. "Help me get her out of here!"

And to his surprise Rhodric did not argue with him or show any shock at all to find her in the midst of this chaos. Instead, the man nodded and ran to her, and Ari followed. With one of them on each side of her, they began the mad exercise of trying to cut through the swath of men who were intent on destroying one another.

There came a point when Arion realized that the loss of his own blood was beginning to affect him. He was feeling a little too disconnected from the battle, he was losing the steadiness of his thoughts even as he was actively fighting. He kept worrying about Lauren beside him instead of the men in front of him . . . the pallor of her face, the darkened red of her hair, wet from snow and blood. She glanced back at him and Arion lost his focus entirely, thinking that he had honestly never seen anything more fair than she was, right now.

Someone pushed into him and he fell over on his back, abruptly seeing the sky instead of Lauren, and then the face of one of the savages, ripped and bruised, snarling. But the man's eyes widened; his mouth opened and blood dribbled out with a prolonged groan. He was gone, and there was Lauren again, beautiful magic. She pulled her dirk from the Viking's back, then leaned over Ari, trying to drag him up again.

"Leave him," Ari heard someone command, and a hand reached out and plucked at Lauren, but she shook it off, her fingers wrapped around the collar of his hauberk.

"Arion, Arion," she was saying, pulling at him, and he tried to follow her, he tried to rise.

The world swam, snow and water and trees mocking him, moving in such a strange whirl that he couldn't easily find his balance. When he was on his feet again he found a new arm around him, and looked to see his steward at his side, helping to support him.

"Go on," said Fuller to Lauren and Rhodric. "Get her to safety. There's a break through the woods over there."

"Yes," Ari said, the word only slightly slurred. "Go."

Lauren began to struggle against the Scot who held her, trying to reach Ari again, but Ari knew that the young Scotsman was stronger than she, and so it proved. He began to shove her roughly to the trees, and another Scot came and aided him, and together they were managing to move her.

Arion closed his eyes. Even the darkness moved and slid, so he opened them again. "Over there," he said, and indicated one of the many rocks.

Fuller helped him stagger to it and lean there. The vast number of bodies lying everywhere turned the beach dark, and then light, as the snow came and covered them.

"A chest wound," said Fuller. "And your arm."

Ari stared down at him, confused. His steward seemed to be speaking through a wall of noise. It grew and faded with rhythmic certainty, matching his heartbeat.

"You must sit," Fuller said now, and eased Arion down to the sand. His face was lined and exhausted. A vicious gash across one cheek had dried to a crust.

"How much longer?" Ari asked, and Fuller knew what he meant.

"Not long," he responded, his hands busy doing something remarkably awful to Arion's upper arm, a tight binding that sent the pain throbbing. "Our men arrived half an hour ago, shortly after the Scots. But there are more Northmen landing. They still outnumber us."

"Damn them to hell," Ari said, with feeling.

"Aye," agreed Fuller, and kept working at Arion's wound.

"Stop." Arion tried to push him away with the arm that still worked. Fuller ignored him, eyes narrowed.

"Go back to Elguire," Arion said. "Barricade yourselves in . . . be ready for . . ."

He lost his thought again, seeing the snow sifting past him, the dim shapes and noises that managed to penetrate the haze of his mind.

"Elguire is ready for a siege, my lord." Fuller did that painful thing again, a cinching agony, and Ari let out his breath instead of yelling, as he wanted to do. "There is naught else to do for them."

"Go back . . ."

"Nay." The steward leaned back at last, his hands on his thighs, and Ari saw that they were completely red, dripping. For some reason it made him want to laugh.

Fuller stood now, his sword and shield raised again, his back to Ari. Arion wondered where his own sword was and was amazed to find it still in his hand, his fingers clenched around the hilt. That was good. That had to be a good sign, that he had not lost his sword. . . .

There was a shift in the constant noise around him, a rise in it, and then a fall and a cheer, unlikely and interesting. It made him sit up taller, and then inch his way up the stone, fighting his own senses now, which told him to bend over and lie down to die.

"What is it?" Ari asked.

Fuller had run a few steps away from him, staring out to the ocean.

"More ships!" he cried.

Arion gritted his teeth together, trying keep his head straight. It was the end. He must meet it with distinction.

"Not longships," Fuller continued. "Not Viking ships! They wave the Scottish flag, my lord! They're cutting off the invaders!"

Ari stumbled out beside him. He had to see for himself.

Out on the high dark waves, past the storm that was turning to sleet, was a battalion of war ships, large and impressive, moving toward and into the midst of the Viking ships. A portion of them split off, racing to Shot. The longships began to scatter.

The battle was turned. Even the invaders onshore seemed to feel it, the renewed strength of the MacRaes and du Morgans, the rebounding hopes.

Arion found himself sitting, something solid at his back, and realized that Fuller was in front of him again, trying to get him to lie all the way down.

"No," Ari protested. "I'm going to fight . . ." But the rest of his sentence faded away, tangled in the weight of his tongue, and he found himself adrift in a whirlpool of snowflakes that swept around him, until they dissolved to dusky nothing.

$\mathcal{S}$HE NEARLY MANAGED TO GET away from Rhodric and the other man when they were broadsided by four invaders, and everyone fought, Lauren forgetting her wounded arm in her desperation, using the dirk to cut her way out of the mess of them. But she could not leave her clansmen to fight alone, so she turned back to defend them, and saw that the Northmen were already down.

"Lauren, we must go on!" called Rhodric, reaching for her. She had already started her race back to the beach, back to Arion. Rhodric was there again, holding her, but Lauren struggled and cried:

"No, look! Look out on the water!"

And they all did, so they all saw the new ships come tearing in, pushing the enemy out to sea. Fire erupted on at least two of the longships, perhaps more, and three others were beginning to sink. It was hard to see past the falling snow but the hulking shadows of them soaring up to shore were unmistakable.

"Praise God!" exclaimed the man on the other side of her.

Rhodric let out a whoop, releasing Lauren and then hugging her to him; she pushed away from him.

"They're running!" Rhodric was laughing, shouting. "Look at them run!"

And it ended just that swiftly. The Vikings ashore had apparently assessed their new situation, and most were breaking off the fights, speeding back toward the water, and their boats there. Even still the Scots and English were chasing them, joined now by this new army of men, and fewer and fewer of the Vikings were making it to safety.

"Let's go," Lauren said, and shouldered past them to return to the beach, not waiting to see if they followed.

"Lauren!" Rhodric was beside her. "You need to return to Keir!"

"It's safe enough now," she responded, still moving.

"You're hurt, you need—"

She stopped, rounding on him. "You go back if you like. I'm going to see those Vikings defeated. Don't tell me you don't want the same thing."

He hesitated, looking at the last of the battle, the fleeing men, the light of something hectic and feverish in his eyes. Lauren kept going.

She pretended to be heading toward where the new forces were landing, the way all the others were. But when Rhodric and the other man drew slightly ahead of her, entranced, she veered off, back to where she had last seen Arion.

Bodies were piled everywhere. Some were not yet dead, eerie moans rising over the wind and surf, and it was this that she feared the most, that he was alive and awake, suffering without recourse. The snow was mingled moisture on her face, cold wetness mixed with the warmth of her tears, her fear for Arion du Morgan.

Oh God, where was he? She couldn't tell, it was all blood and body parts and clouded eyes. There were others moving through the dead, like her, clansmen and du Morgans, finding the wounded, ministering to them. But where was Arion?

She found him slumped against one of boulders, a ragged bit of cloth wrapped around his arm already soaked with blood. Fuller appeared nearby, waving to someone, but Lauren barely saw it.

She knelt beside Arion, easing him down to lie flat in the sand, trying to staunch some of the flow of blood. He looked awful, worse than death, but he was breathing, she saw that right away, and felt a jolt of something severe and grateful jag through her.

"Arion?"

Slowly his eyes opened. The snow had frosted his eyelashes and the rest of his face, giving him the cast of marble, not flesh. She moved a hand to cup his cheek, to brush away some of the flakes.

"Lauren," he said, barely audible.

"Yes." She smiled at him, cradling his head.

"You're . . . alive."

She couldn't stop smiling, though it was more anxiety than happiness she felt. "You're fine," she assured him, and hoped the lie was more convincing than it sounded to her. "You're fine."

"Lauren . . ."

She leaned down closer, trying to shield him from the elements.

"I'm here," she whispered, very near.

He smiled up at her, bloodied and looking almost sleepy, snow falling all around them both.

". . . love . . ."

His gaze moved beyond her, behind her.

"Lauren MacRae."

It was a new voice, one she had never before heard, but it cut off her breath and made her spine go icy. Slowly she straightened away from Arion, then turned her head and looked up.

It was a man she didn't know. He wore a tartan of russet and brown. The brooch at his shoulder was a silver twig of rowan. He loomed above her and held out his hand to her, snow parting around him.

She stared up at him, immobile.

"Take my hand, Lauren," instructed the man, and like a puppet she did so, rising as he pulled her up, feeling everything about her go sinking away to the earth, to where Arion still lay, until she was as empty as a shell.

The stranger brought her hand to his lips and kissed the back of it, and his beard scraped at her skin. There was a gathering crowd of people around them now, a mass of outlines in the coming night.

"I am Payton Murdoch, laird of the Murdochs," he announced, as if she did not know that by now.

She couldn't think of what to respond, only stared at him, his brown hair and his blue eyes and the tan of his forehead. He did not deign to look at the dying man on the ground between them.

"We welcome you, Murdoch," said someone else, a man behind her. It was James, stepping forward. "And we offer you our gratitude, as well."

Payton Murdoch had not released her hand, and Lauren now moved her gaze down to it, his fingers firm and hard against hers, streaks and spots of blood marking her skin.

"She is wounded," said the Murdoch, prompting the others around them to murmur agreement.

Lauren let her look drift past their connected hands, back to Arion in the sand, snow wafting over him, crouching Englishmen beside him. His eyes were green and shadowed. He was staring at her face, his own completely empty, just like she felt.

"Come away, child," said the laird. "You are in need of aid." He released her hand to put an arm around her, heavy and foreign, nothing right about it at all. Lauren broke off her gaze from Arion, looking away to the froth of the ocean, wanting the finish to whatever nightmare this was.

Ari watched the Scotsman move and embrace her, pulling her close against his side.

His world ended then. It was that sudden, and that final: just the sight of another man with his arm clasping her to him, so casual yet so completely possessive.

Arion felt everything in him dry to dust and then scatter. He couldn't look away from it, Lauren standing there next to Murdoch, her head at his shoulder, her fine copper hair blowing gently across the other man's tartan with the snowfall.

Then he looked back at her face, and knew that he had been wrong. Not everything was dust. It couldn't be, because one look into her eyes and all the pain he had ever conceived of flooded over him, an agonizing wash, far worse than any physical wound—misery, hopelessness, rage.

She stared back at him and Arion knew that only he could read her in this moment, only he could translate the faint, anguished curve of her lips, the glimmer of tears shining amid the rare gold of her gaze.

"Come, Lauren," said the Scotsman, and he pulled her away from Arion, from all that he represented. He pulled her away and she let him, moving slowly, her usual grace transformed into halting steps amid the bodies and sand.

She turned her head and threw him one last look, but the copper strands obscured it, masking her face, and Arion couldn't tell if she meant to say good-bye to him or just . . .

Nothing. There was nothing left to say.

She was gone.

Chapter Thirteen

I LOVE YOU.

He had said that to her, she had heard him say it.

The Earl of Morgan had told her that he loved her, and now Lauren had to live with that bittersweet knowledge for the rest of her days.

He loved her. He would say it to her as the lifeblood flowed from his body, as he was most certainly dying, when she would think that he would be considering what truly mattered to him, what his life had meant before it ended. Arion du Morgan was an important man, with a history to him that she could only half guess at, kings and wars and courtiers and estates . . . all those things to consider as life faded away.

But he had told her he loved her.

Lauren hoped no one else had heard it. Certainly not Payton Murdoch, the laird who had arrived at Shot in such grand and lethal style. She didn't think he had; he didn't seem the kind of man to let such a slight go unanswered, to allow another man—an *Englishman,* no matter how noble—to say such a thing to his bride.

The Murdoch was very clearly a man of great pride. She saw it in the way he held his shoulders, so stiff and unyielding, and in the furrow in his brow, which

remained there even when he did not have that pon-
derous look.

She had first noticed that furrow yesterday, when he
had bent down close to her, his eyes fixed on the silver
rowan brooch at her shoulder.

"You are wearing it incorrectly," he had chided her
in front of everyone. "The proper way is so."

And he changed the angle of it so that it looked
crooked to her, a way she never would have thought to
put it.

No, the Murdoch had not heard Arion's whispered
confession on the beach two nights ago. No one else
had, only Lauren. That was as it should be. It was another secret to carry with her, another permanent wound
to the ache that was her heart.

Indeed, no one seemed to want to mention the
battle at Black Beach to her at all, which was strange
enough. Lauren brought it up herself, as she was being
bandaged yet again by Elias, wondering out loud how
her clan had known to come to the aid of the du Morgans just when they had.

Her horse, she was told, after a moment of strained
silence. Her mare had gone galloping home with the
severed reins, and that had alarmed the guards enough
to mount a party to search for her. They had found the
slaughter at the beach instead. Fortunately, Keir was close
enough to send for quick reinforcements.

And that was all she was told. Perhaps it was because
she had been right, and the council wrong: the Vikings
had indeed attacked again. The elders of her clan were
old men firmly burrowed into their ways—to be proven

wrong by a woman had to sting. Perhaps that was why they remained so short with her.

When she tried to bring it up again later, this time to Quinn and a few of the council, she was thrown stern looks and ordered back to her room, to rest. She looked too wan, she was much too thin, it was clear she needed to fortify herself for the upcoming wedding, especially since the Murdoch was speaking of moving up the date to next week.

"Why wait?" he had asked rhetorically to her and the whole clan at supper yesterday, sitting beside her. "We are here now. Naturally, I have brought my own priest for the service, and he has agreed it would be best to do it as soon as may be."

"Why?" Lauren had asked, knowing how it sounded, unable to help herself.

"Why?" repeated the Murdoch, his blue eyes at last landing on her. He pinned her with his gaze, disapproval and censure gleaming behind his smile. "Why, mayhap because I want to be wed to the fairest lass in Scotland sooner rather than later, Lauren."

And this had prompted cheers and laughter from the rest in the hall, the ringing chime of goblets being knocked together in toasts. It seemed that no one but Lauren caught the cold chill from the man she was to wed. No one but she noticed how his gaze was never steady, how even though his hands were large and rough, his voice remained falsely smooth.

She was being stupid. Her perception was affected by her true heart, that was all. After all, Payton Murdoch *had* come, just as all had hoped, and he *had* helped save Shot. That had to be proof enough that he was a worthy ally.

He had taken her hand then and squeezed it—hard. Very hard. Lauren had stared back at him, unflinching, unmoving, incensed but not showing it. Eventually he had relaxed his hold, freeing her. He did not look at her again.

"I was surprised to find Englishmen on your beach," commented Murdoch to the air around him, in the driest tone imaginable.

No one responded immediately, although a myriad of dark looks were exchanged among the council members, and some of the men shook their heads.

"After all, you knew I was coming," Murdoch continued, taking a small sip of his wine, his words almost careless. "It seems a bit . . . odd to me that you would turn to our enemy, even to hold off the Vikings."

James wore a heavy frown. "We did not invite them to that beach. They arrived first. And there were many Vikings. . . ."

Murdoch said nothing, examining his wine as if it held some intense fascination for him. Then he gave a light laugh, looking up. "Aye, and there are not so many Vikings now, are there?"

Laughter echoed around him, relief and forced heartiness.

Lauren glanced over to Hannah, her hands motionless over her plate, her look as cautious and worried as Lauren felt. But the uneasy moment had passed, and the meal once again wound on in pleasant tones.

Near the end of it, when she had risen to retire, the

Murdoch had reclaimed her hand, pulling her closer to him with that same practiced smile as before.

"Do not question me in public again, Lauren," he had said to her, his voice soft and composed.

She had pulled back to stare at him, wondering if he had actually said such a thing, and he only nodded and let go of her, turning away to Quinn, on his other side.

So she had left, quiet, and gone to her room to think about what her life was about to become: wife to a man of prejudice and conceit, who would not allow her to speak out against him, even in the mildest of ways. Wife to a man who had no qualms about using force to control her as it suited him—as witnessed by the throbbing pain in her left hand, the one the Murdoch had clenched. She didn't know how she was going to be able to bear a life of such restrictions.

To distract herself she lay down on her pallet and concentrated on the stars outside her window, becoming lost in their pinpointed brilliance, adrift in the midnight heavens, thin blue clouds. . . .

Arion must still be alive. Of course, no one would mention it to her, and now she dared not even ask. But she had not heard anyone repeating gossip of his death, only of the battle, over and over, and of the glory of the Scots. Nothing of the Earl of Morgan.

Even Hannah had not known, had only shaken her head sadly when Lauren managed to isolate her from the crowd of wedding women and whispered her question to her. Hannah would have told her if he had died. Hannah would not lie to her.

But deeper than that, truer than gossip or rumor or

even hope, Lauren knew Arion was not dead because she had not felt him die. It seemed ridiculous even to think such a thing, but she knew it with all of her being. He lived. He stayed on Shot, at Elguire. His was not one of the lights of heaven she was now surveying.

I love you, he had said to her, defending her with his life.

Lauren sent her reply out to dwell with the stars, silent forever:

And I you.

---------------◦❦◦---------------

*A*H, LAUREN," PAYTON MURDOCH SAID, not bothering to look up from the papers he was studying at the table. "Please close the door and sit."

Lauren hesitated in the doorway to his chambers, uneasy despite the convention of the moment.

She had been told this morning that the Murdoch required her presence in his chamber this afternoon at noon precisely. Since that was the hour when everyone else would be eating, she had assumed he meant to share a private meal with her, perhaps go over the wedding, or her coming duties as his wife.

She had not relished the idea. But this morning when she opened the jewelry box to slip on his ring, she allowed her fingers to brush over the golden brooch of her family badge. It gave her honor. Then, behind it, she found the outline of the sliver of amber cloth, hidden away to all but she. This gave her courage.

Yet she saw now that she had been mistaken after all; there was no meal laid out for them, no food to be seen anywhere, in fact, only her fiancé sitting at the table, papers surrounding him, and a lone goblet of something beside him. His brown hair was swept back into a neat queue, not a strand out of place.

Murdoch looked up at her, inquiry and irritation. "Are you deaf, lass? I said, sit."

She repressed a retort and shut the door, moving into the room, finding a chair that was not too near his. She sat and he watched her now, holding on to his peeved expression. It reminded her suddenly of a horse she had known once, colicky and surly.

Lauren bowed her head, pursing her lips to combat the smile.

"In the future, I expect you to obey me instantly," said Murdoch.

She lifted her head, astonished.

"I am telling you now to be fair," he went on, leaning back in his chair. "I do not wish there to be any misunderstandings between us."

"Obey you?" she echoed, and to her horror the smile came back, and with it a laugh trapped in her throat.

"Aye," he said curtly. "When I say sit, you sit. If I tell you to stand, you stand. It is a very simple law between a man and his wife. I expect you to follow it."

"What law is this?" she managed to ask.

"Naught but the law of God and man. The husband rules his wife with a firm hand. The wife submits."

"But—" She stopped, biting back her protest, and saw him watch her keenly.

"You will submit to me," he said, in the same soft tone as he had used when he had crushed her hand. "Do you understand, Lauren?"

She took a heavy breath, unable to think of what to reply to such absurdity. She had never before known a man to take the word of the church so literally. Yes, men spoke of it, priests sermonized about it, of a woman's weakness, how she must follow the will of her husband, her father, even her grown sons—but she had never known anyone to insist upon it so ardently—

"I asked if you understood me, Lauren." Murdoch stood up suddenly, crossing to her. Before she could move he had yanked her up out of the chair with quick force, using one hand to hold her arm—the wounded one— and the other to pinch her chin to keep her still in front of him.

She stared up at him, furious, not daring to move away.

"In the future," said Murdoch, using the same bland tone as before, "never, ever make me repeat a command to you."

He kissed her then, showing her what was beneath his blandness, the thing she had glimpsed last night: anger and contempt, heated displeasure. It was more of a punishment than a kiss, and he let her drop away from him only when she couldn't breathe, when her lips were hurting, and the place on her cheeks where his fingers had pressed felt sorely bruised.

Murdoch returned to his chair. He took a sip from his goblet, then placed it carefully back onto the table.

"Sit down," he ordered.

Lauren sat.

Murdoch noted it with just a faint nod of approval. "We have much more to discuss, sweet wife."

————————⟶⟶⟶————————

SHE FOUND HANNAH IN HER chamber, embroidering something long and elaborate that spread over her lap in folds of pink and green and gold.

"Oh, you've caught me," announced Hannah, with half a laugh. Lauren paused and looked around the room, startled, but then Hannah indicated the cloth in front of her.

"It's for you," she said, smiling. "Or rather, for your children."

Lauren walked slowly closer, and now she could see that what Hannah sewed was a blanket, soft and pretty, with squares of color on it that made up pictures: sheep and birds, castles and oceans, starfish and dolphins.

"I wanted to finish it in time to send along with you to the mainland," Hannah said to her. "A small gift. For the future."

Lauren tore her gaze from the blanket, from what it meant. "Hannah, I need you to do something for me. It's very important."

"What is it, dearest?"

"Take this note." Lauren held it out to her, the wax seal of it facing upward.

Hannah studied it for a moment, then reached out and took it gingerly, her fingers barely touching the folded paper.

"I know you can get it to him," Lauren said.

"No, Lauren—"

"Listen to me!" She had to stop and swallow, fighting back the babbling fear that wanted to speak for her. "It's . . . it's only a good-bye. I didn't get the chance to say good-bye to him. That's all."

"Are you feeling well? You look flushed—and are those *bruises* on your face—?"

"From the battle," Lauren interrupted, intent on her purpose. "It's nothing. But, Hannah, will you see that he gets it? I need it delivered today, if you can. I need to know he has it today."

"I really don't think this is wise." Hannah shook her head. "I know it's difficult, but sometimes it's best just to leave things as they fall."

"Did *you* get to bid farewell to Fuller Morgan, all those years ago?" Lauren demanded.

Hannah looked down at the blanket on her lap, obviously troubled. "This is really nothing like that."

"You did, though. I know you did. And though you say that you never missed him until now, think what it would have meant to just walk away from him without that final meeting, and your farewell. Think of what it would have been like for you . . . for him."

Hannah was frowning, her hands on her lap, the note between them. She said nothing, staring down at it.

"It's just my good-bye," Lauren said, and she could not disguise the plea in her words. She knelt before her friend, grasping her hands. "I beg you, Hannah, do me this one last thing."

And Hannah looked up at her finally, sighing, releasing the note and the blanket to hug Lauren to her. Lauren closed her eyes, holding tight.

"Please, Hannah . . ."

"I will," her friend said. "I'll see that he receives it, if it means you're more easily able to let go of him."

"Today," Lauren added.

"Aye, today." Hannah sighed again.

"Thank you," Lauren murmured, and felt the gratitude sink into her bones. "Thank you, thank you."

<hr />

*I*T WAS REMARKABLY EASY TO leave Keir.

Much easier than she had expected, or even hoped.

You will come to me when I summon you.

She left through the gate with a party of shepherds and their flock, hooded and cloaked, head always bowed. She carried one of the herding crooks and stayed on the outflanks of the mass of them, trying hard to remain unnoticed. Dogs ran around them all, barking and moving the sheep, and perhaps that was distraction enough for her to become just another shepherdess, out to graze her portion of the sheep. The chill of winter had not abated from the air, and she was not the only one covered from head to toe.

Once outside the castle walls, she followed the flock into the woods, lagging farther and farther behind, slowly separating herself from the group. Eventually, she ducked away behind a group of trees and waited, until the sound of hooves across leaves and the barking dogs faded in the distance.

You will do exactly as I tell you.

Her plan to leave had worked, but it meant that she

had no horse to ride. She dropped the crook behind some bushes and began her long walk, still too tired and sore to run, though the urgency swimming through her kept her steps fleet.

You will stand until I allow you to be seated.

It really didn't look as if it would snow again. It had not since that fateful day at the beach, but neither had it warmed up very much. There were still tufts and drifts of snow on the ground, clinging to the brown autumn leaves. Lauren was careful to avoid them. Patches of snow would leave footprints, and footprints could be followed.

You will speak only when I grant you leave to.

Night was coming fast, a dwindling of light that left the woods shrouded and dark, hindering her progress. But she did not slow. She could not afford to. She didn't know how much time she had.

You will not meet the eyes of other men.

She had told them she was feeling ill, that she wanted to sleep, and please not to send her dinner to her room or disturb her in any way. She had tried to add just the right amount of command and exhaustion to her words, to make them believe her but not be so worried as to send someone up to check on her. Just in case they did, she had stuffed her pillows beneath her covers, a rough outline of a body. It was an old childhood trick, but it was all that she had.

You will not gossip with other women.

If they truly wanted to see her, her ruse would be over that quickly. She had to hurry. She had to walk faster. Twilight was almost gone; the night birds were beginning to stir.

You will yield your mind and your body to my will.

It seemed so much farther than she remembered. That had to be the anxiety in her, making her imagine the distance had grown. Was that voices behind her? No—no. Not yet. It could not be them just yet. Lauren folded her cloak closer to her, picking up her pace, close to a run.

You will bear me sons.

The silver branch of rowan was back at Keir, resting next to the ruby ring in her jewelry box. Should anyone check it, they might notice that her golden clan brooch was missing. But they would not see that she had taken the small strip of amber cloth as well.

You will never complain, never make excuses, never fail me.

She had tied the amber cloth to her belt in a knotted bow, tucked away securely against her waist, out of sight to all but she.

You will listen and be guided only by me.

She was so cold, she was freezing. But she was also hot and flushed at the same time, a dizzying combination that ate away her reassurance, made her breath that much shorter as she ran. She was almost there, almost there, and then she would be truly free, it would be all over then....

Come here to me now, wife.

The meadow was empty.

She stopped just outside of it, trying to breathe silently through her mouth, the air turning to frost before her. Lauren moved until she was well hidden behind a nest of pine trees, and the meadow was fully revealed in spotted checkers of black earth and white snow.

The rock oak stood alone, a cap of snow on top, otherwise untouched by all inclement weather.

Lauren wrapped her arms around herself and crouched down amid the trees, waiting.

 ARION STARED, UNSEEING, AT THE wood of the table beneath his hands.

He made a point to sit at Ryder's table, instead of lingering in his bed. He couldn't bear to stay in the bed. That was where she had slept.

His body was still weak, still pained and slow, reminding him with every breath of the viciousness of the battle he had been in, and the slow encroachment of age that seemed to make mending his wounds a greater struggle with each passing second.

He felt old. He felt hollow. He felt as close to the edge of that infinite void that circled him as he ever had in his life. He was alone, forever alone, and Ari understood, with sort of wearied acceptance, that this was to be his intractable fate.

The void would take him in. If he was lucky, he might not live too long in it. He might die—another battle, a sunken ship, a spoiled meal, perhaps—and then the relief he sought would be found.

And his Lauren, that dazzling flame, would go on in her life with another man, sharing the wealth of her spirit with her husband, giving him herself, and her children, and laughter and love—giving that bastard Scotsman every reason to live, while Arion had none.

Lauren.

She was light and beauty and a sort of transcendent

hope to him. She was his perfect dream, the embodiment of an exact, precious essence his soul craved.

He was so empty without her.

Arion dropped his head into his hands, closing his eyes. He might as well dream of the wind as of Lauren MacRae. Any chance of holding either was mere illusion.

When he moved again he accidentally knocked into the gargoyle inkwell, causing it to skid over the wood and fall to the floor, where it rolled in an awkward loop, stopping against the edge of the rug.

Ink spilled out, a trail of it puddling on the stone, seeping into the fibers.

Arion turned his gaze back to his hands, to the wood beneath them. Time wound on, diffused as light through heavy glass, meaningless.

He became aware, at some point, that there was someone else in the room with him, standing behind him and then beside him. Ari didn't lift his head to see who it was.

"My lord?"

Fuller moved again, obviously seeing the inkwell, caring enough to pick it up, shutting the hinged lid. Arion finally raised his head, breathing deeply to find that stabbing pain in his right side from some Northman's blade. It woke him slightly.

"What is it?" he asked, his voice too gruff.

The steward seemed to be having problems deciding what to do with the inkwell; he held it in one hand, trying to stop the ink from dripping further to the floor and the rug. But his other hand held something that he had not released. A folded piece of paper.

"This is for you, my lord," said Fuller at last, offering the paper to Arion.

Ari turned away.

"Leave it and go. I want to be alone now."

"I think you might want to—"

"I said *leave it,*" Arion growled, scowling at the table.

From the corner of his vision he saw the steward pause, then carefully place the paper on the edge of the table, where Arion could reach it. He bowed, backing away.

"Note the seal, my lord," Fuller said, and then was gone.

Arion closed his eyes. He concentrated on taking more shallow breaths, because that stabbing pain was no longer welcome. He wanted the numbness again. He wanted the void. Why run away now?

Note the seal.

What the hell did that mean? Arion looked askance at the note, at the dark green blotch of wax that had been pressed down into the paper in what appeared to be a bizarre series of interlocking lines.

He could make no sense of it, those lines. He had never seen a seal like it before. Seals were not lines. They were crests. They were lions and griffiths, stars and fields. Not lines.

In spite of himself he was intrigued. Ari pulled the note closer to him, directly beneath his head, so that he would not have to move much to study it.

Yes, lines, but cut off, like just the corner of some greater design, intricate and precise. It did look familiar, now that he could view it more clearly. He had seen this before. The near recognition tickled the back of his mind, a nagging buzz that would not let him alone, pushing away the hollowness that plagued him.

He reached out and touched the cold wax, feeling the raised pattern of it, finding the fold in the paper and breaking open the note just exactly as he realized what the seal was.

Clan crest of the MacRaes. A note from the MacRaes.

Ari felt his heart skip, his blood racing again, and the stabbing pain that came back seemed distant, unimportant.

The note had just a few words. He didn't know the hand, but then, he didn't have to. Firm letters, elegant slant, no wasted space or energy on elaborate script:

Rock Oak, the note said. *Tonight.*

And no name on it, but by God, he didn't need one. Arion pushed away from the desk, the note clutched tightly in his hand. He paced the room, power once more flowing through him, then stopped to read it again, to make certain he had not dreamed it, that it was not merely the product of fervent wishing.

It was not. The words stayed the same, their invitation just as clear.

Arion crossed to the hearth and tossed the paper in, watching it burn to ash, the message curling up into smoky tendrils before vanishing altogether.

He glanced out his window and saw the edge of darkness seeping over the land, and then moved away, looking for his boots.

*A*RION RODE TOO QUICKLY. HE could almost feel his wounds begin to break open, the blood wanting to escape him again. But he had no patience for it now. By the time he had managed to dress himself, to order his destrier saddled and ready for him, too many precious minutes had passed. It had not helped that the stable-master seemed slow and incompetent, that Fuller had arrived while the stallion was still being readied and had tried, unsuccessfully, to persuade Arion to go back to bed—and if not that, then at least to accept an escort.

Arion had forbidden it, mounting his steed with nearly the same ease as he used to know, and then rode away to leave them all staring after him, dark shapes in the twilight.

He was not followed. He knew enough to ensure that; if any of his men had disobeyed such a direct order, they understood the punishment would be swift and sure—and perhaps there was a bit too much of Ryder in him to not make his threat convincing.

He rode alone, remembering the way as if he had traveled it a thousand times over, though in fact he had been to this meadow only once before, back when his alliance with Lauren MacRae had been a new and uncertain thing.

The meadow appeared empty.

Arion fought the disappointment that saturated him, dismounting, walking the steed closer yet staying in the woods, scanning the area. True night was with him now, no moon, just clouds drifting overhead, but it was clear that no one awaited him by the rock oak. He saw no steps in the snow, though it was spotted about in random thatches. He heard no sounds at all, no rustling, no breathing, no birds or wind.

He was early. Or she was late.

Or she couldn't come at all.

No, Ari told himself firmly. She would be here. She had to be here. Everything he was—or ever hoped to be—rested on it.

He waited, feeling his senses honed and sharp, sensitive to the slightest change in the land around him. And slowly he began to realize that there was something different across the bent winter grass, over there, by a thick cluster of trees. Something not right, too soft a shape to be part of the landscape, too irregular to the lines of the trunks. . . .

She stepped away from the forest and Arion released the reins of his steed, uncaring, and began walking to her, faster, faster, focused only on Lauren, the figure of her coming toward him, long steps to him, her hood pushed back, her hair loose, a look of such intensity on her face, her eyes locked on his.

By fate or strange fortune they met exactly at the rock oak, and then he had her in his arms, and his lips were on hers, and she was making some breathless sound that sang to him, that left him stunned and ferocious and wildly joyous.

She tasted sweet and willing, her skin cold, her grasp on him tight. Her breath warmed him, her fingers slid up to enmesh in his hair, keeping him close to her, though he was already half afraid that he might be crushing her with his embrace.

He was saying her name, he couldn't help it, drawing her to him until his back was against the stone tree and she was pressed fully into him, her body a welcome weight against his. He wouldn't let her move away but kept her there, kissing her until he thought he might die from it, and still it wasn't enough, still he had to have more of her, her light, her brightness. She was helping him, she was leaning up into him, matching his kisses, her touch firm, pulling.

Lauren felt his hands slide over the heavy material of her cape, and then beneath it, to skim her breasts, to cup them in his palms. It sent a hot fire through her, the sparks he alone could give her, banishing the chill that had dwelled in and around her. She closed her eyes with it, gasping. Arion smiled against her cheek, his own breath coming hard. She opened her eyes again and took in his face, the dark green heat of his gaze, now slumberous and rapt.

He moved downward, taking her with him, sliding to the ground, his back still upright against the rock oak, until they were on their knees, face to face, and he had a smile that sent more of that sparking fire through her blood. He pushed away her cape until it hung far back over her shoulders, and then his own, and his body was hard and unyielding, his hands at once controlled and supplicating, running over her body—her chest, her back, her bottom and thighs—as if he wanted all of her at once but couldn't decide how to start.

"Lauren," he said into her neck, making her name a rough sound. "Lauren, Lauren, why did you come here?"

But he didn't seem to want an answer, because he was kissing her again, sucking at her lower lip, brushing over her cheeks to her jaw, her neck, causing her body to arch against him on its own. He came back to her mouth and his lips grew softer on hers: another version of that gentleness he had shown her before, on the floor of his chamber in his home. It was tenderness and languid sensuality; it was devotion and reverence.

She had been just holding on to him till now—the force and speed of his want had left her grasping, trying to stay with him, trying not to let go. But Lauren felt something new flame through her now, a dawning awareness of her own power, or else overwhelming desire, she couldn't say which. She touched him as he was touching her, an exploration of him, the pleasing form beneath the tunic, the beauty of him, his exotic unfamiliarity, male lines and solid muscles. Yet for all the newness she knew exactly what to do now, how to caress him, where to stroke him to elicit a dark growl from the back of his throat, all of him paused, focused on her.

Lauren did it again, her hands soft against the hardest part of him, feeling his shape, the urgency of him straining against her.

"Lauren," he said again, only now his voice was broken. He gave a soft, wondering laugh. "What are we doing out here—"

She stopped his words the only way she knew how, a melting kiss, and it worked, it silenced the protest she could feel in him, though not so much as to make him loosen his grip on her.

"Please," she murmured, moving her lips over his cheek, his jaw. "Please, Arion . . ."

He moved swiftly, so fast that she had only a secondary awareness of it, but now she was on her back and he was on top of her, and the rock oak was behind him, pointing up to the scattered stars in the sky, the silver-edged clouds that moved over them.

He came down between her legs and she let him, she bent her knees to keep him there, wrapped her arms around his back and held on, feeling the sparks transform to something stronger, something much more like pain and liquid sun, igniting beneath his touch. The cape was a pillow beneath her, but even if she had been bare on the cold snow, it wouldn't have mattered. Arion was there. Arion was keeping the night far away from her. Arion was moving against her, slow and hot, making the sun in her burn even brighter.

Her gown and tartan were rising; he pushed them higher and she helped him, both of them wordless now, staring into each other's eyes, their breathing matched to short pants.

Even the winter air could not affect her. She felt overheated, she felt as if she would melt the snow beneath her, a river to sweep them both away, far, to someplace where there could be nothing but the two of them, forever.

When he came back down on her again, Lauren realized he had done something to his hose, and his tunic was raised. It was flesh on flesh, and the shock of it made her go still.

It was real. It was truly happening, finally, at last, her joining with Arion, the enemy for whom she would die. Lauren had thought herself ready for it. She had thought she knew what it would mean, to offer herself to him, to taste his sweetness and become his.

But now, with Arion on top of her, sharing the same

air, their bodies so shamelessly intertwined, she felt the reality of what this would mean.

She *would* be his. Her maidenhood, her heart, her soul—all of her. It was terrifying, it was rash and insane. But oh, she wanted it more than anything she had ever wanted before in her life. It seemed she was caught in a terrible contradiction—afraid to move, but wanting to move with every ounce of her being.

Arion cradled her face with his hands. He looked pained, as if what he felt right now was nothing of pleasure but rather agony. The hottest part of him, that maleness, was stiff and still against her, pressed against her thigh by the weight of his body.

I love you, she thought. *I want this.*

Lauren shifted, just a little, and he seemed to grow even stiller, the tension around his mouth pronounced.

"What are we doing?" he whispered.

She raised her leg higher in response, bringing him that much closer to her.

"No," Arion said, closing his eyes, looking tormented. "Wait."

"No," she said to him, soft and sure, and moved her other leg to follow the first.

His body slipped closer, the strangeness of him now probing against her, finding that part of her where the liquid sun burned. Her back arched without her will, a natural flexing, and he responded with a kind of muffled groan, slowing penetrating her, sinking into her.

Lauren felt the unique sensation of his entry, burning and good, and all the air from her lungs fled under the pleasure of it. She could not breathe, she could not replace that air, but she didn't need to, because she had Arion, and he was a part of her now . . . pain and sorcery and passion and him.

But then he stopped.

He stopped, not close enough to her yet. She knew somehow that this act was not done, that there was something incomplete to this moment. Her hands clutched at his shoulders, trying to pull him down to her the rest of the way, insistent. Pleading.

"What are we—" Arion began, and then cut himself off, a hiss of air through his teeth. His eyes were wild and lost; his hand trembled as he stroked the hair from her cheek. "Lauren . . . the snow, and the meadow . . . this isn't right. This isn't how it's supposed to be."

"Yes it is," she said quickly, low and fierce.

He stared down at her, unmoving, so close to her that her heart beat contralto to his, a matching rhythm, both fast and furious. She felt the ache stretching through her, commanding. She flexed her back again, but this time it had no effect on him. He supported himself away from her with his arms, shaking very, very slightly.

There was a change coming over him, she could see it and feel it. The soft focus of his gaze sharpened, grew more keen and clear.

"No," Lauren said again, and to her dismay, this time it sounded closer to a wail, faint and imploring.

"I can't," Arion said, shaking his head, almost to himself. "Not like this."

And to her very great fear and frustration, he pulled fully away from her, leaving her completely, alone on the ground, shivering. He stood up, adjusting his clothes, and walked a few steps from where she lay.

Lauren slowly rolled to her side and pushed herself up to sit, her gown falling back into place, the cloak coming forward to hide the bow of her body. She brought up one hand to cover her eyes.

"It would mean a war," she heard Arion say heavily, his words directed to the trees around them.

She said nothing.

"It would sever you from your clan and your country, from all you hold dear," he continued after a pause, still to the trees. "It would ruin you."

"I don't care," Lauren said, not looking up.

"You do," he countered, turning to her. "Don't lie to me."

"*I don't care!*" she shouted at him, lifting her head, glaring.

He gazed down at her, somber and forbidding, nearly lost in the starlight.

"*I* care," Arion said. "I care *for* you, then."

He walked back to her, crouched down and touched her cheek lightly with his fingers. Lauren was careful not to wince when he brushed the same places as Murdoch had.

"Why did you do it?" he asked, hushed and troubled. "Why did you send me that note?"

Her lips remained locked shut. Pride would not let her speak. She watched his look darken, his face go bleak and stern.

"My God, look at you. You look like you've already been in a war. You're covered in bruises and cuts—"

"Take me to Elguire," she said.

He sighed. "Lauren, whatever it is you think you feel for me, I assure you that it will fade. With time. Right now, you're probably feeling a lot of things that stem from our alliance, from the confusion of battle. But when you are married, and you have a family of your own, all of these things will seem distant to you—"

"You said you loved me."

Pain came and went through him; she felt it so clearly, even as he masked it.

"Was it a lie?" she asked.

He stood up, scowling at the stars.

"Was it?" she demanded.

"No," he admitted, the word sounding angry. "It wasn't a lie."

She stood as well, supple and brisk. "Then let me come with you to Elguire. Let me stay with you. Or take me to your castle on the mainland, or to London. I'll go with you anywhere you want."

"Lauren, you don't know what you're saying."

"I do! I want to be with you, Arion du Morgan. And I don't care if it's right or wrong or even legal. I don't care if you wed me or not. Just take me with you. Let me be with you."

He said nothing, staring at the ground, a kind of violence to the tremors of his hands, the clench of his jaw.

She put one hand on his arm. "I want to stay with you, Arion, and damn the consequences."

He shook her off, spoke with some of that suppressed violence crackling through. "I can't."

"Then you lied when you said you loved me." Her voice was ice, her soul was frost.

"No, goddammit!" Without warning he took her into his arms, holding her firmly over her stiff resistance. After a moment she felt his lips against her temple. Despite the harshness of his hold on her, his words came out soft, hopeless. "So help me, I've never spoken a greater truth. I love you, my grand Lauren MacRae."

"Then—"

"It's why I can't have you. I won't. I will *not* be the one to ruin you. I will not do that. Your life is too dear to me."

The bravado that had sustained her began to crumble. Her arms crept around his waist, her head felt heavy and weary. She rested her cheek against his shoulder, hearing the finality of his decision, feeling it cut through her like the sharpest sword. She was not going to cry.

"My uncle was a man without pity or mercy," Arion said now, remote. "He cared for nothing beyond his own pleasure. He drove his own niece to her death with his constant condemnation of her, his punishment of me and her for every dissatisfaction that came to him. After you left Morgan, after I freed you, he went mad . . . he lost control. So many suffered for it."

He stopped for a moment, mired in his black memories, gone from her though his grip was just as firm. Lauren curled her fingers into his clothing, clutching the cloth, so desperate for him that it left her mute.

After a moment, Arion continued, his voice stronger. "There was nothing I could do to save my sister—but by God, I can save you. I will not be like Ryder. I will not put myself before all others, especially not before you. I will not condemn you to a life of guilt and obligation because you feel bound to me, for how I feel about you. I will not do that to you. I know your heart, my beloved. You don't want a war. You don't want innocent people to die for you. You are too just for that."

She was crying, although she hated herself for it, and she tried to disguise it by bringing up a hand against her mouth, to stop the words that wanted to spill out:

Please don't do this. Don't leave me. Don't send me to him.

"You are the most precious thing in the world to me," said Arion gravely. "And so you must go now. Go home, Lauren. Go back to Keir."

He released her, pulling away from her hands, stepping back. All was shadowed around him, all was dark and dim and relentless cold. He looked as if he might say something more, but then he didn't. Arion bowed to her and turned around, walking away, across the snow and grass to the black horse that waited for him at the other end of the meadow.

She watched him grow smaller, the barest limp to his steps, until the night had taken him completely, and all that was left was obscure and far, dwindling to nothing in the forest.

Only then did Lauren turn away. Slowly she began the long and frigid walk back to Keir Castle.

Chapter Fourteen

———— ∞ ————

*I*T WOULD HAVE BEEN SO simple to persuade him. Lauren realized it afterward, sitting dull and useless through one of the many meals she had to take with Murdoch, her boisterous clan all around them in the great hall.

Simple. A few short words, and Arion would have forgotten his noble intentions, he would have taken her away and hidden her at Elguire, tucked her safely into his chamber, with its sparkling tapestry and tremendous bed. A few simple words:

He hurt me. He wants to do it again.

Just that, and her virtuous English knight would have swept her back with him to the warmth of his home, under his protection, and then . . .

He would die.

Thank the heavens part of her had known that, had raced ahead though the steps of her outrageous plan, however vaguely, and realized that Arion would have indeed gone to war for her, and that her clan and Payton Murdoch would have done everything in their power to destroy him.

She would have been taken away from him by force.

Worse, to greet his body just as she had Da's, broken and torn, nothing at all left of the man she loved.

Aye, if she had stayed with Arion, it would have meant his death. So it was better that it would be her fate, and not his. She would gladly choose her own doom rather than condemn the man who held her heart. Let him gradually ebb from her life, as she would ebb from his.

It struck Lauren as morbidly funny that now that the Murdoch was here, no one seemed to notice her very much. The wedding was all-important, and she became merely a single thread in the greater tapestry of it, nearly trivial.

No one commented on her lackluster spirits. No one asked about the fresh bruises that seemed to bloom on her cheeks, her neck, just where Murdoch's hands would encircle her, complete control of her.

Only Hannah might have noted the differences in her, on her, and Lauren was careful to avoid her. She wouldn't be able to bear to see the sorrow for her on her friend's face. She wouldn't be able to bear her pity.

So Lauren took to wrapping her tartan higher around her neck—as if she felt a constant chill—to hide the telltale signs of his hands on her, because it was easier than thinking up a lie to answer any questions about it.

And the Murdoch was always so careful, despite his hard hands. It was never anything more than a sort of subdued peril with him—nothing severe enough that she could run to Quinn or the council and plead with them for her release:

He holds me too hard.

He threatens me with his eyes.

His kisses taste of ashes and dust.

He hates me.

She could imagine how they might react to that—she would be ordered to her chamber. Again. The marriage was too important to them, too valuable to let go and risk making an enemy of the man they most wanted to befriend. All their hopes and dreams were pinned on this union.

She saw her life as if it were a puzzle all laid out, the pieces almost joined together, every bit of it ready to fit and be finished, and then put away to be forgotten. Yet she kept her thoughts to herself, and followed what they all wanted. She obeyed her fiancé, the will of her clan, and felt herself dying with it.

Being alone with him was the worst. Lauren understood that in those secluded moments with Murdoch it was better not to resist him, that what he wanted was for her to fight him, that behind his chilling words and rough hands was the gleaming snare of a hunter, seeking a challenge. She remained limp and inert, almost removed from her body, no threat at all.

And no one noticed.

She had crept back into Keir that night—was it three days ago now, or four? she couldn't recall—coming through with a returning herd of sheep, going up to her room in the deceptive shadows of the castle, and found her bed undisturbed, no meal waiting for her. Nothing.

Everyone seemed so happy. Everyone talked with such excitement about the wedding, about the feast, the dancing and celebration. The strength of the clan, about to be doubled.

Payton Murdoch smiled and laughed with them, at perfect ease, the honored guest. His soldiers drank Mac-Rae whiskey and ate MacRae food and flirted with so many young women that it appeared, to the delight of all, that there might be more weddings to follow.

Lauren wore the silver brooch of rowan and the ruby ring all the time now, surely the most luxurious shackles she had ever imagined.

She thought about her Da, of what he might say to her. Perhaps it was that she was so very mired in despair—she couldn't hear his wisdom at all.

---

*N*OBILITY AND HONOR MADE COLD dinner companions, Arion found.

He ate his final evening meal alone in his uncle's room, staring at the familiar walls, the furniture. The stain of ink on the rug, pale gray from repeated scrubbings, but still there, his own mark upon this place.

It was all much as it had been days ago, that dusky twilight when her note had come to him, and the hope he had felt then had seemed so bright that it would illuminate the world.

Such different emotions tonight. No hope. Only resignation.

He looked at the trunks pressed back in a neat line along one wall, his clothing, his armaments packed away. They would sail with the morning tide, if the weather was clear enough. He was ready to leave Shot, in body and in mind. Now all he had to do was convince his heart.

Ari told himself he had done the right thing, back in that starlit meadow. He had discovered an amazing aspect of himself, a greatness, even: the sacrifice of his life for that of the one he loved. He had left her so that she would go on, and live well, and follow the path that was expected of her. She would become Lauren Murdoch, and someday he would be nothing but a memory to her, faded and dim.

Ari tilted his head back, offering a bitter smile to the ceiling. No chance of such a peace descending upon *him*. He knew with all his soul that she would never fade from him. The love in his heart, the anguish, would keep her close to him for the rest of his days. But to remain here, trapped on the island, knowing she was so close by, made that pain intolerable.

So he was leaving. After all, the Vikings had fled, defeated. He doubted they would be rash enough to return soon. And if they did . . . he would come back. Or send someone else back for him. It didn't have to be him. He didn't have to see Shot ever again.

A tiny sound captured his attention, off in a darkened corner of the room. He glanced down at it indifferently.

Twin gleams of reflected light gazed back at him, frozen, nearly invisible. Arion did not move, and in a moment the gleams bobbed and shifted—a mouse, staying near the shelter of one of his trunks, firelight caught in its eyes.

A little brown mouse, with tiny folded ears, and whiskers that reached a ridiculous distance from its body.

Nora's pet, he thought, remembering his sister's fancy. *Simon.*

The mouse seemed to stare back at him, unmoving again, only the whiskers twitching, as if it had discovered his scent.

He had not been able to save Nora. All the tricks and sacrifices of his youth had been nothing to her; she had succumbed to the despair in her life despite his love for her. But with Lauren it would be different. It would work with Lauren. He had saved her. He had.

Golden light from the fire flickered over the trunks. He saw the long, sliding sheen of whiskers as the mouse sat up and began to groom its face.

She has to marry him. She should be with him. Her life will be the better for it.

He had a vision of Lauren in the meadow, her face turned to silver beneath the stars, her eyes dark and pleading. How she had felt in his arms . . . how she had grasped him to her, her embrace tight and certain.

She's strong. She'll endure with Murdoch.

The bathing was done. The mouse shook itself, then settled down again, smooth brown fur, liquid black eyes, still watching him.

She'll endure. . . .

"But she wanted *me*."

He didn't realize he had said the words aloud until the mouse started and scampered away, a curving flicker of tail and then nothing but shadows again, empty stone and space.

Lauren might endure. Arion knew that he would not.

*H*ER MARRIAGE WAS TO BE held tomorrow.

Tonight the Murdoch had told everyone that he wanted to dine privately in his chamber with his bride, a short meal before bidding her good night, eager to start their new life together on the morrow.

As usual, Lauren had acquiesced to this seemingly romantic notion. Everyone had kissed her good evening, had smiled at her and congratulated her again and told her to sleep well as she left the hall with Murdoch, her hand resting lightly on his arm.

They ate in near silence. She moved without thought, cutting the meat pie for them both, serving him, then herself. Pouring his wine. Managing just a splash into her own goblet; she did not want to drink.

She kept her gaze lowered, her head bowed, watching with a strange sense of marvel her hands working, how normal they seemed. How they did not shake, or falter, or give away at all the curling ball of panic lodged deep, deep inside her. How amazing, that she was so truly able to hide from herself.

The Murdoch was speaking now. She listened only as much as she needed to. Lauren had found that most of what he had to say was composed of lists and notes he made up in his head. She supposed he spoke them out loud to her as a sort of exercise. Or perhaps he merely enjoyed the sound of his own voice. The steady, even inflection of his tone almost never changed, the words drawn out and shallow.

The ceremony. Her gown. Where to stand. What to say. When to say it.

No flowers, too cold for this time of year. Perhaps hollyhock instead. Something with berries.

Food. Ample fare mixed with rare delicacies. Wine. Ale. Whiskey, enough for all the men.

The boats, fit to sail, fully armed. Weapons replenished, mended.

Land forces, rested and ready. Dead horses replaced, wounded men held back for the second wave of attack . . .

"What did you say?" Lauren asked, raising her head.

Payton Murdoch gave her a brief glance, no expression on his face. "For the second wave of attack. Do not interrupt me, Lauren."

She ignored his warning, felt the panic in her expand with breathtaking speed, wrapping around her chest and then her heart, confining it.

"Attack on what?" she asked.

He stared at her, that terrible blankness on his face still, and she knew that he was summoning his anger, that brutality in him. Yet she couldn't back away now, she couldn't apologize and ask for forgiveness. The writhing panic would not allow it.

Perhaps he knew. Perhaps he sensed that he had at last managed to stir her, to engage her fears.

"On Elguire, naturally," he said calmly. "Where else?"

He smiled at her then—and oh yes, he recognized what her swift intake of breath meant, what fright was living in her now.

"Our good King William has openly expressed dissatisfaction with the English king. It's common knowledge that Henry demands far too much of him, too many concessions. Why, I heard the other day that he accused Henry's ambassadors to their faces of avarice and perfidy. William will not be displeased, I think, to learn that Shot has become entirely Scotland's. Our forces now outnumber du Morgan's. It may be bloody, but it can be done."

She was mute, horrified, bound to her chair with the conflicting instincts to both run and warn the others and to stay and stop this madness in him.

"You can't," was all she managed to choke out.

He raised his eyebrows. "It won't be that difficult. The Earl of Morgan is only one man, with no heirs to seek out revenge. We will make Elguire our own home on Shot. I had thought you might enjoy that. Perhaps I will make it my wedding gift to you. You may thank me later."

His smile was open and malicious now, no effort to disguise his delight at her reaction. Lauren found her will again and quickly stood, outraged.

"We have an agreement with them—one that you cannot violate! They have been our allies! They have fought beside us, defended us!"

"I did not give you leave to stand," said the Murdoch, so gentle.

With one quick move he pushed up from his chair and struck her, taking her by surprise though she should have anticipated it. She fell against the table and then to the floor, jolted and stunned. He came down beside her, bent next to her ear.

"Another gift to you, my wife," Murdoch murmured. "I'll spare as many women and children as I can, and ship them back to England. I'll kill only the earl, and every man under him."

"I won't let you," she swore, and got slapped again, harder now but in the same spot across her cheek, and this time she saw blackness before becoming aware of him again.

"Enough of that, I think," he said, reflective. "We don't want you too marked up for your wedding day. Time for you to retire, Lauren."

"My clan will never agree to it," she said as he jerked her to her feet.

"Oh, I think they will. When I map it out for them, and let them know we will have the unspoken blessing of the king, I think they will. We both know how the MacRaes feel about the English. I am confident they will have the wits to appreciate my brilliance, when I present my plan to them at just the proper moment. Later tonight, perhaps."

"They'll see your *madness!*"

He had a grip on her upper arm that was unrelenting; his face wore the barest frown.

"You are beginning to displease me, wife. You are argumentative and insubordinate. I fear your father spoiled you unreasonably. I always suspected as much."

"Release me!" Lauren twisted against his hold.

He pulled her closer to him with both hands. "I sense you are distraught. It must be the wedding tomorrow that alarms you so. Your nerves are weak and shaken."

He walked her backward, forcing her to move, until she felt his pallet behind her knees. He pushed her down onto the covers, standing over her.

"I think it better that you stay the night here, my bride. I don't want you to go running to your cousin with my plan before I am ready to tell it to him. Clearly you will rest better here, and I will rest better knowing you are secure, with my men outside the door. I shall retire with them. All the better to escort you to the chapel in the morn."

She stared up at him, mute, panting from the struggle. His face remained unchanged, pleasant.

"And then after our wedding, the glory of Shot begins."

"You cannot actually think that my clan would allow you to hold me prisoner here in this room—"

"A sleeping draught," commented Murdoch, as if thinking aloud. "To calm you. Yes, I can see the benefits." And now he smiled again, brilliant. "It would be most unfortunate if you refused it, Lauren. So don't force my hand."

He studied her there on the pallet and she could only stare back, witnessing the transformation of what she had thought was at worst a hard and callous man into something much closer to a monster.

"What, no weeping?" asked the Murdoch, holding his smile. "Are you afraid your womanly tricks won't work on me, Lauren? Do try. Perhaps I might change my mind, to have you fall on me softly and beg me with tears."

Lauren said coldly, "I have wept for better men than you. I will not cry again."

His smile dimmed some, then he shrugged, turning away.

"In the end, what you think doesn't matter in the slightest. You are nothing, Lauren. Tomorrow you will still be nothing, except that through our marriage you bring me one step closer to Shot, and all she holds.

After I win the battle for this island we will leave here; and let me assure you, once on the mainland, you will truly understand me when I tell you that you live only for me."

He moved to the door. "For now, I humor you. You will remain here, docile and calm, and accept the drink I will send you. Else my men will inform me, and you will not like what happens next. I promise you that."

She sat up, arms hugged together over her chest, bedraggled and trying hard not to show him her anger, the panic. He watched her for a moment, then nodded. He walked out the door, had a hushed conversation with the men posted there, then turned back and shut it. He wouldn't have the key to lock it, she knew that, but he didn't need one. There were at least three of his soldiers guarding the room, more formidable than any lock.

Keir did not have a dungeon—she had told Arion the truth, what seemed like years ago now, when she had toyed with the idea of keeping him hostage. But it did have quarters where hostages used to be kept, before both kings had outlawed kidnapping between the two families.

The quarters were in a wing of Keir that was not quite separated from the rest of it, yet not completely a part of it, either. Since castle space was always short, it had been decided that the rooms would be best turned into living chambers, and such effort had gone into making them comfortable that eventually they had become one of the most desirable parts of the castle to live in.

So naturally it was here that the clan had decided to

place the laird of the Murdochs, and his personal guard. And it was here that Lauren was held, in the rooms that used to house English prisoners, far from the main section of the keep, from her family, and their aid.

Would they listen to his madman's rhetoric? Would they give in to hatred and prejudice, and attack the very people who had saved them not a week before?

No. Surely not. Quinn would not listen. The council was not that unwise.

But the thumping of Lauren's heart told her something different. The panic screamed for action—to escape, to warn Arion, to save him.

She ran to the lone window of the room, thankfully enlarged from the narrow slit it had been in the days of prisoners. The wooden frame was firmly secured. She pushed against the hinges, throwing glances over her shoulder at the door. How long would it take Murdoch to find a drug for her? She wasn't certain. She had to hurry.

The window opened with a shudder and she pushed harder, straining. At last it eased open enough for her to fit her head through, and then her shoulders, twisting sideways, looking down at the ground, two floors below her.

Well, she had no choice. She would cling to the stone as long as she could, and if she fell, at least she knew how to roll with it. Who knew that her rough-and-tumble childhood could have prepared her for this?

But she wasn't prepared, and when she was dangling by her fingertips from the edge of the windowsill, she realized there were no grooves in the stone deep enough to provide a hold for her feet or hands. If she stayed as she was, it was only a matter of time before she was discovered.

Lauren let go.

She fell with the fluttering of her tartan and landed hard on her back, instinct taking over to curl up into herself, protecting her head.

Pain slammed through her, blackness filled her vision, all the old wounds of the past few weeks screaming to life again. It was a long while before she could rise to her elbows, gasping in the air.

Nothing broken, as far as she could tell, a precious bit of luck. Lauren rose slowly to her feet, looking around her.

She was out of the keep, but not beyond the castle walls. Worse, she had no cloak, nothing to help disguise herself. At least this side of the keep was cast in shadow. Even at this distance from the main gate, she could hear the chorus of voices from the people milling about in the bailey. Clan members from the outer villages were arriving at Keir for the wedding tomorrow, and the celebration tonight would go on until nearly dawn, she knew.

The weaving room was nearest to her, and blessedly deserted. Lauren quickly crept in and shut the door behind her, feeling her way around in the gloom. She didn't think anyone had noticed her. Her gown was dark, her tartan the same as everyone else's, and no one had cried out to her in recognition.

There was a line of hooks on the wall near the door, meant to hang wet cloaks and tartans, close to the lone hearth in the room. Usually extra cloaks could be found there, forgotten by their owners in the rush to go somewhere else, to make it to the buttery in time for a meal, to the nursery to greet the children. . . .

Yes, fate was smiling on her, at least as far as this. Her hands encountered a mass of material where the cloaks should be, and she pulled down the one nearest to her and felt her way around it until she was certain she had it on correctly. It was slightly too large for her; when she stepped back out into the bailey the hood fell low across her eyes. Perfect.

Lauren hunched her shoulders, moving toward the gatehouse, trying desperately to think of a way to exit the castle walls. It was not time for the sheep to be brought in or led out, and all the shepherds would be gone by now. She could only pray for a hunting party, or a group arriving from the villages. Or perhaps the gate would remain open tonight, in anticipation of late arrivals. . . .

But it wasn't. When she was nearer to the gatehouse Lauren saw that the portcullis had been lowered to the ground, although the massive wooden gate itself was down. She would not be able to leave unless they raised the staked grid of the portcullis as well, however.

She stood still amid the bustling crowd around her, people calling out and greeting one another in hearty tones, MacRaes and a scattering of Murdoch's men, standing in clusters of threes and fours and watching the crowds.

One of them looked over to her and Lauren turned away, head lowered, heart pounding. She began an aimless walk toward a group of her clan, as if she meant to join in their conversation, and then hesitated just outside of them.

People were not really dispersing, only moving about, back to the stables, to the keep and out again, holding mugs and flasks of ale and wine and whiskey. Someone bumped into her and apologized. Lauren only nodded in response, again moving away.

She risked a look at the portcullis, still lowered. Another person stepped into her, this time managing to grab her elbow before she fell; a man reeking of whiskey, who asked if she was hurt and laughed good-naturedly when she shook her head no.

"Have a care, now," exclaimed the man. "You need a drink, lass. It's a celebration, you know."

Lauren replied, "I know," in a husky voice, and walked away as fast as she dared.

She had to get out of here. She was afraid she might be attracting attention, a lone woman amid all these clusters of revelers, but she couldn't very well go up to anyone and join in a conversation. Chances were excellent that some member of her clan would recognize her, and then her game would be finished.

She heard the command for the portcullis to rise. Lauren turned toward it along with the rest of the crowd, everyone eager to see who was arriving now.

It was a party of about fifty people, men and women both, most on foot but a few mounted, and they poured through the gate to the delighted calls of everyone around her. Lauren moved with the group nearest her toward the newcomers, intent on escape.

She brushed by one of the horses just as a woman dismounted, aided by two men. Their shoulders almost clipped but Lauren managed to duck in time, hearing the other woman speak in a soft, happy voice.

"Isn't it grand?" asked the woman, and Lauren was horrified to recognize her cousin Kenna's tones. "I can't wait for Lauren to see the baby."

"Aye, love," replied a man, and they began to walk away.

In spite of herself she turned to watch them, this time not feeling anything like panic but rather something more like pain, remorse. Their heads were close together, Kenna's arms wrapped securely around what Lauren realized was her new child. Lauren hadn't known the babe had come. She didn't even know if Kenna had gotten the daughter she had wanted.

And now, most likely, she would not find out. Not under the joyous circumstances that she had expected.

It hurt. It hurt with a kind of bright intensity, and here, in this perilous moment, she truly understood what it was she was leaving behind her—the goodwill of her clan. Their hopes for her, and for their own future.

She turned back to the gate and began to nudge her way through the people still coming in, all on foot, as if she were looking for someone who had not yet arrived. It was more difficult than she had imagined. She was fighting the flow of people intent upon the keep, and the warmth and hospitality offered there. When a cloaked man knocked into her she was pushed back, hard, and felt annoyance rise through her. The man did not look at her, nor did he offer any sort of apology, not even a nod. He moved on, limping just slightly, leaving Lauren to stare at his shrouded back, a hood masking his hair.

That limp. She knew it. Indeed, she had it burned

into her memory, her very last sight of him, fading off into the night across the meadow.

No, no, she thought, disbelieving. *It can't be him. It can't be.*

She had no time for this. She had no time to turn around, away from the gatehouse, where the last of the people were straggling in. She had no time to chase after this stranger, to risk locking herself into Keir and possibly losing all that she was gambling for just to see the face of a man with a limp. It was insane.

The gate, still open, beckoned to her.

The man, still limping, was traveling slowly through the crowd, as if he were not quite certain of where to go.

Cursing herself, Lauren turned away from her freedom, began a hurried walk through the throng of people, trying to keep the man in sight while at the same time hiding her face from the others.

Stupid, she berated herself. *Fool! You're going to miss it, the gate will close, all because you think you see him everywhere. He would never be crazed enough to come to Keir, not now, not ever. He knows he'd be killed. Turn around! Get out of here!*

But she didn't. She lost him for a moment, an eddy of men stumbling in front of her, ale sloshing from their mugs as they broke into laughter, and when she looked around he was nowhere to be seen.

She took a calming breath and stood motionless on the stones, searching, her hand clenched tight around the hood, holding it close to her face.

There! He was over there, near the entrance to the castle, stopped, looking around. His hood was also low, but when he turned his head she had a glimpse of his jaw—square, firm—and lips set to a tight line.

Lauren went to him as quickly as she could manage, cold fear tingling through her hands, leaving her numb and shaken. Just before she reached him he came to the main doors of the keep, waiting for a group of women to pass though before going in.

Lauren ended up running the last few steps to him. If he went into the great hall, she would be recognized in an instant.

She managed to grab a fold of his cloak just as he began to enter, tugging him back, causing him instinctively to look behind him to see what stayed him.

Lauren moved her hand from her hood, revealing her face to him.

Arion stared down at her, disbelieving.

His eyes widened; a frown appeared, incredulity.

She pulled at him again, wordless, back toward the gatehouse, and she knew her worry must be apparent on her face because he turned at once, taking her arm, leading them back the way they had come. Both had their hoods lowered in place, both walked a little too quickly compared to the rest of the people, but there was no time to be more subtle. The last of the incoming party was entering the gate, and soon there would be no chance to leave. There was no way to tell when or if another party might arrive.

Lauren heard the gatekeeper yell out a command, and the heavy portcullis began to lower, the chain unrolling from its giant spool in metallic clicks that sent a winter touch down her spine.

They were not going to make it. They were about to

be trapped in the bailey, the two of them with almost every member of her clan, and Murdoch's men besides. Lauren knew it would be just a matter of time before she was reported missing, even if Payton Murdoch had not truly planned to send her a sleeping draught. Someone from her family—Hannah, if no one else— would insist upon seeing her, and then the ruse would be over. She could think of no plausible reason to offer for trying to steal out of Keir with the Earl of Morgan at her side.

Lauren and Arion stopped together, watching the crisscrossed wood and metal of the portcullis slowly descend to the ground, preventing anyone from traveling in or out of the castle.

Then they looked at each other. She saw the resignation in his face, the mystery of his green eyes revealed to her: intelligence, determination. He began to look around them, hand still firm on her elbow, searching for some alternative. A rowdy group of soldiers was coming toward them, more ale and whiskey being shared all around, and in desperation she pulled him by the hand toward the wall of the keep, to a spot that held the corner of a shadow from a turret above. They cut through the thinning crowd and stayed there, watching as bit by bit the mixture of people in the bailey headed into the castle.

Payton Murdoch walked out of the keep. He strode with an air of confidence, headed exactly for them, to the group of his clansmen who were standing idle in a circle just beyond Lauren and Arion. He had to pass close by to get to his men. He would, without a doubt, see the couple lingering by the wall.

Lauren turned to Arion and pulled his head down to hers with both hands, holding him there for her kiss, and after a moment of startled hesitation, he put his arms around her, bringing her closer, their faces together, their hoods touching.

He was heat and languid goodness to her, he was strength and comfort. She found herself relaxing against him despite the moment, surrendering some of the outside troubles for this second of stolen joy, for his lips, his touch, so welcome.

He made some soft sound between them, his hands broad across her back, holding her even nearer, and she felt the stinging passion he brought go spiraling through her, lazy and fine, the opposite of what she should be feeling and doing right now, but oh, it didn't matter. . . .

Arion lifted his mouth from hers and murmured, "Was it he?"

She nodded, lowering her head, still wrapped in his embrace, then allowed herself the slightest look down and to her left, to where Murdoch's men had stood.

They were gone. They must have moved off after their laird had come to them, all of them off to some evil business, Lauren was sure. She raised her head a little more, still not seeing them, then turned the other way, scanning the other side of the bailey.

Almost everyone had left for the keep, and Murdoch and his men were nowhere in sight. Pockets of tipsy celebration could still be seen here and there: men and women over by the stables, laughing long and hard. Soldiers by the gate, discussing something in cheerful, loud tones. A few more people walking back and forth, each with a destination, in couples and foursomes.

From inside the keep music could now be heard, more laughter, the din of conversation booming.

The portcullis remained securely lowered.

Lauren gazed back up at Arion, trying hard to think of something clever to save them both, at the very least to get him out of here before they caught her.

"Listen," she began, the barest whisper. "We're going to have to separate. But I have to tell you something before I go—"

He stopped her with another kiss, this one harder, more demanding. Lauren tried to pull away, to finish her sentence, but he was insistent. She gave up her half-hearted struggle and responded to him instead, leaning into him, causing his grip to soften, become closer to a caress through her clothing.

"We're not separating," Arion said after a while, very quietly. "Tell me what you're doing out here."

"Will you listen to me?" Lauren hissed back. "You're in danger! You can't be found near me!"

Three men exited the keep, stood for a moment near the entrance, then began to walk toward Lauren and Arion. He quickly leaned down and kissed her again. She heard the men pass by them, rumbling tones that did not sound pleased, words too low to catch. Then they were out of range.

"You must get back to Elguire." Lauren stood on her toes to bring her lips to his ear, smiling coyly for the sake of the men, who might be watching them. "Murdoch plans an attack on you. You must be ready."

Arion pulled back, his face harsh. "Are you certain?"

She nodded again, her smile fading away to soberness. "I was coming to tell you."

He took a deep breath and let it out, closing his eyes, showing her the strain and fatigue on him that she had not the time to notice before.

"They'll know I'm missing soon," Lauren continued, speaking fast. "You need to be far away from me. They won't suspect you're here."

His eyes opened, ocean deep and beautiful, and she felt a wrenching sorrow fill her, that this would be the end of them after all, that she had come so far and made so many daring choices—only to be caught again. At least she could gain some solace in that she had been able to warn him.

Another set of men came out of the keep, and another, and another. All were soldiers, MacRaes and Murdochs mixed, and they walked with short, impatient steps, coming together in groups and parting again, the mumble of their conversations sounding ominously grim.

Sweet heavens, perhaps it had happened already— Murdoch had gone back to see her and found her vanished. They would be searching for her, forming parties to cover the castle and its grounds with swift efficiency. They would try not to alarm the guests at first— Murdoch would not want a scene from her, not with his wicked plan to pursue—but when she was not easily found they would grow more aggressive in their hunt, and soon all of Keir would join in.

She had to get Arion out of here. She had to find a safe place for him. They were beginning to attract notice again.

The gatekeeper called out a command. Lauren felt her body freeze in hope, in a rush of prayer. And the portcullis began to rise, the clinking of the chain now the most welcome sound she had ever heard. A new party had arrived.

She began to pull Arion toward it but he was already at her side, his hood once again concealing him, her own so far down over her face that she could see only the stones of the ground in front of her. Escape was the only thing she could think of in this moment, the only thing she could feel, taste in her mouth, sharp and bright. The newcomers jostled into them, greeting others in loud tones, and from the sound of it quite a few people were spilling from the keep, flowing around the soldiers of before, laughing and drinking. Arion guided her past them all, his limp growing more and more pronounced.

Lauren watched her feet cross the deep indentations in the stone bridgeway where the spikes of the portcullis would rest. She watched herself take the first few steps out of Keir, past the arched gateway to the road beyond, people and horses still out there, waiting to enter.

They moved slowly and almost easily through these latest arrivals, no hurry, no rush, just a couple looking for friends, perhaps, or family members. They blended in with the confusion, they were nothing strange, nothing suspicious, moving closer and closer to the end of the multitude of people and animals.

The night was clouded and dark, although the wall-walk of Keir was lit with many torches. Firelight fell intermittently around them, actually aiding the disorder with deceptive patterns of shadow and glow.

Her feet came to grass—they were off the road, still walking calmly, their pace unbroken. No one called out after them. No one broke apart from the group, following them.

For the first time Lauren dared to look up at her surroundings, at the tall trees of pine and oak and birch around them, and at the man beside her, his hand warm and firm on her arm. Arion glanced down at her, then back behind them. Lauren followed his look.

Almost all the people were inside the gate. No one turned around to seek them out—they were headed for the golden light and laughter that was Keir right now, with no thought for the darkness of the woods around them.

Arion slipped his hand down her arm until his fingers intertwined with hers. Together they began a stilted run into the depths of the night, where a midnight destrier awaited them, and then Elguire beyond.

Chapter Fifteen

⸺◦〰〰〰◦⸺

*H*E TOOK HER TO A room she didn't know, obviously not his own, this one smaller, more feminine somehow—the bed was made of ash, not oak, and the curtains that fell around it were folds of soft blue and white.

Elguire was a mystery to her, interlocking rooms, narrow turning hallways, people crowded all around them, staring at her, at their lord. Arion said nothing to them beyond sending for his steward, his hold on her hand undiminished as he escorted her to this chamber.

There was a connecting door in one of the walls here. She knew, without asking, that it led to his own set of rooms.

Arion had taken her here and bidden her to rest, few words, a sparse and distracted look to him. Lauren knew he needed to speak to Fuller, to inform him and the rest of the Murdoch's treachery, and that there was precious little time to waste. Aye, she understood when he kissed her hand and bowed away from her, his attention already gone past her and beyond, to a hall filled with his people, and to a battle almost certainly coming with the dawn.

On the ride to Elguire she told him all that Payton

Murdoch had told her, his plans to attack, when and why, and Arion had listened and asked questions. Lauren had been careful not to mention her fiancé's treatment of her; in the anger and urgency of the moment, Arion had not asked. It was just as well.

She tried not to feel remorseful when he left her in this little room in his fortress. She tried to remember that she had done the right thing, that it had to be right to warn him of the attack, that it was what Da would have wanted, what any person of honor would have done.

But here in this foreign chamber, with its pretty bed and dainty rug of flowers and vines on the floor, Lauren felt a misery she hardly comprehended overtake her. She sank down to the stones in front of the hearth, untying and removing her wet and muddied boots because it was the practical thing to do, and a grain of practicality seemed like sanity to her now. She set them aside and let the fire warm her toes until the heat grew painful. Her knees drew up to her chest, arms wrapped around them.

Lauren watched the flames before her, allowing the warmth to bask her skin even as her heart grew colder and colder as she reflected on her actions.

She had done it. She had left Keir, and Payton Murdoch. She had thrown away the alliance she had been bred to create, she had tossed back in their faces her clan's wishes for her and run away with the man they had all been bred to despise.

Slowly her chin came to rest on top of her knees, her eyelids growing heavier.

What an impossible thing she had done. What a mad, impossible thing.

And tomorrow they might all die for it. It would be a war, after all . . . but at least she had made certain it wouldn't be an ambush . . . she had done her best to even the odds. . . .

She must have fallen asleep, because when she looked up she saw Arion standing over her. She was curled on her side on the floor, her back to the fire.

He knelt in front of her, his look one of deep concentration. One hand lifted to touch her face, slow and soft, following the curve of her cheek, stroking under her jaw. She didn't move, she only watched him, his fingers now coming back up to trace the line of her eyebrows, down her nose, to her lips, his touch careful, almost tentative.

"Are you well?" he asked, hushed in the emptiness of the chamber.

She gave a slight nod and he moved his hand away. She felt the coldness of the air take his place, a strange loss. Lauren sat up.

"What happened?" she asked. "What did they say?"

"Elguire is prepared for an attack," Arion responded. "We've been prepared for it for weeks. I don't want it to come to that, however. I don't want to risk the lives of the women and children here. We have lookouts posted throughout the island, a relay chain that will tell us exactly when and where they amass. We will meet the damn Scots in the fields rather than here. They won't find it easy to get past us."

His look was hard and remote; she heard him brand her clan with easy contempt and felt the affront rise through her, though she knew he had good reason for his anger.

"And what of me?" she asked, a shade of tartness to her tone. "Here is a Scot already in Elguire. Are you not afraid I'll turn on you, and let in my fellow countrymen?"

To her surprise, he didn't respond to her challenge, but instead slowly sat down beside her, grimacing, reminding her of his wounds and how he had come by them. She felt a surge of shame, that she would be so hard with him, when all he had done was protect her, again and again.

"No," said Arion, facing the dwindling flames. "Not you, Lauren. I know you too well. You would be honorable, no matter how much it harmed you to do so."

Then he looked over at her, almost a dare in his gaze. She lowered her head, confused and oddly close to some finely strung emotion, something that both thrilled and saddened her. She saw Arion reach out and take her hand, holding it lightly.

A new thought struck her. "What were you doing there?" she asked. "Why did you go to Keir?"

He didn't reply at once, only kept his gaze locked on their hands, and then on her eyes, heated and darkly cryptic. At last he said, "I went for you. For the wedding—for you. To see you again, I suppose." He gave a curt laugh. "It was incredibly foolish."

"Aye," Lauren replied, biting. "And you were lucky you didn't die from it, du Morgan."

"You misunderstand." He lowered his head again, firelight sliding over his features, casting him with flickering gold. "I went to Keir to steal you away, Lauren MacRae. I went to see if I could find you before your marriage took place, and persuade you to come with me to—I don't even know where. Anywhere. I had made a mistake, you see. A laughable, unbelievable mistake. I let you go. I should never have done that."

"Oh," she said, hesitant.

"I came alone. In case you said no." He gave a pained smile to the logs in the hearth. "I didn't want to risk a war, but I couldn't stay away. I couldn't let you do it, marry him. Not without talking to you again, at least one more time. I had to see you—I had to see your face. At first I told myself it was only that I wanted to be certain I had done the right thing in letting you go, that you did not—*could* not—belong to me. But even that wasn't true."

He took a heavy breath; the smile still there, darker than before, a hint of something intense and dangerous in him. "I wanted to reach you, Lauren. To convince you to come back to me."

"You sent me away," she said, unable to stop the words, the hurt that spurred them on, even though her hand was clenched tight around his.

"I was wrong." Arion turned to her, releasing her hand, taking both of her shoulders and pushing her gently down to the floor, until she rested on her back and he hovered over her, so serious, still holding that dark intensity.

"I was wrong, utterly wrong. I was trying so hard to be unselfish, and worthy of you. I was trying to be the thing that my uncle never was, a righteous man. And it took me too long to realize that none of that mattered—not selflessness, or honor, or virtue—not my title, my lands, my knighthood. Nothing mattered without you, Lauren. I'm keeping you now, and to hell with all the consequences. I'm a damned blackguard—and I don't care."

"I don't either," Lauren said up to him, just as serious.

"Good."

He bent down to kiss her, nothing temperate, nothing soft, but instead everything she needed right now—his passion and fervency, his demands and entreaties, his body lowering to hers. Everything hot, everything wanted.

She welcomed him with her touch, with her kisses. She pulled at him and curved beneath him and loved the sound he made from it: a guttural growl, masculine, possessive.

Lauren turned her head and found his jaw, roughness from the growth of new beard, delight in that slight pain, the fragrance of him, the taste of his skin. Her hands felt the coolness of his tunic, straining across his back, the shape of the muscles beneath it, sculpted and taut. He pressed into her, finding their rhythm, leading her to it with him.

She thought, *He may die tomorrow. We all may die.* . . .

But it seemed so far away, the thoughts of another woman, the worries of another time and place. Right now was only Arion, here with him in this room, rising together to their knees, his hands following the lines of her body, to the silver brooch she wore . . . removing it and tossing it aside, letting the tartan fall free to her waist, their chests skimming together, their lips exchanging sweetness.

Her belt was gone next; the tartan slid softly from her, down to puddle between them, and how much closer she could hold him without the weight of it against her. How much more of him she could feel, his form rigid against her. He pulled her nearer, her face tucked in to the heat of his neck, his hands almost frantic on her, roving, finding her shape and outlining it, their breath short and rushed. Lauren held on to him, not knowing what else to do.

He may die, she thought again in some distant part of her, incredulous. *You can't die, Arion, no, no, I love you....*

And it didn't matter that she was inexperienced, that while she wanted all of him at once she didn't know how to achieve it, which way was best to touch him, to hold him. Everything she did seemed right. He let her know with murmured encouragement, with his hands, his legs, his mouth hard on hers and his tongue running over her lips—the back of her gown unlaced, coming loose across her shoulders, offering him more of the paleness of her skin.

He hesitated only when she knew he saw the bruises at her throat, but it was too late to try to hide them. Instead she turned her lips to him, finding the scent of him again, the taste of his skin with her tongue, and it brought him back to her, to the fact of her loosened gown, slipping down her arms.

His kissed her there, he sucked at the slope of her shoulder, across the fine line of her collarbone, his touch now light, almost delicate. It made her crave him more, so Lauren stretched into him, tilting back her head, supported at her waist with the security of his arm, and Arion let her know that this was right, too. His hand came up and tugged at the bodice of her gown, shifting it down, allowing his lips to follow the path.

He sent chills through her, he made the flames before them seem dim. With just a few spare moves her gown was gone from her, and then the thin shift beneath it, and she knelt before him with the firelight gleaming off her skin, abashed and eager together.

Arion paused, his look fervent and sharp, his palms just skimming the tops of her arms.

"Lauren," he said, and nothing more. She felt the barest tremble to his touch. Shyness rushed through her, unexpected and unrelieved. Her head lowered, her hair falling forward in a whisper across her shoulders, concealing her.

His hands moved and found the back of her neck beneath the weight of her hair, cupping her head until she lifted her chin again. He gave her a light kiss that still scorched her, brought a blush to burn across her entire body. "Beloved," he said. "Beautiful Lauren . . ."

He drew her up to stand with him, another kiss, and then before she could fathom it he had lifted her into his arms, taking them across the chamber to the blue and white bed, thick covers and pale furs around her. She fell into the softness, almost laughing, and he was smiling with her, leaning over her, heavy and splendid. The blankets were cool against her back and thighs, and Arion was warm above her. She didn't want him to leave her. When he moved she would be chilled again, bare and vulnerable, and so she twined her arms around his shoulders to keep him there.

His teeth found her earlobe; his breath a murmured rush. "You smell of flowers. You taste like . . . I don't know. Like Lauren, wild and perfect . . ." and he pressed his lips to a place behind her ear that made the air around her seem too thin.

He pulled back despite her hold, leaving her to shed himself of his tunic, the hose and belt and all the pieces of English clothing that held him back from her, until he was as bare as she.

Battle scars and clean lines, bandages and cuts, he was more than what she could have imagined, broader and better defined, so handsome with his dark hair and ocean eyes, and so different from her, so incredible.

But she had no time to admire him, even as the burning blush came back. As soon as he could he was back beside her, lithe and sinewy against her, holding her to him, caressing her, feeling her breasts, her ribs and hips. Lauren felt a measure of her uncertainty fade beneath the magic of his hands, the amazing feel of his skin against hers—and then he stopped, just touching her, his palms a burning heat. For a moment they merely stayed that way, staring at each other, a gathering spell weaving around them.

Then Arion moved; easily and with such grace that it seemed perfectly natural to her—he came over her and she felt his hardness hot against her belly, and then lower, to the part of her that knew him well, that suffused her with the stinging fire of the liquid sun.

Lauren thought she knew what to expect now, and this time her fear of binding to him was gone. All she felt now was anticipation, keen and aching, an impatient desire that opened her legs to him, an invitation.

This was better than before, in the barren winter of the meadow. This was what she had envisioned in her deepest and most forbidden dreams: the sight of him over her, his eyes closed, his face tight with concentration, his hands at her shoulders, holding her . . . and every bit of her stretching to take him in, reveling in the feel of him inside of her. It hurt, but that didn't matter. It was barely there, a new discomfort that still thrilled her.

He did not stop, as part of her expected. He came into her deeper, deeper, until the pain became more distinct, and a cold apprehension broke through her flush, stilling her.

Arion opened his eyes, emerald heat.

"I love you, Lauren," he said, and did something sharp and awful to her, a rough push that buried him into her and made the pain go searing bright.

She gave a small cry but he caught it with his lips, smothering it, holding fast against her sudden resistance to him, clenched and strained above her, the set of his jaw tight.

"Sorry, sorry," he was saying, a broken hush against her skin, and then her hair. "Oh, I love you, my beautiful Lauren. . . ."

And it slowly became bearable like this, with his gasping apology, his body so intimate yet held away from her with just the support of his elbows and forearms braced around her face, his cheek against hers. When she thought it might be safe to try to move, to speak, he did it for her, saying her name again, matching the need in his voice with the stroking of his body, a slow slide out of her, and then back in.

Lauren loosened her hands, which had been braced firmly against him, feeling this wondrous new sensation, and then he did it again, and again. Her fingers unfurled, her back gave a slight arch, and Arion nodded against her, no words now, only the labored release of his breath, rapid and warm. He began to move a little faster, a gradual increase of something, and she felt herself respond without thinking about it, her knees coming up beside him. She turned her head to his neck, tasting the salt there, feeling the blood beat through him and match with hers, with this rhythm they had found together.

It wasn't enough; something was missing, some vital element to him that she had not yet discovered, though it seemed she could hardly encompass more of him. Perfect ebony hair slid over her skin, a silken touch. Their bodies became slick together as he showed Lauren new ways to move, to feel him and let the sparks he gave her blossom in intensity, become lightning.

Lauren arched up again, a shade of demand to her now. Above her Arion's face was closed, lost to her, gone to his own realm of pleasure or pain, she couldn't say which. It made her falter some, seeing the starkness across his features, and she lost the beat of their bodies to her uncertainty, watching him.

Arion came back to her. He focused on her, sudden and almost ferocious with the raw emotion in his eyes, pushing deep and hard, and from nowhere the lightning exploded through her, countless sparks of burning delight, centered on him, all about him. Her head fell back, the soft cry came again, this time holding awe and revelation.

He stiffened above her, then began a series of rapid thrusts that ended as abruptly as they had begun, clenched above her, holding her to him, flooding her with himself until they were both lost to it, each wrapped around the other, panting, enthralled in their closeness.

"I love you, Arion," Lauren whispered, when at last she could speak.

"Yes," he said, and turned his head until their lips were brushing again, a sweet vow of promise and joy. Together they settled down deeper into the blankets surrounding them.

Lauren lifted one hand, a slow stroke across his cheek, an echo of his earlier caress, and he caught her fingers against his lips and kissed them.

Please, Lord—don't let him die.

———————⁙———————

SHE DID NOT THINK THAT she had slept.

It would have been a miracle to sleep with all that had happened, and was yet to happen still, although a new lassitude seemed to weigh down Lauren's limbs, and her body felt sore and warm in the bed, Arion curled beside her.

But Lauren didn't think she had slept until she glanced over at the fire and found it out, cherry embers burning dimly, nothing more. The sky beyond the window, however, was still dark.

When she shifted she found Arion watching her, nearly masked in the dusk surrounding them. Only the faint glimmer of his eyes revealed him to her.

"It will happen soon," Lauren said.

"I know," he replied, after a moment.

"I'm coming with you."

"No." His refusal was instant, absolute.

"I have to," she said. "I must."

"No," he repeated, just as firm.

"Arion, you don't understand—".

"No, *you* don't understand, Lauren." He leaned up on one elbow over her, still graceful, so masculine. "I will not have you in another battle. You will stay here at Elguire. You'll be safe here, as safe as I can make you."

"You *need* me out there. Perhaps I can talk to them, make them see—"

"Stop." His voice was rasped and low, scored with some deep emotion. Arion paused, then shook his head. "Do you think I could suffer it, to watch you harmed again? Do you think I could bear to watch you die, or be taken back to *him*? Don't do that to me, Lauren. Don't do it."

She turned her head away, fighting the betraying shiver in her that wanted to weep and plea and curse at this unhappy ending for them, when they had already managed to overcome so many unhappy things.

The world around them was silent and empty; the blue and white cloth of the canopy above them rustled with some phantom draft, then fell still again.

Lauren kept her voice as dim as the night around them. "Do you trust me, du Morgan?"

It seemed he would not respond, but then he said, "Yes,"—almost angry.

She rolled to her side, facing him. "Then you must let me do this. I have to come with you."

"This has nothing to do with trust."

"You must trust me. You must trust that I know what would be best for me—and, I hope, for us. I don't want to die, Arion. But if I do," she placed her hand on his forearm, "then I want it to be beside you. Not here, locked away. Not trapped in marriage with Payton Murdoch. With you, letting my clan see with their own eyes what their hatred has wrought."

He shifted and moved closer to her, his arms coming around her, their bodies held together again, her face turned to his chest.

"I couldn't endure it," he confessed to her, down to her temple. "To see you injured. To know I was responsible for it—"

"No, not you." She lifted her head. "Not you, Arion. The responsibility falls to them, to Quinn and the council, to Murdoch and his army. To their injustice and cowardice. But never you."

He sighed, still keeping her with him. One hand moved restlessly across her bare back, frustration in his touch.

"Let me come with you," Lauren urged. "We began our alliance weeks ago, Arion du Morgan. Let us end it together, if it must end at all."

She felt his concession in the way he lowered his forehead to hers, resting back onto the furs, his hand now settling into the curve of her neck.

"And mayhap," she continued, determined, "I can change them. Mayhap they'll listen to me, and realize what it is that they think to do."

"God help us all," said Arion.

———————— ⟡ ————————

*I*T WAS THE EARLIEST PART of dawn, the time when the new light was not yet more than a sliver of pale green and rose on the eastern horizon, and if there were stars out, they would shine with hard brilliance above, fighting the new day.

But there were few stars and more clouds, low and heavy, nature's ill omen for this morning. The wind blew in fits and starts, cold and mournful.

Word had come that the united clans of MacRae and Murdoch were riding toward Elguire, a great army of them, horses and archers and foot soldiers, men whom Lauren would no doubt know—their names, their places in the clan, their children and their wives. . . .

It was to have been her wedding day. How curious that she sat on a steed at the opposite end of a long valley from her former fiancé instead, feeling nothing for him but bitter anger.

"Three to one," offered Fuller, on the other side of Arion, his voice empty.

"Aye," responded Arion.

Lauren would have guessed something slightly worse than that. Perhaps it was that she had never witnessed her clan gathered before her as the enemy—had never even dreamed of it—but seeing them now set off a metallic fear in her bones. They looked so fierce, gathered in a rough line across the field, watching her with Arion's army. The dark mass of them stretched out as far as she could see. They looked . . . infinite.

Beside her Arion watched them as well, chain mailed and armed, his eyes piercing and bright. He glanced down at her, at the tunic she wore, her tartan over it. A brooch of emeralds and gold—Arion's mother's, he had said, offering it to her—was pinned to her shoulder. She held the rowan branch and the ruby ring in her hands beneath the reins. She carried no weapon.

Lauren knew she would not be able to lift a hand against her family. To kill one of her clan would be no different from killing herself, and today she hoped that neither of those things would happen. There was only one chance, and she had to take it.

It had upset Arion, of course. He had argued with her and threatened her, then cajoled and pleaded, but she had held firm: No weapon, and aye, she *was* going to face them.

With one last look at all the English warriors spread out behind her, Lauren touched her heels to her stallion and began a slow walk across the valley, Arion on one side, Fuller on the other. She had not been able to persuade him to let her go alone, and finally this was the compromise they had accepted.

She realized Arion planned to be the sword that defended her, even against her clan, if need be. She understood that, and knew better than to argue against it. Should their circumstances have been reversed, she would have insisted on the same thing. So much depended upon her now.

Three mounted men broke apart from the rest on the Scottish side—her cousin Quinn, Payton Murdoch, and James. They began a path that would bring them face to face with Lauren.

Her thoughts became strangely detached, analytical, almost unreal.

She noticed, for the first time, her family's banner snapping in the wind amid the horsemen, another beside it, unfamiliar, yet leaving no doubt as to whose it was.

She had not seen an English banner behind her when they rode out this morning. Perhaps the English did not use such things. Perhaps Arion didn't have a banner.

They had reached the middle of the field and waited there, watching Quinn and the rest continue on until they faced one another, horses snorting and pawing the frozen ground. The air between the two groups became misted with their breath.

Lauren met the deceptive look of Murdoch easily; she had nothing to fear from him. It was her family who could hurt her most.

"Come back to Keir, Lauren," said Quinn evenly to her.

"I won't," she replied.

"Betrayal!" exclaimed James, his voice thin with outrage.

"Not from me!" Lauren cried. "I would never betray my clan—our honor! I would never skulk like a dog and attack an ally from behind! If there is betrayal here, look to your own hearts for it!"

"*He* is not our ally!" spat James, a derisive look to Arion.

"He has been more of a friend to you than that man over there." Lauren pointed at Murdoch. "The Earl of Morgan has acted with integrity toward you, he has defended you and fought for you and me and the entire clan. He has nearly given his life to save Shot, and you thank him for it by planning his death!"

Before James could respond, Quinn held up a hand, silencing him.

"What do you speak of, Lauren? What plan of death?"

She hesitated, her look flying to Murdoch, to the flat

calm of his face. "His plan," she said, nodding toward him. "To attack Elguire. Don't think to fool me."

Quinn only stared at her, and she knew him so well that her stomach seemed to pitch and turn—she read it in his eyes: He hadn't known. He still didn't know. Murdoch had told him nothing of his treacherous plot.

"She is distraught, no doubt," said the Murdoch in his soothing voice. "It is a travesty, this weakness of her mind."

"I am telling the truth," she said to Quinn, trying hard to keep her voice firm. "You know I wouldn't lie. You know."

"Poor child," said Payton Murdoch. "What has he done to you?"

"She is senseless," muttered James.

From the corner of her eye she saw Arion shift in his saddle, his hand clearly held on the hilt of his sword. Tension and danger radiated from him, a closely held restraint that might not last much longer. Lauren turned back to her cousin.

"Last night Payton Murdoch told me over dinner that he planned to seize control of all of Shot, that he and you would battle the English, and kill them, a surprise attack that they would not be able to recover from. He vowed to destroy them, Quinn. He said he would do it with your aid, right after the wedding."

And Quinn looked, just once, back at Murdoch, at the slightly mocking look he now wore.

"Addled," pronounced Murdoch. "You didn't warn me, MacRae, that my bride was prone to such feverish imaginings."

"Lauren," said Quinn, shaking his head. "What are you saying? It's nonsense."

"It's true! He said those things to me! He hates the English, he wants Shot! He said *we* would live in Elguire—that he would make me a present of it—this *after* I protested!" The words left her mouth in a biting rush, too fast, not convincing enough. "Why would I lie?" she asked, much more composed. "Why would I risk *everything* to leave Keir and go warn the English? Why would I turn my back on my father's honor, unless I thought that honor was about to be sullied by you—and by the Murdoch?"

No one said anything, not even Murdoch. The horses moved again, and one of them let out a guttural cry of displeasure. Behind the three men in front of her she could still see the banners, catching the pale light of the sun as it rose.

Lauren looked at Arion and found him watchful, eyes narrowed, his gaze unwavering on Murdoch. His hand was still gripped around his sword, a wedge of steel showing past the scabbard. She could almost feel the readiness of him, tightly coiled muscles, every word and sound a potential end to this moment, and a beginning to the war.

"Despite this insanity I will have her," announced the Murdoch, seemingly to them all. "We can forget this morning, MacRae. I will forgive her. But let us end this now. Come back to me, Lauren. None of us wants bloodshed."

He sounded so normal, almost loving. He looked at her as if she were a child who had merely fallen into some minor prank, and now needed to be lightly reprimanded.

"We don't need a war," lectured the Murdoch, nearly smiling at her. "So come away, Lauren. You will be happy again with me, I promise it."

He was persuading them. He was going to win, to have either her or his war, or both. How could it be that only she was not fooled by his practiced facade?

"Look at what your fine Murdoch has done to me," she said desperately, and tugged at the clasp of the cape she wore until it fell from her, slipping down her body to the horse, sliding to the ground. Lauren stood up in her saddle, pulling the collar of her tunic as far down as she could, lifting her chin.

"Look!" She tilted back her head, exposing her throat.

She knew what they would see, what she had been so careful to hide until now: the even circle of the bruises he had given her, deep and mottled now in the harsh light, doubly strong for the same pressure he had put on her almost every day, both hands around her neck, squeezing. It had been one of his games, a ploy to subdue her or enrage her, she didn't know which. But she knew now what effect it would have.

Quinn looked appalled; even James was shocked. Arion brought his destrier a pace closer to Murdoch's, the fury in him clear.

"You bastard," he said.

"It was the English," stated Murdoch, quick and defensive, backing up his mount.

"It was *you*!" She released her tunic but remained standing, pointing at him. "*You* did this! You and your wickedness! You've been deceiving us from the moment you arrived here—from before! You fooled my father with your lies, you fooled the council and my clan. But I will not let you destroy my family with this battle—not without showing them who you really are!"

Arion drew his sword. "I'm going to kill you," he told Murdoch, a devil's smile and icy conviction.

"It was *him,* I tell you," said Murdoch to Quinn, and then James. His demeanor was at last beginning to crack. "Don't listen to her! She's naught but a woman—she's mad!"

"Are my men ready?" Arion asked Fuller, not taking his eyes from Murdoch.

"Aye, my lord," responded the steward.

"I am the daughter of Hebron MacRae," said Lauren with dignity. "I am not mad, or distraught, or a liar. I speak only the truth. You, Quinn, should know this. I would never side with the enemy, and I will not side with Payton Murdoch now. So kill me if you must. But I will not join with you, or him. I have chosen the Earl of Morgan, who has dealt with us plainly and honestly. *I* have chosen honor."

With that she flung the rowan brooch and the ring to the feet of Murdoch's horse, watching them tumble through the air, flashes of dull silver and ruby, landing with a thud that seemed to echo around them, creating a bubble of silence after it.

Everything stopped, all the noises encased in this moment, the six of them with their armies surrounding them, death hanging above them in the sky, watching, waiting.

It was Quinn who broke the silence. He turned to Murdoch.

"It appears the betrothal is broken," he said, and Lauren felt exhilaration cascade through her, delight and triumph mingled with relief.

Murdoch looked stunned, then infuriated. "You cannot break it! You cannot believe her over me! Where is your sense, man? Take the woman from them and let this battle begin!"

"Do it," invited Arion coolly, his sword leveled in front of him, the tip to Murdoch. "Please. Let me show you how plainly and honestly I will kill you."

"This is your chance!" shouted Murdoch to Quinn, to the men behind them. "This is the place and the moment! We outnumber them! We will win, and then all of Shot will be ours!"

" 'Ours'?" inquired Quinn, an edge of steel to him now.

"Think on it, MacRae! The Isle of Shot belonging fully to Scotland, to our glory! You hate the English as much as I! You know their duplicity, their cunning ways! We unite our clans in marriage *and* in war! We win this battle and it's over—forever! Wipe them out! Show them that we will no longer tolerate them. Kill them all, and let their blood tell their king that *we* are the masters here!"

"Kill them all," echoed James, but it sounded strange, guarded.

"Aye!" Murdoch looked at him. "You agree with me. I knew you would. You see what I do, that Shot and all her wealth can be ours, that we are destined to rule her!"

James looked at Quinn, and then Lauren. His eyes were troubled, doubtful.

"Is it true what you said, lass?" he asked her.

"Yes," she replied.

"No!" countered the Murdoch. "She's a lying whore!"

Arion pushed forward again but Quinn beat him to it, drawing his own sword and holding it against Murdoch, showing Lauren that glimpse of her father in him.

"Enough, I think," stated Quinn. "Gather your men and get off the island. The betrothal is broken. Our alliance has ended."

"You cannot do this," grated Murdoch. "Idiot! You cannot give up what I have fought so hard to gain!"

"Shot is not yours," said Quinn. "And it never will be. That was never what this alliance was meant to be about."

"What do you know of it?" sneered Murdoch, moving his mount enough so that the swords aimed at him were out of range. "I have waited too long for this day— by God, that I should have to betroth myself to that witch just to gain a foothold here! I don't even need you, MacRae. I can do this without you! My men are well trained, they obey me instantly. If you are too weak and blind to rule this land properly, then I gladly take your place. Shot should have been mine years ago. Clan Murdoch should own this island—all of it! It falls into our territory, and it always has!"

"Blasphemy!" roared James, and now his broadsword was out as well.

In the far, far distance, Lauren heard the sound of a

thousand men begin to talk, begin to turn and break the stillness that had held them motionless, watching the drama on the field.

"You will not win," Quinn observed. "But I prefer not to prove it. Save yourself now, Murdoch. I offer you this last chance freely, for the sake of the unity we have shared between our clans until today. Get off of Shot now. Never return."

Murdoch did nothing, and Lauren could almost see him assess his odds, his eyes darting to all the English troops behind her, to his own men mingled with her clan on the other side of the field. His steed backed up another nervous step, shaking its head.

"It appears," said Arion with soft menace, "that we now outnumber *you.*"

Payton Murdoch turned his horse and began a gallop back up to the line of Scots.

"Attack!" he shouted, his sword raised high. "Attack!"

And his men began the run down the slight slope of the valley, a rumbling shout rising from them. Lauren saw Quinn wheel his steed around on the heels of Murdoch's, shouting something as well, but by now it was drowned beneath the cry of the armies, the men swarming toward them. The Scots became splintered, disorganized, her own clan looking to Quinn, following his call. The Murdochs ran past them.

"Get back," Arion was yelling at her, trying to grab her reins. "Get back behind my men!"

She was still unarmed, her stallion alarmed and skittish by the sudden noise and action. It screamed and reared, taking her by surprise, but she managed to hold on, to gain control again and coax it to a run, back toward the English soldiers, who were also running now, coming in for the fight.

It was disaster, it was a nightmare. The Scots would kill the English, the English would kill the Scots, and Murdoch might win—he might be able to take advantage of the confusion and actually win—

Something knocked into her, a vicious pain to her left shoulder, and she was torn from her saddle, landing on the grass and snow in a rolling tumble, blinded and jolted, unable to breathe.

Someone seemed to be calling her name, familiar cries that rang with fury even over the other shouting around her, but right now all Lauren could see was the shape of a man on a horse towering over her, an orange and purple sky behind him. The man dismounted.

"It is your doing," said the Murdoch, no longer trying to control his hatred, the wrath that focused on her. "You betraying *bitch,* you did this, turned my careful plans to this—"

"Lauren!" came the call again, closer.

Murdoch bent down beside her and pulled her up by her hair. Lauren grabbed at his hands, blinking, trying to get back her air.

"I'm still going to win this," he said down to her, shouting to be heard over the din. "You've changed nothing! But what a pity the poison I paid for did not kill you all those years ago, when you were at the mercy of a stronger English earl than this one. With you gone your father would have had nothing to bargain with for an alliance! But no—what a pity I had to try to marry you instead, to gain access to this land. You are a thorn to me, Lauren MacRae, and you have been all your life. But at least I get to kill you now."

He raised his sword to her chest, laughing delight.

"No," Lauren tried to shout, but it was more of a gasp. She pulled at him to no avail, yanking at her own hair, and when that failed, she kicked out at him, finding his groin.

Murdoch bent double with a hoarse cry and Lauren kicked him again, his thigh, his shin. He staggered backward, dragging her with him. She twisted in his grip and reached for his sword—

In an instant she had it, wedging it between the two of them, Murdoch's fist still twisted in her hair. They faced each other, crouched amid the mud of the field, eye to eye.

"Call off the battle," she said, the tip of the sword against his chest.

He gave a snarling laugh, wordless, then pulled at her, and they stumbled in a circle, neither yielding.

"Call it off!" she screamed, and pressed the tip harder against him.

She could see the men behind him, tartans blowing with the wind, men grappling with one another. She could not be certain who was fighting whom. It all seemed almost subdued compared to her own struggle now.

Murdoch's eyes were cold and terrible, reminding her of sharks, of vicious things. His laughter turned into words.

"You'll not do it, Lauren. You haven't the courage. Drop the sword, woman, and let me finish this day the way I should!"

He tore at her hair again and she slid but kept her balance, and her hold on the sword. She offered him her own savage smile, contempt rising through her.

"You don't know me, little man. The death of a traitor is nothing at all to me." She raised her elbows, leveling the blade, increasing the pressure against him. A narrow stain of red began to spread across his tunic. "Call off the battle. Now."

As he stared at her, Murdoch's face seemed to pale, and he stilled.

She was dimly aware that the men beyond them appeared to be breaking apart, separating. Was it really happening? Was the battle ending anyway, even without his command?

Without warning Murdoch twisted, went into a quick, lurching roll, surprising her, pulling her down with him. The sword slipped flat between them; they thrashed across the muddied field and then abruptly he had both hands around her own, angling the weapon toward her, and the blade was lowering to her throat—

A wordless sound came over her head, a terrible, bone-chilling sound, like a monster-demon awakened. A dark shadow flew over her, eating up the sky, enveloping Murdoch as it slammed into him, ripping her along with him, and they all skidded through the mud and grass with frightening speed until they stopped in a tangle.

The demon became Arion, Murdoch beneath him, grasping his sword again. Each had his blade locked against the other's. Lauren picked herself up and darted forward, her fingers groping at Murdoch's waist, finding the dirk there and pulling it away.

His eyes flickered to her, his face contorted with effort. She moved back on her hands and knees with a snarl of hair in her eyes, clutching the dirk.

"Wait," she called to Arion. "Wait!"

Both men ignored her, the swords slipping blade to blade with a metallic *zing!,* long and drawn out.

"He paid for the poison," Lauren shouted now to Arion, to the figures of men running around them all. "He did it!"

Arion gave her one quick glance and Murdoch took advantage of it, his free hand striking out, catching Arion across the jaw. They rolled again; she saw one of the swords slither across the grass. Now Murdoch was on top, murder in his eyes—Arion had lost the sword. Lauren scrambled toward them with the dirk, raising her arm to strike.

Someone pulled her away. She turned swiftly with the blade, ready to fight, but the man shouted down to her as he held her, a voice she knew.

"No, lass! Stay back—"

It was James, laboring to hold her. Suddenly Quinn stood over Arion and Murdoch, his sword resting against the side of Murdoch's neck, pressed under his jaw. In the turn of a second, no one moved.

Lauren, panting, her eyes fixed on Arion, saw him break into a feral smile.

"You've lost," said Quinn to Murdoch. "Get up."

She tore her gaze from the men on the ground to the handful of those surrounding them, du Morgan and MacRae, none fighting, all staring, from her to the earl and the two lairds, the standoff between them.

She saw Murdoch's soldiers in a tight cluster in the

distance, staring with either confusion or open hostility at the MacRaes who held them there, swords drawn. The English were mostly gathered on their side of the valley, Fuller in front of them, his sword held out to his side, preventing them all from going forward, to the Scots. He was watching the scene before him as intently as everyone else.

"It was he who tried to poison me," Lauren said in a ringing voice, only slightly too high. "Back at Morgan, as a child. It was Payton Murdoch who paid to have me killed."

"I heard him," remarked Quinn, unmoving. "I was close enough, although it appears du Morgan was closer." He twitched the sword lightly against Murdoch's neck. "Get up, I said."

And slowly Murdoch did, rising from Arion with a push, Arion pushing back, harder. The smile she had seen before was gone, replaced with the demon intensity of him.

Murdoch stood, surly and silent, in the circle of men around him, Quinn's blade now aimed at the base of his throat. His own sword was held loosely in one hand, lowered to the ground.

Lauren shook off James's grip, crossing to Arion to help him stand, until he had an arm around her, both of them bloodied and covered in the muck of the field. Her hands were numb with cold or emotion; the dirk she had taken felt clumsy in her open palm. Arion's hand covered hers, removing the dirk, letting her release that trouble.

The silence of the field hung around them with an

unnatural pressure, as if even the birds and wind had paused to watch.

"You paid for the poison," Lauren said to Murdoch, still disbelieving. "You—our ally."

"That stupid English serf," said Murdoch, half a scornful laugh. "Imagine if he had managed to give it to you as he should have. I might have conquered this island years ago, instead of having to wait to see who your father would choose you to wed."

"He?" repeated Arion.

Murdoch turned sullen again, ignoring Arion and Lauren, facing Quinn. "So kill me then, MacRae, if you dare. Kill me, and watch the wrath that follows from our king, from our countrymen."

"You've deceived us, Murdoch. I grant you that. But look around you." Quinn lifted his brows, nodding to the men surrounding them. "There is no fighting, not even from your own soldiers. It's over. Most of them refused to battle us at all. At least some of your men will walk away today with their freedom. But you will stand trial for this insurrection, I promise you that."

"It wasn't Nora," said Lauren slowly. "It wasn't her fault. You paid a servant from the kitchen, didn't you? You paid a serf there to put the poison in the soup she made for me. Nora didn't know."

Again Murdoch said nothing, his lips held together in that mocking smile, gazing off past her. Lauren looked up at Arion, dawning realization.

"She didn't *know,*" she repeated. "He *used* her, and she didn't know!"

Movement came from the edges of her vision, the

long cold steel of a sword slicing toward her, silent death so quick she didn't even have time to cringe. But something else smashed into her before the blade entered her body—Arion, shoving her aside. Lauren was knocked wildly sideways, arms outstretched. She fell to the ground, striking her temple hard against the earth, ringing in her ears.

When she was able to see again, Arion was crouched over the prone form of Murdoch. The sword that had nearly killed her was still tight in Murdoch's grip. The handle of a dirk jutted out from his chest.

"I told you I was going to kill you," said Arion, low and flat, wiping a line of blood from his mouth.

Someone helped her up; Arion unfolded out of his position and went to her, holding her to him again with such force that she backed up a few steps. His head lowered to hers, his lips brushed her forehead. Only she could feel the shakiness of his breath.

"I will report to the king that Payton Murdoch was killed in the heat of the battle he provoked," announced Quinn, raising his voice. "By what man, we do not know."

Arion lifted his head.

"It was a just price to pay," Quinn continued, looking over to Arion, "for the injustice he created—for the insurrection he began, and the betrayal of Clan MacRae."

"Aye," came a few voices, deep and muted.

Quinn turned to his men. "And the English fought bravely beside us in the battle. This, too, I will tell our king." He looked at James. "Get his men off our island. Send them to the mainland with a warning: We will not tolerate such deception again. The Clan MacRae has discovered a new allied family—" he glanced back to Arion, offering a slight nod—"and Shot will not fall to any mainlanders soon, not Vikings or rebel Scots alike."

James nodded, moving off, barking orders to the men around him.

Overhead, the sun began a steady warmth, illuminating the sky and the clouds with welcome rays.

"Come away, beloved," whispered Arion in Lauren's ear, drawing her from the sight before them, his hold on her firm and strong.

"Lauren," called Quinn, before they could take three steps.

She turned to him, still in Arion's protective embrace.

"Will you come home, lass?" Quinn asked.

She leaned back her head, Arion's shoulder behind her, the new daylight on her face.

"I am already home," she said, and turned again to her love, beginning the slow walk across the valley with him.

Epilogue

HE DAY WAS CRISP AND bright. A slow breeze came and flirted around the guests, stirring tartans and gowns, pressing back tunics with a light touch.

The wedding was in the exact middle of the beach that bordered the two halves of Shot. Lauren had made certain of that, even pacing out the steps with Arion, both of them starting from opposite ends of the sand, meeting up in the middle, where she had planted a branch of oak, marking the spot.

"Here," she had pronounced, and Arion and Hannah had laughed at her, and then with her. Ari had pushed the wood deeper into the sand, ensuring its hold.

"Aye, here it will be," he had said.

And here it was indeed, Clan MacRae and du Morgans standing side by side, facing the rolling blue and green waves of the ocean, white froth lapping up the sand with each surge to shore.

Ari stood beside Lauren, holding her hand as the ribbon symbolizing their unity was tied around their wrists, noting the slender beauty of her arm, the copper glory of her hair dancing with the breeze.

He had almost died here. It hadn't been that long

ago, that day when he had fallen here in this sand, and watched a tartaned woman defend his life, saving him.

A lifetime lived in weeks, he thought, considering it; an eternity found through her. Just a short while past and his life, which had come so close to ending in every way possible, had been renewed, given joy and hope by the woman beside him. Arion had seen a miracle born on this beach, and he found it perfectly apt that his miracle had chosen this place in the golden sand to be joined together forever.

She looked so serious now, listening to the priest over the call of the sea, amber eyes shaded with dark lashes, so lovely.

Ari's gaze drifted lower, to the bodice of the gown she wore, a low scooping neckline that her tartan didn't nearly manage to cover properly. Her skin glowed pale rose and alabaster. Her breath was even and calm, her voice clear as she repeated the vows the priest intoned.

When she was finished she pretended to adjust a fold of her gown, throwing him a sideways look of mischief at his obvious distraction. Ari smiled back at her, because she could do that to him, bring out in him the peace and happiness that he hadn't even known still lived in him any longer.

Lauren du Morgan, Countess of Morgan. He held her hand tightly, letting the ribbon that bound them together slide back along their arms in the wind, loose but fixed, a long ripple of violet between them.

The celebration lasted all day, well into the night, first at Keir and then Elguire, both families moving freely between the two castles. The initial, guarded well-wishes turned more fulsome with the path of the sun, until by nightfall there seemed to be no true distinction between the many people of Shot.

Lauren slipped in between and around all the guests with laughing flair, stopping now and again to speak to them—the old man from the village of Dunmar, a smiling young woman bouncing a baby in her arms. Whenever his bride came near him Ari made certain to grab her, to kiss her soundly, to let her go again only with reluctance. And the celebration went on.

Ari noted Rhodric sitting by a comely maiden in English dress, his look to her attentive and profound. Fuller stayed beside Hannah, both of them holding an air of serene delight, the perfect ambassadors for the new beginning he wanted the island to embrace.

Two days ago Arion had said to Lauren: "I want a quiet life."

And she had looked up from her rough drawing of the beach, where she had been planning with the precision of a military commander where to place their families. "Well," she had replied, her eyes brilliant. "I cannot promise you *that*."

"No more wars," Ari said, leaning in to her, pushing aside the paper. "No more battles or blood. I have enough scars already."

"No battles," she agreed, ducking around him, reaching for her paper. "But it won't be perfect. Not at first."

"Yes, it will," he had responded, and managed to catch her and kiss her anyway, even in front of Hannah and the women who walked in on them, all of them gasping and covering their mouths with their hands.

No battles today, he saw—not today, their wedding

day, this moment locked in what had to be a sorcerer's dream, his people and hers so amiable, so united in pride. A magical dream . . . no, not that. Dreams faded. Arion had made a vow that his devotion would not.

He proved it that night, stealing Lauren away from them all, hiding with her in the tower room he had secretly prepared for them, away from any who meant to follow and beleaguer them with ritual observation of the wedding night.

Ari made love to his wife on pillows and furs, beneath fragrant candles and a rounded window that offered them starlight and sweet air, hushed and high above the earth, suspended in their union as in thick honey, or clouds, or the gentle wind.

"What were you thinking about, at that meal?" Lauren asked him afterward, her voice drowsy, her hair a shimmering curtain across his chest.

"At the meal?" Ari stroked the copper, his fingers wrapping around the softness. "I was thinking about this. Being here with you, in this room. About the way your lips curve when you're happy . . . like this. . . ."

She gave a smothered laugh, pushing him off her, surrounded by the cushions and blankets he had tossed aside in their passion.

"No, not tonight." Her smile was a delight to him, her golden eyes intimate. "Before, at Dunmar. That night you came to the village, and ate in the common with my clan. You looked to me, over at my table. . . ." Her voice trailed off, suggestive and shy at once, which made him hide his own smile.

"Oh, *that* night." He settled back again into their makeshift paradise, pulling up one of the blankets to shelter them both, finding her beneath it, bringing her close to him. "I was thinking of you, fair Lauren, and of what your children would be like. I was wondering if they would have your eyes."

She was still for a moment. Then, doubtful: "Truly?"

"Aye, truly."

She leaned up over him, sliding under the covers until her body was stretched over his, her heat and suppleness aligned to him, her hair falling down in wild curls around his face.

"Perhaps we should find out," she offered seriously, not quite managing to disguise the way the corners of her lips tilted up.

"Aye," Arion agreed, reaching for her. "We should."

She tried to twist away, playful, but he held her to him firmly, both of them laughing until she subsided and surrendered to his touch, sighing deeply with pleasure.

"Am I your prisoner, du Morgan?" Lauren asked him, teasing.

Ari smiled at her, open and glad. "No, beloved. I believe I am yours."

And he began the kiss that would prove to her his words, that she alone held his body, his heart, and anything at all about him that might be of virtue. He began his worship of her with all the gratitude in his soul that ever lived—and all the grace and goodness in the world wrapped securely in his arms.

Author's Note

Some readers may have noticed and bemoaned the lack of dialect written into the English dialogue of the Scots in *Intimate Enemies.* I decided to forgo such idioms as "ye" for "you," "mon" for "man," "canna" for "cannot," etc., for the very simple reason that I found it distracting to have Lauren speak so differently from Arion.

Once, a long, long time ago—okay, college—I played a Polish character in a Polish play with a Polish setting that had been translated into English. The director had instructed the cast to speak our lines with Polish accents. Everything went as imagined, all of us tripping over our tongues in truly ghastly accents that sounded nothing like they should have, until finally another faculty member asked bluntly, "Why should they speak with Polish accents? Would the Poles be speaking Shakespeare in Polish with English accents?"

Why would Lauren have a Scots accent in her English? Technically, she would not have been speaking English at all, but rather a regional dialect of Gaelic. Even Arion would have spoken no language you or I would readily recognize, but rather a combination of medieval Norman French with a bit of Saxon thrown in.

Obviously, it would not do to have my two main characters not understand a word the other was saying.

So forgive me, please, for my leap into the dramatic, and the smoothing over of the linguistic knots that would have actually occurred between these two people.

And while I'm still immersed in the spirit of honesty, I would like to note that although the distillate *uisge beatha* or *aqua vitae*—the "water of life"—was a cherished part of the medieval Scottish world, the term *whiskey* would have been unfamiliar in the time of Lauren and Arion. Nevertheless, it fit the story so nicely that I could not let it go.

I hope you enjoyed the romance of Lauren and Arion, and that your days and nights will be filled with a love that is even more splendid than theirs.

—S.A.

About the Author

SHANA ABÉ lives in Southern California with her husband, Darren, and two house rabbits. Yes, the rabbits really do live in the house. Shana can be reached through her website at:

www.tlt.com/authors/sabe.htm

Or write to her at:

Shana Abé
PMB 180
2060–D Avenida de los Arboles
Thousand Oaks, CA
91362–1361

Shana Abé's next romance
will be on sale in early 2001.
Read on for a preview of
this hauntingly beautiful love story . . .

Prologue

*T*HE LATCH TO THE GATE came off in his hand.

Tristan stared down at it in some surprise, speckles of rust dotting his skin like dried blood. The soldered seam meant to hold it in place had corroded completely through; he was damned lucky he hadn't cut himself on any of the flaking metal. No doubt the result of the sea air in this godforsaken place.

He remembered now. Nothing lasted here.

Carefully Tristan dropped the ruined latch to the gravel beside him.

The gate itself did not appear much more promising. One half of the barred grill hung at a drunken tilt against the other, offering paltry defense against anyone who actually wished to enter the estate.

It suddenly made him want to laugh. Who would truly want to come here, after all? Safere was the outermost edge of the world—far, far past any prayer of civilization. Surely only the banished or the insane dwelled here.

The thought was so particularly apt that he did laugh now, low and mirthless, but the wind only snatched it away from him. It pushed up off the ocean nearby, a steady tearing at his hair, his skin, drying his eyes to grit. On the journey here Tristan had found himself constantly squinting against it to perceive the land around him, as if that might clarify matters. It had not.

He cupped a hand to his mouth and called out a greeting past the iron bars. It faded off against the bare walls of the buildings beyond. No one responded.

Perhaps there was no one here, after all. Perhaps Safere was as deserted as it appeared to be. He could not fathom why anyone would want to stay here, anyway.

If ever a land was rocky and formidable, it was this place. Whichever of his esteemed ancestors had claimed this seaside territory obviously had not been bothered by the lack of greenery. Perched on its lonely outcrop of rock overlooking the ocean, Safere seemed better suited for a prison than a stronghold: barren, remote, breathtakingly desolate. The water was a steady roar against the cliffs below. The wind never ceased.

He fancied he could hear words in it now—a thin, berating wail that wrapped around him, relentless.

She's gone . . . they're all gone . . . shame . . . shame . . .

He gave the gate a vicious kick. The broken half of it shuddered in place. The other half did not move at all.

Tristan did not like Safere—he never had. Even now, in the peak of summer, vegetation was rare, and trees rarer still. The farther he had traveled on his ride to it, the less and less hospitable the land became. Dirt paths, endless and winding. Pale tufts of grass struggling for life. Faraway birds, tangling into fantastic shapes amid the blue of the sky, dark against white clouds. . . .

But mostly there were rocks. White rocks, golden rocks, even ones tinted pink, which he decided were his favorite. The pink ones did something with the light, a trick of dusk and dawn, capturing the color to create a glow, suffusing the very air around them with warmth. Yes, the pink ones were—

Tristan caught himself with a mental shake, turning back to the problem of the gate.

He might be able to squeeze through the bottom of it. The gap from the angle of the disjointed half was severe enough that he could make it, with a good bit of crawling. He would have to leave his horse behind.

Wonderful. The Earl of Haverlocke crawling back to his wife. What a pretty sight that would be. And nothing less than he deserved.

It was the reproving wind, perhaps, that made Tristan straighten, glancing around him again. Many might laugh at the sight of him on his hands and knees amid dirt and gravel, but it wasn't going to be the ghosts of this place. There had to be another way in. He thought he remembered a garden gate somewhere. . . .

He took the reins of the gelded brown rounsey and began to walk around the walls that enclosed the estate. From here he could see the top portion of the manor, stone and wood, bleached with sunlight. No banner flew to welcome him home. In fact, he couldn't even see the staff for it. The edges of the roof dipped and curved in places it was not supposed to; a few of those shadows might have been gaps in the beams. If the main house was as dismally neglected as the gate had been, he supposed he might be fortunate to find shelter at all tonight.

On the far side of the stronghold the salted rock wall came perilously close to the edge of the cliff, eroded away under the constant assault of the elements. He kept the reins of his horse firmly grasped in one hand, allowing the other to slide along the rough stones of the wall—a thin illusion of security. It would not help if either of them stumbled, but the feel of something solid beneath his palm gave him some comfort.

The gelding snorted and tossed his head against the wind. Tristan pulled him on.

Nothing. No garden gate—only this long, unbroken expanse of wall, stretching on and on. How ridiculous to imagine there might have been another gate. He must have been thinking of one of the other estates. Merllyf, perhaps. Or Layton. They were all mixed-up in his head now, indistinguishable. Mayhap *none* of them had a garden, or a gate. Another fantasy, whirled up out of nothingness.

The wretched portal of the entrance loomed before him once again. *Full circle,* Tristan thought, and for some reason the phrase stuck in his head.

With a sigh he approached it, releasing the reins, grasping the rusted metal of the broken half and lifting with all his might. He was rewarded with a hideous squealing sound, the hinges protesting this rough handling. After a long while and a great deal of sweating effort, the gap had widened enough to fit through without crawling.

He dropped the gate, panting, and absently wiped his hands down the front of his tunic. Rust left smudges of darkness against the gray of it. He had no gloves.

Tristan entered his estate.

Once inside the walls the howling of the wind was drastically reduced, a sudden respite that rang in his ears, close to pain.

No one came to greet him. There was only more dirt before him, and buildings and sky.

He took a deep breath, then called out again—and again he gained no response beyond the mournful cry of the wind.

Shame, shame . . .

An ungentle push from behind reminded him of his horse. The gelding had crossed the entrance after him and now stood impatiently, tossing his head once more.

Yes. Tristan had stolen a mount—he should not have forgotten that. The horse would be hungry. He must see about feeding him. The stables must still be here somewhere.

Safere was fairly sizable, for an enclosed estate. The manor house took up most of it, along with a modest, neat garden—*no gate*—he could see growing along one of the walls. Here at last were living plants, herbs and vegetables, even a scattering of flowers near the back, a decent effort against the thin soil. He supposed it was some sign of hope that there might be more than just ghosts to this place.

Thankfully, he did not have to remember where the stable was to find it. It was the only other structure of any significance, and at first glance appeared just as abandoned as everything else. He found a reasonably clean stall and led the rounsey into it, then had to stop and think about what he must do next.

Hay. Water. Oats, if he could find them.

A rustling sound came from nearby. The delicate head of a bay topped the door of the stall opposite, eyeing him suspiciously.

When he was done with his own horse, Tristan got a

closer look at the other one. It was a mare, a sweetly formed thing, really, with clean lines and a shining flank. One more hopeful sign.

He left the animals examining each other with trembling hostility, walking back out into the bright sunshine of the day.

"Amiranth?"

No one answered him. There was no one here at all. Not a serf, not a servant. Certainly not *her*. He had come to the end of the world and found it just as he had left it all, so long ago—forgotten.

A small noise in the distance caught his attention. Tristan swung around, startled. It might have come from the depths of the manor. Aye. He moved toward it.

The interior of this place was darker than he recalled, cool and musty. A dim hallway of stone and wood paneling stretched out before him, closed doors on both sides. He had to pause to allow his eyes to adjust, until the shadows lightened from black to soft charcoal. The scent of something that might have been beeswax lingered faintly in the air. But the only sound to be heard now was his own breathing, and the occasional creaking of the beams of wood above him.

Tristan walked deeper inside.

One by one he opened the doors, taking care to throw frequent looks over his shoulder—in case *they* came, creeping close behind him; in case *they* had followed and were here as well, ready to drag him back to hell . . . he would die first. He would slay them all—

But there was no one behind him. All he found, in fact, in this soulless place were deserted chambers and scattered furniture covered in a fine layer of dust. Ashes in the fireplaces, long cold. Windows encrusted with dirt, uncleaned. Every single thing spoke of abandonment.

In one room he discovered an elegant little tableau set up: a pair of chairs brought close around a low table of polished wood, the empty hearth just beyond. The edges of a wooden screen closed off a corner of it, creating intimacy. A bit of embroidery lay askew across the seat of the chair closest to him, needle and thread placed neatly on top, as if the seamstress meant to return at any moment.

Tristan picked up the scrap of cloth—a dreamlike scene of the night sky and stars, a swan on a moonlit lake—then shook it. Dust erupted around him in a cloud, clogging his senses. He gave a rough cough, tossing the lot of it back to the chair.

The needle dropped from the side and swung gently back and forth, bright silver suspended by a sapphire thread.

Had his wife begun this piece? What would have caused her to discard it so nearly completed, forsaken to the mustiness of this room?

He felt a chill and shook it off, continuing his exploration.

She would be here. She would be.

There was food in the buttery. That had to be good. Not much, granted: some bread and cheese, flour, roots, dried fruits and herbs—from the garden, he would guess. Certainly not enough to feed all the people that should be dwelling here . . . but enough for a few people, for a while.

Again came that elusive noise, outside now, just past the kitchen door. But when he walked back into the sunshine, there was nothing there—only the dirt of before, an empty sky, the mocking wind. Tristan closed his eyes and let out his breath, setting his teeth.

Alone, alone again. She was not here, no one was. Perhaps she never had been. Perhaps he was not even married at all—it had all been just another dream of his, a delusion conjured up by his mind: that girl, her face, the soft touch of her hand—

No. It had to have happened. It *had* to have been real. If she was not here she would be somewhere else. He would find her. It didn't have to be this place, empty Safere....

But when Tristan rounded the next corner, he discovered that he had been mistaken; Safere was not so empty after all. At the foot of a new garden there was a statue of a marble girl seated upon a marble bench, posed to stare out thoughtfully at the few trees and bushes pressed up against the outer wall.

As first he didn't understand what he was seeing. A marble girl on a marble bench . . . but she wore a black gown that rippled in the breeze. Why had they clothed a statue? Why was her hair so golden?

The marble girl turned her face and gazed back at him, still thoughtful.

Tristan Geraint, Earl of Haverlocke, stopped in sheer surprise.

The woman—not a girl and not marble, but flesh— quickly stood, taking a step away.

"No—wait." Tristan held out his hands, his palms streaked with rust. "I won't harm you." He scanned the area around them, seeing nothing but more of the garden, the pale stone walls beyond that. She was the only sign of life, this figure of gold and white and black.

"Amiranth?" he asked her, but he knew it was not she.

This woman's hair was darker than he remembered his wife's to be, more of a honeyed blonde than the silvery curls that young girl had had. She wore it loose and free, strange for a grown woman—he had not been gone *that* long, to think that a noblewoman would reveal her hair so openly—but Tristan did not regret the sight of it, not when it shimmered in the sunlight as it did, shades of amber and burnished gold, richly layered.

She had not run away, but her hands had come up to shield her eyes from the bright sun; he saw only full lips stained red, like the sunset, and a sweetly curved chin. Long, elegant neck. The tail-end of the wind slipped over the wall, pressing back the shadowed black of her gown, revealing a slender shape in teasing glimpses.

If God had come and placed a desert flower in the midst of this vast emptiness, this woman could not look more out of place than she did.

It was not she. It could not be.

But he said again anyway, "Amiranth St. Cl—Geraint?"

Certainly it was not she. There was no reason to feel disappointment when the woman slowly shook her head in denial, allowing the sunlight to send sparks weaving through her hair.

This would be her servant, then. A handmaiden, perhaps.

"Where is she?" Tristan asked, taking another step forward. The woman did not back away this time, but to reassure her he added in a calm voice, "I am her husband. You may direct me to her."

The handmaiden lowered her hands, not even blinking against the sun. An odd pang of regret ran through him as he took in her face. She was lovely and familiar. He might have seen her at the wedding, all those years ago—

"Where is she?" he asked again, motionless. He would not give in to the urge to come closer to her.

Her head bowed; a slight frown marred her forehead. He watched as one of her hands lifted, very pale against the black sleeve of her gown, her finger pointing into the garden.

Tristan turned, searching past the trees. There was no one else there. Was she jesting? Did she think to test him somehow?

When he glanced back at her she was still pointing mutely to the garden, her stare now direct to his, unflinching. With her golden hair streaming past her shoulders, she was as stern and solemn as any avenging angel.

He felt a strange sense of helplessness come over him. This was it, then. This was what he deserved, after all.

Tristan looked again at the garden.

There it was. A simple plaque amid the plants— actually just a flat rock of that pink shade he had favored, a few words carved roughly into the stone.

Her name had been written clumsily. No doubt it had not been easy chiseling the marker.

AMIRANTH, COUNTESS OF HAVERLOCKE
1326–1349
PEACE, SWEET FRIEND.